Books by Eileen Wilks

TEMPTING DANGER
MORTAL DANGER
BLOOD LINES
NIGHT SEASON
MORTAL SINS
BLOOD MAGIC
BLOOD CHALLENGE
DEATH MAGIC
MORTAL TIES
RITUAL MAGIC
UNBINDING
MIND MAGIC

Anthologies

CHARMED
(with Jayne Ann Krentz writing as Jayne Castle,
Julie Beard, and Lori Foster)

LOVER BEWARE
(with Christine Feehan, Katherine Sutcliffe, and Fiona Brand)

CRAVINGS
(with Laurell K. Hamilton, MaryJanice Davidson,
and Rebecca York)

ON THE PROWL
(with Patricia Briggs, Karen Chance, and Sunny)

INKED
(with Karen Chance, Marjorie M. Liu, and Yasmine Galenorn)

TIED WITH A BOW
(with Lora Leigh, Virginia Kantra, and Kimberly Frost)

Specials

ORIGINALLY HUMAN
INHUMAN

MIND
MAGIC

EILEEN WILKS

B
BERKLEY SENSATION, NEW YORK

**BERKLEY
SENSATION**

An imprint of Penguin Random House LLC
375 Hudson Street, New York, New York 10014

MIND MAGIC

A Berkley Sensation Book / published by arrangement with the author

ISBN: 978-0-425-26387-7

PUBLISHING HISTORY
Berkley Sensation mass-market edition / November 2015

PRINTED IN THE UNITED STATES OF AMERICA

10 9 8 7 6 5 4 3 2 1

Cover art by Tony Mauro.
Cover design by George Long.

Penguin
Random
House

ACKNOWLEDGMENTS

I'd like to thank Richard Manning for helping me get the weaponry right. Any mistakes that remain are, I assure you, entirely my own.

ONE

~

August
West Virginia

THE guards came as a shock.

Demi knew about the alarm system and exterior lights. Those had been in use when she lived in the big farmhouse. She knew about the perimeter alarm they'd added, too, having checked the updated schematics through her back door. No problem. There wasn't a tech system yet invented that she couldn't subvert, given enough time. She'd crossed the perimeter with no problems.

Maybe she'd been cocky. No, definitely she'd been cocky. Tech wasn't the only way to keep people out.

Or to keep them in.

She pressed her back against the big oak as if she could get it to soak her up if she pushed hard enough. Her heart pounded. Her mouth was dry. Nausea stirred in her gut. She didn't deal well with surprises, even the happy sort. This one was not happy. Her mind was a whirlwind, thoughts shooting off in all directions like accidental fireworks. Her fingers began moving in an automatic pattern, fingering an imaginary flute.

Sensei said once that her mind was her biggest friend and her most terrible enemy. Sensei could say stuff like that and no one laughed at him. It wasn't just because he was right, either. You could be right and people would still laugh at you or get mad. She understood the getting mad. It's like Mama used to say: people don't like to feel stupid, and sometimes if you're right, it means they're wrong, or else just you being right makes them feel dumb, and that makes them mad. She knew how that felt. She didn't understand the laughing, but it always made her feel stupid.

She missed Mama so much.

The tree refused to absorb her. Her fingers kept moving repetitively. Gradually her mind calmed down enough to be useful. The situation wasn't what she'd expected. She needed to evaluate it before deciding what to do.

Demi was in a small copse of trees about a hundred yards from the rambling farmhouse. There was some cover between her and her goal—a dip in the grassy meadow that she knew from experience would conceal her as long as she crouched low. That would take her to the barn, which would block her from view of the house as the dip petered out. She'd planned to slip inside the barn, climb to the hay loft, then out the window at the back and into the big elm. From the elm she'd go to the roof of the detached garage; from there to the patio. The motion sensor aimed at the patio was tied into the security system, so that wasn't a problem. She was already hacked into it.

She couldn't hack into eyeballs or the brains and bodies that went with them. The guards had been wearing camo, as if they were soldiers. Maybe they were. Mr. Smith could probably get soldiers if he wanted some.

Why would he want soldiers? What was going on?

She drew a shaky breath. That's what she was here to find out, wasn't it?

The knot of determination in her chest tightened. She wasn't giving up. Nicky was in there. She was ninety percent sure he was. If she was right, all kinds of things she'd thought true were fake and false, lies created to get her to help them do . . . whatever dreadful thing they were doing. Because you didn't lie in order to get people to do wonderful things, did you?

First things first. If Nicky was here, she had to rescue him. Which meant she had to figure out not just how to get in without being seen, but how to get both of them out again. Slowly she sank to the ground, sitting with her knees drawn up. She needed to think. To get her mind pointed in the right direction. If she didn't get all hurried and frantic, she could do this.

First question: Should she abort the mission? Not give up, but gather more data, come up with another plan?

She tried to weigh the risk of continuing against the risk of postponing, but she didn't have enough data to make reasonable estimates. What she needed, then, was more data. How many guards were there? Were they armed? Were they really soldiers? Did they stay put or move around?

She didn't know any of that. She'd seen two guards and panicked and kept backing up until she bumped into this tree. She must have been quiet because they hadn't come after her, but all she really remembered was being scared. She still was, but she was thinking again.

It was three o'clock on a sunny August afternoon. The sun would be up for hours. She had time and a tall tree at her back. She stood, crouched, and launched herself at the lowest limb, grabbed it, and scrambled up.

Climbing was Demi's one athletic skill. Trees, cliffs, walls, whatever—if it went up, she went up it. She scaled that tree like an oversize squirrel, stopping when she reached a convenient fork that gave her a good view of the house and grounds. She straddled it and looked out.

Still two guards, one at the east end of the house, one on the west side. Those sure looked like Army fatigues, with their billed caps and the pants tucked into combat boots. There was some kind of insignia on the sleeve of the closest guard. That made her stomach unhappy. So did the holstered gun.

Grimly she pulled out her phone and tapped in the data: *3:05 Guard 1 by fountain; Guard 2 25 ft. fr. west wall (dining rm)*. Then she took pictures of the guards using the phone's zoom feature and got a fairly good shot of the insignia so she could check it out later. She couldn't do that now. The phone was in airplane mode so it wouldn't ping any nearby cell towers. That was probably excessive caution on her part, but why take a chance if she didn't have to?

For now, the guards were staying put. She set herself to watch. While she watched, she thought about minimum force.

When she first began taking lessons from Sensei, he'd talked about how minimum force was the idea behind every martial art. You learned how to spend the least possible force, often using your opponent's own force to defeat him. This, Sensei said, was what everyone tried to do in every aspect of life: use the least effort possible in order to achieve a goal. No one used one bit more effort than he or she thought was necessary. The trick was in figuring out what that minimum was and how to apply it. That's what people got wrong. That's what they would learn to do in his class.

Demi had been fascinated by the concept. For the next few months, she'd tried to find examples of people intentionally using more effort than was needed. The first one that occurred to her was studying for a test. Some people crammed like crazy, going way overboard. She'd told Sensei that. Sensei had said that she misunderstood the goal of those avid studiers. Their real goal wasn't to ace the test, but to reduce their anxiety about the test. Because they couldn't control what was on the test, they could never eliminate that anxiety entirely, so they kept trying to memorize more and more facts.

Another time she'd suggested that suicide bombers broke the rule. Sensei agreed that they appeared to do so, because giving one's life to achieve a goal could be considered spending the maximum possible. But if your goal is to be a martyr, death is the minimum requirement. And those who sent a suicide bomber out to kill strangers were obviously expending the minimum force. They exchanged one life for several of those they considered enemies and caused fear in hundreds or thousands more.

She'd come up with lots more examples, but after a while she could shoot them down herself with a little thought. When it looked like someone had used disproportionate force, it meant that either (a) she'd misidentified their real goal, or (b) they'd misunderstood their situation and the amount of force needed. The truth was, people mostly weren't very good at estimating the amount of effort needed. They frequently underestimated it, which was why diets failed so often. People tried to make sweeping changes without allowing for how difficult, how against their nature, this was. Incremental change worked better because each step felt like the minimum necessary. On the other hand, when people were scared, they often overestimated the amount of force needed. That's why police departments had rules and training for when it was okay to use deadly force. You couldn't rely on instinct when you were scared. Your instinct might be to shoot whatever was scaring you, and sometimes that was disastrous.

As she sat high in the tree watching the guards and brooding, she fought valiantly to persuade herself she could fix this, could find some way to avoid being seen by those soldiers. Nicky had been missing for three weeks now. She'd wasted a week thinking he'd turn up any minute, and when it was clear he wouldn't, no one would tell her anything. His parents wouldn't even talk to her now, not since she tried to tell them about Mr. Smith. Either they thought she was nuts, or Mr. Smith had gotten to them somehow.

Probably, she admitted glumly, they thought she was nuts.

Nicky must be so miserable and frightened. She didn't think they'd actually torture him. Surely they weren't that depraved, and besides, they didn't want him broken. They wanted to use him. But who knew what kind of pressure they were putting on him to do—well, whatever it was they wanted him to do? Given the nature of his Gift, it was probably something awful. She had to get him out.

Only she couldn't. Not yet. Her chest ached with the knowledge. She hung her head. *Nicky, I'm sorry. I'll be back.*

The dreadful truth was that she'd overlooked the obvious.

The amount of force people use is always in proportion to their goal. She'd been ninety percent sure that Mr. Smith had lied about his goal for the Refuge—that was its official name: "Bright Haven Refuge for Gifted Young People"—but she hadn't reevaluated the amount of effort he might employ to secure it. She'd acted as if nothing had changed, trying to sneak in the same way she used to sneak out.

She had been downright woolly-headed. That stung.

Demi's eyes watered. Angrily she rubbed them. Much as she hated it, today's plan was a bust. She was going to have to go back to campus and come up with another one. At least the guards were staying put, so she should be able to slip away unnoticed. She sighed and began making her way down the tree, going a lot more slowly than when she'd climbed up.

A stick cracked. She froze in an awkward crouch, one foot firmly placed on a thick branch, the other foot reaching below it for the next one. Her heart pounded. That might have been anything—

Faint but clear, she heard the rustle of feet. Coming this way? She thought so. Oh, God, oh God, now what? She was going to be sick. No, she wasn't. She refused to throw up and give herself away. She'd plant herself on this branch and hold extremely still. She was still fairly high up, with lots of branches and leaves between her and the ground. Maybe whoever it was wouldn't see her.

Slowly, careful not to make noise, Demi made herself secure and held very, very still. Even when the pair of soldiers moved into view, heading right for her tree, she didn't move. She may have stopped breathing.

The soldiers carried rifles slung over their shoulders. The man with them did not.

He was a round little man. Not fat, but with a bureaucrat's round little tummy. His slacks were gray, his cheeks were plump and pink, and his head was round as a bowling ball and almost as bald. Even his glasses were round. He stopped at the base of her tree and looked up. Those glasses winked at her as light glinted off them.

"Demi." Mr. Smith shook his head sadly. "You might as well come down."

He sounded like a teacher who'd discovered that his favorite pupil had cheated on an exam. Her cheeks went hot as humiliation washed through her. It felt every bit as bad as fear, only with a sour, rotten tang, and it wasn't fair. She wasn't the one in the wrong! He was the one who'd lied and betrayed her trust and was doing—well, she didn't know what, but something bad. He was the one standing there with soldiers, armed soldiers, and— and he was right. He did have those armed soldiers, so she might as well climb down.

With none of her usual ease, she did. Feeling them watching her made her horribly self-conscious, and she resented that, and clung to that resentment so she wouldn't think about what might happen next. Once she had both feet on the ground, she looked at one of the soldiers so she wouldn't have to look at Mr. Smith. He was tall and young, his skin darker than hers. She said the first thing that came into her head. "What kind of rifle is that?"

"Uh . . ." He looked at Mr. Smith.

"Our Demi has no off-switch on her curiosity. Unfortunately. Demi, do you have any idea how dangerous it was to try to sneak in here?"

That was so unexpected she had to glance at him. He was looking at her with such disappointment that she automatically wanted to apologize. She clamped her jaw tight to keep herself from saying anything stupid.

"I don't deserve this distrust. Why would you work so hard to sneak in here, where you've always been welcome?"

"You—" *You kidnapped my friend.* She couldn't say that, so she asked, "How did you find me?"

He smiled a touch smugly. "How can you ask? You know that Amanda is here."

"Amanda?" She was incredulous—first, that he even brought Amanda up, given the way he'd broken his promise about her. Second, that he thought she'd believe him. "Amanda's Gift doesn't work on me."

"Amanda has discovered many useful abilities since we unblocked her Gift. You must ask her about it sometime. But it isn't Amanda you came to see today, is it?"

She didn't answer, thinking hard. If Amanda hadn't spotted her telepathically . . . and she hadn't. Demi was sure of that. So how had they found her? Mr. Smith and the soldiers had walked right up to her tree. They'd known exactly where she was.

Mr. Smith sighed. "You do possess tenacity. That isn't always a virtue, my dear. You want to talk to Nick, I presume."

Her voice went hoarse. "You admit he's here. That you kidnapped him."

"Oh, he's here, but it's entirely voluntary. Such a dramatic imagination—but it's your age, I suppose. He's not going to be happy with you. Come along, Demi." He turned and started for the house, clearly expecting her to obey.

Reluctantly she did. She hadn't been this scared since . . . maybe she'd never been this scared. "Where is everyone?"

"Field trip," he said. "Were you aware of that when you planned your little visit?"

Of course. She wasn't an idiot. "How come Nicky didn't go on this field trip? If he isn't here against his will—"

"The trip is to the zoo in Roanoke."

"Zoos are nothing more than prisons for animals."

"I'm aware of your views on the subject," Mr. Smith said dryly. "Since Nick shares them, he wasn't included in the field trip."

Nick loved animals the way she did. That's why they were vegetarians, which was how they'd met—at a vegetarian covered-dish supper on campus. Nick's parents weren't vegetarian, but they thought it was cool for him to be one, if he wanted. They saw it as an extension of their beliefs. They were Quakers, and so was Nicky. Which made it ridiculous for Mr. Smith to claim Nicky was here voluntarily. He was a dedicated pacifist.

A few months ago, she'd told Nicky about Mr. Smith. She hadn't told Mr. Smith about Nicky because he didn't want anything to do with the NSA. That was one of the few things they'd argued about. He'd wanted her to cut her ties to the agency.

"You've stopped, Demi." Mr. Smith sounded exasperated. He was several feet ahead of her.

She flushed and scowled. "Why are you here today anyway?" He hardly ever was. Dan and Sharon took care of everything.

"That's hardly your concern, is it? Now come along."

Slowly she did, somewhat reassured. If he didn't want her to know how he'd tracked her, maybe he wasn't planning to shoot her, or have one of his soldiers shoot her, or whatever. Because she was pretty sure he was here because of her. He'd found out what she planned to do and come here to stop her. Only how? She'd never found a precog for him, except for that one boy whose parents hadn't wanted him to leave home, so he hadn't been tipped off that way. And even if Amanda could read her mind, which she couldn't, Demi had been too far away until today. Amanda might have increased her range, but not that much.

As for more prosaic means . . . she'd been so careful! Surely if they knew about her back door, they wouldn't have left it open? And she'd paid cash for her bus ticket, and she didn't see how they could have known about the bike she'd borrowed to come the rest of the way. She supposed that someone could've been following her, but the NSA was all about electronic surveillance, not the in-person kind. And she'd left her phone in airplane mode the whole time, so . . .

Wait a minute. Look at it the other way around. How would she track someone's phone when it was in airplane mode?

That had her thinking furiously until they reached the porch, where the two soldiers peeled off, going back to whatever they did when they weren't helping Mr. Smith collect trespassers. Demi felt a little sick, a little scared, and altogether weird as she went up the three stairs.

The farmhouse had started out big, with ten rooms plus a finished basement that held the classrooms, a couple of half baths, and the housekeeper's room. When she first came here, she'd had a bedroom of her own, but that hadn't lasted, and she'd moved out before the addition was finished. That had nearly doubled the house's size. The two-story wing had a rec room, the teachers' bedrooms and shared bath, plus lots more bedrooms, restrooms, and shower rooms for the kids. The kids' bedrooms were dorm-style. There were twenty-one "Gifted young people" living here now, most of them below the age of thirteen.

It felt so odd to walk inside the Refuge . . . and that's what it had been when she first came here. Not a home, but a refuge. The place looked like it always had—the same scuffed floorboards, with one that squeaked three steps inside the entry hall. The big, square living room on her right still had that squishy couch where she'd liked to curl up with a book. The TV was new, but she'd bet they still weren't allowed to turn it on until after supper.

Three kids were in the living room playing some kind of board game. She knew two of them because she'd found them. Adrian was fourteen—two years younger than her—and a strong farseer. Susan was fourteen and a Finder. The other boy, the one she didn't know, looked about twelve.

All three were staring at her. She looked away.

"He's upstairs," Mr. Smith said. "Second bedroom on the right."

Not in the new wing, then. The only way into that was down the hall on her left. Demi's heart pounded as she started up the stairs. Mr. Smith came up behind her. "Adrian and Susan and that other kid aren't on the field trip."

"I'm afraid they're grounded. Minor infractions, but the rules exist for a reason. I've always thought you agreed with that."

It was true that Demi liked rules. Rules kept things fair and orderly. Because she followed most rules scrupulously, everyone thought she was a good girl, not the sort to cause problems. It had never occurred to Dan and Sharon that she might sneak out sometimes at night. But Demi had needed time alone more than she'd needed to follow the house rules. To her surprise, she'd turned out to be good at sneaking.

Not good enough, apparently. She paused at the top of the stairs. "Why isn't Amanda on the field trip?"

"A stomach virus. Please keep moving, Demi."

A virus?

Her heartbeat picked up, but not with fear this time—with that little thrill she got when she found the answer to a hard problem. It wasn't Amanda with the virus. It was Demi's phone. Her phone must be infected with a virus that made it ping the cell towers even when it was in airplane mode. That's how Mr. Smith had known she was coming here. He must have them tracking her phone. That wouldn't be hard for him to arrange. He'd had more distance to travel than she had, but he hadn't had to travel by bus and bicycle. He'd had time to figure out where she was going and get here before she did.

All of a sudden she was at the door. Second bedroom on the right, Mr. Smith had said. This used to be Laura's room. "Where's Laura?"

"California. She's twenty now, so she isn't with us anymore."

"Nicky's twenty."

"Nick has made different decisions than Laura did. Do you want to see him or not?"

Mr. Smith was so sure of himself. Demi was so . . . not. Her mouth was dry. Her hand shook a little when she raised it to knock.

TWO

~

NICKY sat at the desk with a laptop in front of him. There was at least three days' worth of bristles on his pale skin; his hair had needed a trim two months ago; his jeans were ragged, his feet bare. He wore the same black-framed glasses he always did. She'd seen that T-shirt dozens of times. On it, a cartoon cow and chicken held out a plate piled high with green peas.

All in all, he looked scruffy, malnourished, and one step away from homeless. That was normal. The stony face he turned toward her with was not.

Her gaze skittered away from that unwelcoming face to take in the room. It was barely big enough to hold the bed, the desk, and a chest of drawers, which was why it was one of the private bedrooms. It didn't look like Nicky, either. None of his stuff was here. It couldn't be, because everything was back at college or at his parents' house.

Almost everything. She still had his copy of *Hitchhiker's Guide to the Galaxy*. He'd loaned it to her, and she hadn't been able to bring herself to give it to his parents like she should have. "Nicky?" Her throat closed up. She couldn't get another word out.

"Shit." He shoved back his chair and stood. "I should've known you'd pull something like this."

She felt worse than she had since Mama died.

"Oh, God, now with the puppy dog eyes." He ran a hand through his hair. "Listen, Demi, I'm fine, okay? I changed my mind about some stuff. No biggie. Mr. Smith told me you were out there trying to sneak in. What did you think, that I needed to be rescued?" He snorted. "If I had, you wouldn't be my first pick. A team of commandos maybe—"

"What are you talking about?" she burst out. "Your parents are worried sick! You just vanished without a word to anyone. Your advisor didn't know where you were, and neither did Mike or Sean. You stopped coming to classes, and you left all your stuff, and—"

"For crying out loud—look at my T-shirt! I wasn't wearing it when I—when I left. And here. Look here." He strode to the closet and threw open the door. "There's my stuff."

Demi took a few stiff steps toward the closet. She knew that dark blue T-shirt. It said, I SUPPORT HABITAT FOR A MANATEE. And the gray one next to it—that's the one she'd given him that said, STOP MAKING CHEMISTRY JOKES. ALL THE GOOD ONES ARGON. She got it because his dad was a chemist and a punster and he'd always been really nice when he and Nicky's mom came up to campus to visit and . . .

"My folks boxed everything up and sent it to me," Nicky said.

Bewildered, she shook her head. "Your folks didn't know where you were. They asked me if I knew." They hadn't liked her answer, but they'd asked.

"I didn't handle it very well, all right? I should've told them right away, but I knew how they'd react. I knew. And I was right. They don't want anything to do with me now."

Slowly she turned around. "What are you talking about?"

"You're just going to keep poking and poking, aren't you?" Abruptly he turned away. "My Gift got away from me."

"Oh, no, Nicky!" Instinctively she moved closer and reached out—then paused, her hand hovering uncertainly in the air between them. "What happened?"

"It was that damn Wayne Diamond. He was talking—bragging!—about this girl that he got drunk and I told him that was rape, and it was, but he just laughed, and when I said I was going to report him, he hit me, and he kept hitting me, and . . .

and that's no excuse. I know that, but . . ." She heard him swallow.

She vaguely remembered hearing something about Wayne Diamond getting hurt. He was a jock, a football player, and she never paid attention to them, so she didn't remember what had happened to him. "I'm pretty sure," she said cautiously, "that he didn't die."

"No." He still wouldn't look at her. "Your Mr. Smith was on campus that day. He'd come to see you, but you were out. When he saw the EMTs, he . . . we talked."

"I assume," Mr. Smith said dryly, "that's why Demi decided I'd abducted you. She knew I was on campus and yet I didn't talk to her, so I must have been there to kidnap you."

"But—but Nicky, you don't want to work for the NSA! You always said—"

Now he looked at her. Glared at her, really. "That's why I didn't want to tell you. I knew you'd throw that in my face. I changed my mind, okay? Mr. Smith is helping me get my Gift under control, and I need that."

"But—"

"Geez, Demi, can't you take 'you were right' for an answer? You told me Mr. Smith was different and I should trust him."

No, she hadn't. She hadn't said anything like that. She opened her mouth to remind him of what she'd really said—that Mr. Smith had helped her a lot and she thought he was helping the others, but she wasn't sure anymore, not since he broke his promise about Amanda.

"I don't want to hear 'I told you so,'" he said quickly. He took two steps and closed his hands around her arms. That startled her as much as all the odd, angry things he'd said. "Look, we had a good thing going, the two of us, but everything's changed now. Though I should've known you couldn't take a hint." His mouth cocked up on one side, and for a moment he looked like the Nicky she'd known. "Hints just blow right on past you. And I guess you deserved to hear from me in person, so here it is. I'm breaking up with you, Demi. I like you. I think you're a great girl. But we aren't a couple anymore."

Nicky had lost his mind. Had he gone crazy when he lost control of his Gift and hurt someone? He couldn't break up with her because they'd never been a couple. They'd been friends, and that was better than—

He bent and brushed her mouth with his, shocking her into utter stillness. "There's your good-bye kiss," he said firmly. And then, with his face still close to hers, he looked at her and suddenly his eyes were wild. And he whispered very softly, "Run."

THE other thing Demi had figured out about disproportionate force was that no one ever expected it. If someone was selling his car, he didn't expect anyone to offer him twice as much as he was asking. If a woman was rude to a clerk at the store, she didn't expect the clerk to shoot her in return.

Mr. Smith hadn't hurt her. He hadn't locked her up. He hadn't even forced her to return to the Refuge to live where she'd be more under his control, and he could have. She was underage and Bright Haven Refuge for Gifted Young People was her legal guardian—which was the same as him being her guardian, because they did whatever he said. No, he'd used what he considered the minimum force necessary to get Demi to stop making trouble. He wanted her to keep working for him. He even said something about it.

But he didn't say one word about her back door. Not one. He didn't know. She was ninety-five percent sure of that.

So Demi did what he expected. He expected her to be upset about Nicky, and she was. She was upset all the way down. When she refused his offer of a ride back to school, he looked sorrowful and disappointed, but not surprised. Then he took away everything she had with her except for her phone and ten dollars for Cokes and snacks. That was supposed to show that he was being strict but not mean. He gave her bus ticket to one of the soldiers and sent the man with her to return the bicycle and wait with her at the bus stop. The soldier handed over her ticket and watched as she got on the bus, but he couldn't buy a ticket there, so he didn't come with her.

And at the first stop, she quit doing the minimum necessary. She got off the bus and started walking. She had a ten-dollar bill in her pocket. She left her phone and her life behind.

Nicky had said "run." She did.

WHITE HOUSE DENIES VIOLATION OF DRAGON ACCORDS

Term in Accords Allows for Dragon "Sabbatical"

By GORDON SHELLEY and JENNIFER MARKUM
JUNE 22

In an effort to refute claims made by some on Capitol Hill that the apparent absence of Mika, Washington, D.C.'s dragon, constitutes a breach of the Dragon Accords, administration officials made the rounds of the Sunday talk shows. U.N. Ambassador Harvey Farrow, appearing on *Face the Nation*, downplayed the idea that the dragon is missing. "Just because we haven't seen Mika for a while doesn't mean he's gone. Dragons have ways of going unseen. New Yorkers rarely see their dragon—standoffish fellow, apparently. Won't even tell them his name. More importantly, the ambient magic level here in the capitol remains low. Our tech's not in any danger." Asked why Mika, who is considered one of the more approachable of the world's twenty-three dragons, might have started masking his presence, Farrow shrugged. "I'm no expert on dragon psychology. Maybe he's having a bad hair month."

On *Meet the Press*, Secretary of State Amanda McCutcheon also pointed out that there was no evidence that Washington's resident dragon had in fact abandoned his lair, adding that, "Even if he is temporarily gone, there is no violation of the Accords. Per that treaty, dragons may absent themselves briefly from their assigned cities for communal or personal reasons." Asked if a month's absence could be considered brief, McCutcheon said there was also a provision in the treaty providing for a more extended absence due to "de'zell afianim ayi'ah veeshun." McCutcheon was unable to define this term or identify the language used. She said that Sun Mzao, the black dragon who negotiated the Accords, had insisted on its inclusion, although he refused to provide a translation. "I believe it refers to a sabbatical related to their spiritual practices," she said. The provision, which appears in Article IV of the Accords, allows each dragon to vacate his post for an indefinite period once every forty-two years.

Efforts to contact Sun Mzao outside his lair near San Diego were unsuccessful. None of the reporters involved in the attempt were injured, and all but one have woken from their magically induced sleep. A shaman and physician connected to the Nokolai lupus clan, Dr. Nettie Two Horses, offered a firm assurance that the man's health was not affected and that he would wake eventually. "I'm told he actually tried to enter Sam's lair," Dr. Two Horses said. "Under the circumstances, Sam showed great restraint." "Sam" is the nickname bestowed on Sun Mzao by some members of Nokolai Clan, which has close ties to the black dragon.

The Dragon Accords, which were signed by the president eighteen months ago, were a response to mounting levels of ambient magic after the Turning. The effect of high levels of ambient magic on computerized technology had resulted in plane crashes, power failures, intermittent cellular outages, and last year's brief panic on Wall Street. Dragons' ability to absorb large amounts of magic convinced a large, bipartisan majority in both the House and the Senate to back the president's proposal to permit dragons sovereign status within their lairs along with more tangible payment. In exchange, dragons agreed to remain within their assigned territories, with exceptions as noted above. Since the Accords were signed, no significant technological problems due to ambient magic have occurred in the dragons' territories.

———————

THREE

July
Washington, D.C.

LILY woke slowly in a bed that wasn't hers. The bed was soft. So was the early morning light. The man pressed up against her back . . . wasn't.

"I had a wonderful dream," Rule murmured, his thumb idly circling her nipple. "It was a sunny day, and you and I stood on opposite sides of a bridge. We both walked out onto it until we met in the middle. There, in front of our families and friends, we agreed we were married."

"Never happen," Lily said, rolling over so she could see his face. "Everyone knows your people don't believe in marriage."

And then she just lay there smiling at him while he smiled at her. She loved the way Rule looked in the mornings. Messy. Which was funny, because she didn't like mess anywhere else. But when he first woke up, with his face all stubbled and his hair every which way, he was hers. Once they left the bed, he'd be Rho of Leidolf Clan, Lu Nuncio of Nokolai Clan, and second-in-command of a highly secret group fighting a war the rest of the world didn't know about. Here, he was just hers.

Funny, Lily thought, how unimportant she'd thought weddings were before she had one of her own to look back on. Not very far back, of course. They'd returned from their honeymoon a little over two months ago. It had been a busy two months, but relatively peaceful until . . .

A waking-up yawn overtook her, making her need to stretch, so she did.

"Do that again."

Her mouth twitched. "Yawn?"

"You can do that, too, if you like," he allowed, "but I was referring to the part where you pressed up against me."

"Oh, you mean like this?"

He confirmed that and added another request. She asked for clarification, so he gave her a hands-on demonstration. Suddenly she was wide awake. He began trailing kisses down her torso, pausing here and there at points of interest, making her wish she could purr. She combed her fingers through his hair.

And shrieked, jerking her hand back and shaking it.

His head came up in alarm. "What?"

She closed her eyes. "Your hair turned into spiders."

"Spiders."

"Hundreds of them. Thousands. Crawling and waving their nasty little legs around."

"I'm guessing that's a mood killer."

She nodded, her eyes squeezed tight.

"Headache?"

"Not this time."

"Then if you kept your eyes closed—"

She opened her eyes to glare at him—and promptly shut them again. "I hate spiders."

"You're afraid of spiders." There was a hint of amusement in his voice.

"Don't even think about teasing me."

"You've fought demons, dworg, a chimea, a wraith, a god, a sidhe lord, and God only knows how many gun-wielding bad guys, but spiders—"

"Shut up, Rule."

"—make you shriek like a little girl."

She couldn't hit him. She might get one of the spiders on her. They weren't real—she knew that—but they looked and felt real, and would for another . . . shit. She'd forgotten to note the time the hallucination started. "Take your gloating and your creepy spider-covered head elsewhere. But first tell me what time it is."

A short pause. "Six fifty-eight. How is it I'm just now learning about this phobia?"

"It's not a phobia. I can handle them one at a time," she said with dignity. "Just not in the thousands."

The bed shifted as he stood up. "I'm going to go wash my spiders."

"No, wait, I need to log how long it lasts, and if I don't see them go away, I won't know—"

"Your eyes are shut. You won't see them go away anyway."

Oh, God, she was going to have to look at them again. She forced her eyes open long enough to confirm that the episode was not over. "I can take quick peeks."

A man spoke on the other side of the bedroom door. "Is everything all right?"

"Lily was startled by one of the hallucinations," Rule said. "She's fine."

"I see. The coffee's ready when you are. I'm going to stir up some pancakes to go with it. We've got maple syrup and a blueberry syrup that Deborah makes from the bushes out back." Ruben's feet made almost no sound on the hardwood floors as he moved away from the door.

Great. Her boss had heard her yell. Not shriek like a little girl. Rule had exaggerated. Yelling was a perfectly natural response to seeing your lover's hair turn into spiders. Seeing and feeling it. Teeny little spider legs on her hand . . .

Lily tossed back the sheet and sat up. Scowling, she reached for her notebook on the bedside table. She jotted down the approximate time the hallucination had begun, what she'd seen—and felt—and added "no headache." Then she snuck a quick peek at Rule, who was contemplating ties. He'd already slipped on a pair of ragged cutoffs to make the trip to the bathroom and selected the day's armor: a suit the color of wet charcoal.

His head still squirmed with horrid little spiders. She looked away and checked the time.

Keeping a record of when each episode hit, what she saw, and how long they lasted might not do a damn bit of good. Sam had called the episodes unpredictable, and the black dragon used words with the precision of a surgeon's scalpel. But he'd also said that both the duration and the nature of experiences during the adjustment period were "highly idiosyncratic," which was why he couldn't tell her how long this would last. Between a few weeks and a few months, perhaps. Though it might be shorter. Or longer.

Given all that uncertainty, Lily really wanted Sam to be wrong about one thing. Maybe her version of the hallucinations would turn out to be predictable. It couldn't hurt to try, and she had learned one thing. When a hallucination was triggered by her connecting with Rule's "frequency," she didn't get a headache afterward.

"Red or blue?" Rule said.

"Hmm?"

"I'm leaning towards red. Politicians often wear red ties, and people are more comfortable if you seem to be like them."

"The honorable representative is not going to think you're like him in any way, no matter what you wear."

They were on this side of the country for several reasons. Representative Jack Brownsley was one. He was on the committee where the Species Citizenship Bill had languished for over a year, and was among those who'd kept pressure on the chair to prevent the bill from coming up for a vote. He was also one of the politicos screaming loudest about the disappearance of Washington, D.C.'s dragon, which was why he'd agreed to talk to Rule today. He knew Rule had a connection to the dragons.

"Not consciously," Rule said, "but I'll use other tools to influence his conscious mind." A pause. "I am not looking forward to this."

Surprised, she glanced up—and quickly looked away again. This one was lasting awhile. "I didn't realize you found dealing with Brownsley that unpleasant."

"I find it unpleasant to have our mate sense scrambled."

And he'd be well over half a mile away, so it would be messed up, but . . . "If we don't 'look' for each other, we won't notice."

"True."

Something in his voice bothered her, mainly because it made her think he was bothered. "Do you want me to go with you?"

A pause while he considered that, then a chuckle. "I might not have a problem dealing with Brownsley, but he'd annoy you. He has some things in common with Leidolf—notably his attitude towards women. At some point he'd try to figuratively pat you on the head. You'd wither his manhood with a glance, and then where would we be?"

"I do not wither manhoods with a glance." Though she liked the idea. Grandmother could wither pretty much anything with a glance, and she wanted to grow up to be like Grandmother.

"Of course you do. I've seen it."

"Now you're just flattering me. Why not go with your silver tie? It's perfect with that suit. Makes you look like a celebrity, and that's a different kind of power than the representative wields."

"True, which is why Washington is fascinated by celebrity. Silver it is. Are you going to accompany me to the shower so you can track the duration of the episode?"

"I . . ." She looked up. And smiled. Rule's head was once more topped by the shiny, mink brown hair she loved. "I won't have to."

"Excellent. In that case, you should definitely come watch me shower."

She laughed. "Forget it. It's seven thirty."

"It's Sunday. Millions of people sleep in on Sunday."

"Ruben didn't. He's going to make us pancakes. After which I'm going to work out with Deborah."

"I'll be quick," he promised.

She snorted. "Sure you will. I want pancakes."

He sighed. "Rejected in favor of pancakes."

"With Deborah's blueberry syrup."

"There is that." He smiled and crossed to her and dropped a kiss on her head. "I'm glad the spiders are gone."

"Me, too. Everyone dislikes spiders, Rule. It's not a phobia. It's a perfectly natural reaction. I do not want to be teased over a perfectly natural reaction."

"I wouldn't dream of it."

"Shit."

He laughed and headed for the door.

She jotted down the time the episode ended, set down her notebook, and stretched. She'd take her shower later, after her workout. There'd be plenty of time for that, she thought gloomily. She was on sick leave. Indefinite sick leave.

Most people did not stay with their boss while they were on sick leave, and Ruben Brooks was Lily's boss twice over: in an official sense, since he headed Unit 12 of the FBI's Magical Crimes Division; and in a highly unofficial and not precisely legal sense. Ruben was also the founder and head of the Shadow Unit.

The Shadow Unit was Ruben's quiet conspiracy to stop the Great Bitch from swallowing the world, most of which didn't know she existed. Things had been quiet on that front lately. The Great Bitch hadn't made a move since her agent, Robert Friar, had been sent to hell—otherwise known as Dis or the demon realm—in late April. This lull would end at some point, but it was welcome, especially with the current communications problem.

Normally the dragons handled the Shadow Unit's communications—you couldn't get more secure than mindspeech—but with Mika AWOL, Ruben had been forced to fall back on more cumbersome and less secure methods involving either encryption and the Internet or burner phones. That was reason number two Lily and Rule were in D.C. As the Shadow's second-in-command, Rule had two primary duties, one ongoing and one contingent. He managed the Unit's finances, and he stood ready to step in as head of the Unit if Ruben were killed or incapacitated.

Reason number three was Leidolf Clan. Ever since the mantle for that clan had been forced on Rule, making him Rho, they'd crossed the country to visit that clanhome as often as possible . . . which hadn't turned out to be all that often. The mate bond made it impossible for Rule to go without her, and often Lily's job made it impossible for her to get away. She knew it worried Rule. All lupi needed the occasional presence of their Rho and the mantle he carried; some needed it more than others.

This time, they planned to spend at least a week at Leidolf Clanhome. Longer, if her hallucinations continued.

Lily heaved a sigh and stood. She'd unpacked as soon as they arrived last night, so it took only a moment to pull on her workout things and head for the bathroom to brush her teeth. Deborah and Ruben's home was large and lovely, but back when it was built, people didn't see the need for more than one bathroom per floor. They'd added a master bath after they moved in, but the only one available for guests was at the far end of the hall. On the way she met a wolf coming up the stairs. He was pale gray with a grizzled muzzle—a rare sight. Rare, too, was that he seemed a bit winded from climbing the stairs.

He stopped and ducked his head.

"I'm afraid I don't recognize you," Lily said apologetically. He must be Wythe—Ruben's clan—and he looked old, but beyond that she couldn't tell. "We must have met, but—"

He shook his head once.

Her eyebrows went up. "You weren't there when I supposedly met every Wythe clan member?"

"That's Charles," said the man at the foot of the stairs. Ruben Brooks did not look like a Washington power broker—or a werewolf, for that matter. More like a modestly successful geek. His black-framed glasses weren't held together by duct tape today, but Lily had seen them that way in the past. "Charles Dupree. You've seen him, but you didn't actually meet him because he was in sleep at the time. I gather," he added dryly as he moved lightly up the stairs, "he wanted to amend that."

Charles nodded.

Now she knew who he was. "You're the one who was hurt by the bear." Hurt saving two human hikers who never knew what he'd done. "I'm honored to meet you, Charles."

He shook his head, then bowed in a way that born-wolves don't, going down on his front knees and lowering his head.

Because of the mate bond, the lupi saw her as a Chosen—chosen by their Lady, the Old One who'd created them over three thousand years ago. Lady-touched. "I know you're honoring the Lady, not me, but it feels weird, so could you get up, please?"

Charles huffed and stayed in his bow.

"I think he's honoring you, not just the Lady," Ruben said. "You preserved Wythe's mantle at great risk to yourself."

Eight months ago, Lily had played temporary host to the

Wythe mantle when the clan's Rho—the mantle-holder—was killed without an heir. Eventually Lily had found the person the Lady wanted to pass the mantle to: Ruben Brooks. Who was her boss at the FBI and—at the time—not a lupus at all. Turned out he had a teeny trace of their blood in his ancestry, and that had been enough. Like all of the Old Ones, the Lady was barred from acting directly in their realm, but she could act through the people she'd created. The lupi. She could, within limits none of them understood, act on the lupi.

She'd used that trace of lupi blood to turn Ruben fully lupus, then she'd bestowed the Wythe mantle on him. And now the head of the FBI's Unit 12, a man who had the ear of the president, turned furry at times.

The mantles were the lupi's deep, dark secret. A clan's mantle gave the Rho his authority; it united the clan; it helped lupi maintain the balance between wolf and man. Mantles also ensured that no lupus ever felt entirely alone. That sounded partly good, partly awful to Lily, who needed time to herself now and then. She'd said something like that to Rule.

"I can't really relate to your need for time alone," he'd admitted. "I try to respect that need, but I don't feel it myself. But mantles aren't intrusive, no more than clothing is. You don't spend your days thinking about how clothed you feel. We don't notice the mantles every moment, but they garb us, keep us from ever being naked, stripped, isolated."

Interesting, she'd thought, that he compared being alone to being stripped. As for her, she might not notice her clothes most of the time, but she always enjoyed removing them at night. Especially her bra.

"Charles," Ruben said, "Lily appreciates the honor you do her, but she's embarrassed."

The wolf huffed again and lowered himself to lie on the floor next to Lily. He sniffed her leg, then settled his head on his forepaws with a sigh of what sounded like satisfaction. And promptly dozed off.

"Charles is one of Wythe's elders," Ruben said softly. "Last month he celebrated his one hundred and fiftieth birthday."

Lily blinked. "He fought a bear when he was a hundred and forty-nine years old?"

"He told me he was glad the bear didn't kill him because he always wanted to go out on an even number." Ruben regarded the sleeping wolf wryly. "Charles has spent much of his century and a half mastering the art of stubbornness. He's good at getting what he wants. He wanted to remain wolf for his last days, so of course I granted that. He also indicated—strongly—that he wished to spend those days near his Rho instead of at our elder home. He persuaded me to allow that, too."

In other words, the wolf dozing at Lily's feet was dying.

Lupi lived longer than humans. A century and a half wasn't unusual. Some lived even longer, and they were healthy and vigorous almost up to the end. But there came a moment, a distinct point, when they began to fade—"like a switch was turned off," one of the Nokolai elders had described it to Lily. They called the remaining span of their lives the waiting time. Some waited only a few days. For most it was a couple weeks, and a few lingered for a month or two. But for all of them, after that point the Change was too taxing without help.

Help was available. A Rho could propel any of his people into the Change, even those who'd passed into the waiting time.

The bathroom door opened and Rule stepped out. He wore a dress shirt with the almost-black slacks, but hadn't yet donned his suit coat or tie. His hair was still damp. "Ruben." He nodded once.

Ruben matched his nod. "Rule. You slept well last night?"

"Very well, thank you. And you?"

"I slept well, also."

Charles snorted.

Lily glanced down, her eyebrows raised. He still looked like he was sleeping.

"Charles," Ruben said dryly, "does not approve of our little experiment."

Nokolai Clan was the majority owner of a perfectly good house in Georgetown, which was somewhat closer to the political action than the Brookses' home in Bethesda. Lily had stayed there several times. Rule was the public face for his people, and he came to D.C. occasionally to advocate for them. The house had recently been renovated, too—the basement could now sleep up to sixteen guards. But she and Rule weren't staying there this time. Ruben had suggested that they could sell the Georgetown house and stay with him and Deborah when they needed to be in Washington.

War was expensive. The clan could use the profit from the sale. First, though, they had to find out if two Rhos could share space comfortably—with "comfortably" being the key word. Rule and Ruben could share space if they had to. They were both aces at control, they liked and respected each other, and neither of them would attack or knowingly offend the other. But lupi need hierarchy. They need to know whether they're the dominant in the room, and each man's instinct would push him to test the other in subtle ways. When they asked about each other's sleep last night, they weren't being polite. They were gathering data.

After a pause Ruben added, "Though I did have an odd dream."

"Shit," Lily said. She and Rule looked at each other. When an off-the-charts precog said he had an odd dream, you wanted to pay attention. Ruben's Gift usually manifested as hunches. Crazy accurate hunches. Lily knew of only one time that Ruben's Gift had escalated into out-and-out visions. Then, the fate of the world had hung in the balance. But those had been visions, not dreams. "Or maybe not. I hope not. Is a dream the same as a vision?"

He smiled, but it was a bit crooked. "No. For some reason, on the rare occasions that my Gift tries to tell me something about my own future rather than larger events, it often manifests as a dream. Precognitive dreams are distinctive in that they're unusually vivid and memorable. Also, they tend to recur, and are often couched in symbolic terms. This one certainly was." Ruben's tone indicated that he did not approve of dreams that failed to state their meaning clearly. "It may be that I have an enemy I'm unaware of. There were a lot of masks in the dream. But that wasn't what I came up here to discuss. Deborah wishes to know if you'd prefer cantaloupe or strawberries."

"Strawberries," Lily said. "Maybe if you told us what, exactly, you dreamt—"

"I don't think that would help." Ruben looked abstracted, as if he were listening to another conversation. His face cleared. "At least that much is plain. It won't help to tell you more at this time. Strawberries, you say?" He gave them a pleasant nod and headed back downstairs.

FOUR

~~~

IF Ruben Brooks looked like the stereotypical geek with a splash of nerd, his wife, Deborah, was a dark-haired version of the cheerleader every geek is supposed to lust after. She might be past the age for turning cartwheels in front of the crowd at the big game, but her type of beauty didn't diminish with the years.

Books and covers, Lily thought as she followed Deborah down the basement stairs, heading for the workout room. It wasn't that the packaging didn't matter. People responded to it, so it made a difference—but only because of how it affected what was inside, not because it reflected the inside. She knew without asking that Deborah had never been a cheerleader. Deborah was rich, beautiful, and painfully shy.

Lily had been glad to learn that because at first she'd thought her boss's wife was stuck-up. That might have been partly her own bias—it was all too easy to assume that rich and beautiful meant stuck-up—but not entirely. Deborah did freeze with those she didn't know well. Once she got past her shyness, though, she was warm and funny and brutally honest. Turned out she could shut down completely with people or she could be wide open. She had trouble with anything in between.

"You're sure you don't mind if I go first on the treadmill?" Lily asked.

"Not at all. I'm hoping you'll run so long I won't have time to get on it at all. I hate the stupid thing."

"I'd much rather run outside," Lily agreed. That, unfortunately, was out of the question. She'd gotten one bodyguard—and friend—killed because she wanted to go for a run when she was away from home. No way would she put her people at risk like that again.

"I meant that I hate running."

"Oh."

Deborah paused at the foot of the stairs to glance over her shoulder with a dimpled smile. "You don't understand that at all, do you?"

"No," Lily admitted. "I love running."

The stairs ended in a short hall. Deborah headed to the right, toward what was obviously the workout room. Lily followed her. "My friend Cynna feels the way you do. I sort of get it. Some parts of working out are tedious. Take crunches. Who could enjoy crunches?" Lily did them because she needed to, not because she enjoyed it. She ran because she needed it, too, but that need was only partly about staying fit.

"I certainly don't. I used to enjoy Pilates class, though."

Lily's hostess had had to give up a lot when her husband was turned into a lupus and inherited the Wythe mantle. Pilates class was the least of it. "I'm not much for exercise classes. Sometimes I get competitive."

"No! You?"

Lily grinned. "Hard to believe, I know."

"I would have thought competing with others would make you enjoy classes more, not less."

"No, because it puts my head in the wrong place. I would've thought classes would be a challenge for you, too."

"You don't have to talk to anyone when you're working out. Just smile and nod. I can do that. Here's your indoor running machine. Shall I show you how to use it?"

"Nice," Lily said. The treadmill was top-of-the-line, as fancy as anything she'd seen at a gym. The other equipment in the small room looked like good quality, too—weights, a pair of reclining benches, a stationary bike, and a big exercise ball. Lily started playing with the settings on the treadmill. "Looks like it does everything but move my legs for me."

"It was my parents' Christmas gift to Ruben. Their way of apologizing for the way they reacted to the unpleasantness last year."

Deborah's voice was tart enough to make Lily think she hadn't entirely forgiven her parents for their assumptions. Ruben had been framed for a nasty murder, part of the Great Enemy's plans for world domination, and Deborah's folks had believed the frame. "Your feathers are still ruffled."

"I'm working on it. This was a thoughtful gift," Deborah admitted. "They have no way of knowing that he's not in a constant state of rehab for his condition anymore."

And there was the reason all the upheaval of Ruben's conversion to lupus had been worth it for Deborah. The condition that had been slowly killing him was no longer an issue.

Deborah lingered beside the treadmill. "Um . . . may I ask you something?"

"Sure," Lily said promptly, though she considered that among the world's silliest questions. The idea behind the question, she supposed, was to warn someone that your question might be offensive and get forgiveness in advance. But if the question was offensive, it would still offend. And why would you want to warn someone anyway? It just put them on their guard. That was no way to get answers. But Deborah was being diffident, which was right on the edge of shy, so Lily didn't explain any of that.

"It's about your health," Deborah confessed. "The condition that has you on indefinite leave."

"Okay. What did you want to know?"

Deborah blinked as if she'd expected more. "Um . . . what's wrong?"

Lily's eyebrows shot up. "Ruben didn't tell you?"

"No. He said it was temporary, that it would resolve itself in time, but he didn't say what it was. He wouldn't," she said matter-of-factly. "Ruben sees health issues as very personal, not something he could repeat without your permission."

"It's not a big deal. A big pain, yes, and it's secret as far as most of the world goes, but not from you. I'm, ah, having hallucinations. Not all the time," she added hastily. "Sometimes I don't have one all day." And sometimes she had two or three, but never mind that. "It's a side effect of my mindspeech training."

Deborah blinked again. "Your what?"

"With Sam. The black dragon. Ruben didn't tell you about that, either?" Obviously not, from the look on Deborah's face. "It turns out that a capacity for mindspeech is part of the package that comes with my Gift."

Deborah's brow wrinkled. "I've never heard of touch sensitives being able to speak mind-to-mind. I don't see how the two are related."

"I can't explain it." To explain she'd have to tell Deborah where her Gift came from, and she wasn't supposed to do that. Which was just as well, because then Deborah would want to know how she could be magically descended from a dragon, and she didn't understand that, either. "Normally touch sensitives don't know about the mindspeech deal because the ability remains latent if it isn't trained. Sam offered to help me train mine."

Deborah looked puzzled, then nodded. "Because of your grandmother. There's some kind of tie between them, isn't there? But this . . . your condition . . . it's temporary? You'll stop having these hallucinations soon? I've always heard that telepathy is hard on the person experiencing it."

That was a nice way of saying that telepaths always went crazy. "Mindspeech and telepathy are both aspects of mind magic, but mindspeech isn't telepathy. They seem to us as if they're the same thing because they both deal with thoughts, but . . . well, the way Sam put it once is that all colors look the same to a person blind from birth. He's certain I won't turn into a telepath, even if I do develop real mindspeech."

"That's in question?"

Lily nodded glumly. "Sam doesn't know how much I'll be able to do after this period of adjustment is over. Or how long the adjustment will take." Probably more than a week, he'd told her. Probably less than a year. The thought of it lasting anywhere near that long made Lily break out in a cold sweat.

"Oh, dear. That's so vague."

"Yeah. I am not good at being on medical leave."

"You hate it."

"I'd rather get a root canal. Or talk to reporters. Or fight demons. Or be locked up in a small room with my Aunt Jei." Lily paused. "Strike the last one. That would be worse."

Deborah laughed and patted Lily's arm. "Remember that it's possible this will only last a couple weeks. Though I can see by your expression," she added, a dimple quivering at the corner of her mouth, "that you consider optimism unnatural. I'll quit bothering you now. I did want to know what was wrong, but you don't have to talk about it."

"It's good that you know. This way I can bitch about it if I want to."

"Feel free." Deborah moved over to the bench. "I'm going to get those annoying crunches out of the way."

"You're not an eat-dessert-first person, I take it."

"No, I want my spoonful of sugar after I've taken the nasty medicine. Don't you?"

"That's an optimist's view. I think you noticed that I'm not an optimist." The treadmill wanted to know all about Lily. Her weight, her age, her height—and why did the machine need to know that?—her resting heart rate. Desired speed, intensity, and length of workout.

This was like speed dating. Any second now it would ask for her astrological sign.

"What do you mean?" Deborah asked.

"You trust that there will be a spoonful of sugar." And a "later," but Lily was trying not to be too much of a downer. She must have succeeded because Deborah laughed again—albeit a bit wheezily, because she'd started her crunches.

Lily finished telling the nosy machine what it wanted to know and hit start. It did. As her feet fell into an easy rhythm, her mind went back to her last session with Sam. As usual, they'd been at his lair just outside San Diego, in the wide, shallow cave he'd excavated in the west side of San Miguel Mountain. The white candle she'd grown to loathe was stuck in the sand. He'd lit it with a thought, then told her to find him in the flame.

That was all he ever said. She'd been trying to find him in the candle's flame for months. Nothing ever happened. Oh, when she first started the lessons, she'd thought she'd "found" him a couple times, but she must have imagined it. Either that or she was going backward, because for months now there'd been nothing. The same nothing had happened at that session, too, for minute after slow, dragging minute . . .

IF she weren't so bloody stubborn, she'd quit, but she hated to give up. Maybe, like Cynna said, she was congenitally incapable of giving up. But if Sam still thought she had some chance of learning something . . . unless he was playing an obscure dragon joke on her, dragging her out here week after week for no—

The candle melted. Between one heartbeat and the next, it turned into a puddle of wax. The rock walls of the cavern melted, too—turned liquid and shiny as they ran and reshaped themselves into an enormous mouth. The inside of an enormous mouth spiked with teeth taller than she was, and there at the back of the mouth was the gaping hole of the throat. She was sitting on the tongue, which rolled beneath her, propelling her back toward the dark maw of the gullet—

Obvious, a cold mental voice said, *yet powerful.*

The mouth was gone. She was sitting on the sand again, with the black dragon coiled at the back of his cave. The candle was intact, but unlit. A wisp of smoke drifted from its wick. "What—what—"

You have made progress. There was, for once, a hint of emotion connected to that crystalline voice, but it was so faint Lily couldn't identify it.

That was progress? Lily's mouth was dry. Her hands shook, and her head was starting to throb. "The mouth—being swallowed—that was an illusion?"

It was a hallucination elicited by an experience that your brain lacks the referents to process. You are now on a cusp. You will continue to experience such mental states intermittently until your brain is able to process the unfamiliar input it is now receiving. There is a small chance that your brain will be unable to adapt, in which case your nascent mindspeech will become permanently blocked. Human brains are quite elastic, however, within certain parameters. It is your minds that resist change, and your mind has now accepted this new input. I estimate the chance of a permanent block forming at less than five percent.

Now she knew what that faint thread of emotion was. Satisfaction. "You were expecting this to happen. You wanted this to happen."

A goal is not an expectation. Today's breakthrough was the goal of this stage of your lessons. You have frequently wondered what purpose was served by sitting in a dim cave staring at a candle. I will now explain. Human brains are heavily weighted towards visual processing. They also seek stimulation while preferencing the familiar. The candle provided a visual focus that engaged your visual processing center. Staring at it became familiar to the point of boredom, while repeated exposure to my mind gradually stimulated your nascent ability into what might be called wakefulness or openness. Both are imperfect metaphors for the process, but your language lacks a precise term. This combination of boredom plus awakening was necessary. On those few occasions when you have briefly accessed your ability, you were not sufficiently bored. Your brain shut off the unfamiliar stimulus before your ability could fully open. Or fully wake, if you prefer.

She had no damn preference which word he used. She wanted it to go away. "And now it's awake and I'm going nuts. And this is what you wanted?"

You are not "going nuts." Neither your brain nor your mind have been damaged, nor should they be as long we avoid contact during your period of acclimatization.

"I didn't hallucinate when I mindspoke with Drummond, and my alert brain didn't shut that down."

He was a ghost. Your connection was largely spiritual. Spirit is exempt from logic, so I do not attempt to explain it.

Lily scowled. Her head hurt, dammit. "How long will this go on?"

Your experience of this period will be unique to you and is therefore unpredictable, though I would be very surprised if it were less than a week or more than a year. It is likely that most sensory distortions will be not be as disturbing as the one you experienced a few moments ago. My mind is exceedingly stimulating to a human mind. Such stimulation was necessary to wake your mindspeech, but is now dangerous and will remain so until your brain learns to process the input it is now receiving.

Wait a minute. Her brain was receiving that input right now? She didn't notice anything. Nothing but a damn headache.

The headache is a product of your having established contact with my mind, however briefly. For now, I am suppressing certain paths. This is an emergency measure, as such suppression has a dampening effect on other brain functions.

"Then once you stop suppressing it, I'll start hallucinating?" Panic hit. If Sam's suppression was the only thing keeping her from hallucinating now that her mindspeech was awake, and her "period of adjustment" went on for months—

Stop. Think instead of reacting. I told you that "waking" was an imperfect metaphor. Your ability was not truly asleep before, nor is it now awake. At the risk of providing you with another mechanism for drawing incorrect conclusions, I will offer a different metaphor. Mind is a product of consciousness which interacts with matter and with magic in detectable ways. Your Gift has always sensed magic. It has now developed a channel—attempt to remember that this is metaphor—through which it senses minds due to the way they interact with magic. There are millions of frequencies available on this channel. Many of them will remain inaccessible to you; you will not acquire the ability to truly read minds. It is quite possible that you will never do more than sense them. It is also possible that, depending on what form this sensing takes, you will eventually be able to initiate mindspeech with a few, many, or even most of the minds you encounter. During the period of acclimatization, your Gift will be constantly, randomly sampling nearby minds. Most of the time you will be unaware of this, but occasionally your Gift will encounter another mind that resonates with yours in a way which stimulates it. When this happens, you will hallucinate until your Gift stops sampling that mind. This process cannot be placed under your conscious control until your brain has acclimated.

Okay, that didn't sound as bad as she'd feared. Not great, but not overwhelmingly awful. She rubbed her temples with both hands. "When I 'found' you, then . . . metaphorically speaking, that means I found the frequency your mind is on?"

My mind is present on all of the frequencies.

Oh. Wow. Shit.

This is why my presence was able to stimulate your Gift

sufficiently for it to claim this new channel. It is also why you cannot be in my presence during your acclimatization period. You are currently unable to stop sampling my mind, which causes a degree of stimulation your mind is unable to sustain without damage.

"But what am I supposed to do? I—"

Leave. I have contacted Rule Turner. He was upset at the sudden distortion of his sense of you, but—

"His what? What do you . . . hell!" Automatically she'd checked for Rule, using the nameless sense the mate bond provided that let her know where he was and roughly how far away. She found him, too, only it didn't make sense. The mate sense said he was fifteen feet away, which would put him in solid rock. Then that he was a hundred miles to the east. "The mate bond's messed up, and it can't be!"

Strive for calm. Your bond is not damaged. The part of your brain which processes your directional sense has, until now, only been used to locate Rule Turner. It is now being employed to process additional input. This creates what you might think of as static. The condition should resolve when your brain completes its adjustment.

"But that's happening in my brain, not Rule's, and you said he was affected, too."

I do not claim to understand the processes of the bond, but there appears to be something similar to a feedback loop. I would appreciate a chance to study it, but at the moment Rule Turner is not inclined to indulge my curiosity. He will arrive in approximately seven minutes to take you home. It would be unwise to drive while you are unpredictably subject to sensory distortion.

She'd left. What else could she do?

That was two weeks and two days ago. Much to her relief—and Rule's—they'd found that the mate sense continued to work normally when they were near each other. Distortion crept in as the distance between them increased. At a hundred feet, no problem. At two hundred feet, the directional sense became less certain. By the time they were half a mile apart, it was completely scrambled—though the scrambling wasn't the same for Rule as it was for Lily. She simply got random locations for him. He usually sensed her in multiple locations at the same time.

Lily had been forced to tell Ruben about being "unpredictably subject to sensory distortion." So far she hadn't had a problem separating hallucination from reality, but she couldn't prove that. Hence the medical leave. The worst defense attorney on the planet could get his client off when the agent in charge of the investigation suffered random hallucinations. When Rule suggested this might be a good time for him to head to D.C. for a bit of lobbying, she'd agreed.

Maybe she could talk Ruben into giving her some kind of desk work. It would be wrong to pester her host, of course, but she could mention the possibility. No more than once a day, she promised herself. Twice a day would be pestering.

The nosy treadmill tilted as it started her up yet another pretend hill. Lily was not a marathoner. She seldom had time for a long run, and besides, what was the point? If she couldn't catch a perp in the first ten or twenty minutes, another hour of chasing wouldn't help. The treadmill had translated her desire for an intense thirty-minute run into lots of hills.

She checked the time . . . almost twenty minutes down. Good. The hills were a bitch. Automatically she checked something else and frowned. Rule was still here. She could have sworn he intended to leave right after breakfast. Representative Brownsley must have called to postpone their meeting. She hoped that didn't mean—

"Pardon the intrusion, Deborah." A red-haired man who looked about thirty stepped into the doorway. Lily had met him when she arrived last night. His name was Alan Jones—a lot of Wythe clan members were named Jones—and he was older than he looked. "It's about Charles."

Deborah didn't sigh. Lily wasn't sure why she had the impression she wanted to. "Yes?"

"I told him to go back to the barracks, but he won't. Not on my word." A tightness around Alan's mouth announced his opinion of that. "The Rho has already left. I could have Charles carried over there, but—"

"He'd probably just come back."

"He's a stubborn cuss."

"I'll speak with him when I go upstairs."

"Thanks." He left as quietly as he'd appeared.

"I . . . met Charles." Lily had to work to find enough breath

to talk. The bastard treadmill had saved the steepest fake hill
for the end of her run. She could reduce the speed or the incline,
but that would be letting the machine win. Seven minutes to
go . . . "He'll listen . . . to you?"

Deborah had finished her crunches plus some lunges and
moved on to weights. "Charles agreed to accept my authority
when Ruben wasn't present. That was one of the terms Ruben
set for allowing him to return with us. I am so glad to see you
out of breath."

Six minutes, forty seconds. Surely a couple of those minutes would be cool-down. "Why?"

"Because I thought you never would be."

Lily snorted. She didn't have enough breath to laugh. Six
minutes, six seconds . . . "Hey," she panted as Rule's presence
nudged into her awareness. He was close enough for the mate
sense to work just fine, but he wasn't supposed to be. A moment
later he appeared in the doorway. "Thought you'd be gone."

"Something came up." He looked easy, comfortable. He
wasn't. That certainty came from a type of knowledge older than
the mate bond. Lily lived, slept, fought, and made love with this
man. She didn't always know his mind, but she knew his body,
and right now his muscles were loose and easy because he
wanted them that way, not because he felt relaxed. She couldn't
tell what emotion he was hiding, but he was hiding something.

The smile he gave Deborah looked like any other smile . . .
if you weren't watching his eyes. "Please excuse us a moment.
My father called. I need to discuss some clan business with
Lily."

"Of course. It must be important if he called at this hour.
It's not much past six in the morning there, is it? I'll head
upstairs so—"

"No, no. You stay and finish your workout. We'll step outside."

FIVE

OUTSIDE meant the backyard, though Lily considered it a stretch to call a space like this a yard. Deborah, like Lily, loved to garden. Maybe that's why she hadn't reverted to shy last night. It's hard to be shy with someone when you're talking compost and mealy bugs. Unlike Lily, Deborah was Earth-Gifted. It wasn't a major Gift, but the size of a Gift didn't always determine what could be done with it, and Deborah worked with hers all the time.

A lot of public gardens would envy the results. Deborah had said she'd let Lily play in her dirt while she was here. She was looking forward to it.

José fell into step several yards back as Rule left the rear deck. Lily wasn't sure where he'd come from, but clearly he wasn't about to let Rule wander around without him, even on land watched by other guards. They were Wythe guards, after all.

His attitude wasn't entirely chauvinistic. Wythe, like most lupi clans, hadn't trained its guards to use handguns the way Nokolai did. Ruben was changing that, but it would take time. Most of the guards patrolling the house weren't armed.

Arranging the guards hadn't been easy. Ruben understood that Rule had to have his own guards; that wasn't the issue. But the guest house he'd built to accommodate his Wythe guards wasn't large enough to house the number of additional guards Rule considered necessary. Plus there was the face issue—at least that's how Lily thought of it. Rule was Rho to one clan and Lu Nuncio, or heir, to another. Both clans needed to be included in the job of guarding her and Rule. In the end, Rule had brought four guards with them, all Nokolai. They'd be joined later today by four more guards, all Leidolf. Leidolf's clanhome was close enough for them to drive up, so they hadn't had to fly any of the California contingent out with them. Two guards would stay on the Brookses' property, with that duty rotated. The rest would stay in a nearby hotel, ready to accompany Rule or Lily when they left the property. And José would be in charge of them all, Nokolai and Leidolf alike. It wasn't an easy job, but he'd done it before.

The path Rule took was mossy stone. It led to a gazebo. A few meters beyond that, the tame area some would call a yard ended and trees began—a long, narrow stretch of old-growth forest. The Brookses owned a small slice of that forest. The rest was a jumble of property lines that the lupi enthusiastically ignored when they went for a run.

"Should I be worried?" Lily asked as they approached the gazebo. There was a breeze, which felt good on her sweaty skin.

"I'm not sure."

That meant no one had died, which was good. Whatever else it might mean, Rule was serious about wanting privacy. He didn't stop at the gazebo, heading on into the forest on an earthen path unsullied by weeds or grass. Lily suspected Deborah had told them not to grow there. There wasn't room to walk abreast, so Lily followed behind.

She didn't mind. Rule had a great butt. Dress slacks didn't do it justice, but the view was still good.

Rule walked in silence about fifty paces inside the trees, then stopped. "We should be private here, if we keep our voices down."

Only he didn't. Speak, that is. Lily waited, but the silence stretched out farther than her patience. "Unless you brought me here to make out—"

"No. Although that's always a lovely idea." A smile skimmed his face without reaching his eyes. "You know about Nokolai's agreement with Sam."

"Sure." Per the Dragon Accords, all dragons were supplied with food—mostly cattle, goats, and sheep, delivered live to a holding pen near their lairs. But eating was not the same as hunting. Sam had arranged to hunt deer occasionally on clan land. In return, Nokolai got a favor or favors. The tricky part of the agreement had been how often Nokolai was required to cash in those favors. Sam didn't want his debt piling up.

"Sam contacted my father. He wishes another deal with the clan. If we agree, he'll show Cullen how to make his array work without side effects."

Lily's eyebrows went up. She thought that over.

Until the Lady turned Ruben lupus, Cullen Seabourne had been the only Gifted lupus in the world. He possessed one of the rarest of Gifts, too: the Sight. In other words, he was a sorcerer, able to see magic. The array was his best attempt so far to protect tech from excess magic. Ever since the Turning, the level of ambient magic had been rising, and magic did not play well with anything that used a computer chip. Unfortunately, while the array did soak up excess magic, it leaked a peculiar form of mind magic that created hallucinogenic memories. If Cullen could make the device work without leaking, it would be worth big money.

She spoke slowly. "He's not wanting a small favor, then. Unless Sam has decided he doesn't object to money after all?"

"No, he doesn't want any of the profits from the device. Those would be divided between Nokolai and the Shadow Unit." Rule's voice remained even, but his jaw was so tight it was a wonder he could push the words out. "In return, he wants you to go to Ohio."

She cocked her head, puzzled. "Ohio pisses you off?"

"Specifically, he wants you to go to a small town called Whistle. You're to be at a park just east of that town at six P.M."

"Six o'clock today?"

"Yes. That's why he wants a decision quickly." A muscle jumped next to his mouth. "He does not want me to go with you."

Okay, that explained Rule's attitude. It didn't explain anything else. "I'm not sure how far away Whistle, Ohio, is, but the mate bond might not agree with Sam about me going there without you."

"Isen negotiated the deal. Naturally he thought of that. If the mate bond disallows our separation, that stipulation is void."

"So what's up? Why does Sam want me to go to Ohio, but not you?"

"It's something about the patterns he monitors. He couldn't or wouldn't explain."

Lily did not understand Sam's patterns. They weren't the same as Ruben's precognitive ability, though Ruben's hunches often matched what Sam read in those patterns. They were what patterners manipulated—she knew that much—but that didn't tell her what they were. "I thought Sam watched the patterns in California, not Ohio."

"Perhaps he's spread his nets more widely that we knew. Perhaps the patterns in California connect to those in Ohio. I don't know. My father wants to accept the deal. I agreed to present it to you."

He hadn't had much choice, if his Rho told him to do it. Maybe that's why he was pissed. "Why did he call you instead of . . . never mind." She'd left her phone in their room. Lily never went anywhere without her phone, but there'd seemed so little point to keeping it with her while she worked out. She wasn't going to get a call about her job. "I'll have to go, of course."

"Dammit, Lily, Sam is manipulating you! You're so antsy about being on sick leave that you're grabbing his offer the way a toddler reaches for candy."

"Of course he's manipulating me. He's manipulating all of us. That doesn't mean I shouldn't go. I wonder why he did it this way? As an exchange of favors with Nokolai, I mean. He could have just asked me. Not directly," she added, "since he can't mindspeak me right now, but he could have passed word to me without going through Isen. I should call—"

"I'm going with you."

Lily told herself not to react. He was worried about her. Ever since the hallucinations started, Rule had been a tad protective. Mostly he kept it under control, but this was pushing his buttons. "If Sam said you shouldn't—"

"Do I tell you what to do?" he demanded. "Have I ever interfered with what your job requires of you? Not that this has anything to do with your job, but if you are foolish and bored enough to accept, I go, too."

Temper sparked. "I'm not the one saying you can't go. Sam is. I need to call—"

"You can't even drive. You aren't safe on your own right now, and I don't give a damn what Sam says."

"I don't have to be able to drive! I'll take guards with me, of course, so one of them—"

"And will you have a guard with you every moment? In the bathroom? In your room at night? What happens if you see a demon at the window? If you think it's a hallucination and it isn't—"

"I can tell the difference. And if you interrupt me one more time—"

He did.

Things went downhill from there.

"OF course I know about it," Grandmother said.

She said it in Chinese, which meant she expected Lily to speak Chinese, too. Which Lily could do, but not all that well, and Rule didn't understand it at all.

She and Rule were still on the forest path, but no longer yelling. At least Lily had stopped yelling. Rule hadn't started. He never raised his voice, no matter how mad he was. It drove her crazy to be the only one yelling. Lily had pointed out— rather loudly—that she'd been trying to tell him she'd call Grandmother before officially agreeing to anything. She'd borrowed Rule's phone to do that, since hers was in their room.

In careful Chinese, Lily said, "Would you object to speaking English, Grandmother? Rule is here."

"The two of you are arguing. Good." That was in English.

Grandmother often baffled, annoyed, or confused her. This time she managed to do all three at once. "How do you know? And what in the world is good about that?"

"Your wolf is fairly wise about women. He knows nothing of marriage. You are wondering why Sun makes this request."

Sun Mzao was Sam's Chinese name. Grandmother, who had a long—a very long—history with the black dragon, called him

Sun. But when Lily met the black dragon, he'd told her to call him Sam, so she did. "Yes."

"I can tell you very little. First, Sun has not perceived the Great Enemy's hand in the patterns which concern him."

"Good to know."

"However, he also has not perceived anything which would definitely rule out *her* involvement, perhaps through multiple intermediaries."

"That's less reassuring."

"Ohio is a long way from California."

Meaning, she supposed, that even Sam had his limits. "Can you be more specific about why he wants me to go to Ohio?"

"The patterns suggest that your presence there is highly desirable."

In other words, no. Though Lily suspected Grandmother knew more, she wasn't sharing. "Why did he arrange the deal through Nokolai?"

"So it would not be a family matter. If you do not agree to the deal on behalf of Nokolai, however, I will ask it of you."

That put a whole different spin on things. She couldn't refuse to go if Grandmother asked her, so she might as well go as a representative of Nokolai and let the clan benefit from it. She looked at Rule, eyebrows raised. "You heard?"

He looked grim. "Yes."

"Rule does not approve?" Grandmother asked.

"He's unhappy because Sam wants him to stay here. Do you know why?"

"If Sun says Rule should stay in Washington, he should stay in Washington. I will go eat my breakfast now." Grandmother disconnected.

Lily looked at Rule. "You knew the Great Bitch isn't behind whatever Sam wants me to investigate."

"No, I knew Sam couldn't detect her in his patterns. That's not the same thing."

"And you didn't tell me." All of a sudden Lily wasn't mad anymore. Emotion flowed into the vacuum left by the departure of anger, but it was too complex to hang a tag on. Silently she held out his phone. When he took it, she turned and started for the house.

This time he followed her. Neither of them spoke until they

reached the rear deck, when Rule broke the silence. "You're going."

"Yes. If I can," she added. "There's no telling how the mate bond will react." The mate bond was essentially physical. It was also capricious. Sometimes it allowed them to be miles and miles apart. Sometimes it didn't, and it let them know that by making them pass out when they crossed some invisible line. "Where is Whistle, anyway?"

"The southwest corner of the state, about four hundred miles from here."

"Then there's a good chance you won't have to worry about Sam's dictum that you stay here."

"Since I'll be with you, the issue won't arise."

She stopped, turned, and frowned at him. "What's going on? Is it you or your wolf that's being so pigheaded?"

"I am my wolf," he said, and then, "I don't know."

She huffed out a breath. "We need to talk about this. About . . ." She waved a hand vaguely. Rule was protective, no doubt about that. But his reaction today was over the top. Out of balance. As protective as he could be, he was also driven by duty. "Whatever it is that's making you act so weird. But I don't have much time. If I'm going to be there by six—"

"We can talk about it on the way there."

Lily stared at him, frustrated. She could point out that if he went with her, the deal with Nokolai would be invalidated and the clan would get nothing. She could repeat that it would be stupid to ignore the advice of the black dragon, who wanted Rule in D.C. But he knew those things, so why bother?

Stone would be more yielding. Shit, his brother Benedict would be more yielding, and Benedict made granite look like a pushover. She shook her head and went into the house.

Ruben was in the kitchen, sitting at the table in the breakfast nook. Lily had vivid memories of that nook—of the whole kitchen, really. Some of them were not such great memories, but one of them . . . here, she'd passed the Wythe mantle to Ruben. Here, she'd heard the Lady's voice.

Today Ruben was reading the morning paper. He put it down when they came in. "Deborah said you were discussing clan business. Your faces suggest it's not good news."

She glanced at Rule. He didn't offer to explain, but he didn't signal any objections to her doing that, so Lily told him about Sam's proposed deal. ". . . so I need to leave, and pretty quickly, too."

"*We* have to leave," Rule corrected her.

"You're going with her?" Ruben asked sharply.

"Of course. Sam's stipulation about my remaining here is unacceptable. Isen will have to renegotiate."

Ruben's eyes went unfocused for a moment. "That would be . . . unfortunate."

"You've got a hunch," Lily said.

"Yes. It's difficult to read because it involves my own future as well as larger events, but I believe the Shadow Unit will experience a crisis soon. Given our communication problem, I will need Rule here."

For a long moment Rule neither moved nor spoke, looking like a storm cloud just before it cuts loose and hurls down floods and lightning. Then: "I'm going for a run." He shot Lily a hard look. "A quick run. You'll still be here when I return." And he took off.

Ruben frowned at Lily. "What was that about?"

"I just won the argument," Lily said. Pity that made her feel like shit.

SIX

JOSÉ needed more time than Rule to complete the Change back to two legs, so Rule made a couple phone calls while he waited.

The run hadn't helped as much as he'd hoped. Anger still churned inside him, a dark and roiling mass without a target— or with too many targets. He didn't want to poke at it. He didn't want to examine whatever slurry of need and fear fed the compact storm inside him. He'd have to, but he didn't want to.

He didn't understand.

Neither did Lily. What had she said? A great many things, he thought with a flash of dark humor as he buttoned his shirt. Some of them reasonable, which had infuriated him. Some of them not so reasonable, which had been both infuriating and satisfying. He hadn't wanted to be angry alone, had he?

Whatever has you acting so weird. That's what she'd said, and she was right. He was acting weird. Unlike himself. It was always a struggle to hold back when Lily hurled herself at some deadly opponent, but his mate was a warrior. He couldn't shield her from what she was, and trying would only make them both miserable without making her one bit safer. She'd do what she had to do anyway.

As she was today.

He rolled up his sleeves. José was pulling on his jeans now. José's first Change—the one from two legs to four—had been plenty fast. Also involuntary. Rule had switched to four legs with such brutal speed that he'd pulled José into the Change with him.

Appalled by that lack of control, Rule had been careful not to repeat his mistake when he switched forms this time. With the power of one full mantle and a portion of another, he could have Changed back and forth between wolf and human all morning. He wouldn't have enjoyed it, and he would have grown extremely hungry, but he could have done it.

José couldn't do that. Unlike some, however, he could switch from four legs back to two quite soon after making the initial Change. That's why Rule had been careful not to pull him into Change the second time, though that would have been easier on José. When a Rho or Lu Nuncio forced the Change on one of his people, the mantle helped power it. But doing so would have been an insult. It belittled a man to do for him what he could do for himself.

It belittled a woman to do that, too.

Rule's mouth stretched thin. He was needed here in D.C. He wanted to dispute that but couldn't, not with Sam and Ruben making the same claim. And Lily would go on Sam's mysterious errand whether he liked it or not. If he insisted on going with her, he wasn't just tossing duty aside. He was announcing that he didn't trust her to handle the situation without him.

Rule gave José instructions as they walked to the house. When they reached it, José split off to get ready. Rule paused in the kitchen. Lily was close enough for him to use their bond's directional sense without much distortion, so he knew that she was upstairs. His ears told him that Deborah was, too.

Perhaps Deborah heard him as he came up the stairs because she excused herself on a rather flimsy pretext. When she passed Rule in the hall, she gave him an encouraging smile. Encouraging him to apologize, no doubt. He nodded, agreeing grimly that he should.

Rule stopped in the doorway to their room. Lily was tucking her toiletries bag into the corner of the suitcase. She spoke without looking up. "I called Isen."

Isen had mentioned that when Rule called him while waiting for José to finish Changing. He hadn't deigned to tell Rule
anything about the conversation. "I called Alex. He'll send a
squad to meet you in Whistle. They should be there by eight
or nine this evening. Until then, you'll have José and Carson.
José will be in charge of the guards."

Alex was Lu Nuncio or second-in-command for Leidolf. He
ran things when Rule couldn't be at Leidolf Clanhome—which
was most of the time, unfortunately. Rule had brought a number of Leidolf to California to serve as guards, but most of the
clan still lived on this side of the country. One of the things on
their to-do list for this trip had been spending time at Leidolf
Clanhome.

"A full squad?" Now Lily looked at him, eyebrows raised.
"That seems excessive."

"We have no idea what you'll be facing."

"Is that why you're so . . ." She gestured vaguely.

"Weird, I think you said?" His mouth twisted. "I don't
know. And I don't care to talk about it."

Lily cocked her head. Then she walked up to him and put
her arms around him.

He grabbed her back—grabbed her and held on as if she'd
been struggling to escape, rubbing his cheek along the top of
her head, trying to breathe in so much of her scent that it would
stay with him.

Slowly she ran her hands up his back and down again. Over
and over. Soothing him the way he sometimes soothed her.
For once, she asked no questions. Slowly, some of the tension
eased out of him.

She leaned back to look at him. "Are we still mad at each
other?"

"I'm sorry for losing my temper. I don't want to talk about
that, either."

That made her snort. "You sound like me when I'm being
a pain."

He laid his hands on either side of her face and tipped it up.
Her eyes were dark and worried. "I love you. I'm angry, but I
love you."

"And I love you, even when you're freaking out. I told Isen
that you staying here wasn't part of the deal."

"You—" He stopped. Knocked the biggest prop for his anger right out from under him, hadn't she? "I didn't think that was an option. Sam insisted I stay here. That's what Isen agreed to. That's what you wanted me to do."

"Sam can insist on whatever he wants. Isen can agree. Doesn't mean I have to agree, and without me there's no deal. But I hope you'll stay in D.C. even if it isn't part of the official deal. Not because I don't want you with me, but if Sam and Ruben both think you'll be needed here . . ." She shrugged. "Black dragon. World-class precog. It seems like we should listen to them."

Rule grimaced. "Yes. Did I say anything unforgivable when we were arguing?"

"It's never what you say when you're mad. It's the way you say it. Did I say anything I should apologize for?"

"There was something me being a pigheaded idiot."

"Yeah, but that was true. Was there anything else?"

"You didn't react right." The words came out before he knew they were true. It hurt. He hadn't realized that. At the center of the storm in his gut was pain. "You weren't upset. I wanted . . . I don't know what exactly, but you accepted our separation so calmly, so reasonably, and I—" His eyebrows snapped down. "Why are you grinning like that?"

"Because for once I get to be the grown-up. It's downright childish to expect someone to follow your script without having a clue that it exists, then get all pissy when they don't."

This time his eyebrows shot up. "Now I'm a childish, pigheaded idiot?"

She just smiled and patted his cheek. "I love you."

He sighed. The storm hadn't gone away, but it was less virulent. "I won't be able to feel you. To sense where you are."

She nodded. "Which sucks."

"And I can't have your back when we're separated by four hundred miles."

"For all we know, I'll get twenty miles out of town and we'll both pass out."

"God, I hope so." Which was pathetic. He took a slow, careful breath, then glanced at the bed. "You're packed."

"Packed and ready."

"Then I'd best be ready for you to go, too."

*   *   *

THEY headed downstairs together. Rule carried her suitcase; she had her garment bag. They'd packed for an extended stay when they came here, and she seemed to be taking everything with her. That did not mean they'd be apart as long as the amount of clothing she was taking suggested. He was firm with himself about that. She was just being practical.

When it really mattered, Lily had managed to refrain from asking questions. On the way downstairs, she reverted to normal. "Do you think Sam has some way of knowing that the mate bond will allow us to be separated?"

"I don't see how he could."

"If the mate bond does allow the separation, does that mean the Lady approves?"

"I don't know."

"Ruben thinks the Shadow Unit's involved in whatever you're needed here for. That suggests the Great Bitch is going to try something here, not in Ohio. If so, I'm the one who ought to be worried."

He had managed enough rational thought to reach that conclusion, which was why he'd suddenly needed to run. When he set his fear of being parted from Lily up against stopping the Great Bitch, stopping the Great Bitch won. Barely.

Ruben and Deborah were waiting outside for them. So was the Mercedes that Rule had rented last night. Clearly, José had hustled. He was riding shotgun with Carson behind the wheel. Lily liked to tease Rule about his fondness for Mercedes, especially when it came to rental vehicles. She didn't understand why he'd pay that much when he could rent "a perfectly decent sedan" for half the price. Rule didn't understand why anyone who could afford it would trust their lives to less than the best. The most dangerous places in America weren't the slums of any city, but the roads and highways where its citizens blithely risked life and limb every day.

Carson popped the trunk. "You'll need to rent another car," Lily told Rule.

"Of course." He tossed the suitcase into the trunk, which already held the rifles and ammo he'd told José to bring. They came from the Georgetown house, retrieved last night. The other addition to the trunk, he assumed, had come from Ruben. "You'll need to call me. Often."

"Of course." She laid her garment bag on top of the suitcase. Her eyes lit up. "Hey, that's an M4. Or an M4A1?"

"It's the A1," Ruben said.

Which meant it was capable of switching to fully automatic fire. After the incident with the dworg, Lily had announced a "don't leave home without one" policy for submachine guns. Fortunately, her boss had seen the need as well.

Ruben could, on a whim, call out the Army, but obtaining submachine guns for his field agents turned out to be more difficult. However, FBI SWAT teams already used M4s, which meant most of the *i*'s had already been dotted, the *t*'s crossed, for those weapons. Ruben had made bureaucratic magic and gotten the automatic version of the rifle approved for use by Unit 12 personnel. The M4A1 was not, Lily had informed Rule firmly, a true machine gun. It was a carbine rifle capable of firing an average of 825 rounds per minute when set to automatic fire—which sounded like a machine gun to Rule, but he hadn't argued.

Lily had qualified on the weapon two weeks ago, but hadn't been issued one yet. She gave the one in the trunk an approving pat. "I don't suppose you've gotten approval for the grenade launcher attachment."

"Not yet."

"Pity, but I am very glad to see this." She closed the trunk and slanted Rule a glance. "I don't know about you, but I feel better."

He spoke dryly. "I'm hoping you won't need a machine gun."

"Well, sure, but it's better to have it and not need it than the other way around. Not that the M4A1 is really a machine gun. Leaving aside the kind of ammo used, it's not designed for the kind of sustained fire that . . . oh, hi, Charles."

The Wythe elder had apparently decided to see Lily off, too. He wagged his tail once, sat next to Lily, looked at the car door.

"I guess you heard that I'm leaving?"

Charles nodded.

Ruben wanted Lily to sign a form accepting receipt of the

weapon. Deborah wanted Lily to know that she planned to install asters and other plants whose names Rule didn't recognize—a treat Lily was invited to share if she got back in time. José wanted Lily to know that while he and Carson could carry their weapons in Ohio due to the reciprocity agreement that state had with California for concealed carry permits, the Leidolf guards wouldn't be able to.

Rule wanted everyone but Lily to go away.

Lily signed the form, hugged Deborah, then just looked at Rule. Apparently now that they came down to good-bye, she didn't like it, either. After a moment his mouth quirked up. "You'll do fine. I may be a wreck, but you'll do fine."

She hugged him without speaking. It was hard to let go, but he did. She turned and opened the car door. "Hey!"

Charles had brushed past her and jumped into the car. When he lay down, he didn't leave much room for Lily. He was a very large wolf.

She shook her head. "Charles, I'm sorry, but you can't go with me."

Charles laid his head on his paws and lowered his ears—a submissive posture, but he didn't follow through by obeying her.

"Charles," Ruben said sharply.

Charles twisted around and grabbed tip of his tail with his teeth.

Oh, shit, Rule thought.

Lily said, "Is that supposed to mean something? Because it doesn't. At least not to me."

"It looks like he's trying to make the sign for the Lady," Carson said. "Normally he'd curve his body so that he shaped a circle to stand for the moon, but it's hard to do that in the backseat."

"I know you're excited that I'm Lady-touched." Lily sounded exasperated. "But you can't go with me."

Rule fought a brief but fierce battle with himself. One of the them won. "Ruben, I don't wish to intrude on your business, but with your permission, I'd like to ask Charles a couple of questions."

"Very well."

Lily gave him a questioning glance, which he ignored. She

moved aside so he could bend down and address the stubborn elder. "Charles, you made the sign for the Lady. Were you referring to the fact that Lily is Lady-touched?"

Charles let go of his tail and shook his head.

He did not want to ask the next question. "Are you saying that the Lady wants you to go with Lily?"

He nodded.

"Is that what you feel she wants?"

The wolf shook his head.

"Did she speak to you?"

His nod this time was quick and definite.

"Did she tell you specifically to go with Lily?'

Another nod.

Rule sighed and straightened. That's what he'd been afraid of.

Lily watched him with a small frown. Ruben's frown was more pronounced. "You believe that?" he asked.

"Sometimes the Lady speaks to an elder in his waiting time."

Ruben exchanged a look with Deborah—the kind outsiders couldn't interpret. "Is this something I'd know if I'd been born lupus?" he asked.

"Probably. Many elders experience the Lady's presence in their waiting time, sometimes quite keenly, but few actually hear her voice. Those who do . . ." Rule paused, remembering Gregory Lawson, who'd died five years ago. Gregory never would repeat what the Lady had told him. When Rule asked, he'd just shaken his head and smiled, but that smile . . . Rule could only hope that, if he survived to reach his waiting time, he would be as fortunate as Gregory. "Those who receive the blessing of her voice don't always reveal what she said, but some do. The Lady often uses that moment of clear communion to acknowledge an elder's service in some way."

Ruben's frown lingered. "I should have been told about this possibility."

"I've never heard about it, either," Lily said. "They're forever forgetting to mention stuff. Partly that's because they're so used to keeping secrets, but also once you've been clan awhile, they don't realize that no one's told you this or that because it's something that 'everyone knows.'" She tipped her head, looking at Rule. "You believe Charles. You think the Lady told him to stick with me."

"He wasn't lying." Rule had been close enough to smell a lie.

"And you don't think he's fooling himself?"

"You've heard the Lady's voice. Could you mistake anything else for that?"

She shook her head. She looked wistful.

"We hear the Lady's song carried on the moon, and we . . . I think . . ." He stopped, struggling for words. There were no adequate words for the Lady's song. "Hearing her song is not the same as having her speak directly to you, but it's still her voice. I can't imagine any lupus could confuse her voice with anything else."

Lily's gaze went to the huge wolf in the Mercedes's backseat. "Looks like I'll have four-legged company for the drive."

SEVEN

THE office was large, but far from plush. The desk was large, too, but old and battered. Not the space or the furnishings of a mover and shaker, not in this town, where appearance counted for so much.

The man seated behind the desk fit his office. He was pale and plump and looked like any modestly successful bureaucrat on the shady side of fifty. His head was round, bald, and shiny in the glare of the overhead fluorescents. His glasses were round, too, and rimless. His navy tie matched his slacks and the suit jacket hanging on the coatrack just inside the door. The white shirt he wore was the one hint of personal extravagance, being made of especially fine Egyptian cotton.

He was tapping away at the keyboard in front of him when the office door opened.

The man who entered was seven inches taller and twenty years younger. Something in his carriage suggested the military, though he was dressed much like the older man. His hair was dark and thick, his skin swarthy, suggesting a Mediterranean heritage—Spanish or Italian. "I had a feeling you hadn't left yet," he said with a small smile.

"What time is it?" The round little man glanced at one of the computer screens and shook his head. "Six o'clock already. I should let Helen know I'm running late." But for all the distracted regret in his voice, he was smiling, too. "I suppose Mrs. Ellison has gone home?"

"Yes, sir. I thought I'd see if you want to check out the latest tests on the Prism system."

"Oh, are those ready? Certainly." He pushed his chair back and stood.

The two of them left the large, ordinary office. As they headed down the hall, they chatted in a mix of tech-speak and bureaucratese about Prism, which apparently had something to do with cell towers. Most of the offices opening off that hall were dark, but a couple held people working late. Their conversation turned more personal as they reached the elevator. The younger man asked the older one about Helen's recent foot surgery. They discussed bunions as they rode down four floors.

When the elevator stopped at the ground floor and the doors opened, neither man got off. Instead the younger man inserted an unmarked key card into a slot. The doors closed and the elevator descended again, although the indicator stayed on the ground floor. When the doors opened a second time, they stepped off.

There was no hall this time. They stepped directly into a large room where a couple dozen people sat at workstations watching displays. About two-thirds of the stations were manned; the displays at the unmanned stations were dark. Several of the workers wore headphones. The two men spoke about text messages again as they skirted the perimeter of the big room, stopping at one of the doors along that perimeter. The younger man used his key card a second time, inserting it into a slot where a doorknob would normally be. There was a faint click. He pushed the door open.

Three people sat at the round table inside—two men and a woman. The woman and one of the men wore versions of the bureaucratic uniform. She was blond; he had carroty red hair. The third man had at least one Asian parent. His jeans and black silk shirt set him apart from the others, as did the way he lounged back in his chair. A large screen hung on one wall.

No one spoke until the door closed. "We're tight," the woman announced. She was watching at a handheld device that resembled a touchscreen phone.

The younger man pulled out a chair and sat. His superior remained standing as he addressed the others. "The curtain goes up tomorrow," Edward Smith told them. "Chuck, please bring everyone up-to-date on your end."

"Yes, sir." The red-haired man pointed a remote at the screen, which lit up. A flowchart appeared. "As some of you are aware, we weren't able to create the optimal routing due to the unexpected addition of magical protection on Target Duo's accounts. Weng believed he could disable those protections, but couldn't guarantee he could do so without being detected, nor was he able to determine what would happen if the ward was triggered. It was decided that the risk was unacceptable."

The two looked at the Asian man, who shrugged. "Hey, Seabourne's good. Not as good as me, but it's always easier to set a ward than to eliminate one without getting caught."

"Wait a minute," the blond woman said. "You're saying he warded a bank account? How is that even possible?"

Tom Weng's upper lip lifted in a sneer. "And of course magic can't be used on electronic records. Otherwise we'd be able to do things like, oh—maybe change the history of how funds were moved through a particular system."

The woman flushed with embarrassment or anger. "A ward by definition is fixed. Electronic data is fluid."

Tom shrugged. "Obviously this isn't a conventional ward. I call it that because it serves a similar function, not because it's constructed along conventional lines."

"But how—"

"Give it up, Sharon. Nowhere in my contract does it say I'm obligated to instruct you."

The woman smiled unpleasantly. "Meaning you don't know how Seabourne did it, either."

Smith broke in before the discussion could devolve into an outright argument. "Since we weren't able to implicate Target Duo directly, we'll be using the secondary plan. I'm not going to brief you on that right now, but it's proceeding as planned."

"And Target Tres?" she asked.

"Remains on sick leave and so not our concern, though we will assist Tom if he chooses to act. At this time, he does not require our assistance." He looked at the Asian man. "Tom, please apprise the others of your implementation of the attack on Target Prime."

He shrugged. "I did what I said I would. Your geeks implanted the changed data, and I made all traces of the tampering go poof and spread the changes around."

"That's not a briefing," Carrot-top complained. "It doesn't come close to explaining anything."

Tom looked bored. "I'm not obliged to explain. If I tried, you wouldn't understand one word in ten. Maybe I'm wrong. Maybe you do know something about the effect of trans-zero substitutions on immaterial matrixes."

Carrot-top scowled. Before he could speak, the woman did. "Don't bother, Chuck. He's being obscure on purpose. He doesn't want us to know how he does what he does, just in case one of the kids might learn how to do it, too, and then where would he be?"

"Still employed," Tom drawled, "since none of your kids have or ever will have a clue how to make the potion."

The woman lifted her chin. "You're sure of that? We know what the key component is."

"You probably know the key component in a nuclear bomb, too. Doesn't mean you can make one. Though you could do that long before you could duplicate my potion. Unless," he added so politely it registered as sarcasm, "you've managed to locate a kid with the Sight and haven't mentioned that to the rest of us?"

"Tom is and will remain an invaluable part of our team," Smith said firmly. "Now, Greg tells me he's completed testing the results of Tom's magical cleanup." He nodded at the younger man who'd come to get him. "If you'd let the others know the results?"

Greg spoke in crisp, jargon-rich sentences, ending with, ". . . all negative, in other words. Tom has done exactly what he said he would. No one will find any sign that the files were altered."

There were grins, a few words of congratulations. "This is it, then," Carrot-top said. "Are we green to go?"

"If the girl follows through on her threat," Carrot-top said worriedly.

Smith brushed that off. "I am confident she will, but if I'm wrong, it's hardly a disaster. The public pressure will be less, but you can trust me to see that Eric acts."

Carrot-top grimaced. "I suppose so. Still, he'll be more motivated if the reporters are screaming. I guess we can count on her to remain a traitor, but she's also a coward. What if—"

Smith spoke with sudden sternness. "She's not a traitor."

"Oh, come on. She turned on us. She puts those weirdos of Sharon's above the good of the country. If that's not—"

"The children are not weirdos!" Sharon snapped.

"Enough." Smith rapped the table with his knuckles. "Demi is misguided and squeamish. Her actions make her our enemy, but that is not the same as treason. If we delude ourselves into thinking that those who oppose us are traitors, we will fail. We will fail because we won't understand our enemies' goals and motivations." He looked around the table, holding each pair of eyes briefly. "Most civilians aren't capable of putting the country first. They aren't capable of making the hard decisions. They need us to do that, whether they realize it or not. We're their protectors, and if we must do much of our work in secret, so be it."

Heads nodded. Eyes glowed with fervor. Greg murmured agreement.

Tom Weng looked sardonic. "So would you say that Target Prime is an enemy or a traitor?"

Smith stood. "Oh, he's both. No question about that. Ruben Brooks is very much our enemy. He is also a traitor to this country. We've known that for some time. People with nothing to hide don't go to such extremes to make sure we can't listen in on their calls."

"That drove me crazy," muttered Chuck. "I still don't know how he blocked me on some of his calls."

Smith waved that away. "It hardly matters now. Thanks to Tom, we know what form his treason takes. And soon everyone else will know, too." He smiled. "It's time for me to give Eric a call."

EIGHT

THE piercing alarm made Demi scowl and pull her pillow over her head. It didn't help. Muttering to herself, she threw the pillow off, reached out, and slapped the button on the cheap clock. She sat up on the edge of the narrow bed and rubbed her face.

One forty-five. Time to get up. She'd hadn't even tried to go to bed until six this morning, keeping herself busy by playing online games and reading posts in the forum and at her favorite fan site. She'd needed something to do in between checking over and over for a response that hadn't come.

Today it would. It had to. Today was the last day for Mr. Smith to respond. If he didn't, the first file was going out, and he couldn't afford to let that happen. She'd sent him part of that file so he'd know she meant business, that she could take him down if she had to.

Her stomach hurt. Slowly she stood, wishing she liked coffee. That had to be a nicer way to wake yourself up than with a jolt of fear. Though fear did the job pretty well.

The twin bed opposite the one she slept in held a pile of dirty clothes and a top-of-the-line MacBook. Oh, shoot. She'd forgotten. Her favorite screensaver was showing, the one that switched among her collection of Rule Turner photos. Usually she didn't leave that up because she was being a guy now. If anyone saw it, they'd think she was gay. She wouldn't care about that if it weren't for the "getting beat up" aspect. Lots of people in high school and college had thought she was gay, which she wasn't . . . and why wasn't it okay to wear a pin saying "I'm straight"? She'd thought that was a great idea, but Nicky talked her out of it. He claimed it would send the wrong message, which made no sense. Apparently she was sending the wrong message without the pin.

The Aspies in the forum thought pins were a great idea and that everyone should wear one: "I'm straight," "I'm gay," "I'm bi," or "I'm asexual." They couldn't agree on if trans people should modify their pins—"I'm trans straight" or "I'm trans gay" or whatever. Most of the gay and straight Aspies thought it depended on whether or not you'd had the full surgery; to them, it was only fair to let a possible sexual partner know up front if you didn't have the type of genitals they expected. The bi's thought it was unnecessary to announce a variance between appearance and identity, since there were plenty of workarounds. And the asexuals didn't care.

Demi thought the reason they couldn't agree was that none of them were trans. Aspies weren't good at imagining themselves into other people's feelings. They all agreed that pins would work for most people, though.

Normal society did not see it that way. Normal society liked to make things complicated. And unfortunately, some people in normal society liked to beat up on gay guys. Demi usually didn't leave her Rule Turner screensaver up.

She moved to the bed holding her laptop and sighed. He was so pretty, but looking at him didn't make her feel one bit better today. She hurried through the security protocol and checked for flags. Nothing. She logged into the IRC server . . . several new messages, but nothing directed at her. Her heart pounding, she hopped over to the gardening forum where she'd directed Mr. Smith to post a response.

Still nothing. How could there be nothing?

The forum wasn't down. There were new messages on other threads, but nothing on the one she'd started. The one where Mr. Smith was to respond by two o'clock today. It was 2:05.

She didn't understand. She'd planned for all sorts of possibilities, everything she could think of. Everything except silence.

How did silence make sense? Mr. Smith was a terrible person, but he wasn't stupid. He had some reason for not responding, but for the life of her she couldn't figure it out.

He'd be trying to find her. That much she was sure of. But he'd been trying to find her for eleven months and hadn't managed it . . . except for last March. He'd come close then. Way too close. Maybe he was close again. Close enough that he thought he didn't have to answer her.

But he shouldn't think that. She'd told him. If she didn't send a certain code, the first file would be released automatically. The others would follow on a preset schedule. Grabbing her—even killing her—wouldn't stop that.

Why hadn't he answered?

When Demi's stomach growled, she realized she'd just been sitting there, hugging herself and rocking. She let out a shaky breath. Bodies were weird. How could her stomach be upset and hungry at the same time? It was, though.

At least today was Sunday. She took a deep breath, stood, and stepped carefully around the fan that was trying valiantly to cool things off. She liked a lot of things about the little Airstream trailer that was home for now, but not the lack of air-conditioning. At least she'd be at work by the time the interior temperature hit "oven."

The bathroom was only a few steps away. She'd decided years ago that sleeping naked was more efficient, so she didn't have any pajamas to deal with. She turned on the hot water, emptied her bladder, then adjusted the water temperature in a shower designed for munchkins. Demi was five feet, ten inches tall. She hadn't fit under the original shower head, so she'd replaced it with a handheld.

Not that her landlord knew about the alteration. The old witch would have a hissy fit if she found out, though it was clearly an improvement.

Mrs. MacGruder was the other thing she didn't like about her current home. The woman had mean eyes, a mean mouth, and a cold heart. Otherwise, the place suited Demi. It was cheap, close to the gas station, the utilities were included in the rent, and there weren't any roaches. Give Mean-Eyed MacGruder that much—she was a demon for clean. The little trailer might be old and worn, but it had been spotless when Demi

moved in. And it was nice outside. Mrs. MacGruder's property
was right on the edge of Whistle, and if the ground between
Demi's trailer and her landlady's home was more weeds than
yard, it had looked really pretty in the spring with all the wild-
flowers. They'd stopped blooming now and the mix of grass
and weeds looked tired and dry, but the woods that bordered
the land on one side were green and soothing to look at.

Almost everything in the trailer worked. One of the two
burners on the stovetop was out, but that wasn't a biggie. Demi
only cooked twice a week, on her days off: a pot of soup on
Saturday and a pot of beans on Wednesday. She fixed rice to go
with the beans, but that could wait until the beans were done,
so making do with one burner wasn't hard. She didn't have an
oven, which was a shame; she'd like to be able to make corn-
bread. But otherwise, she was set up okay here.

Especially when it came to Wi-Fi. Her landlady's old frame
house was over seventy feet away, but Mrs. MacGruder had a
really strong router and no imagination. Her password was one,
two, three, four, five. Demi snorted at such stupidity and tow-
eled off.

She brushed her teeth, humming the alphabet song to time
it, then took the six steps that put her in front of the vanity
tucked next to the closet opposite her bed. She ran both hands
over her cheeks, frowning at her reflection. Her skin was
slowly reverting to its usual smooth, hairless state. For the
tenth time she considered getting more of the testosterone gel
she'd used when she first went on the run. For the tenth time,
she voted it down. Too risky. In Cumberland she'd been able
to steal it . . . poor Jake. She spent a moment in sympathy for
the man who'd been her boss at the warehouse. Jake hadn't
been that much of a jerk. And even if he had, she told herself
virtuously, that didn't make it right to steal from him. Necessary and right were not the same thing.

But she didn't know anyone here she could steal the cream
from. She could get some online, but you couldn't be sure what
you were getting from those places.

She grabbed a clean pair of tightie-whities. Even without the
testosterone, she thought she made a great boy. Some people
thought she was younger than the eighteen she claimed, and

they were right, which was funny because when she'd been a girl . . . well, she still was a girl. When she'd publicly been a girl, a lot of people had thought she was older than she was.

People mostly saw what they expected to see. When she'd been just herself, people had expected her to be older because she was in college. Now she wore boy's clothes and walked differently—that had taken a lot of practice—and worked at guy jobs, so people expected to see a boy. Not once in the eleven months she'd been on the run had anyone guessed that she was a girl. It helped that she had narrow hips and no butt, plus her voice was kind of deep for a woman.

Demi wrapped the wide elastic bandage around her chest. She'd never grown beyond a double-A, so it was easy to smush her boobs all the way flat. Then she pulled on a pair of baggy jeans she'd bought at Goodwill, an equally oversize T-shirt, and her shoes and socks. She didn't have to do anything to her hair. Now that she was being a guy, she just kept it really short, which meant twice-a-month visits to Faylene's at $10 a pop. Faylene's was the only place in town to get a haircut, so both men and women got their hair done there.

She was ready, yet not ready. She stared at her computer. Maybe she should send the code to delay the release of the first file and try to contact Mr. Smith again. Maybe he was in the hospital. Maybe he'd died. Maybe . . .

Maybe she'd better do exactly what she'd said she would. This was why she'd broken the data up into three files, after all. She hadn't expected Mr. Smith to stay silent, but she'd planned what to do if he pleaded for more time.

Demi grabbed two dog biscuits and a bag of M&Ms and headed for the door. The M&Ms went on the rickety front porch behind a pot with a dead plant. No sign of Harry, but there usually wasn't. The biscuits were for Samson and Murphy. Samson was a bulldog mix. Murphy was just a mix, a charming clown of a dog with ears just like Zipper's had been—one all perky, the other flopped down. Having to wait and wait and wait to have a dog of her own again was hard. Visiting Samson and Murphy helped.

She hummed the theme song from *Frozen* as she set off down the twin ruts that passed for a driveway along the east side of Mrs. MacGruder's half acre of land, heading for Elm Street. Three blocks up Elm, then she'd turn onto Main. Two more blocks and she'd be at the Tip-Top.

Now that she was up and moving, she felt better. The sky was a bright, bright blue. She'd made the right decision about the file. And today was pancakes day.

Five days of the week she ate her first meal of the day at the Tip-Top Café. Monday was oatmeal with blueberries. Tuesday was an omelet. The Tip-Top didn't offer a lot of options for vegetarians, but Frank made excellent omelets. She skipped Wednesday because it was her day off and one of her cooking days. After that came grilled cheese and fries on Thursday, the special on Friday, skip Saturday, and pancakes on Sunday. The pancakes were pretty good, but the syrup wasn't. She'd asked once if it would be okay if she brought her own syrup, but Jamie had given her one of those looks, so she let it drop.

It was extravagant, eating out so much: $38.83 a week. Friday was the most expensive. That's when she had the meatloaf special with double vegetables and no meatloaf. With tax and tip it cost $9.73, which was almost half her grocery budget. Demi had spent some time figuring out if she was supposed to tip based on the menu price or the real, after-tax cost of a meal. In the end, she'd decided it wasn't fair to use the before-tax price. The special was $7.95. Sales tax here was 6 percent, which brought it to $8.43, and 15 percent of $8.43 was $1.26, but Demi tipped a full $1.30. She always rounded up on the tip because it was probably annoying to get pennies, and besides, Jamie worked hard. Her mom lived with her and Jamie still had one kid at home. A teenager. Teenagers cost a lot more than toddlers, Jamie said, plus they were more trouble and not nearly as cute. "Present company excluded, sweetie," she'd said, and for a minute Demi had thought Jamie was going to pat her on the head. Sometimes Jamie acted like Demi was twelve, not eighteen, but that was just her way. She mothered everyone, even Frank, who was her boss.

Demi made $241.04 a week at the gas station, and that's if she worked all the hours she was supposed to. Sometimes Mr. Burgenstein cut her hours, and once she'd missed a day because she'd been puking her guts out. So she had to watch her pennies, but she loved eating at the Tip-Top. She hadn't been able to eat out at all in Washington, unless you counted the soup kitchen. Demi refused to count the soup kitchen. Washington was expensive. The room she'd rented there had cost more than she paid for her trailer now and she'd had to buy a hot plate and a mini fridge, which had come out of her emergency funds. She'd eaten a lot of beans and rice and peanut butter. Vegetable soup had been a treat.

But she was in Whistle now, headed down sunny Main Street on her way to the Tip-Top Café, and Mr. Wilkins from the hardware store gave her a friendly nod when she walked by. People did that here. She'd been in Whistle five months and three days and pretty much everyone knew who she was. Who she was supposed to be anyway, but that was okay. She liked being Danny Stone.

The Tip-Top was pretty empty this time of day. Old Mr. Hawthorne sat at the counter drinking coffee and there were two deputies at one table, a man and a woman. Demi had seen them in here a few times, but hadn't ever talked to them. Their uniforms made her nervous.

Jamie was refilling the napkin dispensers. She looked up with a crimson smile. Jamie liked to wear bright red lipstick. "Hey, there, Danny. You have a seat and I'll put your order in. Pancakes, right?"

Demi smiled and nodded. She liked it that Jamie knew what she wanted without her having to say a word. She went to the counter and sat three stools down from Mr. Hawthorne. That's what she'd decided was a sociable distance without being pushy. The old man gave Demi a nod that she returned. Mostly Mr. Hawkins didn't talk to her, but mostly he didn't talk to anyone. Demi figured he liked people okay, or he wouldn't come to the Tip-Top every day. He just didn't like to talk.

Demi knew that other people didn't eat a fixed menu the way she did, and that made her stand out. Standing out wasn't good when you were on the run. But other people did a lot of things differently than she did. It couldn't be helped. She needed routine, and really, she was proud of how flexible she'd been. She'd had to completely reinvent her routine twice now. Three times if she counted moving off to college, but the two hardest ones were when she'd first gone on the run and, later, when she'd nearly been caught in Washington. If she hadn't run across Harry . . .

He'd claimed he'd been waiting for her. Maybe he had, but he wouldn't explain what he meant, and Harry liked to joke, so he might be pulling her leg about that. But he'd steered her to the right place. Whistle fit her really well. Not that she blended in. Even if she could have faked normal perfectly, she'd still stand out in southern Ohio. This had to be the whitest area in the whole country.

Demi thought she had pretty skin. It was a pale caramel color that the sun sprinkled with freckles—a lot like her mom's really, only darker. But put that with her kinky hair and she did not look like anyone else in Whistle. In spite of that, she hadn't run into prejudice here the way she had in D.C. At least she didn't think so, but she missed out on some social cues, so it was possible she just hadn't noticed.

She was pretty sure Mean-Eyed MacGruder was nasty to everyone, though.

"Here's your water, sweetie." Jamie set the glass in front of Demi. "Pancakes will be up in a minute. Listen, you like beans, right?"

"Sure." Jamie knew that. She'd given Demi some tips for cooking them. But Jamie, like a lot of people, liked to ask questions that she already knew the answer to.

"My pole beans and limas have come on like gangbusters this year. Cucumbers didn't do much, but I've got beans coming out my ears. More than I can pick, and that's a fact. I thought you might want some. You'll have to pick 'em yourself, mind."

"Oh, I—I'd like that, but I thought you were going to freeze your extra."

"Got to get 'em picked before I can freeze them, and I can't get 'em all picked, what with Craig staying with his sister and me working doubles. I sure hope Susie can start picking up some of the supper shifts again soon, but she's at the age where you don't bounce back fast, and that surgery took a lot out of her. Now, if that young niece of Frank's would just—but never mind that. My mother keeps threatening to go pick those beans so they don't go to waste, and she doesn't have any business doing that, not with her bad hip."

Demi immediately resolved to pick all the beans, not just however much Jamie was giving her. If she was still here, that is. If Mr. Smith hadn't grabbed her. "Thanks, then. Uh . . . I've never picked beans."

Jamie chuckled. "You are a city boy, aren't you? You're off Wednesday, right?"

Demi agreed that she was.

"You come over about four, then, and I'll show you how to pick beans."

Demi knew where Jamie lived because she'd gone there once to see if she could fix their computer. Turned out the hard drive was damaged, but Demi had been able to recover most of the data—why did people never back up their stuff?—using Linux. It was a tedious job, but nothing special, though Jamie and Craig had made a fuss about it. That was her youngest kid's name, Craig. Craig usually ignored "Danny Stone," but that night he'd been impressed. He and Jamie had acted like she was some kind of tech wizard.

Well, she was, but not because she could build a bootable Linux system on a USB stick. Anyone could do that. You just had to be able to follow instructions. But Jamie had been happy that she hadn't lost all her photos and had insisted that Demi stay for supper, which had been fried chicken, which of course she didn't eat, but there'd been mashed potatoes and corn on the cob, too, and a salad with cucumbers and red onions. When Demi went back a few days later to install the new hard drive (which she'd ordered for them so they wouldn't get soaked), Jamie had paid her for the drive and given her a whole pan of peach cobbler to take home. Really good peach cobbler.

The deputies left just as Demi's pancakes were ready, so while Demi ate, Jamie hung around and talked, mostly about Craig and Lisa—Lisa was her married daughter—and her son Roger, who was in the Army. Their father was dead. He'd died in a car crash fourteen years ago, leaving Jamie a small insurance policy and three kids to raise. Which she'd done, though Craig was worrying her. Demi wasn't sure why, but it had something to do with the crowd he was hanging out with, plus he hadn't gotten a summer job the way Jamie wanted. That's why he was staying with his sister, Lisa, this summer, to keep him out of trouble. Mr. Hawthorne even chimed in at one point with advice.

Then it was time for Demi to leave for work, so she counted out $7.52 and told Jamie she'd see her Wednesday for those beans. And hoped she was telling the truth. She nodded at Mr. Hawthorne and headed out.

The gas station where she worked was only a hop and a skip away. It was a boring job. People pumped the gas themselves, so she was mostly there to sell them cigarettes and candy and sodas. Now and then someone wanted a tire or their oil changed, or their battery or wiper blades replaced. Demi could do that sort of thing because of Nicky. His dad being a mechanic, he thought everyone should know how to do basic stuff like that, so he'd taught her.

A pang shot through her, so sharp she stopped walking. She hadn't thought of Nicky for days. She'd thought about Mr. Smith a lot, but not about Nicky and the others. She was so comfortable here in Whistle, and it hurt to think of him. Of them.

But he was the reason she was here. It won't be long now, she told him fiercely as she started moving again. While Jamie had been telling Demi about her son Roger's overdue promotion, the first packet of data had gone out. One lucky reporter was getting a fantastic scoop. She wouldn't get everything, not yet, but enough to make Mr. Smith wish he hadn't ignored her. Enough that he'd see he had to make a deal to let Nicky and the rest of them go.

If he didn't, another file would go out—to two reporters this time, in case Mr. Smith had somehow silenced her first choice. Then the third file, to three reporters. They'd get get everything she had except for the Lodan files. She didn't dare let anyone know about them. But she didn't have to. The financial data should put Mr. Smith in prison for a long, long time.

He had to know that. It was going to work, she promised herself. She just wished she knew what he was up to.

NINE

~

As it turned out, Charles wasn't much company. Mostly he slept. He did wake up when they pulled into a drive-through in Cumberland for lunch, where he demonstrated that being in the process of dying hadn't hurt his appetite. He skipped the fries and ate six quarter-pounders.

He woke up again when they pulled to the side of the road twenty miles outside Cumberland. The right-rear tire had gone flat. That shouldn't have slowed them down too much, and Mercedes Benz used full-size spares, so they wouldn't even have to drive on a donut. The problem was the jack. It was missing. The lug wrench was where it should be, but no jack.

They could have worked around that if she'd had more guards with her. José and Carson could lift the rear of the car, but José wasn't sure they could hold it up long enough for Lily to change the tire. Lily might have talked him into trying if she hadn't started seeing little birds. Dozens and dozens of them. Each was the size of a gypsy moth and the bright turquoise blue of a swimming pool, and they circled her head like in an old-time cartoon. The air was so thick with little blue birds that she couldn't see the damn car.

The hallucination didn't last long. Nor did the headache it triggered. But it convinced José it was not safe for her to change the tire, and he refused to lift the car so she could try, which made her regret telling him about the damn blue birds. They waited a full forty-five minutes for roadside assistance to arrive, leaving them barely enough time to make it to Whistle by six . . . if they kept to the speed limit. So they didn't. They didn't dare push their speed too much—getting stopped would slow them down even more—but Lily wanted some margin of error in case the park proved hard to find.

Normally she would have spent some of the drive-time learning more about the case she was headed to. Normally she'd spend time just thinking about the case, too, lining up the questions she needed to find answers to, maybe talking to Rule about it. Normally he'd be with her.

He wasn't. And this wasn't a case.

She hadn't realized how often she checked on Rule's whereabouts, how habitual that had become. She kept doing it without thinking and getting back that he was alive and a thousand miles to the west. Or sitting on the hood of the car. Or several miles due north. Or floating a dozen feet overhead. Every time that happened, it derailed whatever train of thought she'd been pursuing.

She tried to keep her mind busy. She had no idea why she was needed in the hamlet of Whistle—founded in 1821, with a population of 1,356 as of the last census. She did learn that much by cruising the Internet. She also learned that the town adjoined the Crown City Wildlife Area, a state-managed tract of over eleven thousand acres, almost half of it forested, with ponds for fishing and "both game and non-game wildlife," according to the state of Ohio.

Whistle was roughly equidistant from Portsmouth, Gallipolis, and Jackson, so she looked up newspapers in those cities. She read about a meth bust, a car fire, and a lecture at the Madding Center for Welsh Studies. A man's body had been found in the Ohio River. The Jacksonville City Council was considering revising statutes concerning dilapidated or condemned houses. Three Lawrence County correction officers had been arrested for inappropriate treatment of a prisoner, and the annual River Days Festival was only a month away.

Lily read the piece about the correction officers closely because there was little she hated as much as bad cops of whatever stripe. She read what she could find about the body, too, but there wasn't much. It had been in the river feeding the fishes awhile, so no ID yet. No cause of death yet, either, but a source "close to the investigation"—probably a cop with a big mouth—said there were no obvious signs of foul play.

She texted Rule a couple times. She did not pass out. She hadn't expected to, not once Charles joined them. She had no idea why the Lady wanted Charles to accompany her, but it seemed unlikely she'd send him along if the mate bond was going to make the separation impossible. The bond was of the Lady, so she could probably make sure it cooperated.

Which seemed to mean the Lady approved of this separation.

Could Sam have known that? She didn't see how . . . unless he and the Lady were both acting based on those mysterious patterns. Maybe Sam had counted on the Lady seeing the same things he did and making sure the mate bond didn't interfere. If so, would it have killed him to tell them that? Or something, anything, about her errand in Whistle? Lily was not feeling happy with the black dragon when they pulled into the tiny town at five thirty-five that afternoon.

There wasn't much to see. Typical small rural town, she supposed. They came in on—surprise—Main Street, which was brick-lined and boasted two gas stations, a tiny post office, Chrissy's Beauty & Supply, a hardware store, Sunny's Market, the Tip-Top Café, two empty storefronts, an antique store, an accountant's office, and a handful of similar establishments.

They'd driven past the park on the way in, so finding it wouldn't be a problem. That meant they had just enough time to drop off the flat tire at one of the gas stations. They also filled the tank and emptied their bladders—at least, the two-legged among them did, taking turns in the only restroom. Charles would have to wait for a less public venue. While Carson grabbed a few snacks to tide them over until supper—with "a few" being defined in lupi terms—Lily found out that the closest hotel was thirty miles away, in the county seat.

The attendant at the station was painfully young. Biracial, she thought, which made her wonder briefly about his story. Southern Ohio was overwhelmingly white. He was shy, keeping his head ducked most of the time, but did answer Lily's question about hotels, going so far as to offer that the Hampton Inn in

Gallipolis was "supposed to be pretty nice." She sent Rule another text, letting him know they'd arrived and suggesting that the Leidolf guards meet them at the Hampton Inn in Gallipolis.

Then they headed for the park. That took a whole four minutes.

They were the only ones there. The grass looked tired from the heat. Otherwise, it was a pretty little place with three picnic tables, a swing set, a pair of slides, and a metal trash can. A barbeque made from a metal barrel was welded to a post sunk in concrete. No one would be carrying it off, not without a cutting torch. A creek trickled along the east side of the little park, shaded by trees.

José got out first. No one shot at him and he must not have smelled anything threatening. He gave a nod, so she and Carson got out; she held the door open for Charles. He jumped down, and if he landed more heavily than lupi usually did, it didn't seem to cause him any pain. He trotted straight for the tangled field along the park's western boundary, probably seeking the pit stop he hadn't been able to take at the gas station. There was a narrow path, maybe a game trail, leading into the uncut grass and weeds. Really tall grass. Charles was a big wolf, but it was over his head. She could follow his movement in the twitching of the grass.

Nothing else happened. Lily checked her watch. Five fifty-eight.

It was July. It was hot. Hotter than San Diego, which seldom got above eighty, thanks to the Pacific Ocean. It was more humid than she was used to, as well. There was a bit of a breeze blowing east to west. Locusts serenaded them from the trees.

Nothing continued to happen. "You smell anything I should know about?" she asked the lupi with her, and got two head-shakes in answer. She walked around, looking. Someone had cooked on the barbeque without cleaning out the ashes. They'd burned wood, not charcoal. The metal trash can held an assortment of trash and more ashes. She sighed, checked her watch again. Straight up six o'clock. The shade under those trees looked inviting. Might as well wait there as anywhere. If nothing kept on happening, she decided as she headed for the creek, she'd take off her shoes and walk around barefoot. Maybe she was supposed to check for magic.

Charles yipped three times. It sounded urgent.

"Carson, with me. José, go!" By the time she finished speaking, Lily had her weapon out and was sprinting toward the weedy field.

José, of course, pulled ahead immediately. Carson ran at Lily's side. If she hadn't told Carson to stay with her, José would have. The extra two seconds that would have taken could make a difference. Or not. Maybe Charles had just found a rabbit.

José crashed into the brush at top speed and didn't slow much. Being on two feet, he remained visible, so Lily saw him stop maybe ten yards in, then move ahead slowly.

As she reached the path, she motioned for Carson to take the rear. It wasn't much of a trail, more like the memory of one, overgrown in spots and narrow where it existed at all. She couldn't take it at speed the way José had, but she did her best. When she reached Charles, she slowed. José was ten feet ahead of her on the path, not moving. His weapon was pointed at the ground. He looked at her. "He's dead."

A few more steps and she saw what he meant.

The grass and weeds were trampled and flattened here, making enough room for an army-green sleeping bag with a plaid lining. The man lying on his back on top of that sleeping bag wore filthy blue jeans and a T-shirt that might once have been white. He was barefoot; a pair of ragged athletic shoes were set neatly beside the sleeping bag with the socks stuffed in them. A tan canvas backpack rested near his feet. His hair was long, an unkempt tangle of brown and gray, as was his beard.

Where it wasn't red or rusty from blood, that is. His throat had been cut.

No other visible wounds. No signs of struggle.

She glanced around the small, flattened area. The grass and weeds didn't look disturbed anywhere else. Most likely whoever killed him had come down the same path they'd just trampled all over. "Charles. Do you smell anyone else on the path? Someone other than us or him?"

One quick yip. With a Nokolai wolf, that would mean no.

She didn't know if Wythe used the same signals. She glanced over her shoulder. He shook his head.

Old humans often lost some of their sense of smell. Maybe Charles had, too. He hadn't smelled the body until he got close to it, had he? Or maybe it was just that the breeze was blowing the wrong way. "Carson. I need you to Change and see what you can sniff out about whoever did this. Check along the path first." Better to use Carson anyway. Charles couldn't Change back into a form that could communicate clearly. "José, how close did you get?"

"I stopped right where you see me. I thought you wouldn't want me putting my big feet all over everything."

"Good thinking." She slid her weapon back in its holster, took out her phone, and took a quick picture. The time-stamp would confirm when she found the body. She stepped forward, careful of where she put her small feet. She didn't have booties with her, so every step she took contaminated the scene. Couldn't be helped.

The blood was mostly confined to the area right around the body, having leaked out rather than been pumped out. His heart would have stopped quickly. She crouched within arm's length of what used to be a man.

Brown eyes. Pug nose. Big, square, yellow teeth. One was missing—the incisor next to his lower left canine. No visible scars, but between his hair and his beard, not a lot of his face showed. The skin she saw was weathered and dirty. He wasn't young, but beyond that she couldn't guess his age. Living rough added years. He was a big guy, over six feet, with broad shoulders. A bit gaunt; he hadn't been eating well. He stank, but it was the sour odor of BO, not the rancidness of decay. In this heat, that meant he hadn't been dead long. She took two more pictures, getting a close-up of his face, then his throat. The crime scene people would do a better job, but they wouldn't be here for a while and she wanted to be sure she had photos. She'd had a corpse vanish once. Those circumstances weren't likely to apply here, but she'd take no chances.

His sleeping bag was saturated with blood, much of it still wet. The wound looked to be singular and devastating—one blow with a large blade, maybe a machete or sword. The cut was angled, deepest on his left, where the carotid artery was. It had taken a lot of strength to cut so deeply with a single blow, slicing through skin, muscle, and cartilage to sever his windpipe, probably the carotid and jugular vein, too. She couldn't tell if the cervical vertebrae were damaged, but it wouldn't surprise her.

If he'd been standing or sitting when he was struck, his head would have fallen sideways as he fell. That hadn't happened, so he'd been lying flat when someone took a machete to him. Napping, maybe, to get through the heat of the day. Maybe he'd gone from sleep to death without ever waking up. Maybe he'd never known someone killed him.

She sighed. Plenty more to be learned here, but most of that would be up to the crime scene team. One thing only she could do, though, and best do it now, before she called it in.

Lily steeled herself, dreading this part. Normally magic was like drugs or guns—neither good nor evil in itself, only in how it was used. But there was one exception. Death magic was so wrong that she felt its foulness. That's what she expected to find here—death magic. Not that this looked like a ritual killing, and ritual was usually necessary to create death magic. But Sam had sent her here for a reason, and this guy seemed to be it. The most obvious reason she'd be needed at a homicide was that magic had been used to kill. That wasn't the case here. A blade of some sort had opened this man's carotid and windpipe to the summer breezes. That left death magic as the likeliest reason for her presence.

She stretched out a hand and touched his. Her eyebrows shot up. The buzz of magic was too faint to identify, but one thing was sure. It was not death magic. That was unmistakable, no matter how tiny the trace she touched.

There were several reasons she shouldn't touch the bloody wound and only one reason she should. That one was compelling, however. Magic usually spread throughout a living body even when its effects were localized, but it didn't spread evenly. And this man had died quickly. If he'd been killed with some sort of magic-imbued weapon, the magic would be concentrated at the wound itself. She pressed her fingertips to bloody flesh.

Huh. Weird. If—

"We've got company," José said, then raised his voice slightly. "Carson, get out of sight."

Lily glanced up at him. He was frowning, but he didn't raise his gun. She rose and looked where he was looking. A moment later, a black-and-white sheriff's car pulled in next to their Mercedes.

"José, put up your gun and come with me." Lily started back toward the park. She spoke softly to Charles as they passed him. "Stay here, stay out of sight. Keep an eye on the body."

Two people in khaki shirts, dark slacks, and the usual accoutrements of law officers got out of the car. Probably deputies, though Lily couldn't see their badges clearly from here. One was female, maybe late thirties, dark hair, pale skin. She'd been riding shotgun. The driver was male, also in his thirties, built short and square like a fire hydrant. Ruddy skin, sandy hair.

Both of them reached for their weapons. "Halt!" the man cried. "Hands up!"

"FBI," Lily called out. She ignored half of his order, continuing forward on the sketchy path, but obeyed the other half, raising her hands. She trusted José to do the same.

The woman lowered her gun. The fire hydrant didn't. "I'll need to see some ID," he said loudly as he and his partner started toward them. More quietly, "For Crissake, Gwen, keep 'em covered. Anyone can say 'FBI.'"

"Pretty sure she's Lily Yu," the woman said. She didn't put her weapon away, but she kept it aimed at the ground.

"Who?"

"Damn, boy, don't you ever watch the news?"

The fire hydrant did not like being called "boy," but he sucked it up and kept his gun and his attention on Lily and José.

"I won't retrieve my ID until you can see my hands," Lily told him, "but she's right. I'm Special Agent Lily Yu. I assume you got some kind of tip."

"You don't need to be assuming anything."

"Oh? Do you draw on civilians every time you see one?"

His eyes narrowed. "You claim you aren't a civilian."

"Got me there. Of course, that leaves you drawing your weapon on federal agents." She'd reached the edge of the brushy area. The deputies were about twenty feet away and approaching cautiously. "I'm going to reach for my badge now. It's in my jacket pocket." She did so, slowly.

"Toss it on the ground and step away."

At least he was a properly trained idiot. The other kind were more dangerous. Lily did as she'd been told. José stayed with her. The female deputy came close enough to pick up the folder without being jumped—at least, the distance would've been safe if José had been human—then retreated a couple steps and opened the folder that held Lily's badge and ID. "Looks pretty damn official, Ricky. Lily Yu, Special Agent, Federal Bureau of Investigation, Magical Crimes Division, Unit Twelve."

Ricky scowled. Slowly his gun lowered. "Unit Twelve?"

"That's right," Lily said. "You want to put that weapon away now. The man we found in the brush was killed by magic. This is my scene."

TEN

~~

IT took forever for Demi's heartbeat to settle down after the Mercedes drove away. She consulted her "get the hell out" list several times, but of course she'd never expected Lily Yu to drive up and buy gas from her and ask about hotels, so that wasn't on her list. FBI agents were, but only if they were asking people about her—the original her, that is. The one who was female and seventeen.

Finally she decided that if Lily Yu had wanted to arrest her, she would have done so instead of driving away. This wasn't a "get the hell out" situation, which meant she was probably okay, as long as she didn't do anything to draw attention. So she stayed at work, and everything was just like usual, only better. She kept smiling, thinking about how she'd actually met Lily Yu and spoken to her. Lily Yu was a genuine hero. She was brave and smart, plus she was married to Rule Turner. That was beyond cool, but it wasn't why Demi read everything she could find about the FBI agent.

Lily Yu was like *her*. Like she might have been, that is, if not for Asperger's.

Most of the time she liked herself the way she was, Asperger's and all. Being an Aspie had its good points, like being orderly and logical and able to immerse herself in things that interested her. But there was no denying that some things were hard for her, such as making eye contact and understanding body language, social cues, and facial expressions. She'd make a terrible FBI agent. She always thought people were telling the truth. She knew that wasn't so, but she had no idea how to apply that knowledge to individual people. FBI agents needed to be able to tell when people lied to them. So she'd never be like Lily Yu, not really, except maybe in some ways . . . she was brave sometimes. She hadn't panicked today. She'd used her lists to get her mind working instead of bumblebee-ing around, and she'd been able to reason her way through.

Demi felt happy as she sold gas and cigarettes and candy. Instead of worrying about Mr. Smith and what she should do next, she thought about meeting Lily Yu. She thought a lot about how to figure out if the wolf she'd glimpsed in the back-seat of the car had been Rule Turner. If it had, that would make today just about perfect.

ELEVEN

THE sun was hot, the freshly cut grass smelled sweet, and the push of Ruben's mantle was annoying. Rule could live with it, but it was annoying. He was, he admitted, a bit on edge. The storm in his gut had never really gone away. It was quieter now, but not gone.

Had anyone been watching, it would have looked like they were sitting on Ruben's rear deck enjoying a couple glasses of lemonade and a chat. The hypothetical watcher wouldn't have heard them, however, no matter where he stood or what Gift or technology he might be using. The crystal Rule had set on the table was brand new and, at the moment, one of a kind. It was based on a silence ward Cullen had recently learned from a former hellhound.

The crystal had two drawbacks. First, those without the Sight couldn't tell when it ran out of charge. Second, it needed to be employed within a circle to contain the effect. Rule couldn't set a circle. With very few exceptions, the power that resides in lupi can't be used for spells.

Ruben, however, was Gifted, and that type of power was available in ways Rule's magic wasn't. He'd chalked a circle around the table and chairs before they sat down to enjoy the slant of the late afternoon sun, the tart lemonade . . . and their chat.

One of Rule's duties as second-in-command of the Shadow Unit was to function as CFO. He'd just finished going over the books and was briefing Ruben on the protections Cullen had recently put in place. ". . . can't guarantee anything should a large-scale magical attack on the bank's computers be mounted, but any individual tampering with our accounts will now be blocked."

Ruben didn't look happy. "I wish you had consulted me before acting."

Annoyance mounted. Rule told himself firmly that Ruben was not challenging him. "Given the current communication difficulties, that would have meant waiting until we spoke in person. I judged that an unnecessary risk. Was this not within my authority as CFO?"

"Would you have acted unilaterally on similar Nokolai business without discussing it with Isen?"

"If for some reason I couldn't reach Isen, yes. Would you be acting as if I'd challenged your authority if we weren't sitting so close with our mantles pushing at each other?"

"You're making unwarranted assumptions."

Rule gritted his teeth. "You're leaning forward."

"I don't see what that—"

Rule leaned forward, too. "Don't you?"

Ruben froze. After a moment he sighed and leaned back in his chair. "You're right. Being around you—or being so near the mantles you carry—reinforces instincts I'm not yet accustomed to. My apologies. You were unable to discuss it with me and felt there was enough risk that you wanted to go ahead, and you do have the authority for that."

It was harder than it should have been to lean back and let go of the need to defend himself. Rule did it anyway. Long experience let him keep the difficulty from his voice. "You don't agree with my decision."

"It seems unnecessary. Unit Twelve has investigated a number of cases in which practitioners tried to shift money into their accounts magically. Often the mere use of magic on electronic records either shuts down the bank's computers or causes multiple glitches without making the change the thief desires. Sometimes funds do magically appear in the thief's account, but not in the amount intended, or the funds are withdrawn instead of deposited. On the rare occasions when the thief gets the result he's after, the tampering is easy to spot and quickly rectified. Finding sufficient evidence for prosecution can take time, but the problem itself is fixed quickly."

Rule shrugged. "Perhaps that's true with most practitioners, but if Cullen can undetectably alter electronic records in a manner that is not 'easy to spot and quickly rectified,' someone else might be able to."

Ruben's eyebrows shot up. "He's done this?"

"Yes." Two years after the fact, Visa still didn't know why the credit card they'd issued to one Cullen Seabourne had gone overnight from a thousand-dollar limit to none while the minimum payment remained twelve dollars a month.

"Ah. I see why you considered this more of a threat than I did. I still don't see how it's possible. Any use of magic to ward an account should set off the same problems an attempt at tampering would."

"I can't explain what I don't understand, but apparently using sympathetic magic makes a difference. The ward isn't installed on the bank's computers, but on a symbolic representation of them."

Ruben considered that a moment. "He put these protections on Nokolai's accounts two months ago, you said?"

"Yes. There have been no problems."

"I see. Or rather, I don't see how it works, but if you and Cullen say it does, I'll take your word for it. It would be inconvenient to have our funds suddenly disappear."

"That it would." Surreptitiously Rule checked his watch. Five minutes until six. Whatever Lily was needed for in Whistle, she should encounter it soon, if she hadn't already. Such a large word, "whatever." He tried not to think about how many grim possibilities it covered and carefully did not check for her. The utter wrongness of the distorted mate sense seemed to reach him at a deeper level than it did Lily.

If Ruben noticed Rule's preoccupation with the time, he didn't comment on it. "Before we discuss the communications problem, I'd like to brief you on a few situations. Two of them involve Shadow agents. The other one is a case Unit Twelve is investigating that could become of interest to the Shadow Unit, depending on how things develop."

And so they left the legal part of the discussion for murkier regions.

The Shadow Unit had three great strengths any clandestine organization would envy. First was the instant, untraceable communication the dragons provided. Wars have been won or lost due to communication. Their second strength was Ruben's position as head of Unit 12, which gave him access to the vast information-gathering resources of the FBI. It was, of course, illegal for him to use those resources that way, which underscored the need for secure communications.

Their third strength was Ruben himself.

Precognition wasn't well understood. Many dismissed it as useless because it was so often wrong. Precogs whose Gift manifested only in dreams or visions couldn't be tested in a laboratory—but most precogs were hunchers, like Ruben. The experts had derived a test for them. It involved randomly generated three-digit numbers and was scored based on statistical models that accounted for sequencing and partially correct answers.

Using that weighted scoring system, most precogs tested between twenty and thirty percent—well above pure chance, but nothing anyone would want to bet the farm on. A few of the strongest ones had hit in the forties.

Ruben had tested at seventy percent.

Tests are not real life, of course. In real life, Rule had never known Ruben to be wrong. That was partly due to the strength of Ruben's gift, but just as important was that he knew when he had a hunch.

Ruben had told Rule once that being a strong precognitive was like having background music on all the time . . . music made by a couple dozen different bands, each playing a different tune. Fast or slow, faint or loud, familiar or eerily alien, the songs all had one thing in common: they were instrumentals. No vocalist, Ruben had said wryly, ever added a spoken refrain to explain things. It was a music composed of feelings, not notes. That's why precogs often mistook their own unconscious fears or fantasies for the prompting of their Gifts.

Ruben didn't. For him, it was like the difference between listening to music and humming a song himself. He couldn't mistake one for the other. That accounted for much of his uncanny accuracy: he knew when he didn't know.

". . . mystifying and potentially connected to *her*, given the nature of the cult," Ruben finished. "I've had trouble deciding who to send. Suggestions?"

"That's Ybirra territory. Is there some reason you don't want a couple of Manuel's people checking them out?"

"Nothing concrete, but I suspect that whoever I send will need good spellcasting abilities."

"You've thought of Cullen."

"Not him." Ruben was certain. "Someone I haven't yet considered."

"You must have considered all the usual active Ghosts." Rule glanced at his watch again. Six ten. He wanted badly to call Lily. That would be stupid, potentially interrupting her at a key moment, so he didn't do it. But he wanted to. "Arjenie isn't active. She is skilled, but bear in mind that if you send her, Benedict will go, too." Benedict would never let his Chosen go into danger by herself the way Rule had been forced to do.

"Not Arjenie, but . . . ah, that's it. Someone connected to her." Ruben nodded briskly, pleased. "Her cousin. He's done some off-the-books work for Unit Twelve and I've been considering recruiting him for the Shadows. This is the right time and the right job."

"I don't know anything about him."

They discussed the man briefly, then moved on to the meat of their discussion. With Mika gone, the Shadow Unit effectively lacked two of their three strengths. Ruben couldn't lead effectively without quick, clear communications. "The solution," Ruben said, "is obvious. While Mika is absent, I need to leave D.C. for another dragon's territory. With you here—"

Something happened.

When it finished happening, Rule was on his feet. His chair lay on its side behind him. His entire being seemed to vibrate like a gong a second after being struck—the sound had passed, but the reverberations continued.

He felt settled. At peace.

Ruben clearly did not. He was on his feet, too—his shoulders hunched, his head lowered, his eyes fixed on Rule. The posture of a wolf prepared to attack. "No?" he said very low.

Rule smiled at him. "My apologies. I take it I reacted very suddenly?"

Ruben's posture didn't change. "You don't remember?"

That would strike Ruben as deeply suspicious. "No, but it's all right. It was the Lady."

Ruben's posture eased slightly, but he still looked ready to attack or defend. "The Lady spoke to you?"

"Not precisely. Not in words." But he would need to find words to express her message, or the man across from him would think he'd been possessed or placed under compulsion or some such. "She . . . agrees with me. Or approves of my instinctive response, or . . ." He shrugged. "You know how you feel on full moon night, when you open completely to her song? Just before the pain hits, when there's nothing but her song . . . it was like that."

Silence, except for the distant sounds of birds, a car with its radio on driving along the street in front of the house, a dog a couple houses away, Deborah humming in the kitchen . . . and the elevated heartbeat of the man across from him. Who gradually relaxed the rest of the way. "What did the Lady agree with you about?" he asked dryly.

"I can't be trapped here." There was more . . . the warm glow of her approval, the sense that she regretted something . . . and the utter certainty that his instincts were correct.

"My going to Wythe Clanhome would make you feel trapped?"

"I have to be free to go to Lily if she needs me."

Ruben spoke slowly, as if unsure of Rule's ability to understand language. "You agreed not to go with her."

"Yes. I didn't agree not to go to her."

"I don't understand why my leaving traps you here."

Rule opened his mouth to explain . . . and closed it again. He couldn't explain. He didn't have a reason.

"I feel that you're needed here," Ruben went on. "Sam believes you should stay here. But that's true whether I'm here or not."

"When will I be needed here?"

Ruben's eyebrows lifted. "I don't know."

"Perhaps I'm needed now but won't be later. I don't know. I can't explain. But I have to be free to go to her. If you leave—"

"If you—" Ruben's phone buzzed. He took it from his pocket. "It's Lily." And touched the screen. "This is Ruben. Rule's with me."

Ruben hadn't put his phone on speaker. He didn't have to. Rule heard Lily clearly. "Good. I'm at the park outside Whistle. So are a couple of deputies and a body. The deceased is male . . ."

It was good to hear her voice. He listened closely as she described the body she'd found. ". . . jeans and a T-shirt. Barefoot. His shoes were next to his sleeping bag. Age between . . ."

His own phone dinged. He grimaced and checked to see who it was. Cecily Alvarez. Cecily handled Rule's website, social media, and public e-mail account. She had excellent PR instincts. She knew how to respond to most e-mails and posts and when to ask for guidance, but she texted, she didn't call. Whatever the problem was, she must consider it urgent. He accepted the call. "This is Rule."

It was, as he'd suspected, bad news, but nothing major. He'd have to put in a call to one or two of the reporters he'd cultivated. Rule caught snatches of Ruben's talk with Lily while listening to Cecily's explanation, which was more technical and detailed than he required.

". . . discern the type of magic?" Ruben asked.

"That's the weird thing," Lily told him. "I'm pretty sure—"

"—want me to do other than the post I already made?" Cecily asked.

"No," Rule said, pulling his attention back to the problem at hand. "I'll deal with it. Let Isen know right away, then find out how it was done . . . I understand, but there must be consultants who can. Contact Arjenie Fox. If she doesn't already know, she'll be able to find out. Yes. Thank you for letting me know right away."

Rule disconnected, frowning. Someone had tampered with his Facebook page, posting a number of pornographic photos as if they came from him. That could be dealt with, but the sophistication of the attack was worrying. Cecily didn't know how the hacker had gotten in. Rule used a random-generated password, and Facebook's software should have shut down the account before a brute force attack was able to hit on the right combination.

He turned his attention back to Ruben's conversation with Lily. Ruben was asking if she'd spotted the weapon.

"No," she said, "but that doesn't mean there isn't one, given how high the brush and grass is. I figure that search should be left to CSI."

"That's logical. The deputies arrived very quickly after you found the body."

"Within minutes," she said.

"How timely of them."

"Yeah. I'm betting they received a tip, but I wanted to speak with you before I question them about it. I took control of the scene, but I don't know if you want me to handle the investigation."

"Hmm. Give me a moment." Ruben fell silent. His eyes went unfocused. After a long moment his gaze sharpened again. "Very well. It's your case. Consider yourself restored to active duty. I'll see that Ida sends you the contact information you wanted. Felix Thompson has a strong TK Gift and manages a chat room for others with that Gift, so he's quite knowledgeable. He's wary of speaking about his Gift to those he sees as outsiders, however. You'll need to be sure he knows I referred you to him. Is there more?"

"No, sir."

"Report when there is." He disconnected, tapped the screen a couple times, and looked at Rule without putting his phone down. "I heard very little of your conversation, but I gather there's been a security breach?"

"Nothing earthshaking. My Facebook account was breached and the hacker posted some unpleasant pictures." He waved that away. "Lily found a body. Homicide? And I gather magic was involved."

"Yes—in, as she said, a weird way. The . . . Ida, I'm sorry to interrupt your Sunday. I need you to send Lily Yu contact information for Felix Thompson. Yes. Thank you." This time Ruben put his phone in his shirt pocket when he finished the call. "The victim's appearance suggests he was homeless. His throat was cut very deeply. The nature of the wound is such that, had Lily not been sent to that park, no one would have suspected that magic was involved."

Which was why Ruben had put Lily back on active status. Rule had mixed feelings about that. He didn't voice them. "Sam doesn't ordinarily take an interest in the death of a single human."

"No, clearly this is significant in some way. Perhaps the means of death is the important element. Lily believes it possible that no physical weapon was used."

Rule's eyebrows lifted. He remembered another time when someone had killed at a distance, using magic rather than a conventional weapon. An ancient artifact had been involved. "Did she find death magic?"

"No, she found TK."

Rule's eyebrows shot up. "Telekinesis?"

"Or a magic with a similar feel. She detected some difference between what was on the body and what she has felt in the past when she touched that Gift. She isn't sure what that difference means."

"Using a sword with your mind instead of your hand is an odd way to kill, but still involves a weapon."

"Perhaps not. Because of the way the magic was concentrated at the wound itself, she thinks the killer may have magically removed an extremely narrow slice of the victim's neck."

Rule's eyebrows flew up. "Is that even possible?"

"I don't know."

"Lily's right. That is weird." Rule paused, shifting gears. "Are you going to go to Wythe Clanhome?"

Ruben looked at him steadily. Too steadily, given the way his mantle pushed at Rule's, but Rule had his head straight again. He didn't react. When Ruben spoke, his voice was mild enough. "What will you do if I say yes?"

He smiled. "Leave. Immediately."

Ruben sighed faintly. "I suppose I'd best stay here, then. For now."

TWELVE

～

THE dark-haired young man with a military bearing closed
the door carefully before speaking. "Sir, we've got a situation.
I'd like you to listen to the intercept we just picked up from Target Prime."

The round little man paused with his hamburger in one
hand. A big glop of shredded lettuce and mayonnaise oozed
out from under the bun and fell on the paper towel he'd spread
on his desk in lieu of a plate. That desk was large and cluttered,
all but overwhelmed by its piles—of paper, folders, and tech
paraphernalia. "Target Prime?"

"Yes, sir. I just sent you the audio file."

"Very well." Smith put down his lunch, wiped his hands
carefully on a paper napkin, and tapped at his keyboard. A
moment later, Ruben Brooks's voice came over the speaker.
The two men listened intently. The one behind the desk cursed
briefly when Lily Yu reported that she'd claimed the scene, but
didn't speak again until the audio file reached its end.

"Damnation," he muttered. "How in the hell did she turn
up there?"

The other man shook his head. "I don't know. Unless there's
a leak—"

"If anyone who knew anything was leaking information, we'd already be under arrest."

"I don't believe in coincidence," the younger man persisted. "Target Tres has been on sick leave. Now suddenly she's in Ohio, stumbling across the remains from the last training exercise."

"Target Prime specializes in inexplicable coincidences. He's a precog. Clearly, he had a hunch that Target Tres needed to be in Ohio." The smaller man drummed his fingers briefly on the stack of folders to his left. "Still, the possibility, however unlikely, has to be checked out. Put Roberts on that. I want you to activate the Humboldt identity."

"Yes, sir. Who's going to be using it?"

A cold smile. "Time to wrap up loose ends, Rudy. The body was found by someone we very much didn't want to find it, but we can make that work for us. The dead man will assume the Humboldt identity."

Revelation dawned. "Of course. You want to go after the girl."

"The terrorist," he corrected his subordinate. "A deranged young woman with a terrible Gift. Agent Humboldt has been pursuing her for weeks now, but she must have realized he was on her trail and killed him. Tragic, really."

THIRTEEN

~

THE deputy who'd recognized Lily was named Gwen Orlander. The one who'd drawn his weapon on her was Rick Savage. Lily had learned that much about them before she called Ruben. She'd also shaken their hands—an obvious ploy, maybe, but she wanted to know if either of them had a Gift.

They didn't. While she spoke to her boss, Deputy Savage— God, what a name!—called his boss, then relayed the gist of that conversation to his partner. Lily didn't catch all of it, but enough to know that the sheriff wasn't going to make trouble.

Ruben told Lily to report when she knew more and disconnected. When she put her phone up, Deputy Savage gave her his best thousand-yard stare. "You're that FBI agent who married that weer," he informed her.

That's what he fixed on? Of all the things she'd done, everything she'd been part of . . . and sure, the press didn't know everything, but they'd reported on some and speculated about more, like her connection to the return of the dragons. Or to the collapse of a mountain. Or her role at the Humans First massacre at the D.C. Mall, which had also been attended by demon-ridden doppelgängers and an Earth elemental. Next month she was supposed to receive a presidential medal for that. Not that she deserved it, and the vast majority of her fellow citizens had no clue what the Presidential Citizen's Medal was, but you'd think a cop might.

Nope. What got Deputy Rick Savage's attention was the fact that she'd recently gotten married.

"You are," he insisted, as if she'd been arguing instead of staring at him. "You married that rich weer."

Deputy Orlander sighed. "They went to France for their honeymoon. I've always wanted to see France."

"It's lovely," Lily said dryly. "You want to call them lupi, Deputy. Lupus in the singular, lupi in the plural."

"Same difference. Listen, the sheriff says you've got the authority to claim the scene, but—"

"No, it's not the same. It's clear you've had good training." Otherwise the idiot would probably have shot her. "Surely that training included a caution against using racial epithets."

"It's not an epithet. It's just what we call them around here."

"José, would you explain to the deputy why 'weer' is a derogatory term?"

"Sure. It's what we'd been called in most of the shoot-on-sight states before the Supreme Court made them stop. The word has a real bad connotation for us."

Savage's eyes bulged. "Wait a minute. You mean he's a—"

"Lupus," Lily said. "Yes. So are the two wolves I haven't introduced to you yet. Carson? Did you finish checking out the trail?" A very large gray-and-tan wolf emerged from the brush and shook his head. Lily added to the deputies, "Do not draw your weapons again. That would deeply annoy me."

Savage's hand hovered over his holstered 9mm, but he didn't draw. His eyes were all bulgy. Carson gave Lily a wolfish grin.

"Deputies, this is Carson Forrester. Carson, Deputy Savage and Deputy Orlander." Orlander's eyes were wide, but she gave Carson a nod. Savage just stared. Lily told Carson to finish checking out the trail, Change as soon as he was able, and report. Then she asked the deputies why they were here.

Like she'd thought, they'd gotten a tip. The caller—who'd sounded male, young, and shook up—had said "someone got his throat cut out at Whistle Creek Park." He'd declined to identify himself.

"He thought he was anonymous." Orlander snorted her disdain for that assumption. "What do they think—that everyone but us has Caller ID? He used a mobile phone, so it will take a bit longer, but not much."

Savage, naturally, wanted to know why Lily was there. She admitted she'd gotten a tip also, and refused to say from whom. "Though I'm 99.9 percent sure it's not the same as your guy. My source used, ah . . . something similar to precognition." Then she showed them the picture she'd taken of the body.

"I don't recognize him," Orlander said, "but I bet Wheeler will."

"Wheeler?" Lily repeated.

Orlander looked at Savage. He scowled at Lily as if she'd accused him of something. "There's some homeless guys camped out over in the Wildlife Area. They're not supposed to, but— anyway, Wheeler is their leader. He keeps them in line. You're thinking we ought to roust them out."

"No, I'm not." Though she wondered why they hadn't. Not the sheriff's department, maybe, since the wildlife area was state property. But someone. "Is Wheeler his first name or his last name?"

Savage shrugged.

"I don't know, either," Orlander said. "Thing is, Special Agent, you might want to get Father Don to go with you. He's got a relationship with those guys. Anyone else shows up, they're gonna scatter. They don't trust people much."

After that, things fell into the familiar rhythm of most police work. Waiting, in other words. They waited for CSI and for Carson to be able to Change. Lily got contact info for Father Don, aka Donald Perkins, minister at a nondenominational church nearby. She encouraged the deputies to talk—you never knew what might prove useful, and Orlander, at least, was happy enough to chat. Then the sheriff showed up. Sheriff Franklin Boone was the sort of man who fills up a room with the sound of his voice alone. He was just under six feet tall with the shoulders of a fullback, a luxuriant mustache the color of strong tea, and thirty years on the job. He had a firm handshake and no magic. He didn't like having feds come in and take over. Who would? But he wasn't actively hostile.

"We'll have the identity of our caller soon," Boone said. "I doubt it's the perp, but you never know. What kind of magic did you say was involved?"

"Telekinesis or something similar."

"You aren't sure?"

"I'm sure magic was used. Not a hundred percent sure what kind it is, but it felt more like TK than anything else. There's some variation in the way a Gift feels from one individual to the next. It's sort of like the way different kinds of leather can feel—soft or stiff, smooth or textured."

"And this magic felt like—"

"Warm, mostly smooth, and lively."

"Lively."

"You ever touched a pane of glass when someone's cranked the bass up way too high? Kind of like that, only this glass had little bubbles in it."

Boone grimaced. "You feeling magic is pretty damned squishy. Subjective. I prefer to deal with facts."

"Not all facts can be objectively confirmed. Doesn't mean they aren't facts. Take eyewitness reports. If . . ." She stopped, frowned.

A small, round face peered out at Lily from behind one of the trees. The person it belonged to might have reached Lily's knee. Her skin was the color of hot chocolate with lots of milk. Her hair was an ash brown that blended with the bark of the tree, cut short except for a single thin braid dangling below her shoulder. Lily couldn't see her body so didn't know what she was wearing, but it was undoubtedly brown.

There was a reason brownies were called brownies.

"What is it?" The sheriff asked.

The only non-brown thing about the little woman were her eyes. A brilliant green, they widened as she realized Lily had seen her. She ducked back behind the tree.

"Wait here a minute," Lily told the sheriff. She gave José the signal that meant "follow" and headed for the trees.

The sheriff ignored her instruction and tromped along with her and José. She gave him a look. If it withered his manhood even a tiny bit, she couldn't tell. It certainly didn't stop him.

When they got to the trees, no one was there.

". . . DIDN'T see her again, so maybe it was a hallucination."

"Could be," Rule said." You're sure about the braid?"

"Positive."

The braid—*nuli ahm* in brownie-speak—meant the brownie was a mother. Without it, Lily wouldn't have known if the brownie was male or female. Brownies lacked obvious secondary sexual characteristics—beards or breasts, that is; both sexes wore the same clothing; and male and female faces looked equally cute to human eyes. Or lupus eyes, for that matter. Brownie men had skinny little butts while the women's were subtly rounded, but Lily hadn't seen the brownie's body. "Hmm. Well, brownies are good at going unseen, even without the *dul-dul*. With both trees and brush to hide in . . ."

"Yeah. Maybe I saw her, maybe I didn't."

Rule took another bite of the ham sandwich he'd made so he could eat with Lily. She was four hundred miles away in a hotel room. He was in the Brookses' guest bedroom. They might not be sharing a table, but they were sharing a meal. Or food, at least. The French dip sandwich she'd picked up before reaching her hotel was supper for her. His sandwich was a snack. "What did the sheriff say about the brownie?"

"You think I told him I was seeing brownies?"

Rule smiled. "I take your point."

Everyone knew that brownies never left their reservations. Everyone was wrong, but that's how the brownies liked it. They called their ability to go unseen dul-dul. Dul-dul blocked scent as well as sight, but not hearing. This bugged Lily, he knew. She'd asked the brownie who liaised with the Shadows why it worked on scent but not hearing. Harry had rolled his big green eyes and said, "Because we need it to work on scent, of course. We can learn to move silently, but we can't learn how to not smell."

Brownie logic did not precisely align with the usual kind.

Dul-dul didn't work on Lily, so maybe she really had seen a little brownie peering at her. Or maybe she'd hallucinated three bloody damn times today. Rule did not want that to be true. "Their reservation isn't far from Whistle. She was probably just wandering."

"Maybe, but nothing's missing. I've still got my ring, wallet, watch, badge—everything I had with me. That suggests it was a hallucination, doesn't it?"

"They only play 'the game' in a space you claim as yours. A park wouldn't count."

"Are you sure? Because I claimed that damn crime scene. If that little puddle of cute took anything from it—"

"If she hasn't asked for a forfeit, she didn't take anything. Did you find out who called the tip in?"

"Yes. Talked to them, too."

"Learn anything useful?" he asked.

A small sigh. "Yes and no. There were two of them, both boys, both sixteen. I'm pretty sure they're just what they seem— a couple of kids who were planning to do things their parents wouldn't like out at the park. Weed, most likely. José smelled it on them."

"That's the 'no' part of the answer, I assume. What's the 'yes' part?"

"The bit that's useful but puzzling. Carson had already found their scents on the trail. The thing is, those were the only recent scents he found anywhere near the body, aside from ours."

Rule frowned, trying to make sense of that. "Doesn't someone using TK have to be close to the object they manipulate?"

"That's my understanding. I tried calling the contact Ruben gave me—a guy with a strong TK Gift—but he's getting some kind of medical procedure done. His wife didn't say what, but she said I could call back tomorrow. I think you have to be able to see what you're manipulating with TK, though. That's what someone else with that Gift told me once. I haven't figured out how anyone could have seen the victim without leaving any scent near the body. Not unless they were also able to levitate."

"I've never heard of a levitation Gift. There's nowhere nearby they could have attained enough height to see over the grasses in that field?"

"There's some trees, but none of them give a clear view of where the victim was killed. José didn't find any scent up in the trees, either. Admittedly, he was two-legged at the time— wolves don't climb trees well—but still, if someone had been up there today, he should have smelled them."

"Hmm." He took a last bite of his snack, chewed, and switched the subject. "I wonder if the Lady sent Charles with you so he could find the body."

"I wondered about that, too, but it doesn't add up. If Charles hadn't been there, someone still would've found the body. Maybe it would've been the deputies instead of me, but I'd have claimed the scene anyway. I don't see that it would have made much difference."

"Unless it mattered who found the body."

"I don't see it. Say the deputies show up and I'm still wandering around, wondering why I'm there. They'd check me out, same as they did. Once we'd all shared ID, I'd have learned why they were there and probably would have sent Carson looking for the body. Even if I didn't, I would have looked with them. It all would've ended up about the same way it did." She hesitated. "There's something I need to ask you, but he's right here."

"Charles?"

"Yeah. He decided there was room for him on one side of the bed, and I can't figure out how to tell him to go find his own damn bed. Good thing it's king-size."

Rule grinned. Charles was milking his status for all it was worth. "I take it this is something you don't want him to hear."

"No, but he's asleep." She lowered her voice anyway. "Is there anything I should know about . . . you know. What I should do."

"There's little you can or should do," he assured her. "Charles passed into his waiting time six days ago. There's no saying how much longer he has, but generally, an elder doesn't suffer much, even at the very end. He'll grow tired easily and sleep more than usual. He may have bursts of energy when he seems normal. He may have periods of confusion. Ah . . . humans sometimes treat their dying differently than we do. Charles will make his own decisions about what he eats and when and whether he feels well enough to go for a run."

"I get that," she said. "I don't make his choices for him just because he's dying. But I'm not sure about . . . well, he might die while he's with me."

"You're not sure what to expect? Sometimes an elder's heart simply stops. He's here with one breath and gone with the next. Sometimes there's a period of respiratory distress as his body shuts down more gradually. Though it doesn't last more than two or three hours, it can be difficult for those who wait with them."

Lily huffed out an impatient breath. "His body, Rule. That's what I'm talking about. If he dies while he's with me, what am I supposed to do with his body? I don't think a regular mortuary will take him when he's in wolf-form—"

"For God's sake, no embalming."

"I know you don't usually do that, but how am I supposed to get him back to Ruben? Or to Wythe Clanhome, if that's where he's supposed to go."

"Lily." He paused, trying to understand why this bothered her. "You're talking about a body, not about Charles. You know we don't have the same reverence for empty flesh that humans do."

"But you do bury your dead! And surely someone's going to want Charles's body."

"Charles didn't have any children, and I don't see how possessing his body would comfort those who grieve for him. If Charles dies before you finish this investigation, José will see that his body is taken care of."

"He'll dispose of it somewhere, you mean."

"Of course. That's what burial is."

"It's not the same. Sneaking his body into an unmarked grave somewhere is just—shit."

"What?"

"He's laughing at me," she said darkly. "He wasn't asleep after all, and now he's grinning like he thinks I'm funny."

Rule carefully kept his own amusement out of his voice. "We do find human attitudes about empty flesh rather odd."

"All right, all right, I get it. I'm the only one who doesn't like the idea of just dumping his body somewhere, so I can just get over it."

"I wouldn't put it that way."

"You don't have to. What's on your schedule tomorrow?"

"Quarterly taxes," he said dryly. "I suspect you'll have a more interesting day. I'll also want to talk with Ruben and see if he's made a decision."

"About what?"

"He's considering heading up to Maine to see his healer."

He could almost hear the wheels turning in her head as she deciphered that. Ruben had been treated by a reclusive healer at one time, which had come in handy when he needed to explain his current robust health. The healer was also a convenient excuse for going to Wythe Clanhome in Maine—supposedly he needed ongoing treatments. "That's probably a good idea."

"He told me I was welcome to stay here if he leaves, but I don't think that's a good idea."

"You don't?"

"It's just a feeling I've got."

Silence. Then: "He's not having any particular problems, is he?"

Was she asking if Ruben had had a hunch? "Nothing specific." Some might think it a surfeit of caution to speak so obliquely on the remote chance someone was eavesdropping, but he considered paranoia a healthy survival trait.

"If you—huh. Either nature's calling, or someone else is."

"Pardon?"

"Charles just headed for the door." Faintly he heard a knock. "Not nature. Someone's here."

"Let José check it out before—"

"I'm betting the two guards in the hall have already checked them out, Rule. I'd better go."

"Be careful. I love you."

She told him she loved him and disconnected. He sat on the big, comfortable bed, his phone in his hand, and missed her. Worried for her.

Someone needed to. She didn't worry about herself. But it probably wasn't helpful to feel half-sick with anxiety for no reason whatsoever . . . save that she wasn't with him.

He sighed and put the phone down and started stripping. "Mike," he said to the guard on the other side of the door. "I'm going for a run. You'll want to Change if you're going to keep up with me."

FOURTEEN

~⌇~

LILY grabbed her weapon from where she'd set it on the night-stand. Another knock. "Coming," she called. But when she reached the door, she didn't open it. "Who are you?"

"We'd prefer to identify ourselves after we're inside, Special Agent."

Another voice spoke, but the words were muffled by the door. It sounded like Carson. "Human ears here," she reminded him.

He raised his voice. "Two men, both human, both armed. They wouldn't identify themselves."

The first voice spoke firmly. "Special Agent, we'd prefer to keep our presence here quiet."

Another door opened—the one to the room next door, which was shared by several of the guards. José stood there with his Glock ready. Lily gave him a nod, and opened the door with her left hand. Her right held her weapon.

Two men, as Carson had said, both on the shady side of forty. One was skinny, white, and balding, with black-rimmed eyeglasses. He carried a briefcase. The other was all-over bland—bland suit, bland tie, a bland blend of English and Irish in his features and skin tone.

Bland Man glanced down at her gun with neither surprise nor offense. Skinny Guy wasn't as sanguine. "What are you, crazy?

You answer the door ready to shoot?" He spoke fast, shooting the words out like bullets. "What kind of damn cop are you? That's not the way you were trained. Pretty damn paranoid, if you ask me."

"I didn't. Who are you?"

In answer, Bland Man held out an ID folder much like Lily's. He was blessed with a most unbland name: Aloysius A. Griggs. The card that offered the information he hadn't wanted to state out loud was not from the FBI, but it was federally issued. Lily's eyebrows lifted. "Homeland Security?"

The other man rolled his eyes. "Which part of 'we'd like to keep our presence quiet' did you not understand?"

"You're mistaking understanding for giving a shit. I haven't seen your ID yet."

Skinny Guy was named William Rutherford. He was also with HSI, the investigative branch of Homeland Security. Usually Homeland Security played well with others, that being a big part of their mandate, but some agents from their investigative branch liked to pretend they'd never gotten the memo about interagency cooperation. Rutherford seemed to be of that ilk.

Or maybe he was just naturally judgmental and obnoxious. Lily held out the hand that didn't have a weapon in it. "Agent Rutherford."

She got another eye roll from Rutherford, but he did shake her hand. Dry palm, no calluses, no magic. Griggs had a firm grip and a smidgeon of an Earth Gift, so small she could barely detect it. He probably had no idea it was there. She told them to come in and stood aside.

Two paces into the room they both stopped. This was a reasonable reaction to having a wolf place himself across your path, especially when his hackles were raised. "Charles," Lily said sharply. "Back off."

He didn't.

"Not very well trained," Rutherford said disapprovingly. "A large dog like that can be dangerous if he isn't properly trained." He held his briefcase in front of him as if he was trying to shelter behind it.

The bland Griggs snorted. "That's not a dog, Will."

"You mean he's a—" Rutherford stopped. His hands tightened on the thoroughly inadequate shield of his briefcase.

Lily frowned at Charles and spoke under the tongue, a type of subvocalization only lupus ears would pick up. "You embarrass me by disobeying."

His tail drooped. He gave the two men a quick growl—a warning to behave themselves probably—and reluctantly moved a few feet away. Lily wondered if they smelled especially aggressive, or if he just didn't like Rutherford.

"He can't remain," Rutherford said. "Neither can your man there." He scowled at José, who still stood in the door to the other room, though he'd put away his weapon.

"Guess what? You aren't in charge here. I am." She reminded herself to be professional. Rutherford was making that difficult. "But José can go watch TV for—no, wait. We need another chair. José, if you wouldn't mind?" Her room was standard hotel fare. Aside from the bed it held a dresser with the television, a nightstand, and by the window was a round table with two chairs.

José brought a chair from his room . . . which held a couple more lupi who were keeping quiet, staying out of sight. He then went back to his room and turned on the TV, but without closing the door. The HSI agents didn't like that. Aloysius A. Griggs went so far as to frown. Rutherford nattered on at her in a way that might drive her nuts if she had to listen to him for long.

Lily sat down and put her hands on the table. "I'm not going to ask José to shut the door. You might as well have a seat and tell me why you're here."

"The wolf—"

"Stays. He's suffering from a condition that doesn't allow him to Change, so he won't be able to repeat anything he hears, if that's your concern."

Griggs stepped up, pulled out a chair, and sat down.

Rutherford frowned. "I don't like it."

"TV's on," Griggs said in that deep, melodious voice. "They won't hear us if we keep our voices down."

"The wolf will." But after shooting Charles a deeply suspicious glance, Rutherford did finally take a seat. He set his briefcase on the floor beside him and looked at Lily the way most people would eye a bug in their beer. "They warned us you'd probably have lupi with you, but this is over the top. You really are freaking paranoid, aren't you?"

"Funny how even a handful of attempts on your life can do that. Why don't you tell me why you're here?"

Griggs answered before Rutherford could. "The victim you found. The one you say was killed by magic. He was one of ours."

Lily blinked. "HSI? He sure didn't look like it. You don't get that kind of ground-in dirt unless you've lived rough awhile."

Rutherford sneered. "He was undercover. On the trail of a suspected domestic terrorist. We need to know everything you've learned."

"Pretty damn little, at this point. He was killed by a type of magic that either is or strongly resembles telekinesis. How do you know he was your guy?" The body hadn't been autopsied yet.

Rutherford didn't answer the question. Instead he leaned down, opened his briefcase, and pulled out a thin folder. "His name was Jason Humboldt." He tossed an eight-by-ten photo on the table.

It was a head shot and looked like it had been blown up from a much smaller picture. An ID photo maybe. The background was plain white. Lily picked it up. The man in the picture was both clean and clean shaven, which made it hard to compare the photo to her memory of the dead man. She tilted her head, studying it. "That could be him."

"It is."

Her voice softened a bit. "You knew him?"

Rutherford shook his head. "No, but he's been positively identified."

"By who?"

"That's irrelevant."

She tried another tack. "Who's this terrorist he was investigating, and why did that require him to pass as a homeless man?"

"We can't give you many details, which is why we'll be handling the investigation into his death."

"No, you aren't."

"We aren't asking your permission."

"You'd have to ask Congress's permission. They're the ones who gave me, as an agent of Unit Twelve, the authority to take charge of any investigation into felonies involving magic."

Rutherford and Griggs exchanged a look. Griggs shrugged. Rutherford scowled at her. "We'll see about that. I can oblige you in one way." He pulled out another photo but held on to it. "This is one of our suspects. We had reason to believe she was in Georgia—but we thought Humboldt was, too. His cover doesn't allow him to report regularly, but he's been following her, trying to ID other members of her cell."

"By pretending to be homeless? Is she homeless?"

He ignored the question. "If we were wrong about our man's location, chances are we were wrong about hers, too. It's possible Humboldt identified and followed someone else from her cell here, but we consider that unlikely." At last he handed over the photo. "She's had Lasik surgery since that was taken, so she won't be wearing glasses now. Do you recognize her?"

This photo had the grainy, out-of-focus look of a low-resolution photo blown up too large. Snapped by a phone camera maybe, and not one of the newer models. In it, a skinny girl with dreadlocks and thick glasses sat on a narrow bed, grimacing at the photographer. One hand was raised, her fingers spread, as if she'd tried to block the camera. She'd failed, but given the glasses, the picture quality, and her expression, she needn't have worried. Her features weren't clear.

Lily raised her eyebrows. "Homeland Security is in hot pursuit of a kid?"

"The picture's two years old."

"Making her at least fifteen now."

"Seventeen. I know it's hard to believe, but some terrorists don't actually look like terrorists."

Lily grimaced, acknowledging that the sarcasm was warranted. She picked up the photo, frowning. Something about it . . .

Rutherford leaned forward. "Have you seen her?"

Lily shook her head. "Something about her strikes me as familiar, but I can't put my finger on it. Maybe I saw an alert about her."

"We haven't distributed her picture. I can let you have that photo, but I need your word that you won't show it around."

"Why not?"

"We don't want to spook her. Notify us immediately if you see her."

"What's her name?"

"It doesn't matter. She won't be using it."

"Seriously? You aren't going to tell me the name of your terrorist?"

Rutherford stood. "You need to consider her very dangerous. Either she or someone from her terrorist cell killed Humboldt. It's believed that there are at least three more in her cell. All of them are Gifted."

The silent Griggs pushed his chair back and stood, too, so Lily did the same. "What are their Gifts?"

"That's all I'm cleared to tell you. We didn't want you stumbling across her without being aware of the danger, but I can't give you any more than that."

Apparently they were done. She got a nod from Griggs, a scowl from Rutherford, and the two men left without another word.

She shook her head as the door closed behind them. "That was weird."

José came through the door to his room. "What did they want? Did they really think you were going to meekly hand over the investigation?"

"Beats me." José had, of course, heard everything. Humans almost always underestimated lupi hearing, which wouldn't be bothered by a little TV noise. "Couple of things stuck me as odd. First, they were surprised by Charles, but neither of them jumped to the conclusion that he was Rule. Seems like they would unless they already knew where Rule was. Second, they refuse to tell me anything about their investigation into a terrorist cell . . . except for identifying this girl as the leader." She tapped the photo they'd left.

He glanced at the picture. "You think that was the real point of their visit?"

"I don't know. Maybe Ruben will."

He didn't, though he did find it interesting that he hadn't heard from Homeland Security himself. If HSI wanted to try to kick her off the investigation, they weren't going about it through the usual channels. He told her he would call his counterpart in the other department. Eric Ellison had recently become executive director of HSI, after a bit of a shake-up. Ruben said he didn't yet have a feel for the man, but the way he said it made Lily think that what feel he had was not positive. Still, he'd get in touch with Ellison. They needed to know a helluva lot more than Rutherford and Griggs had been willing to say.

Lily studied the photo again after making that call to Ruben. A nagging sense of familiarity lingered, but she couldn't get anything to rise to the top of her brain. After wrestling unsuccessfully with her memory, she set it aside. Maybe her subconscious would work on that overnight. She wanted a shower. Usually she preferred to shower in the morning, but this time she wanted one before bed.

It wasn't until she was standing beneath the driving pulse of hot water, reluctant to turn it off, that she realized she was putting off going to bed. That she felt sad and scared and lonely and hated the thought of sleeping in that big hotel bed alone.

How foolish. Surely she wasn't so needy she couldn't spend one night away from Rule. It was okay to miss him. It was not okay to be so damned pathetic about it. On a scale of one to horrible—and she'd experienced the truly horrible—such a brief separation barely nudged the needle. She told herself those things. It didn't help. She took her time drying her hair and wished she could reach for Rule through the bond, but when she tried, the disorientation was worse than ever.

She could call him. It was only a little after eleven. He wouldn't be asleep yet.

He'd think something was wrong. He was already anxious about them being separated. She didn't want to make that worse.

This sucked. She opened the door and saw that she'd been wrong about one thing. She wouldn't be sleeping alone. Charles had resumed his spot on the king-size bed. She shook her head, but didn't try to make him leave. Maybe his bones ached too much for the floor. She climbed into bed and turned off the light.

It took her a long time to fall asleep. When she did, she dreamed about hell.

Hell was cold, not hot. It was stony and barren, yet it was a place for the living, not an afterlife repository for errant souls. Only the living had to worry about dying, and a lot of dying went on there. Hell—the real place, the one Lily had experienced— was also known as Dis, the demon realm, and demons ate the living, not the dead.

The dream mixed memory and imagination, jumbling past horrors with present confusion. In reality, Lily had arrived in hell shorn of clothes, memories, and her name. In the dream, she knew who she was, but not how she got there. She was just as naked as the first time, though. The rocks she climbed cut her feet and slithered beneath her as if they wanted to dump her back down the slope. Way down, to where the demons waited.

At first that was all there was to the dream—climbing those cold, treacherous rocks in a fever of fear, trying to escape the waiting demons. She pulled herself up and up. Gradually, in spite of her terror, the conviction grew that this was wrong. Why was she here again? She couldn't be. She remembered hell. She remembered escaping it. How could she be here again?

Without Rule this time. Without anyone. She was alone in the vast, rocky desolation. She stopped and looked up.

Not really alone, after all. High in the sullen sky, a dark shape spiraled down. A dragon. The black dragon, who'd carried her away in his talons the first time. He'd do that this time, too, and it would crack open her mind and spill out whatever sanity she'd collected in her thirty years of living, and it wasn't right. It wasn't supposed to happen like this.

Why? she screamed at the sullen sky and the stooping dragon.

Get out of my head! the sky screamed back. *Get out!*

Rocks and sky disappeared, fading to black . . . the black of her closed eyelids. She felt the weight of the blanket drawn up over her body and the chill of the air on her face and understood that she'd been dreaming. Now she was awake. Mostly awake . . .

She felt something else. *Who are you?*

Nothing. The voice, the sense of presence, had been a product of the dream, nothing more. She . . .

I'm going crazy.

Despair coated that thought. And it wasn't hers. Not her despair. Not her thought, either.

FIFTEEN

~

"**YOU** did what?" Rule stopped moving, phone in one hand, sock in the other.

"Mindspoke someone. I could be wrong, but I'm pretty sure I did. I was half asleep when it happened . . . well, at first I was all the way asleep. I had a nasty dream about hell, complete with rocks and demons. You weren't there."

Perversely, that made Rule smile. He shouldn't have. His *nadia* had clearly had a nightmare, and he hadn't been there to hold her. But he couldn't help but appreciate the unsubtle message her subconscious had sent. "I wonder what your dream meant," he murmured.

"I have no idea. The point is, in the dream the black dragon was swooping down to get me. I yelled at him and someone answered, told me to get out of their head. That woke me up, but I still felt . . . I don't know how to put it. A connection, I guess. I asked who they were and I 'heard' their reply. It felt like mindspeech."

"Are you saying 'they' because you don't know which pronoun applies?" He finished pulling on his sock and slid his feet into his shoes.

"Of course. Mindspeech isn't sexed. Whoever it was thought they were going crazy."

"Understandable, especially if they'd never experienced mindspeech before." In Rule's experience, it was impossible to mistake mindspeech for his own thoughts. It was like the difference between imagining eating chocolate and actually biting into it. "What happened next?'

"I got a headache," she said wryly.

Rule slid his wallet and a couple more things into the appropriate pockets. "Better now, I hope."

"God bless ibuprofen. I hope whoever's party I crashed isn't still freaked out this morning. Maybe they persuaded themselves they were dreaming."

"Very likely. You got a headache, but no hallucinations?"

"Nope." She sounded cheerful about that. "I'm trying not to get all crazy optimistic, but I can't help thinking that's a good sign. Maybe my brain is getting itself sorted out."

"We can hope." Fully dressed now, Rule left the bedroom where he'd almost slept last night. Every time he'd dozed off, some part of his mind had reached for Lily. Every time, the resulting disorientation had woken him. "What's on your schedule today?"

"Did Ruben tell you about those HSI guys who dropped by last night?"

"He did."

"Did he tell you they left a couple photos with me? One of their man, taken from his ID badge. One of a girl—seventeen now, fifteen when the picture was taken. She's supposed to be a terrorist."

"Supposed to be?"

"Something's fishy. I have no idea what. Ruben checked out my visitors, and they're genuine HSI agents. Everything they told me is accurate—what little of it there was," she added with disgust. "But they're up to something. I'm going to see if I can find out what."

Downstairs the doorbell chimed. Odd. It was early still, not yet eight. Couldn't be anyone too alarming, though. The Wythe guards wouldn't have let a potentially dangerous visitor reach the door. "How will you do that?"

"There's a minister who's supposed to know the homeless guys around here. I called him yesterday. Didn't get him, but I left a message. I'm hoping he'll go with me to talk to some of them. I want to know more about this undercover HSI guy. What's on your schedule today? Did you get that meeting with Brownsley rescheduled?"

"We're having some difficulty matching our schedules." Primarily because Rule refused to commit to a day and time because he had to be free to go to Lily. He was behaving irrationally. He knew it, and couldn't seem to care. "Today I'll be working on Leidolf's quarterly taxes."

"I thought you had an accountant for that."

"Her estimate is substantially different from what I'd anticipated. I need to go over her documentation." Vaguely he noted that Deborah had answered the door. His own door was closed, so he didn't hear her words clearly, but her voice sounded puzzled.

"I'm going to have a better day than you will."

"Perhaps, although I'm fairly sure I won't be shot at." Curious, Rule moved toward the bedroom door and opened it a crack. Mike stood in the hall, listening intently. He met Rule's inquiring glance with a small head shake.

"True, but unless I actually get hit, I'll still have a better day than you. If you . . . I've got a call. Can you hold?"

"No need. I should go, too."

"Okay. Love you." She disconnected.

Rule slipped his phone into a pocket. With the door cracked, he could hear Deborah better. She told the visitor to wait here, please. A man replied in a deep, gruff voice that he couldn't do that, ma'am, and where was Rule Turner?

Rule's eyebrows lifted. He opened the door fully.

Ruben joined Deborah and whoever-it-was by the door. "What's this about, Officer?"

Officer? Rule moved quickly and quietly to the head of the stairs. From here he could join them—or make an exit through the window opposite the stairs, which were at the back of the house. It would be an easy drop. He signaled for Mike to stay with him.

The officer asked Ruben to identify himself. Ruben did, including his position with the FBI, and repeated his question.

"I understand you have a guest staying with you, sir. Rule Turner."

"That's correct."

"We need to speak with him."

"Again, I'd like to know why."

There was a pause in which the officer spoke quietly to someone else—another man. Probably a second cop. The two kept their voices so low Rule couldn't make out all their words, but what he caught suggested they were trying to decide how much to tell someone who was much higher than they on the law enforcement scale, though not part of their own hierarchy. Finally he said, "We have a warrant for his arrest."

Well. That presented him with an interesting question. Rule's heartbeat zoomed straight up into racing mode. His mouth went dry. He'd spent time in a cell once. It was worse than an elevator. Much worse. He glanced at the window.

Ruben was delaying, giving him time by asking the officers for their identification. Rule breathed in, breathed out, doing what he could to slow his heartbeat, to control the physical aspects of fear, so he could think. The first thing he thought of was Lily. If he allowed himself to be arrested, he'd be locked up for an indefinite period of time. Probably not too long. This was Monday, so it shouldn't be hard to arrange bail, assuming the charges were such that bail was an option. But for some period of time, long or short, he wouldn't be free to go to Lily if she needed him.

He waited for the panic to hit. It didn't.

Oh, he feared being locked up, no doubt about it. Most lupi disliked small, enclosed spaces, and Rule had to admit his own discomfort was above average. But that was about him, not Lily. The lack of panic was a relief, but it was sure as hell confusing. He shoved the confusion aside for now and considered his options: stay and get arrested, or go on the run. He had so little information upon which to base a decision . . .

"I need to see the arrest warrant, also," Ruben said.

. . . but there were very few circumstances in which it was better to be on the run from the cops. Rule sighed, pulled out his phone, and called up the number for the attorney Nokolai used here in the capital. As the phone rang, he started down the stairs. "So do I. I'm sure my lawyer will, too."

"**THEY** what?" Lily blurted out.

Ruben repeated it. "Arrested him for distribution of child pornography."

"That's insane."

"To anyone who knows him, yes."

"Or anyone who knows anything about the lupi." When it came to sexual predators who targeted children, lupi thought "dead" solved the problem really well.

"True. Not that the Justice Department will take our word for it."

They wouldn't. Of course they wouldn't.

Who had done this? Who had set Rule up to be charged with a crime so vile? One that might eventually be disproven—would be disproven, she corrected herself. But the taint to his name would linger. Even when he'd been legally cleared, people would remember that he'd been charged. Lily's hands clenched. "Give me a minute."

"All right."

"I am really, really angry." Blind with fury. She'd heard the words lots of times and thought she knew what they meant, but until this moment she'd never felt them.

"Lily." Someone touched her arm. "Breathe."

It was José. He sat up front with Carson, who was driving. He'd twisted around so he could touch her, get her attention. She almost punched him.

The call that had interrupted her conversation with Rule had been from Father Don. She was on the way to meet him now, at the wildlife preserve. Carson was driving; José rode shotgun. She sat in back with Charles, who'd lifted his head and looked worried. She had to get a grip, stay in control. Lupi needed their leaders to be in control. So she did like he said and breathed in and out slowly, until the red tide began to retreat. Not entirely, but enough.

"I'm putting you on speaker," she told Ruben. "José and Carson are with me, and they're listening anyway." Might as well be sure they heard clearly.

"All right. They also had a search warrant, which allowed them to seize his laptop. I trust there's nothing on it they shouldn't see."

He meant Shadow Unit business. "Of course not, unless someone else put it there. We'd better assume that's possible." Lily rubbed her forehead. She knew damn little about computer security. Rule's laptop was supposed to be protected, but good hackers could get into most anything. "Dammit, I don't want to be here."

"You wouldn't be able to do anything if you were here. He chose to allow the arrest, Lily. I gave him time to get away if he'd wanted. Instead, when he came downstairs, he was already on the phone to an attorney."

"Do you know who?"

"Miriam Stockard."

"Ah." That made her feel somewhat better. Lily knew from personal experience that Miriam Stockard was every bit as good as her reputation, and prosecutors all along the East Coast hated her. Prosecutors on the West Coast weren't too fond of her, either. "Good. That's good. I thought she didn't take cases involving any kind of child abuse." Kiddie porn sure fell into that category.

"She won't represent someone accused of harming a child if she believes they're guilty. Rule gave her his word he was innocent of these charges. Apparently that convinced her."

Stockard must know more about lupi than Lily had suspected. "She's top drawer. She'll see that he gets a bail hearing promptly. Maybe even get the charges dismissed. There can't be anything to them."

"He thought it might be related to his Facebook account being hacked yesterday."

"I didn't know about that. What happened?"

"I don't know the details, but apparently someone posted objectionable photos. He spoke with a reporter or two about it yesterday, I believe. Over the phone, not in person. I didn't see any mention of it on the news last night."

Neither had she, and Rule hadn't mentioned it. They'd talked twice on the phone and texted several times, and he hadn't told her that his Facebook page had been hacked. He must have considered it unimportant. It sounded like the media had agreed, but still, he should have told her. Lily rubbed her head some more. She couldn't yell at him about it until he was free. "There has to be more to it than that. They wouldn't arrest him based on a Facebook hack."

"I agree. The arrest was odd in one respect. He was picked up by local police, not federal marshals."

"Maybe the local cops were tasked with the arrest because

they thought marshals might tip you off. It's a federal crime. You're a big-deal fed."

"If they were sufficiently ignorant to suspect that, we should have an easier time disproving whatever frame they've arranged. I've no connection to the marshals or to CEOS."

CEOS was part of the Justice Department. "They've got that Unit—HTIU, right? High Technology Investigative Unit? They investigate child pornography on the Internet. You don't have any contacts there?"

"None who've returned my calls," he said dryly.

"Which judge signed off on the warrant?"

"Bernhardt."

Bernhardt was a no-nonsense type. She wouldn't have signed the warrant if there wasn't evidence of a crime. Anger made Lily's head throb. "Any ideas who cooked this up?"

"Not yet. But if Rule's presence in D.C. is important to the Unit for some reason, it seems likely that whatever enemy is moving against us is behind this."

Ruben hadn't specified which Unit he meant. He didn't have to. "If they keep him longer than overnight, I need to be there when he's released." Rule had claustrophobia. He refused to call it that, but just riding in an elevator was a strain. He did it all the time, insisting on taking the elevator even when it would easy to use the stairs. He hated having a weakness and challenged his as often as possible, but that didn't make it go away. Being locked up for any period of time would be hard on him. Being locked up for too long might be hard on his jailers. If he lost control . . . "Are you in touch with his lawyer? Tell her he needs bail, stat. If they hold him too long . . . I need to be there, that's all. Deal or no deal." Sam would just have to understand.

"Lily, you know lupi ways better than I, but they take the giving of one's word very seriously. You might want to think about the consequences if you were to go back on yours, however good your reason."

Now she wanted to punch Ruben. "I'll think about it. Have you contacted Isen? What about Alex?" Rule's second-in-command at Leidolf needed to know his Rho had been arrested.

"Mike is talking to Alex now. He wishes to speak to me as well. I'll call Isen after I talk to Alex."

In other words, Lily needed to stop pestering Ruben about the obvious—if he'd had any idea who set Rule up, he'd have said so—and let him handle things. "Right. I guess I'll go."

"I'll be in touch," he promised, and disconnected.

Lily hung up her phone and didn't say a word for the next two miles. As they drove by rolling grasslands, heading for a lightly wooded area, she did what she'd told Ruben she would. She thought about it.

More like she argued with herself. One of her mental voices sounded a whole damn lot like Ruben. That one pissed her off, but it didn't win the argument until Rule chimed in. Not really Rule, of course, but the part of her that knew him, the part that rose from her gut. What's the worst that can happen? she asked the tight, twisty feeling in her gut. Sam knew she wasn't a dragon or a lupus and didn't have the same attitude toward deals and such. He knew . . .

Sam wasn't the problem.

Trees surrounded them when Carson slowed a few minutes later. New-growth forest, noted one corner of Lily's mind—a mix of conifers and deciduous trees, some tall but none thick-girthed. Lots of saplings and underbrush, but not as thick as some she'd seen, where the forest made a wall you couldn't enter.

"Six-point-two miles," Carson said. "This should be it, according to the reverend." He turned off onto a dirt road.

Lily sighed and spoke. "I'm not going to back out of the deal."

José nodded. "We knew you wouldn't. You were pissed, that's all."

He was right. She'd been pissed, yes. He was also wrong. If Ruben hadn't reminded her to think about consequences, she might well have broken the deal. And she couldn't. Even if Rule needed her desperately, she couldn't go until she'd done whatever Sam sent her here to do. She'd tried to persuade herself that putting her investigation on pause long enough to rush to D.C. didn't violate her word, not as long as she hurried back. She might even think that was true.

The lupi with her wouldn't. To Lily, keeping her word was a high priority. To them, it was the highest. The way lupi saw it, if you swore to do something, you did it or died trying. Literally. If it cost your life or someone else's—tough. Once you gave your word, you were bound by it. Rule had granted Lily a great deal of authority, telling the guards to obey her as they would him. They wouldn't understand it if she broke her word, no matter how good her reasons. If she did, she'd still be their boss . . . but she wouldn't be their leader.

The difference between a boss and a leader could be measured in lives. She knew that because it had happened.

They'd been attacked by dworg—her, Cynna, and the guards with them. One guard had decided it was okay to disregard her orders in order to protect her. Because she'd been his boss, not his leader, he'd placed his judgment above hers. His decision had cost at least one life and endangered others, including hers.

"This should be the spot," Carson said, slowing again as they reached a small clearing in the trees. A second, much rougher road, no more than a pair of ruts, ambled off into the grass, aiming for the edge of the clearing. José pulled off onto the two-rut-road. The car behind them did, too. It held four more guards from the Leidolf contingent who'd arrived last night.

"No sign of the reverend," Carson said. "He said he'd be in a pickup, right?"

"A 2004 Silverado, red with one fender primer gray." Which clearly wasn't waiting for them like he'd said he would be. "I'll call and see if—" Her phone dinged. She checked it and found a text from Perkins: delayed by congregant. sorry. 30 m. "He'll be along in about thirty minutes."

"Good. Gives us time to check out the area," José said, and: "Not you, Lily."

She'd had her hand on the door, ready to get out. He was right. As unlikely as it seemed, it was possible the reverend had set them up. A sniper could be waiting. Or a Gifted person able to send knives flying through the air. Or a demon. Lily never forgot the possibility of demons, though she hadn't seen one for quite a while now. So José was right, but— "I need to move."

It was a need any lupus would understand. "Give us five minutes to check out the area."

She could do five minutes, dammit. Lily grabbed the folder that held the photos she planned to show Father Don and any of the homeless men she could find. It held two shots of Jason Humboldt—the glossy headshot the HSI agents had given her, and a print made from one of the photos she'd taken of the body. Looking from one photo to the other, Lily could see the resemblance more clearly than she had at first. The beard made it hard to be sure, but it sure looked like the same guy. Aside from the dirt, that is. Could that much ground-in dirt build up in only a couple months of undercover work?

That was one of the things she wanted to find out. If Humboldt had started out clean, or with only superficial dirt, the men he hung out with would have noticed.

She had a lot more questions. Why had the HSI agent decided that a homeless man was a great cover? It was a hard way to live, and it didn't let you mingle with most people. Did HSI think their alleged terrorist was living rough? Seventeen-year-old girls who ended up on the streets didn't usually hang out with a bunch of homeless guys, especially not out in the woods.

Speaking of teenage terrorists . . . Lily looked at the last picture in the folder, the blurry one of a fifteen-year-old girl. And suddenly memory clicked into place.

"Ross is giving me the clear signal," José said.

"Good." Lily handed him the folder. "I may have seen our teenage terrorist. You two have a look, see if you recognize her."

José opened it. Carson leaned close to look. José shook his head. Carson said, "I dunno. She looks kind of familiar."

"Yesterday, at the gas station," Lily prompted.

"Oh, yeah! That does kinda look like her. I can't say for—"

José interrupted. "The gas station attendant was a boy."

"No, she wasn't," Carson said, looking up in surprise. "Oh—you probably didn't smell her. Him? I guess we're supposed to say 'him' if that's how someone thinks of herself. I mean himself. Shit, you know what I mean. It's hard to remember to say 'he' about someone my nose says is female."

That was pretty good confirmation. It was possible the attendant was trans, as Carson assumed, and her resemblance to the alleged terrorist was coincidence. Lily didn't think so. "Looks like we're going to need more gas really soon."

"You going to notify those Homeland agents?" José asked.

"No. Not yet anyway. I'm going for a walk."

A run would be better, but she didn't want to stress out her guards—four of whom took up positions around her the moment she got out of the car.

It wasn't a very big clearing, so she set off along the dirt road. A large, aging wolf fell into step beside her.

How much of what she'd thought of as "Rule being weird" had been because he was lupus? Not because he turned into a wolf and she didn't, but because he knew he could not go back on his word. No matter what. And she . . . well, she'd never consciously factored in the possibility of breaking her word, but that might be because she hadn't thought the issue would come up. Rule was supposed to be safe in D.C.

Easy enough to risk herself. So much harder to risk him. Yet she'd expected him to be able to risk her, hadn't she?

Lily scowled at an innocent tree, turned, and started back. She knew how to set aside fear for her own life. She'd thought she'd gotten a handle on how to keep moving when she was scared for Rule, too. She'd faced that fear more than once . . . but she'd always been in a position to do something about it. To act.

Well, she was still supposed to act, wasn't she? Only not in a way that helped Rule, dammit all to hell. He'd be okay, she told herself. He might do better if she was there, but he'd manage. Assuming he wasn't locked up too long . . .

What was that? Lily stopped. And stared.

Once was odd. Twice was too damn much for coincidence. "What the hell is she doing here?"

SIXTEEN

~

RULE stank. Surely even human noses would wrinkle at the smell clinging to his skin and clothes. Not the noses near him, however. The drunks, gangbangers, and drug users sharing space with him were the reason he stank.

Lupi didn't have the same scent aversions as humans. Most smells were either pleasant or interesting, including many of those humans considered offensive. To Rule, urine smelled interesting, most perfumes stank, and sweat smelled good . . . except for alcohol sweat. He heartily disliked the smell of stale alcohol oozing out through human pores.

It was neither the first nor the worst time he'd spent in jail, but this incarceration was unusual in one respect: he'd been placed in a holding cell with the general jail population. Normally authorities were very cautious when they locked up lupi, using a high-security cell if possible, often with the addition of shackles. Rule was glad to do without shackles, but a crowded holding cell was not a good place for a wolf. Though it did have one advantage: it was larger than a regular cell would be. He was locked in, but at least the walls weren't unbearably close.

His fellow prisoners were, however. Though they kept away from him as much as they could, they were still too close. And they smelled like . . .

Yes, he told his wolf, but do not think about it. Instead he'd count up his advantages. No one had beaten him—always a plus. And he'd been fed. Not well and not enough, but the sandwich had kept hunger at bay. For a time anyway. He hoped supper would arrive soon. When it did, he would need to acquire extra portions. Preferably meat. He could simply take what he needed from his cellmates, but his jailers were apt to react poorly to that. Perhaps he should explain to his fellow prisoners how much more comfortable he'd be if he was well fed. They weren't an altruistic bunch, but they knew who and what he was. Phrased properly, such a request might motivate them to share.

Best if they did. Best if he didn't spend the long hours of the coming night pushing away thoughts of how much those around him stank of fear and sickness. Perfect prey. Easy.

He dragged his mind away from wolf thoughts, focusing on the man's concerns. Those were complex enough to require concentration. The main question: why was he here?

Two Justice Department agents had questioned him once his lawyer arrived. His lawyer's associate, that is. The interview had been fairly perfunctory, since the associate advised him not to answer any questions until Ms. Stockard could discuss the case with him. Miriam Stockard was handling the issue of bail herself.

That raised questions, too. Rule had dealt with the criminal system on behalf of clan members often enough to know what to expect, and the most junior of legal associates could have gotten his bail hearing on the docket. The hearing itself wouldn't occur for at least another day, probably longer. He might hope for twenty-four hours, but realistically he had to expect it to take longer.

Maybe by then Lily could be here. Maybe she'd be waiting for him when they released him, and he could touch her, hold her. And be touched and held.

No, he told himself firmly. She was in Ohio, and there she'd stay until she'd fulfilled the terms of the deal. She'd want to come to him, but she couldn't break her word.

Lily, his wolf pointed out, didn't see the giving of one's word that way.

He was not going to wish for her to break it, however.

His wolf wished very much that she was here now.

But then she'd be trapped, too. Locked up with people who might be a danger to her.

I would protect her. And she doesn't mind being trapped the way I do.

She does mind it, however. This is a bad place. Better that she isn't here.

She wouldn't agree. She'd rather be trapped here and be together than be separated, knowing I need her.

His wolf could be a selfish bastard. Accurate maybe, but selfish. And he was sliding too much toward the wolf. He yanked his thoughts back to the man.

Perhaps the enemy who'd framed him had somehow arranged for him to be placed in a holding cell? That was possible, he supposed. His enemy might hope he'd lose control and rack up more charges against him. More likely, though, that reality lay behind door number two, where bureaucratic inertia overwhelmed all reason.

The locals were holding him as a courtesy to the feds, so they'd put him where temporary jail residents always went—a holding cell. And the feds seemed in no hurry to take him into their own custody. No doubt there was paperwork involved. In his time with Lily he'd learned that law enforcement ran on coffee and paperwork. Cops drank gallons of the former and loathed the latter.

Rule would have killed for a cup of coffee right now. He sighed and leaned against the wall of the cell and reminded himself to breathe through his mouth.

It didn't help as much as he would have liked. One of the ways in which lupi differed from humans was a fully functional vomeronasal organ, meaning that he smelled through his mouth as well as his nose. Not as intensely, however. He'd gotten one good whiff through the nose of the pungent man passed out on the floor a few feet away. One was enough.

If an enemy had arranged for him to be here, he'd miscalculated. Rule could put up with the smell. He'd endure the lack of privacy, too, though he wouldn't sleep. That was too much to ask of his wolf, who was quite . . . restless. One might even say agitated. Doing without sleep was annoying, but better than the way his wolf was apt to react to being startled awake if he did doze off.

He wouldn't be here long, surely. Twenty-four hours tops, he was guessing, and he'd either make bail—if he was very lucky— or be moved to a private cell. That was likely to be much smaller than this one. The last time he'd been held in one, they'd left the lights on constantly. Between that and the extremely small space—

Don't go there, he told himself firmly. He'd survived. He'd survive this, too.

The smelly man groaned. Rule hoped the man wasn't going to throw up. Again.

The holding cell held twelve people at the moment. All of them except the smelly man—who hadn't woken up enough to realize what Rule was—kept away from him. That helped. The fear-scent he inhaled with every breath did not.

Earlier, before his wolf had grown quite so agitated, he'd interacted with a couple of his cellmates. A pair of gangbangers. Not because they'd tried to give him a hard time; they seemed well aware of the stupidity of taking on a lupus. No, their target had been a skinny kid, barely eighteen, who'd been all too visibly terrified of them. Rule had explained to the larger of the two gangbangers that he disliked bullies. He'd been pinching the man's inner elbow at the time. Done right, that grip causes a great deal of pain, but no lasting damage.

Rule remembered well the first time that grip had been used on him—by his brother, course. Benedict had an active teaching style. When he—

"Rule Turner," a correctional officer said as he approached the door. Another officer—a woman—was with him. She watched Rule closely, one hand resting on her holstered weapon.

Rule stood. "Here."

"You're out. The rest of you, step back from the door."

"Out? I'm being transferred?"

"Released. You must have one hell of a lawyer."

He did, but he was still surprised. He couldn't imagine how Miriam Stockard had gotten a bail hearing so quickly.

They wanted him handcuffed. He tolerated that and the gun the female officer held on him while he was cuffed. *Out. I'm getting out.* Both officers were afraid of him. The smell was very interesting to his wolf, who growled and paced inside him. But he was getting out. His wolf understood and tried to settle.

They took him to a dingy room with a table and four chairs

where his lawyer awaited him. Miriam Stockard was a small woman, even shorter than Lily, with an outsize presence. Rule had met her twice before. She liked immaculately tailored suits, basic black glasses, and winning. Today's suit was a shade of rose that hovered between pink and red. She looked smug. She did not smell of fear.

"Good to see you, Ms. Stockard. Lovely suit. I'm being released on bail?"

"No. You've been remanded to house arrest at the Brookses' home. You'll wear a monitor, of course."

His eyebrows shot up. "That's . . . unusual."

"Judge Carter dislikes incompetence."

Whatever she'd meant by that remained a mystery, for they were joined by another officer, who carried the small bin Rule had emptied his pockets into when he was first brought here, and someone in civilian clothes. One of the officers read Rule a list of terms and conditions and required him to sign a form. This was awkward with the cuffs still in place, but he managed. The civilian placed a monitor on Rule's right ankle and explained all the ways it was impossible to circumvent the system without setting off an alarm. The officer with the bin needed Rule to sign another form stating that he'd received his belongings. His phone wasn't among them. It was being held for evidence.

Signing that last form achieved the necessary bureaucratic magic: they removed the handcuffs. And they left.

He looked at his lawyer. "I'm not being escorted in handcuffs to the Brookses' home?"

"As an officer of the court, I've been entrusted with your transport." A very small smile. "I explained how tense you were likely to be after being incarcerated and advised them to use female officers to transport you to the Brookses' home, since lupi are much less likely to offer violence to a woman. We discussed the wisdom, or lack thereof, in having placed you in a holding cell. The result of that discussion was the decision to charge me with your transport."

"It must have been an interesting discussion."

"Moderately, yes. I've been advised by your father on several points. He said to tell you that you are instructed to respond honestly to the following question. What kind of shape are you in?"

"Tense," he said, surprised to find himself smiling as he echoed her word. "But I'm in control. It wasn't a lengthy incarceration." No matter how long it had seemed. "What time is it?"

"Six fifty-two. Will you be all right riding in a car? It will be driven by one of your men, with another along for security."

"I'm eager to ride in that car."

"Very well. We'll leave a roundabout way. Reporters."

As they moved quickly through a large common room, she told him how she'd been able to spring him so quickly. It all came down to paperwork. "The locals messed up yours," she said dryly.

"It seems like that would slow things down, not speed them up." His stomach growled. That sandwich had been a long time ago.

They'd left the large common room for a short hall that ended in a door he thought opened on a stairwell. Miriam stayed two brisk paces in front of him. He allowed that. She was a woman who needed to be in control. "Normally, yes. But Judge Carter, as I said, dislikes incompetence. He agreed to hear me after I got word to him that you were being kept in a holding cell." She snorted, opened the door to the stairs before he could, and headed down. Her heels clicked on the stairs. "That was stupid of them. Using locals for the arrest so they could drag things out might have seemed clever, but putting you in a holding cell infuriated the judge. He knew right away what they were up to."

"He knows more than I do, then."

"They wanted to delay bail. Can't hold the bail hearing without all the paperwork in order. Officially, the marshals who were supposed to take custody of you were temporarily delayed, so the arresting officers placed you in temporary detention in the holding cell. Unofficially, you were dumped there because it was the simplest way to slow things down. There's a fair amount of paperwork involved in transferring a prisoner from local detention to federal."

At the bottom of the stairs was another door. "Easy to forget some small bit, I suppose?"

"And then they can drag things out correcting the mistake. They do that sometimes, usually because their case isn't really ready for prime time."

Rule chewed on that a moment. They were below ground, he thought, and approaching a steel door. An exit. The sign said so. "Why arrest me if they weren't ready?"

"That's the question, isn't it?"

Rule tried to step around her. "Let me get the—"

She slapped the bar on the door and shoved it open before he could. Miriam Stockard was not accustomed to having anyone open doors for her. She didn't care for going second, either. She charged through the doorway as if it led to the promised land.

It did. Today's version of that fabled place was an underground parking garage.

This wasn't freedom, not really. He wore a damn monitor on one ankle, and once he'd been delivered to the Brookses' house, he wouldn't be able to leave it. But the garage smelled of exhaust, concrete, and gasoline instead of fear, sweat, and vomit. There were no locks. No one stood by, weapon drawn, ready to shoot him if he took off running. For a moment he savored that thought. He could run. He wouldn't, but he could. "This seems to be for official vehicles only."

"It is. Your men should be—ah, here they come."

A white Mercedes cruised toward them. Paul was driving. Mike rode shotgun. Another knot of tension in Rule's guts unwound. He'd feel better with his people near.

Both men were Leidolf, not Nokolai. Rule didn't know Paul well yet, aside from the basics: he was thirty-nine, thin, a bit jumpy—not a good trait in a guard—but he had a good tactical sense and excellent reflexes, which made him a good choice for driver. Rule nodded, approving Mike's decision.

With José gone, Rule had put Mike in charge of the guards here. A year ago that would have unthinkable. In addition to the very large chip on Mike's shoulder where Nokolai was concerned—many Leidolf clansmen were like that, the two clans having been enemies for so long—he'd been damaged more than most by his previous Rho. Rule had had to take him down hard.

He'd followed that discipline by placing Mike with the guards entrusted with Lily's protection. It had worked out well. All the guards knew that only the best of them were entrusted with Rule's mate. And Lily, in turn, had taught Mike to respect

her—not easy with most of Leidolf lupi, and especially difficult with one as stubborn as Mike. Lily couldn't toss him into
a wall the way Rule had, but she didn't need to. She was a natural dominant. Lupi couldn't help responding to that. And even
hard cases like Mike eventually understood that she was also a
warrior, and a damn fine one.

Mike proved his worth this day by handing Rule a sack con-
taining four roast beef sandwiches the moment he slid inside the
car. Miriam Stockard got in on the other side without speaking.
"The others?" Rule asked.

"They'll fall in behind us when we leave the parking garage,"
Mike said.

Rule nodded and began demolishing the sandwiches. Traffic
was heavy. Rule finished them well before they reached the
highway leading to Bethesda, and Mike proved his worth a second time. He handed Rule a large foam cup filled with steaming
black coffee.

Rule closed his eyes in pleasure as he inhaled the fragrance,
then took a sip.

Stockard let him finish half the cup before she spoke. "Better?"

"I'm much improved, thank you."

"Good." She scowled. "Then tell me what the hell is going on."

His eyebrows lifted. "I've been framed for distributing
child pornography. I rather thought you knew that."

"That's not what I'm talking about—though we will. The
government's case is surprisingly flimsy. I'm tentatively willing to accept that it's a frame—"

"I gave you my word on it."

"Your word means something to you, so it meant enough to
me to take you on. It does not prove anything. Never mind that
for now. I want to know why Ruben Brooks has been arrested,
too."

Rule went still. "You need to tell me what you're talking
about."

"Two hours ago, Brooks was picked up by Homeland Security."

Rule's mind spun, settling slowly into the obvious. "That's
too much of a coincidence."

"I agree. Which is why I asked what the hell is going on. If you and Brooks are together in this—if you're part of some conspiracy against the government—"

"We are not." Rule spoke with the easy conviction of truth. The Shadow Unit was a conspiracy, but against the Great Bitch, not the government.

"If you are," Miriam repeated inflexibly, "I need to know. Now. It won't affect my decision to represent you, but it will strongly affect whether I've got any chance of winning this case."

"We are not involved in anything that might harm the government or the country," he repeated. "What is Ruben charged with?"

"He hadn't been charged with anything when I spoke with his wife, but one of the agents used the word 'conspiracy' in her hearing."

"How can I be placed under house arrest at the Brookses' home if he's suspected of conspiracy?"

"Possibly the judge isn't yet aware of Homeland's actions."

In spite of himself, Rule snorted. "You remind me of my father." Devious, in other words.

"Isen Turner is a smart man. If you're as smart as he is, you'll level with me."

"You seem convinced that I'm not."

"On the same day that your host is picked up by Homeland Security, someone frames you for a noxious but unrelated offense? Please." She waved that away. "I'd rather not believe that my government is in the business of framing people they know to be guilty yet lack the evidence to convict, but I'm not naïve enough to think it's impossible. It's certainly not as unlikely as coincidence."

"You have a low opinion of coincidence." Rule fell silent, thinking hard. As hard as he could in his current state, that is. He'd eaten. He was no longer locked up. Those things helped. They helped because they made control easier, but implicit in that was the need for control. He hadn't thrown off the effects of being trapped for so long. He still stank. He still needed a shower. And a run. A run would clear his head better than anything.

Almost anything. He needed Lily.

Tough. He couldn't have her, not anytime soon. He'd call her, though. She'd be waiting to hear from him. He'd borrow a phone in a moment and call her, but right now he needed to make a few decisions. Clearly, whoever had moved against him had also moved against Ruben. Possibly the charges against Rule existed primarily to keep him locked away while Ruben was taken down . . . by Homeland Security? How and why were they involved?

It looked very much as if someone had found out about the Shadow Unit. He couldn't imagine how. He didn't see what evidence they might have . . . but a lack of evidence hadn't kept them from getting Rule arrested, had it? Smearing him with one of the worst crimes in existence . . . and never mind that. The nature of their enemy's actions suggested a group, one with remarkable reach, rather than an individual. The next obvious question was whether their enemies were part of Homeland, part of the Justice Department, or were separate yet able to manipulate those arms of the government in ways Rule couldn't at the moment fathom.

He rubbed his face. "All right. I'll tell you one more time: Ruben and I are not involved in a conspiracy against the government. We have at times acted in ways that needed to be kept from the public. I can't tell you more unless you obtain approval from the president."

"The president." Her voice was flat with disbelief.

"Yes." Not that the president was aware of the Shadow Unit. Rule was intentionally conflating two secrets—that of those covert actions Ruben had undertaken with the knowledge of the president, and that of the existence of the Shadow Unit.

"You expect me to believe that whatever you and Brooks are up to, the president is aware of it?"

"'Expect' is the wrong word. I've spoken truthfully, and that's as much as I can tell you. Our most pressing need right now is for information. With Ruben out of the picture . . ." Rule was in charge of the Shadow Unit. Which meant he'd better get word to the other Ghosts, and quickly—without leaving D.C. Without leaving the Brookses' house.

Abel. Abel Karonski. He was an agent of the other Unit, the legal one, as well as a member of the Shadow Unit. He might even now be someplace where there was a dragon who could pass word along. "I need a phone. Mike, the throwaway, please." It was SOP for the leader of off-site guards to carry an untraceable phone as backup.

Mike didn't let Rule down. He twisted around to hand Rule the phone and spoke quickly. "I need to tell you something first. It's about Lily."

"Hold on," Stockard said quickly. And for the first time, she smelled faintly of fear. "Isen said to wait until—"

Mike gave her a hard look. "Isen isn't my Rho. Rule is. And—"

"No! This isn't what I agreed to. This isn't—"

"Miriam," Rule said very softly, "shut up. Mike, what about Lily?"

"She's missing."

SEVENTEEN

~~

A great, gaping chasm opened between one moment and the next. An emptiness. Rule hung suspended in that non-moment, expanding into it, knowing without thinking that this was the instant when the ocean retreats, abandoning the shore. The pause before the tsunami hits. As automatically as a falling man throws out a hand to catch himself, he reached for Lily.

And found her. Above him. At his feet. A thousand miles off to the west. A mile north and speeding along at the speed of a jet. Splinters of Lily everywhere—

The tsunami slammed home.

"What is it? What's wrong with him? His eyes—"

Out, out, out—

"He won't hurt you."

Out! Go to Lily!

"He's not right. He's doubled over. What's happening?"

A woman's voice. Upset. Not Lily. He ignored her. He had to—

"He won't hurt you, dammit. Man or wolf, he's not going to hurt you."

Wolf and man alike knew that voice. Mike. Mike was his. So was the other one, Paul, who was driving . . . who would surely be pulled into the Change along with him. Rule's need was too fierce, too strong. He'd pull both Mike and Paul with him if he Changed now.

The wolf didn't think the same way the man did, but he wasn't stupid. Paul controlled the car. If he Changed, no one would be controlling the car. That would be bad. The car . . . oh, but he wanted out, wanted desperately to leave this metal trap and go to his mate.

He didn't know where his mate was. She was alive. Their bond still existed, so he knew she was alive. But he didn't know where she was. He didn't know how to find her.

The man would. Slowly the wolf curled up, retreating, allowing the man . . .

"Mike," Rule said, straightening. He still gripped the phone Mike had handed him. Carefully he loosened his fingers, hoping he hadn't damaged it. Were his eyes still black? Probably. The wolf had pulled back, but the man was only in control at the moment because the wolf allowed it. "Tell me what you know."

Mike was still turned around in his seat. He kept his gaze down, carefully submissive. "After you were arrested, José and I stayed in touch by text. He let me know what was happening at his end. Some of this I got from his texts, some from when he called me after it happened. Lily was real upset about you being arrested. She even talked about breaking the deal and coming back here. Didn't do it, of course, but that's how upset she was. They were on their way to a nature preserve where they were supposed to meet with this preacher. Ah—Perkins, that's his name. Father Perkins. He was late, and Lily wanted to walk around. She needed to move. José sent four of the guys with her, and that elder—Charles—he went, too. She walked up the road a ways. She saw . . ." Mike hesitated. "Lily said it was that brownie, the little female she'd seen yesterday. José doesn't think it was a hallucination, because he heard the brownie's voice, too, when he got there. None of them could smell or see her, but they heard her talk. José says brownies can do that . . .?"

Rule nodded. "Their dul-dul works on scent and sight, not hearing."

"That's what José said. So the men heard the brownie—if that's what she was—ask Lily to come with her, but she had to come alone. The men refused, of course. That's when José joined them, and at first he said no, too. He can't tell Lily what to do, but she can't tell the guards to stop guarding her, either. José could, but he wouldn't, not until the brownie said Charles could come with them. Lily . . . she can be pretty persuasive. So José agreed to keep the men with him. Lily and Charles went off into the woods with the brownie. They didn't come back."

"José has searched." Rule said that calmly. He was calm now, his mind clear and spacious. All unplanned, he'd slid into certa, the battle state, a place of perfect readiness and balance. "He found no scent trail?"

"Her scent trail ended about half a mile into the woods. So did Charles's. He didn't smell anyone else there, no one who might have grabbed her, but their scents just ended."

"You said 'if that's what she was' when you referred to the brownie. Is there reason to believe that it wasn't a brownie who met Lily in the woods?"

"Nothing concrete, but—a brownie?" Mike's incredulity was obvious. "A brownie who kidnaps people?"

And who was apparently able to render both Lily and Charles unconscious or otherwise unable to resist, and then cart the two of them away somewhere. Rule couldn't see how a whole troop of brownies could have pulled that off, much less why they would want to. Brownies were their allies.

He tabled that question for now. "Paul, you have permission to exceed the speed limit, but not too much. We need speed. We don't need a traffic cop tailing us with siren blasting."

"Same destination?"

"Yes." Bethesda was more or less on the way to Ohio, and he needed to organize his departure. "Mike, I've got calls to make. I need you to call—" His mind clicked through the names of the guards who should be there. "Andy. He is to take all of my clothes, both clean and dirty, to the cleaners immediately. Everything but the socks and underwear. Those should be washed immediately, along with the bedding I've slept on, and anything else a handler might use to give his dogs my scent."

"Wait a minute," Miriam Stockard said sharply." You're not thinking of breaking the terms of your release."

He looked at her. Her fear filled his nostrils. Fear was a reasonable response to him in this state. Meeting his eyes like that was not. He looked at her until she dropped her gaze. "Ms. Stockard, I require you to be quiet and patient for now."

"I put my reputation on the line for you. You can't—"

"My mate has been taken." That came out low. Almost a growl.

"Missing does not equal kidnapped."

He took a few seconds to consider that, then shook his head. "José hasn't found her. Her scent trail stopped. Even if Lily for some reason decided to ditch her guards without leaving a message for them—highly unlikely, but not impossible—she couldn't arrange to stop leaving a scent trail. Someone took her."

Miriam swallowed and stopped arguing. Good.

This phone didn't have any numbers in memory, so Rule got José's number from Mike. José gave basically the same report Mike had, then added information Mike lacked. Some of it was extremely interesting. ". . . didn't know if I should tell Adler or not," José finished. "Lily hadn't intended to tell the HSI guys about their supposed terrorist, though, so I decided to keep it to myself until I talked to you."

Brent Adler was the Unit 12 agent Ruben had sent to look for Lily and take over the investigation into the Homeland agent's death. He was a Finder, which was good. He not a member of the Shadow Unit, however, and Rule knew nothing about him. "Best not, for now," he decided. "We don't know what Adler might feel compelled to share with Homeland, and they do not seem to be our friends at the moment. Your impression of Special Agent Adler?"

"Seems competent," José said, "as far as I can tell. He's out there now, trying to Find her, but his Gift only has a radius of a couple miles."

Rule hoped to import another, much stronger Finder. He didn't say so, or tell José about his other intentions. José would know what Rule had to do, and there was no point in taking chances. The phone Rule was using shouldn't be on any governmental list, but it was barely possible that José's was. He disconnected.

While he'd talked to José, Miriam had been trying to get Mike to talk Rule out of breaking the terms of his jailing.

"Not my call," Mike said now. "But I doubt they'll even know he's gone, unless you tell them."

"They'll know. He can't remove the tracker without tampering with it. The moment it's tampered with, it will send a signal."

Mike snorted. "Putting one of those things on a lupus is silly. Unless they asked for his word that he'd stay—"

"They didn't," Rule said.

Miriam scowled at him. She didn't smell frightened anymore. Good. "They certainly did. You signed papers stating that you understood and accepted the terms of your release."

"I did and do. A judge has determined that I'm legally obligated to remain on the Brookses' property. If I don't, I will be breaking the law."

"And your word."

Rule shook his head and tapped in a number he knew by heart into the phone. "Think about the wording, Miriam. I wasn't asked to pledge that I will remain where the court placed me, but to acknowledge that if I don't, there will be legal consequences. You may see that as morally binding. I don't."

He could see how badly she wanted to argue, but he knew exactly what he'd signed. When your word is binding, you're careful about how vows are worded. Finally she huffed out a breath. "You signed in two places. One of those signatures was a promise not to tamper with the tracking device."

Mike snorted. "He won't have to. The minute he enters the Change, the tracker will fall off. That's not tampering. Unless the magic involved in the Change fries it?" He turned to Paul. "What do you think?"

Paul shrugged. "Don't know. That Nokolai sorcerer might. I don't."

"Think," Rule advised them as a phone rang in California. "Your phones don't stop working when you Change. Clearly, our magic doesn't scatter itself in a way that fries tech. I don't know if the monitor will send a signal when it falls off, but— Isen," he said when the phone at last stopped ringing. "It's good to hear your voice."

It was good. Rule wasn't angry with his father for having told Miriam to wait to speak of Lily's disappearance. It had been good advice. Rule had nearly lost it. But Mike had been right, too. Isen was Rule's Rho. He had the right to temporarily withhold such information. Mike did not.

"And I'm very glad to hear yours," Isen said. "You didn't use your own phone, however."

"It's being held as evidence. I need you to send me some phone numbers."

Isen, like José, knew without being told what Rule intended to do. Any lupus would, and none would argue with him about it. Rule's mate had been taken. The drive to find and free her overcame all else. "Of course. Before I do, you need to know about a remarkable coincidence. Cullen has also gone missing."

Rule's calm wobbled. He breathed slowly and thought of Lily. Reaching her was his goal. Everything else was data. "Tell me."

Isen did, very briefly. Yesterday Cullen had headed into Mexico to investigate some kind of magical anomaly in the mountains across the border. When Isen learned of Rule's arrest, he'd tried to contact Cullen to tell him he was needed. That's how they learned he was missing, as were his guards. A few hours ago, Cynna had left with two squads of guards to look for her husband.

Cynna was the clan's Rhej. She was also the best Finder in the nation—one of the best Finders anywhere, he suspected—and Rule had no doubt she could locate Cullen. Dead or alive, she'd Find him. Alive, he told himself firmly. Assuming the worst wouldn't help. But dammit, he'd wanted Cynna here. Cullen, too. Cynna to Find Lily, and Cullen to deal with whatever magic was involved.

That wasn't happening. "This changes my plans."

"I thought it might. Is there anything I should know immediately? Anything you need to ask?"

Not on a line that theoretically could have been tapped. "I don't think so."

"Very well. What phone numbers did you need?"

Rule told him, then asked about Toby. Isen told him his son was fine and was in class now, but would appreciate a call from his father later, if that was possible. He finished by bidding Rule *t'eius ven*—a phrase that meant both "go in the Lady's grace" and "good hunting"—and disconnected.

A moment later the first of the phone numbers Rule needed arrived. He called it and was in luck. Abel Karonski answered right away. "Abel. This is Rule. Where are you?"

"Near Portland."

"Good. The forecast is dark. You understand?"

"Yes, but—"

"Ruben's been taken away by HSI. I was arrested for an unrelated matter. In one hour, not before, you are in charge. At that point you are to call Deborah."

"Hold on, hold on! What do you—"

Rule disconnected. A dark forecast meant that the Shadow Unit was in danger and its members were to go dark—cease all communications save those passed through dragons. He'd not passed on command in the proper way, through the dragons, but that couldn't be helped. He didn't want to spend the time or the circumlocution necessary to tell Abel what was going on, so he left that to Deborah. The hour's delay was to ensure that by the time Abel assumed control of the Shadows and called Deborah, he'd learn that Rule was gone—too late to order Rule not to break his house arrest.

An hour was generous. He was aiming for twenty minutes. They were ten minutes from the Brookses' home. With luck, he'd have ten minutes there to arrange matters, and then he'd run. On four feet.

Better if he stayed two-footed, of course. Cars were faster than legs, especially when there was so much distance to cover. But he couldn't take this car. He couldn't take Ruben's or Deborah's. He'd be caught, and quickly. And he couldn't wait long enough to acquire a vehicle. Literally could not.

He estimated he had roughly twenty minutes before the Change overtook him.

Certa had many advantages. It was a dispassionate state, the eye of the hurricane from which he tracked all the changing variables of battle . . . including his own condition. His body was charged with adrenaline, taut and ready to engage the enemy, while his mind remained cool and calm. But certa was temporary. It was a battle state, and there was no one to fight.

Yet. "Mike, tell me exactly what happened when the HSI agents came for Ruben."

SEVENTEEN minutes later, Rule ran.

Wolves could run for hours. Wild wolves brought down

prey that way, with the pack running a deer or elk into exhaustion. Rule was not a wild wolf. He ran through these woods alone. He had—barely—managed not to drag any of the others into Change with him by inviting it instead of waiting until he'd been robbed of choice, but that had used up the last of his control. Now he raced through the trees at top speed, surrendered to the urgency of his need.

The wolf was in charge, but this was a wolf with a man's knowledge, even if he didn't think in the same manner. He understood why he was alone, where he needed to go, and how to get there. He knew roughly how long it would take and that he would need to pace himself—later. Most of all, he knew why he ran.

Lily.

But he didn't think about the how, where, or why. He didn't even think about Lily. She was the stretch and flex of his body, the wind whipping by, the terrified rabbit he didn't chase. He ran. Trees flew by in a blur; his body exulted in motion and the rush of scents. The woods that touched the back of the Brookses' property stretched nearly to the Potomac, and he ran their length full-tilt, slowing only as he neared the last of the trees. He made himself stop, whining softly with regret at the necessity. He wanted to keep running and running, but at least he'd burned off the worst of the urgency.

Time now to think.

Humans would be surprised at how readily a wolf could go unnoticed in their towns. Slums were difficult, for they lacked green spaces, but Bethesda was a prosperous place. Lots of green. It would have been dead easy to navigate after dark, but night wouldn't fall until after nine in this latitude in the summer. Still, he'd planned for this next stretch. Three of his men were busy laying false trails—two in fur and one in a car with Rule's credit card. He hoped they'd draw away any immediate pursuit, but he still needed to cross the next few blocks without attracting official attention. An animal his size couldn't go truly unnoticed on a city street, but as long as no one called the police, it should be okay. That's why he wore a disguise: a bright red collar with a short length of leash dangling from it.

A few people did see him trotting across lawns, driveways, and parking lots on his way to the river—only they didn't, not really. They saw a very large dog who'd escaped from his owner. He helped their misperception along by behaving like a loose dog, pausing to sniff here or lift a leg there, but he was bigger than any dog and his proportions were wrong. It didn't seem to matter. People mostly see what they expect to see. The mantles he carried may have given his disguise a boost. They seemed to do that at times.

At a boatyard next to the river a brave if foolish Good Samaritan approached him, telling him what a good dog he was, clearly intending to grab the truncated leash so he could return Rule to his owner. Rule wagged his tail, gave the man a doggy grin, and loped away.

Once he reached the river's bank, he stretched out and settled in for a long run. There were long swaths of protected green space along the Potomac. Houses, too, but they were mostly set well back from the banks, and traffic on the river was light at this time of day. If any boaters did get a glimpse of him, he was running too fast for them to take in details. Not that he ran flat-out, but he didn't settle into the easy lope he would have used for a really long run, either. He aimed for a speed about that of a human's top sprint. His goal was sixty-five miles away by road, slightly longer on the winding river route he'd take. He wanted to cover those sixty-five-plus miles in three hours.

After reaching the Brookses' home, Rule had politely separated his lawyer from her phone, then stashed her where she couldn't overhear before calling Alex to arrange for a vehicle. A lot of Leidolf's clan members weren't "out" as lupi, so no one should be able to link them—or their cars—to him.

He hadn't had to come up with an escape route, fortunately. Ruben was a man who planned for contingencies, including the possible need to evacuate his home. He'd mapped out several possible escape routes depending on how many needed to evacuate, what form they were in, and whether they wanted to leave the city or just the immediate area. He'd shared that information with Rule last night, and while Rule hadn't had time to memorize everything, a quick talk with the Wythe clansman in charge of Ruben's guards had refreshed his memory of the route he wanted. He was headed for a truckstop-style

diner just outside Charles Town, West Virginia. Three Leidolf
lived within an easy drive of Charles Town. One of them would
meet him at the diner with a vehicle he could use and other
necessities. And then . . .

Find Lily. Find the enemy. Sink his teeth into the enemy's
throat.

How?

For the next hour he chewed over what he knew. It was
clear that one or more branches of the government were his
enemies or were being used by his enemies. This was bad,
but the need to evade the authorities didn't disturb him. It
felt normal. Human governments had always been hostile to
his people, and the U.S. government's change to a more neutral stance hadn't been around long enough for him to trust it.
But the wolf was fuzzy about some aspects of human authority. He knew "arrest" meant being locked up and "taken in for
questioning" might lead to arrest. Both involved human laws,
but they weren't the same thing, and he couldn't track the
implications of that difference. He knew HSI was not the same
as the Justice Department, yet both entities had acted against
them.

He decided to leave that part of the situation for the man to
sort out. Omitting the governmental tangle allowed other
things to spring into focus.

Sam had not perceived the Great Enemy in the patterns.

Ruben had had a strong hunch that the Shadow Unit would
experience a crisis.

The Lady had allowed the mate bond to stretch enough for
Lily to be separated from him. She had also spoken to Charles,
sending him with Lily.

A man whom HSI said was one of their agents had been
killed by magic, possibly telekinesis. Sam had apparently
wanted Lily to discover this.

The Lady had let Rule know she approved of his determination to go to Lily if she needed him.

Rule had been framed for a vile crime. His lawyer considered the case rushed and flimsy.

HSI had picked up Ruben for questioning while Rule was
in jail.

Lily and Charles had been taken by someone who could remove them without leaving a scent trail.

A brownie had either conspired in the abduction or had herself been taken.

Rule-wolf did not think about these things in the linear manner of the man. He held each thought in his mind, allowing it to open and bloom until it had grown as large and intricate as his current understanding allowed. He spent some time considering the meaning of crisis in this way, some time contemplating brownies, and quite a bit of time remembering as clearly as possible the way he'd felt in the first few seconds after receiving the Lady's approval.

After about an hour he remained unsure of much, but a few things were clear. First, the Lady was extremely interested in whatever was going on. This was not comforting. She might keep a close watch on her people, but she almost never communicated directly with them. Either Sam was wrong about the Great Enemy's involvement, or the situation was extremely dire even without *her* participation.

Second, he clearly had human enemies to deal with, whether or not any of them were *her* agents. He had no idea who, but the scope suggested an organized group, not an individual. HSI was involved, either complicitly or as unwitting tools.

Third, the dead man was key. Sam had wanted him found by Lily; Lily had been taken soon after finding him. The dead man was connected to HSI. He might or might not be their agent as they claimed, but there was some connection.

Therefore, if he found out why the dead man mattered, he'd have a trail to the enemy. The enemy would lead to Lily.

Rule whined, greatly disliking that conclusion. That trail would take too long. He wanted to find Lily first, then go after their enemy. But he didn't see how. Maybe he should check, make sure he still couldn't use the mate bond. Sam didn't know how long it would take for Lily's brain to adapt, resolving the interference that played havoc with their bond. Didn't that mean it could happen at any time?

Maybe it had already happened. He came to a complete stop. Gingerly he reached with the mate sense . . .

It was all he could do not to tip back his head and howl.

Splintered Lilys were everywhere. He heaved a sigh and started trotting.

Up ahead, the island divided the river into two channels. He compared what he saw to what Ruben had told him and the map he'd studied. Farther up the river there should be a bridge. Harpers Ferry was just beyond that. He needed to be on the opposite bank before he reached the bridge, and Ruben had mentioned this as a crossing spot. He jumped into the water. It felt good, cool and refreshing. He swam that channel, crossed the island to the next, and swam again.

He'd come about a third of the way and was getting tired, but this area was wooded, with good concealment. He pushed his pace while he could, running almost flat out until he drew near the bridge. He stopped and rested at the road that fed onto the bridge, catching his breath and waiting for a gap in the traffic, one large enough that he might not be spotted. Eventually one appeared.

A couple miles later he reached a spot where a tributary dumped itself into the Potomac. He abandoned the Potomac for the tributary. He had to mix running with trotting now. After about five miles he took another swim to get to the other bank of this river. Then it was time to strike out across country, heading west-southwest.

He soon left the woods behind, forcing him to go slower. That was okay. He was hot and tired, ready for an easier pace. This stretch involved a lot of open fields broken here and there by small copses, left in place or planted as windbreaks. Although the sun was headed down, it was still light out and his coloring didn't blend well with the greens of summer. He found what he hoped was the right highway and followed it west, staying well back from the road. Most people driving by at seventy miles an hour or more wouldn't notice him, but a few would. Some of them might even think "wolf" for a second, but he was betting they'd quickly discount that. There were no wolves in this area, and it's hard to get people to see something they know can't be there. It helped that his size would be less obvious from a distance.

Eventually his nose told him he was drawing near human habitations. He angled toward a cluster of trees along the highway. If he'd plotted his course correctly, the truckstop should be close.

It was. On the other side of the trees was a parking lot and a building with a sign—the number 354 in blue centered in an orange circle. The diner had been named for the highway it served. The parking lot was full of semis huddled together like oversize sheep sheltering from the wind. He needed to circle around, find the section of parking used by normal vehicles.

He hesitated, reluctant. Hating to give up this form. As soon as he became two-legged, the man would begin *thinking* again—thinking about what might be happening to Lily and mistaking what he thought for reality. Reality was this moment, with him crouched low to the ground, his nose full of messages—fried food, a nearby squirrel, the sour reek of exhausts. Earth. Leaves. The scent of a lone man walking slowly toward his rig. The tang of days-old dog urine from that shrub at the edge of the concrete.

Lily had been taken by some enemy. That, too, was reality. The pain of that truth, the urgency, had been part of the run he'd just made . . . but so had relief. At last he was acting to end their separation. Why had the man allowed it in the first place? He knew the reasons. He even understood them. He did not understand why the man had deemed them sufficient. Foolishness, to be parted from her. Look at what had happened.

For now, she was alive. He didn't wonder if she'd been hurt, if she was hurting now. He had no way to know, and until he did, there was no point in dragging his thoughts around in the mire of maybes. The man knew this, but knowing wouldn't help. He would still think about all sorts of bad things that might have happened, might be happening, to Lily. He would still react to those thoughts as if they were reality.

To the wolf's way of thinking, the man was slightly insane.

He didn't have to Change yet. He could have his clansman drive while he rested in the backseat . . . except that the speed of a car wasn't all he needed.

Find Lily. Find the enemy.

He'd cleared the mental brush and found a target, but taking that trail meant finding the enemy first. He did not want to do it that way. Sometimes the man's maybe-thinking cracked open possibilities the wolf hadn't seen. He needed to give the man a chance to come up with something better, faster. With a trail that led to Lily.

He started moving again, heading around to the other side of the parking lot. His Leidolf clansman should be waiting. He'd have cash, a vehicle . . . and the clothes Rule would need when he was two-legged once more.

EIGHTEEN

~

ONE second Lily was in a sleep so deep no dreams could find her. The next, her eyes popped open.

Rock. Rock above her—dim, craggy, with orange light dancing shadows into the crevices. Rock beneath her, too, rock she'd been lying on for quite a while, judging by the way she ached where flesh met stone. Her bladder was full to bursting. She was warm. Too warm, and downright hot along her left side. Someone was lying next to her. Someone furry. Rule. As automatically as breathing, she reached for him—with her hand, her mind, and her mate sense.

Turned out Rule was a mile directly overhead. No, he was immediately behind her, which she barely noticed because the rocky ceiling abruptly grew hands. Lots of hands. Some of them sprouted arms and reached down for her and she tried to shove them away, but a pair of them got through and wrapped around her throat and—

And were gone.

A hallucination. She'd had another hallucination. She lay still, breathing fast, feeling terrified and horribly alone. But she wasn't alone. The furry presence at her side might not be Rule, but he wasn't a hallucination, either. At least she didn't think so. She turned her head. A wolf lay with his back pressed against her.

Charles. Rule was in D.C., and Charles had been with her when . . . what had happened? How long had she been lying here? Where was *here?*

Lily remembered where she'd been—following the little brownie through the woods in the nature preserve. Charles had been scouting ahead when she stepped out into a clearing, and . . . nothing. She had nothing beyond that moment. No memory of someone knocking her out, and her head didn't hurt. A dart? She didn't remember being hit by one, but it was the only thing she could think of.

Her stomach felt sore. She slid a hand over it. Definitely tender, but in a superficial way. Not cracked ribs, just a bruise. Had someone kicked or punched her while she was unconscious? More quick explorations let her know she still wore her jacket, slacks, and tee. No shoes. No shoulder harness. Her pockets had been emptied.

Charles hadn't stirred. A flicker of panic made her lay a hand on his shoulder and shake him. He didn't wake, didn't respond at all, but she felt the distinctive pine-needles-and-fur of his magic, so she knew he was alive. She took a shaky breath and began taking more careful stock of her surroundings. Her fingers found rough fabric beneath her. She wasn't on bare rock after all. A wool blanket separated her from the stone . . . relatively smooth stone. She and Charles lay in a smooth indentation in the stony floor of a small rock chamber. A cave.

Lily had bad memories of caves. Those memories swam up and drowned the present, turning her breathing fast again. *Stop that.* She made herself take several slow, careful breaths and pay attention to now. To here, wherever that might be. A cave, yes, and one that didn't have the decency to block her inadvertent attempt at mindspeech. Earth and rock were supposed to block mind magic. It should have kept her flailing Gift from touching another mind.

Which meant that either she'd brushed against Charles's mind to trigger the hallucination, or there were more people down here with her.

If so, they were really quiet. She couldn't hear a damn thing.

Lily sat up, wincing at the soreness in her stomach, and looked around. Directly ahead, the stone was smooth and rounded. To her right the rock was more jagged and was interrupted by an opening. The source of the flickering light lay out of sight around that corner. Firelight? Sure looked like it. The stony floor where she lay sloped down toward the back of the cave, lost in shadow in the dim light. The ceiling was extremely uneven, but there was room for her to stand up.

She did. And stared. Was that what it looked like?

Lily stepped carefully over Charles. Four feet away a primitive porta-potty sat on the floor—a camping stool with a hole in the seat. A plastic bag was fastened to the hole and a roll of toilet paper sat on the floor beside it. A small plastic glass sat next to the toilet paper; it held a toothbrush and a travel-size tube of toothpaste. And her shoes were lined up neatly beside the plastic glass.

She immediately sat down and put them on.

What did it say about her captor, that he or she had provided minimal sanitary facilities? She frowned and decided she didn't have enough data yet to make a guess. Now, if she were to find soap and a makeshift shower around the corner, where that flickering light came from . . . and her purse. And her phone. And maybe a little bell she could ring to summon room service, she jeered at herself, for thinking of a shower had made her realize how thirsty she was. Once she'd noticed, she couldn't stop noticing. She licked dry lips. She needed water.

She didn't have any. Check out the source of the light first, she told herself. Find out if she was alone. Everything else could wait, including her bladder. She headed around the corner.

Another, smaller chamber. No one here. The ceiling sloped down abruptly; the walls narrowed and the floor rose, so that all sides converged in what had to be the exit from her stony cell— a narrow opening she'd have to duck or crawl to get through.

She'd also have to be fireproof. It was blocked by a curtain of flames, the source of the flickering light. Flames that put out heat and light—it was warmer in here, uncomfortably so—but no smoke. A fire that burned without any visible fuel.

Magic fire.

Lily grimaced. She hadn't really thought she'd be able to just

walk out—or crawl out, as the case might be. But magic fire
was not good news. Cullen could create and maintain a fire that
didn't require conventional fuel, but he was unusually good
with fire . . . as he'd gladly tell anyone who asked, and often
those who didn't. She wasn't happy to learn that her abductor
possessed skills equal to Cullen's.

Near the fire curtain were two plates. One held what looked
like trail mix. The other was piled high with jerky. A plastic
bucket sat next to them, as did a dented mental canteen. She
licked dry lips and headed for it, ducking low to avoid the low
ceiling. The bucket was full of water. That would be for Charles.
He couldn't drink from a canteen.

She grabbed the canteen, verified with a shake that it held
water, and sighed in relief. Then stared at the other items that
had been left for her: a thick puzzle book and a pencil.

Lily sat back on her heels, perplexed. Food, water, crude
sanitary facilities, a blanket. A puzzle book and a pencil. Magic
fire across the exit. Someone with substantial skill at magic had
gone to a fair amount of trouble to set up a livable cell for her,
which meant—good news!—they didn't want her dead. Not
right away, anyway. As for the puzzle book . . . she picked it up,
leafed through it. None of the puzzles had been worked. Was
her captor thoughtful enough to give her something to pass the
time? If so, that was a depressingly thick puzzle book. It suggested a long stay.

She frowned at the canteen in her hand. Could she risk
drinking? Eating? Either or both might be drugged.

She felt so damn shaky. Thirsty and shaky. Some of the
shakiness was fear, sure. She was scared. But some might be
from hunger. Her blood sugar was probably in free fall, even if
she didn't feel especially hungry. When you were really thirsty,
you didn't notice hunger. She rubbed her face and tried to think.
If her captor wanted to drug her again, the water was an easy
way to do it. The food might be drugged, too, but the water
would be a sure thing. At some point she'd have to drink.

The thing, then, was to choose that point. Do what she
needed to first. She took the canteen and the plate with trail mix
back into the other chamber, then emptied her bladder and
checked on Charles. He seemed okay, for a value of "okay" that
meant he couldn't wake up. His heartbeat was slow but strong,

about right for a sleeping lupus. Then she began exploring the dark end of the "bedroom."

It went back over twenty feet. She tried not to rush her exploration, which was more by touch than sight. No spooky hands formed from the rock to grab her, though she kept expecting that. And her own hands didn't find a tunnel or crack she could slip through. By the time she finished, she didn't much care if the water was drugged or not. She sat down next to Charles and unscrewed the cap on the canteen.

The water tasted stale, metallic, and wonderful. She drank about half of it before she could make herself stop. No telling how long it would have to last.

Charles would be thirsty, too, when he woke up. If he woke up. God, she hoped he'd wake up. Was that selfish? He was dying anyway. He might be better off passing away quietly in his sleep instead of enduring whatever . . . no. No, that was giving up. Somehow, someway, she'd get out of here, and she couldn't take him with her if he was unconscious. And if part of her wanted him to wake up just so she wouldn't be alone, well, that part wasn't in charge.

Why had she woken up, but he hadn't?

That should have occurred to her before. Her head was fuzzy, and that might be due to hunger. She frowned and tried some of the trail mix. Dried apples, peanuts, and some kind of crunchy bits. It tasted wonderful. She made herself nibble instead of shoving in handfuls.

She'd save the jerky for Charles, who would need the protein if he woke up. When he woke up. He hadn't been drugged. That was obvious now that she thought about it. Drugs didn't work on lupi, so he must have been spelled into sleep. Or charmed? The sleep charms Cullen made had to be held in place, but she shouldn't assume that was the way all sleep charms worked. Maybe she'd better make sure there was nothing hiding in Charles's thick fur. She dug her fingers into the ruff around his neck, hunting for any kind of foreign object.

It seemed as if she was dealing with a versatile and well-equipped bad guy. He or she had knocked both Lily and Charles out, but he'd used magic on Charles, a drug on Lily. She knew that because magic didn't work on her and drugs didn't work on Charles. Apparently the bad guy knew it, too.

Bad guys, plural, she decided, continuing to run her fingers through Charles's fur while she nibbled trail mix. One person might be able to knock both of them out and haul away her unconscious body before José came looking for her, but it was unlikely one person could carry them both off that quickly. Charles probably weighed in around two hundred pounds.

No foreign objects on his head, neck, or chest. Stomach next.

Why in the world had Charles been taken? Surely it would've been easier to kill him. Or to just leave him behind, sound asleep. Maybe this wasn't about her. Maybe she was the add-on, and Charles was the real target. But that didn't make sense. They wouldn't bring in a porta-potty for a wolf . . . unless their captor didn't realize Charles couldn't Change. But if Charles was the real target, why take her? And why take both of them, but not the brownie?

There was one obvious answer to that last question. It just wasn't easy to believe. Lily grabbed another handful of trail mix with her left hand, felt carefully along Charles's hind-quarters with her right, and thought about brownies.

Everyone loved brownies. They were cuter than a litter of kittens and amazingly athletic. Who hadn't watched clips of their gymnastic feats? Everyone thought they knew a lot about brownies, too. They were shy little beings, timid and easily frightened. They loved milk and they never left their reservations.

Most of what everyone knew wasn't true.

They acted shy—at least most of them did—but Lily wasn't sure their behavior meant the same thing it would with a human. They liked chocolate a lot better than milk. And they sure as hell weren't timid. She'd seen a squad of brownies scale a giant Earth elemental, form a living chain, and dangle in front of its gaping maw so they could chuck a magically charged item down its throat, thus saving a lot of lives.

They definitely did not all stay on their reservations, either. They enjoyed people watching in towns and cities all along the East Coast. Between dul-dul and their athleticism, they found it easy to hitch rides on car bumpers, pickups, even the backs of motorcycles without anyone noticing.

Brownies were also talented pickpockets who loved to play a game revolving around the theft of small objects. That thought had Lily checking her fingers, then breathing a sigh of relief. Her captors had taken her weapon, shoes, and phone, but not her rings.

Lily knew more than most about brownies because they were allies of the Shadow Unit. They were aces at gathering information, not much for fighting. They admired her cat, for crying out loud, because Dirty Harry had sounded the alarm when he sensed a demon—then run away. A brownie bad guy was hard to imagine.

Was she letting all that cuteness skew her judgment? God knew that not all humans were dependable. Why would she think all brownies were? Too, there was always the possibility that the bad guys had somehow forced the brownie female to help them.

Brownies could be a lot of help. She knew that from experience. Not that she had a clue what these bad guys wanted, other than to imprison her and Charles in a damn cave that didn't do much to block mind magic, considering the way—

Dark—vastness—swallowed whole—spinning down—who? oh, you aren't supposed to—down down into heat—burning burning BURNING—

The last of the trail mix spilled from her hand as darkness rose up and swatted her.

NINETEEN

~

THE Leidolf clansman whom Alex had sent to meet Rule was named Robert Burns, but he preferred to be called Rob. Alex had chosen him because he was close to Rule's size. The jeans he brought were a trifle loose, but the legs were long enough and the T-shirt roomy. Rob's spare shoes were not a good fit, but by omitting socks, Rule could get them on.

Rob worked as a bartender in "a riverfront dive. Doesn't pay much, but it's steady." He owned an eighteen-year-old Honda Civic. Like Rob, the Honda looked like it had seen better days, but everything worked. Rob made sure of that, having been a mechanic at one time. He'd worked a lot of different jobs, being seventy-two years old and on his third name. Lupi often had to take on a new identity when they failed to age the way a human would.

He'd brought Rule all the cash he had on hand: one hundred and twelve dollars. The small sum embarrassed him; Rule assured him it was sufficient and much appreciated. They spent some of that on hamburgers at the diner—four for Rule, a modest two for Rob—and Rule used Rob's phone to research his destination. When he left, he took the rest of the money with him, but didn't take Rob's phone. He'd connect with José soon enough and didn't like to leave the man broke and without means to contact anyone. It might be several hours before someone arrived to pick Rob up and reimburse him.

For the next five and a half hours, Rule drove and thought. Just as he'd assumed while four-footed, some of those thoughts were dark. Some were sheer frustration; Rob had replaced the radio in his car with an MP3 player, so he couldn't get any kind of news. And he wasn't able to come up with a way to find Lily without first locating his enemy. The man was as unhappy about that as the wolf had been. But some, at least, of his thinking was constructive. By the time he drove into the little river town of Gallipolis, Ohio, he had a plan.

It was just after four in the morning. Gallipolis might be the county seat, but it was a small town with a small town's habits. The streets were empty. He felt very conspicuous, especially when a police car cruised by. He found the Hampton Inn without trouble, having picked up a map when he stopped for gas. The hotel was just the other side of the highway from the Ohio River.

He drove on by.

José would be expecting him. Unfortunately, so would the authorities. Even if the false trails Mike and the others had laid down had worked perfectly, they were a temporary distraction. Miriam must have reported that his goal was to find Lily, so the local cops would be watching for him. Possibly state or federal cops, too. This made connecting with his men tricky. He'd originally planned to call José on Rob's phone, but in the end decided in favor of healthy paranoia. It was possible the authorities had a tap on José's line. Not likely, perhaps, given the procedures that were normally involved in obtaining a legal tap. But he hadn't noticed a great deal about recent events that was normal.

The solution he'd come up with was to let his men find him. According to Google Earth, there was a large wooded area near the hotel. That turned out to be true. The hardest part was persuading himself to park where he knew damn well he ought to. The Holzer Medical Center was a large facility for such a small town, no doubt because it served the surrounding area as well. Out-of-town cars must park there all the time. But it was five miles away, and it had been a long, exhausting day. After a brief struggle—his brother's imagined voice, incredulous that he might balk at such a short distance, played a part—he drove the five miles. His borrowed Honda blended in nicely with the other vehicles in the hospital parking lot.

He made his way back toward the hotel on two feet at first. When he reached the wooded area, he stripped and knotted the legs of his jeans around his T-shirt and shoes so he could carry the bundle in his mouth. The Change hurt more than usual; he was nearly spent. He kept to a tired trot as he followed the highway back, staying out of sight within the trees.

Those trees approached but didn't reach the hotel's parking lot. He sniffed, hoping that José had stationed someone in the woods . . . apparently not. He sighed and fell back on Plan B, moving along the edge of the woods, pausing to mark here and there. José would know these woods were a likely destination for Rule. Unless he and the other men had suffered some calamity, he'd have them checked periodically. They couldn't miss Rule's scent.

At last he could move farther back into the trees, where he curled up in the hollow left by an uprooted elm. Only when he did, when the weight of exhaustion pressed him into the loam, did he realize how much he dreaded sleeping alone. Alone was wrong. Wolves need other wolves; he needed Lily. But he was too tired to do more than whimper softly, grieving his solitude, before sleep yanked him down.

He dreamed of Lily.

It was a strange dream. Nothing happened. For a long time he lay quietly with his arms around her and listened to her breath and her heartbeat, inhaling her scent with every breath of his own. He couldn't have said if they lay in a bed, on a couch, the ground, or a particularly dense cloud. There was nothing else in the dream, no sounds or sights or scent. Just him and her. He felt entirely at peace.

A bird's song broke through his sleep, waking him. The light was strong, though he couldn't tell the hour. Trees blocked the sun. He felt rested, easy . . . as if Lily really were next to him. He knew it was no more than a hangover from the dream, but for a moment he didn't move, hanging on to the illusion.

The birdcall—it was supposed to be a lark—sounded again.

He stood and shook out his fur. He was in the wrong form to reply, so he opened himself to the moon's song. A moment later he gave his own imitation of a lark's call. He was pulling on his borrowed jeans when José arrived bearing a pair of paper sacks and a large foam cup.

"Ahh." He took the foam cup first. He was hungry, but his nose told him he'd be eating hamburgers again. Repetition made them less interesting than the coffee, which he sipped with pleasure. He wondered if Lily had coffee, wherever she was. Or food. If she was conscious and well or . . . his wolf growled at him. He forced his thoughts away from speculation that *did not help*. "How much of a hurry am I in?"

"No rush. The locals are following us, but it's embarrassing, how bad they are at it."

José spoke lightly enough, but something about the way he held himself . . . "You have bad news. Is it—"

"Not about Lily," José said quickly. "But yes, I've bad news about one of your Leidolf men. Andy's dead. A head shot."

The sudden burning on his hand told Rule he'd crushed the cup. He didn't move. "What happened?"

"When you escaped, Homeland Security put out a bulletin that you were to be considered extremely dangerous. It was an engraved invitation to every cop in the nation to shoot you on sight. It was the Virginia State Police who took them up on it, just outside Fairfax. Imagine the trooper's surprise when it turned out he'd killed the wrong wolf."

"Goddammit." Rule shoved to his feet and stalked away. "No heroics. That's what I told Mike. He was to send decoys out, but they were to be cautious. The ones on four feet were to let themselves be seen a few times, but not by the police."

"I don't know exactly what went wrong," José said quietly. "Mike texted me, but it was just the bare bones. According to the news, the trooper claims the wolf charged him."

"That's bullshit."

"I figured it was."

"'Extremely dangerous.'" Rule stood very still, letting his rage ice over. "That's true enough, but not in the way they meant it. Did you say Homeland Security put out that bulletin? They had nothing to do with my arrest."

"Homeland seems to be running the show now—or they think they are. Bunch of damn idiots," José muttered. "The regular FBI agents here don't seem to have a clue, either, but at least they're professional. Those HSI goons act like—"

"What do you mean?"

"I mean that they're idiots. They—"

"No, about them thinking they're in charge. I haven't heard any news. First I was jailed, then I was on the run. The car I borrowed lacks a radio."

"Shit. A lot has happened. Let's see. To start with, Unit Twelve has been pulled off the hunt here. Both hunts—the one for Lily and the investigation into the death of that guy Lily found."

"What?" Rule stared. "Croft wouldn't—"

"Croft isn't running Unit Twelve. They put someone in charge who's regular Bureau. Jim, ah—Madison? No, Mathison. He just keeps rolling over and showing his stomach, no matter who's growling. First he handed over the investigation into that guy's death to HSI. It was their guy who was killed, so I guess there's some justification, but Lily sure wouldn't have let them take over this way. That wasn't enough for those assholes in Congress, though. They screamed too loud for Mathison, I guess, because next he suspended all Unit Twelve investigations, and a bunch of Unit agents have been removed from duty 'pending the results of the investigation.'"

Rule felt cold. "Abel Karonski? Martin Croft?"

José nodded. "Among others. Isen says they're going after the whole Unit, not just Ruben."

"They? Who?"

"Half of Congress and a lot of the media. The elected idiots keep coming up with conspiracy theories, which the press reports on with great glee. It's a real shitstorm. Isen says the president had no choice but to put someone from outside the Unit in charge of it for now. Politics." José shook his head, disgusted. "So far, Lily's about the only one who isn't being smeared. Homeland's hinting that she was the target of the bad guys, by which they mean Ruben and the rest of the Unit. The prevailing theory seems to be that they killed her to keep her from exposing them."

Rule scowled. "She's alive."

"I know. But that's the slant they're taking, and it's HSI's excuse for trying to shut out the FBI—who, to give them credit, haven't given in. Both groups are looking for her—or they're supposed to be, but mostly they're tripping over each other. And since they can't use any Unit Twelve personnel, they're doing it without a Finder or anyone else with a shred of magic. Is Cynna going to—"

"Not anytime soon," Rule said grimly. "Cullen is missing, too. She's gone to look for him."

José let out a low whistle. "Who could do all this?"

That was the question, wasn't it? Rule scowled and wished he had more coffee. Absently he reached for the paper bag José still held and took out a hamburger. As he ate, he thought.

He could see Congress going on a witch hunt. Give them one whiff of the existence of the Shadow Unit, and half of that distinguished body would be howling for blood—the administration's blood, preferably. Nothing else added up. If the Shadow Unit was the enemy's target, why had Rule been framed for an entirely different offense? The cops hadn't asked him anything even vaguely connected to the Shadow Unit while they had him in custody. Miriam Stockard had suggested that he might have been framed for one thing because they couldn't prove his guilt about the other. That seemed a stretch, but not impossible. Could his arrest have been intended to soften him up so he'd accept some kind of deal to testify against Ruben?

But Miriam had also said the case against him was both rushed and flimsy. Why the rush, if they were about to launch a major takedown of Unit 12? If they waited, they could have hoped to get evidence against him for what they'd consider his real offense—being second-in-command of the Shadows.

And none of that gave him a hint why Lily had been kidnapped. *Look at the outcome*, Lily often said when she was investigating. What happened because of the crime? Who benefited?

Two things had happened because of Lily's disappearance. HSI had assumed control of the investigation into the death of the man they claimed was their agent . . . and Rule had become a fugitive.

Which of those had their enemy wanted? Both? Or something else? Automatically Rule finished the second hamburger, thinking hard. He looked at José. "What about Abel? Has he or any of the Unit agents been charged with anything?"

José shook his head. "No, but I only know what's on the news. I'm sure they're being questioned, but Ruben's the only one the reporters have named."

He needed to talk to Abel, but he had to make sure that conversation couldn't be overheard. Right now, he wasn't sure how to arrange that. "Do you know what kind of evidence they have against Ruben?"

"He's been tied to some kind of covert operation at a house in West Virginia, though if anyone knows what went on there, they aren't saying. That doesn't stop everyone from speculating—and God, you should hear some of it. It's like the Internet exploded, and its stupidest bits rained down on the regular news. They're talking about everything from aliens to horrible medical experiments to that old favorite, the UN plan to take over the country. But it sounds like the only solid evidence is the financial trail this one reporter found."

Rule's eyebrows drew down. "I handle the Shadow Unit's funds."

"This wouldn't be anything you did," José assured him. "Apparently Ruben diverted federal funds to finance whatever you had going on at that house."

"No. He didn't. The Shadow Unit has no connection to a house in West Virginia. And the last thing Ruben would do is draw attention to the Shadow Unit through the misuse of federal funds."

"Then what the hell is going on?"

"I have no idea. But," he said with a grim smile, "I know what we need to do."

TWENTY

〜

DEMI hated lying. Sure, some people someone might say she'd been doing that for months and months, living under other names, but she didn't see it that way. Pretending wasn't the same as lying, and she'd always liked role-playing.

One reason she hated lying was that she was so bad at it. *Sound feeble*, she reminded herself as she picked up her phone. Not panicked. Panicked talked fast. Feeble talked slow.

She stared at her computer monitor, where a news program was playing, while the phone rang. And rang. Finally Mr. Burgenstein picked up. "This is . . . it's Danny," she said, working hard not to pant into the phone. She didn't want him to think she was dying. "I'm . . . really sorry. I'm sick."

"Sick?" he said suspiciously. "What kind of sick?"

"I'm sorry," she repeated. "I keep throwing up." That was almost true, though so far she'd swallowed the bile that tried to come up.

"Why are you calling me? If you think I'm gonna come over there and hold your hand at fucking eleven o'clock at night—"

"No! No, I just . . . I won't be able to come to work tomorrow."

She wasn't sure Mr. Burgenstein believed her. He thought it was odd that she'd called in sick ahead of time—"How d'you know you won't be just fine in the morning?"—but finally he agreed that if she was still throwing up tomorrow, she didn't have to come in. By then her stomach really was aching. Panic plus a huge heaping helping of sad were not good for the digestive track.

Her eyes filled as she looked around her little trailer. Maybe it wasn't much, but she liked it here. She liked the way she'd fixed the shower. She still had most of a batch of black beans in the refrigerator. They were in the cast iron pot she'd bought at the Driscolls' garage sale, and she wished she could at least take the pot with her. She really liked that pot. But even if she could've fit it in the backpack, which she couldn't, it was way too heavy.

Properly speaking, she ought not leave a pot of beans in the refrigerator. She ought to empty and clean the refrigerator and the bathroom and everything else. But filling up the trash can with so much of her stuff would surely tip off her landlady and spoil her getaway. With luck, now that she'd called in sick for tomorrow, no one would realize she was gone for at least another day.

She was leaving things behind that wouldn't fit in the trash can. People. She liked a lot of the people in Whistle. One had even become a friend, and she didn't make friends easily. She hated not being able to say good-bye. Not in person anyway. She'd written Jamie a letter saying she'd had bad news and had to leave right away, which had the benefit of being true. She hoped Jamie wouldn't be too mad at her.

". . . admitted that talks between the countries have stalled," the news anchor said, "but said that it is too early to give up on negotiations. Here at home, Senator Webster renewed his call for a special prosecutor to investigate the growing scandal connected to the FBI's powerful Unit Twelve and its chief—"

Demi flinched.

"—Ruben Brooks. Brooks has not spoken to the press, but . . ."

How could it all have gone so wrong?

She'd spent the whole day trying to figure out what had happened so she could fix things. She'd even snuck her laptop into the gas station when she went to work so she could keep looking in spite of Mr. Burgenstein's ban. He didn't mind if she read a book when there weren't any customers, but he refused to let her bring her laptop. He was convinced she'd use it to look at porn. He seemed to think that was all anyone did with a computer, which had made her wonder if that was all he did with his computer, and then wish she hadn't. Mr. Burgenstein was sixty years old and fat and smelled like old socks. The image she got in her head of him getting hot and bothered over pictures of naked young women had stuck with her way too long.

It would've been hard to look at Internet porn while at work even if she'd wanted to. There wasn't any Wi-Fi at the station. To get online today she'd created a hotspot with her phone, which was expensive when you used a prepaid phone. But this was an emergency, so she'd gritted her teeth and used up a lot of minutes.

Not that it had helped. What she found didn't make sense. Nothing made sense.

". . . still no word on the whereabouts of Rule Turner," the news anchor said. "In a statement earlier today, his attorney appealed to him to return, claiming that the charges against him were absurd and would be quickly disproven. In a related story, the search continues for Mr. Turner's wife, Lily Yu. The missing FBI agent had been due to receive the Presidential Citizen's Medal this fall for her actions—"

Why was she listening to this? It hurt. It hurt a lot. It wasn't as if she could help anyone by staying here and getting caught. Quickly Demi shut down her computer. There were federal agents all over the place. Mostly FBI, but Mrs. Hawkins had talked to two men from Homeland Security. It was Homeland Security who'd nearly caught her before. They wouldn't be fooled by her disguise. She had to run again.

The reporters said the Refuge was empty. Abandoned. What had Mr. Smith done with the kids? With Nicky?

Demi swallowed and unplugged her laptop and slid it into the padded pocket in her backpack. The backpack had cost nearly a week's wages, but it was worth it. She was experienced at running now and knew what was important. The first time she'd run, she'd had nothing except the ten dollars Mr. Smith left her. That had been terrible. The second time she'd still been pretty broke, but she'd been able to plan ahead some. She'd bought a cheap backpack at the Salvation Army Store and kept a change of clothes, some trail mix, and a toothbrush in it. All she'd had to do was stick in her computer, zip it, and go, which had sure helped because she'd been in a major panic. But when she got caught in a rainstorm later while walking along the highway, her spare clothes had gotten wet. If the rain had lasted longer, her computer could've been damaged.

So "highly weather resistant" had topped her list for a new backpack once she'd saved up the money, along with decent ergonomics to distribute the weight properly. Even when correctly packed, a backpack got heavy after the first couple hours. She went for weather resistant instead of waterproof because truly waterproof bags cost a fortune and were heavy and awkward. Research suggested that adding an additional nylon cover in case of heavy rain should work. She'd found one that folded up real small for only $4.99; the same place had sold her a rain poncho for herself, too, for the same price. Both were tucked into pockets in the backpack.

At least she hadn't had to use her "get the hell out" list, she thought as she carefully checked list number four.

Demi kept four lists in her wallet telling her what to do if she had to run. They were titled: (1) get the hell out; (2) fifteen minutes when NOT at home; (3) fifteen minutes when at home; (4) thirty minutes or more. Experience had taught her that if she had to run, she'd likely be panicked and not thinking straight, so having the lists helped. "Get the hell out" meant leave with only what she had on her. That always included a fifty-dollar bill and a prepaid Visa with the last of her savings, but it might mean abandoning her computer, so it was a list of situations when it wouldn't be safe to go home. The "fifteen minutes when NOT at home" list told her which places were within fifteen minutes of her little trailer. Whistle was small, but when you were on foot, some spots were more than fifteen minutes away. Lists three and four told her what to add to her backpack, which always held a change of clothes, extra socks and underwear, and a box of vegetarian protein bars. Those lists were identical, except that number four included things she'd like to do if there was time, like writing the letter to Jamie.

She'd had time. Demi checked her list now, making sure she hadn't missed anything. Her backpack bulged. Briefly panic tried to make her go back and rethink everything. Maybe she'd made it too heavy. Maybe . . . *follow the list,* she told herself. She could always dump something along the way, but she couldn't come back and retrieve anything. What she left behind now was gone forever.

Quickly she added the one thing not yet packed: the power cord for her laptop. Drawing a deep, shaky breath, she slid her arms through the straps and headed for the door. Stopped. Turned around and went to the cupboard she used as a pantry.

There were five little bags of M&Ms left. Tears filled her eyes when she grabbed them. She'd hoped that somehow Harry would figure out she was leaving and show up so she could tell him bye. Maybe she'd even hoped a little bit that he'd be able to help her again, but the little brownie hadn't come. She hadn't really thought he would. She'd just hoped . . .

Demi sniffed and stuck one bag in her jeans pocket. The rest would be her farewell present to Harry. She stepped out on her tiny porch and locked the door for the last time at 11:17 P.M. She sighed and wiped her leaky eyes and tucked the bags of candy behind the dead plant, straightened, and looked up.

One advantage of being a night owl was seeing the stars more often than a lot of people did. Admittedly, she was mostly messing around on her computer instead of stargazing, but on warm nights she liked to take a break now and then and go sit outside and just look up. Mrs. MacGruder went to bed at ten o'clock every night and she was too cheap to leave the porch light on, so the stretch of ground between her house and Demi's trailer was dark.

The moon was high overhead and three-quarters full. Its light would make walking easier. But it wasn't the moon she needed to see.

The best thing about the stars was that she always had them. No matter where she went, the stars would be there, too. She gazed up for several moments before sighing again and stepping off her little porch. She had her route all mapped out. If it had been daytime she'd have headed for the woods that lined the west half of Mrs. MacGruder's half acre, but in the dark she was apt to get turned around. She had a small flashlight, but she didn't want anyone to see its glow bobbing around. The whole idea was to leave without anyone knowing she was gone.

So she'd take Elm Street for a couple blocks to get to that big field just past the Pattersons' house. Cut across that and she'd hit the dirt road that led to—

One second she was walking along all alone. The next she'd been slammed up against a man's hard body—one arm clamped around her waist, one hand over her mouth. The bulge of the backpack between them left her bent slightly over.

Terror shot through her, slick and cold. She didn't think. She was way too scared to think, her mind whited out in the fear-blizzard, but her body didn't need any help from her mind. Her arms lifted as her feet shifted into base stance. Her knees flexed and her hip swung to the right. She stepped back and in with her left leg, staying low, slapped her hands behind his knees and straightened, lifting and releasing—

He went down just like he was supposed to. Only somehow she went down, too, landing on top of him in a discombobulated tangle of knees and elbows and backpack. He rolled so fast she barely registered the motion. And then she was on the bottom, ungainly as an overturned turtle, the lumpy backpack her shell, with him straddling her. One of his hands gripped both of hers. When had he gotten hold of them? His other hand covered her mouth—again? Still? Her lips tingled. Everywhere his skin touched hers tingled with magic. It wasn't a type of magic she'd ever felt before, but . . .

Moonlight fell across his lips and jaws, but shadow made mysteries of the rest of his face. "Good takedown," he breathed.

Terror somersaulted into anger. It wasn't fair! It wasn't fair at all! It *had* been a good takedown. She'd executed it just right. He should be on the ground, not on top of her. She should be running away as fast as she could. And her laptop—if her laptop was damaged—gods, what would she do without it?

His voice was a silky thread of sound in the darkness. "We need to talk. We're going to get up and go back inside where you can tell me—no?"

She'd shaken her head frantically. Or tried to. The hand that covered the bottom half of her face hadn't let her head move, but apparently he'd gotten the idea.

"You don't want to go back inside? Perhaps you'd rather stroll off into the woods with me."

She tried to nod.

He stared down at her. "You'd rather go into the woods with a man who's assaulted you than go back in your trailer."

She almost-nodded again.

"Did you plant a bomb in there, perhaps?"

She stared at him. Was that supposed to be a joke? It wasn't funny.

"Come along, then."

But he didn't let her get up and stroll off into the woods. He pulled a scarf from his pocket and gagged her, then lifted her easily to her feet. He leaned in close. "No tricks," he whispered. "I'm bigger than you, faster than you, and so much stronger. You haven't a chance."

She glared at him, but tears stung her eyes.

Neither the glare nor the tears affected him one bit. He tossed her over his shoulders like a bag of laundry and set off at an easy run. It was horrible. Her head bobbled with each step. He held both of her legs and one arm, so she hit him in the back with the other. He ignored that. She thought she should try to wiggle free, but what would happen if she did? She'd fall to the ground. She knew how to fall without hurting herself, but her computer was in her backpack. She couldn't risk hurting it.

At least he ran toward the woods, not back to the trailer. It was creepy dark under the trees. He hardly slowed at all, dodging around things she couldn't see. He ran for a long time. Finally he slowed and stopped and set her on her feet. She wobbled, so dizzy she hardly knew how to stand up. His face was a pale blur in the darkness. She couldn't see his features, much less his expression.

When he spoke, he didn't bother to keep his voice down. It was so silky it seemed to be made out of shivers. "Let's have that little chat. No one will hear you but me . . . no matter how much noise you make." With one hand he pulled down the gag.

"This," she said in a voice that wobbled even worse than her legs, "is a huge disappointment."

TWENTY-ONE

RULE blinked. That was not the reaction he'd been expecting. He'd decided to handle this encounter himself because he didn't think his men would be good at threatening a woman. Apparently he wasn't, either. "Disappointing?"

"I don't suppose you fantasize much," she said bitterly. "I don't suppose you need to, so maybe you don't understand how awful it is to have one of your favorite fantasies ruined. Fantasies aren't reality, but they still require verisimilitude." When he didn't respond right away, she added, "'Verisimilitude' means—"

"I know what the word means, Miss, ah . . . ." He couldn't keep the amusement out of his voice. "I'm afraid I don't know your name."

"I know yours, Mr. Turner." She sounded sulky.

He could have sworn he'd kept his face in shadow. That was strike two for tonight's plan. "Call me Rule. What should I call you?"

"Danny."

"You aren't a boy."

"You didn't ask if I was a boy. You asked what you should call me, and I told you."

"True. So tell me, Danny, where were you going in such a hurry tonight?"

She jolted as if he'd goosed her. "My computer!" Quickly she slid the backpack off her shoulders. "I can't believe I forgot—if you've damaged it with all your grabbing and rolling and running, I'll—I'll—I don't know what I'll do, but you better not have hurt it."

He watched, bemused, while she unzipped the backpack and carefully pulled a laptop out. She dropped onto the ground, legs crossed tailor-style, opened her precious computer, and powered it up. It seemed, to his inexpert eyes, to be working fine. "Now that you've reassured yourself, perhaps you could answer a few questions. Let's start with why Homeland Security believes you're a terrorist."

"I expect Mr. Smith told them that." She didn't seem bothered by the idea. Her whole attention was focused on her computer. "That works . . . the drive's okay . . . but there's no Wi-Fi here. I can't check the modem."

"Is Mr. Smith with Homeland Security?"

"No, he's NSA. I've been on the run from him for eleven months, one week, and three days."

"Have you now." Should he add the NSA to his list of federal agencies who were out to get him, Ruben, and one or both Units? Or was that one of her fantasies? Or a simple lie, he reminded himself, but he didn't believe it. She didn't smell like she was lying, and instinct agreed with his senses. She was telling the truth—or what she thought was true. "And are you a terrorist?"

She snorted and at last looked up, but only for a second. Her gaze skittered away from his face. "About as much as you're a distributor of child pornography."

Rule considered her for a long moment. Frightening the girl hadn't worked. Try another tack. "It seems you and I are both on the run. I've got a place to hide and a great many questions. Would you care to hide with me for a time?"

She shook her head, slid the laptop back in its pocket, stood, and slipped the straps of her backpack in place. "I'd better stick to my plan. It never works if I change plans when I'm panicked."

She assumed he'd just let her walk away. That wasn't an

option, but he decided not to point that out. "Are you panicked? You don't smell like it."

That startled her. After a moment her eyes narrowed, as if
her current lack of panic was highly suspicious. "Not as much,"
she said grudgingly. "I think I need to think."

His lips twitched. "All right."

Thinking apparently involved staring over his shoulder
while her fingers moved in an odd, deliberate pattern. Spellcasting? It didn't look like any spell he'd seen Cullen use, but
to be safe, he moved a few silent paces away. Most impromptu
spells had to be aimed, and he doubted she could see him. It
must be very dark here for her.

Not for him. The light was dim, but he saw her face clearly
and marveled that everyone had taken her for a boy. Even Lily
had done so, from what José had said, and she wasn't easy to
fool. Perhaps his sense of smell informed his viewpoint too thoroughly for him to see what others did, but she simply didn't look
like a boy to him. Not that she was conventionally pretty. Her
features were more intriguing than that. Her mouth was as Anglo
as his; her buzzed-short hair was pure African; her skin and nose
split the difference between the two continents. Her face was
long rather than rounded, which must have helped her disguise.
So did her build. She was a skinny thing, all angles. But her eyes,
with those long, curly lashes, struck him as innately feminine. So
did the curve of her chin.

Her fingers paused in their repetitive motion. "Where are
you hiding?"

"In the wildlife area south of Whistle. It will be a bit of a
hike, I'm afraid." Not that they really had to walk the whole
way. Kevin and Tucker were in a car parked on a nearby road
and could easily meet them. He didn't mention that.

Find Lily. Find the enemy.

His wolf's priorities were clear. They were the man's priorities, too. Rule had two reasons for not taking the car. The
first was obvious: cars travel on roads, and so do cops. But he
had a second, equally important reason. He didn't just want to
hear whatever she decided to tell him. He needed to learn the
things she didn't plan to tell him, too—everything he could
about this girl who wanted him to call her Danny. How could

he know what to believe, what to check out or dismiss, without context? And she herself was the context.

She didn't trust him, and no wonder, given how he'd treated her. He needed time to change that.

After frowning into space for several moments with one hand hovering in midair, ready to resume its motion, she dropped that hand and shook her head. "I was planning to walk, so hiking is not a problem, but I'm not much for camping out. I like nature, but I like showers and toilets more. And Wi-Fi." She sighed regretfully. "I won't get any of that for a while. But I guess I should tell you about Mr. Smith before I go. You won't believe me, and it isn't going to help you much since you're on the run, too, but I guess I should tell you. You probably don't know what's going on."

That was certainly true. "I'd appreciate that."

"All right." She continued to look over his shoulder rather than at his face, took a deep breath, and began. "For many years Mr. Edward Smith, a special assistant to the director of the NSA, has illicitly channeled federal funds to support a clandestine operation that purports to help children with magical Gifts learn to control their Gifts. Operating through a nonprofit organization called Bright Haven Refuge—"

"Bright Haven? In West Virginia? That's—"

"Don't do that!" She cleared her throat and resumed what was clearly a prepared speech. "—Bright Haven Refuge for Gifted Young People, which obtains legal custody of orphaned and abandoned minors who meet his criteria, he's conducted experiments on the children. These experiments include the administration of a secret drug that greatly increases the strength of their Gifts. He controls these children—and their Gifts— through a combination of psychological brainwashing and mind control."

Rule was silent for several heartbeats before saying softly, "You really are going to have to come with me, you know."

TWENTY-TWO

~

DEMI didn't know what she felt. Everything was such a stew—a hot, lively stew, zingy with spices that tangled in her gut and tingled in her brain. "You believe me?"

"I believe you're speaking the truth, as you know it," Rule Turner told her.

Rule Turner. It was hard to believe he was right here, in front of her. Talking to her. Listening to her. It was as if Gandalf had stepped out of the pages of *Lord of the Rings*, or Jean Luc Picard had stepped out of the screen, to have a little chat.

Or Darth Vader. "I don't want to." She was almost sure of that.

"Danny, do you even know where you are?"

She didn't answer.

"You can't follow through with whatever your original plan was. I interfered with that. Even if you could figure out where you are, you can't see where you're going. It's too dark for you."

She scowled and looked down. "I brought a flashlight." Which she did not want to use in case someone saw it. But maybe that wasn't an issue. Maybe she was too deep in the woods, too far from any road, too *lost* . . . a bubble of panic rose, stopping in her throat. Her hand lifted, playing the flute she hadn't actually held in eleven months, one week, and three days.

"You're fingering an instrument," her fantasy-destroying companion said suddenly. "A flute?"

No one had ever guessed correctly. Mostly they just told her to stop being weird. Maybe the fantasy wasn't entirely shattered, after all. "It used to be. Now it's just stimming, to help me calm down. Why did you grab me? Were you trying to scare me into telling you things?"

"That was the general idea."

"It was a stupid idea."

"Yes," he said meekly. "But I didn't yet know you. What if you'd really been a terrorist?"

She snorted. After another moment's thought she asked a hard question. "Am I your prisoner?"

"I'd rather not do it that way."

What did that mean? That she wasn't his prisoner now, but she could be? Demi swallowed. "You don't break your word. Not ever, not for anything."

"That's true."

"If I go with you voluntarily, will you promise not to make me your prisoner? Or—or give me to Mr. Smith or to Homeland Security. Or to any law enforcement. Or let them get hold of me."

He answered slowly. "Because my word is binding, I'm careful about how I phrase my promises. If you come with me and place yourself temporarily under my authority, answering my questions freely and honestly, I will offer you the same protection and privileges I would provide for a child of my clan."

"I'm not a child."

"You are, however, a minor under human law and according to the custom of my people."

His people. A thrill shot through her. She forced herself to think carefully about the meaning of each word he'd used. "There are things I don't want to tell you, and 'temporarily' is too vague."

"Very well. If you come with me and place yourself under my authority for the next forty-eight hours—"

"Twenty-four."

"—for the next twenty-four hours, answering my questions

honestly—and 'I don't want to tell you' is an honest answer—I will give you the same protection and privileges I would a child of my clan."

Demi swallowed and held out her hand. "All right."

He took it. Her skin tingled from his magic. He shook hands, sealing the deal, but he didn't let go.

She tugged. "I don't much like touching."

"I can guide you better if I hold your hand, but you could hold on to my shirt instead, if you'd rather."

"That would be better."

He let go. "May I carry your backpack for you?"

"No."

"We've got about twelve miles to cover."

"No."

"Let me know if you change your mind." He turned his back to her. "Grab hold of my shirt."

She had to move uncomfortably close to him to do that, adding a new ingredient to the stew, one that made her heart pound. At least it was dark. She latched on to the stretchy tail of his T-shirt and they started off.

She expected him to start asking his questions right away. He didn't. He didn't say anything, except to tell her things in a quiet voice now and then, like to watch out for a branch or step over a big rock. She couldn't hear anything except the sound of her feet scuffing along behind him.

Normally Demi was fine with a lack of conversation. It bothered her this time. "How did you find me?"

"Two HSI agents showed Lily an old photo of an alleged terrorist. Shortly before she was kidnapped, she realized where she'd seen that face."

"Is she why you're in Whistle?" That must be it. He hadn't known Demi existed until . . . "I'm really sorry about Lily Yu."

His voice stayed even and low. "What do you know about her?"

"Lots," she assured him. "But she isn't my fault, even if it feels like . . . but it's all tangled up together." She hesitated, then went on in a very small voice, "I think Ruben Brooks is my fault. I don't see how they did it or what I did wrong, but somehow I must have messed up."

"Oh?"

"Don't do that! Your voice sounds . . . don't do that."

"I'm not trying to be scary, but I really need to hear what you know about Lily."

Her brow wrinkled. "Everything I know?"

"Start with why it isn't your fault that she's missing."

"I didn't make Mr. Smith kidnap her, but he probably did it because he couldn't find me. I'm not responsible for what he does, so it's not my fault and I shouldn't feel guilty."

"You think your Mr. Smith has her?"

"That's a theory, not a fact, but it fits the facts."

"Why would he consider Lily a good substitute for you?"

That was one of the things she'd decided she could tell him. "Because I'm a touch sensitive, too. Just like her. That's how I recognized you." The second she'd felt his magic prickling along her skin, she'd known her attacker was a lupus. Lily Yu had described the feel of lupus magic in an interview she'd given *People* magazine: like fur and pine needles. "You could have been some other lupus, but I saw the bottom part of your face, too."

"You stopped being scared then."

"Lupi don't hurt women. Even if I was wrong about which lupus had grabbed me, I knew I wasn't going to be hurt." She added with remembered indignation, "I did not know you were going to throw me over your shoulder."

"You seem to know a lot about me. Or about lupi."

That wasn't a question, so she didn't say anything. Maybe it was okay to tell him she was in his fan club. She wasn't sure, though, so for now she wouldn't.

"Why does Mr. Smith want a touch sensitive?"

"Because that's how he finds them. The kids. Or how he used to. I found them for him." Guilt swamped her, as it sometimes did no matter how often she told herself she wasn't responsible for what Mr. Smith had done. "It's my fault he has them. I've been trying to fix it, but everything's g-gone wrong." Tears welled up.

He stopped, turned, and put his arms around her.

She stiffened. "I don't much—"

"—like touching. I know. I'm fulfilling my word. There's no way I would let a child from my clan cry and not comfort them. I'll let go of you the second you tell me to."

His arms were warm. He was warm all over. Demi felt stiff and awkward like she always did when someone hugged her. She was supposed to hug him back, but she couldn't. She was doing it wrong. She always did it wrong. But it felt okay to stand there and let him do the hugging. It felt . . . not alone.

She didn't start sobbing. Demi didn't know how to cry all-out that way. Her eyes burned and her nose ran, but she didn't sob. She stood there all stiff and awkward and sniffed several times, and her nose got stuffy, and then she told him that was enough comforting.

He stepped back right away and waited while she dug a tissue out of her backpack so she could blow her nose. Instead of asking her more questions about Mr. Smith, he told her to grab hold of his shirt and went right back to leading her through the trees. He didn't say anything at all for a while. Then he confused her all over again. He asked if she was an orphan.

So she told him about her mother, who'd been Mr. Smith's secretary at the NSA. "Officially she was an administrative assistant, but that's not what she called herself. She used to say that a secretary by any other name will still be underpaid." As they walked through woods, where owls hooted and her feet stirred up the rich perfume of leaf mold, she talked about HER2-positive breast cancer and how she came to work for Mr. Smith.

She remembered that day so clearly, which was funny, because there were big gaps in her memory. But the parts she remembered were as clear as if they'd happened yesterday . . .

FOR the last two days, Demi and Zipper had been staying with her mother's friend Sara, who already had two kids and two cats in her two-bedroom apartment, so Demi slept on the couch. Sara was a hugging kind of person, but she'd known Demi all her life so she mostly managed not to hug Demi. Not always, but mostly. Demi liked her a lot. She liked Sara's kids, too. They were a lot younger than her, but that was okay. She liked playing with little kids, even if they were really loud sometimes. But she did not want to stay with Sara and her kids and her cats, who did not like Zipper. She wanted to stay at home, in her own room and her own bed, until Mama was better. Zipper would be happier at home, too. Demi knew how to do everything she'd need to do, how to take care of herself and Zipper, but no one would listen to her.

She'd cut school that day, which she never did, and taken the bus to the hospital. When she walked into her mother's room, Mr. Smith was there, too. The bed was cranked up so that Mama was almost sitting up. She hardly looked like Mama anymore, with her beautiful red hair gone and her skin so pale. Even her freckles were pale. She wore a green scarf on her head. Sally was African-American and knew how to wrap and tie scarves so they made really cool turbans. When Mama started radiation, Sally had taught her and Demi how to do that, but Mama didn't have the energy for that anymore, so she just tied the scarf at her nape. Sometimes Demi rewrapped it for her, making a cool turban.

Mama still sounded like herself, though. When Demi walked in, she was saying something to Mr. Smith about Zipper. She stopped, looked at Demi, and instead of asking why she wasn't in school, she told Demi to say hello to her boss and shake his hand.

Demi frowned, confused. Mama knew she didn't like to touch people. But she'd used the voice that meant Demi had better not argue, so she didn't. She held out her hand and shook Mr. Smith's. His hand was soft with stubby fingers and a little tingle of magic.

"Now," Mama said, "tell Mr. Smith what you felt."

"But, Mama—do you mean—"

"Yes. Tell him."

That was unprecedented. They never, ever told anyone about Demi's Gift. She darted a glance at Mr. Smith. "You've got a little bit of a charisma Gift. It's really small," she said apologetically, as if it might be her fault he had so little magic.

Mr. Smith's eyebrows climbed up on his forehead. "Remarkable."

Mama said in her don't-argue-with-me voice, "Zipper, too. In writing."

Mr. Smith had laughed, shaken his head, and said, "You win, Margaret. If you'll sign, I'll waive the no-pets rule—in writing. She can take her dog with her."

Then Mama had said, "Light of my heart"—she called Demi that sometimes—"come here."

She did. Mama looked so tired.

"I won't be here to take care of you much longer. No, don't phase out on me! I love you more than the moon and stars. You know, that, don't you?"

Demi nodded, her throat so tight she couldn't squeeze a single word through it.

"And you love me," Mama said as if Demi had spoken everything that was stuck in her throat. "And you don't want to hear this, but you have to. The damn cancer is winning. Now, we've talked about Sally taking you in if worst comes to worst, but she doesn't have much money, and my life insurance isn't going to stretch very far. There sure won't be enough for college, and you're going to go to college. So after I'm gone, you'll go stay at a place Mr. Smith operates called the Refuge. You and Zipper. You'll work for Mr. Smith two weekends a month, and he'll see that there's money for college."

Mr. Smith had told her about the Refuge then, but she didn't remember that part. If you aren't paying attention, your brain doesn't make any memories, and Demi hadn't been paying attention. She couldn't think about anything except "after I'm gone." She knew vaguely Mama had said that before, but this time was different. This time the words were like marbles she couldn't put down. She kept rolling them around in her mind, trying to make sense of them, but their meaning was sealed up inside glass. She couldn't touch it.

Six days later, the glass shattered.

Three days after that, she left home forever, moving to the Bright Haven Refuge for Gifted Young People. Her and Zipper.

ON a moonlit night four years and four months after her mother died, Demi walked with Rule Turner down a dirt road in a river of silvery moonlight banked by the dark shapes of trees and told him about Asperger's. She used the short explanation, the one Nicky had helped her work out because, he said, people stop listening when you tell them too much at once.

But Rule Turner didn't seem to get tired of listening. She

told him about Mr. Smith—"Edward Smith, no middle name. He's fifty-six. He's worked for the NSA for thirty-one years. He graduated from the University of Cincinnati in . . ."

As they crossed a small, grassy meadow, she told him how she'd set up her back door into the NSA's computers, but not why. Well, she did slip up and mention Amanda's name, but she stopped because she didn't know how much she should say. And as they set off down a path she couldn't see into another sprawling patch of woods, she told him about her plan. How long it had taken her to get the financial data that she'd sent to the reporter. Why she'd sent it. What was in the other two files—and how key data had inexplicably changed overnight to implicate Ruben Brooks instead of Mr. Smith. "I thought if he knew that I had solid data, he'd have to shut down the Refuge and let the kids go, but it went wrong somehow. I don't know what happened. It all went wrong."

Demi had thought she was in good shape. She'd walked every day in Whistle, and almost every week she'd taken a long hike to build her stamina. But even on her long hikes she hadn't walked for twelve miles. She hadn't walked through woods dense with darkness where ups and downs, roots and stones, conspired to trip her.

Twice more he asked if he could carry her backpack. Twice more she said no.

It was good that he asked. It reminded her that she couldn't trust him. She needed the reminder, because he was awfully easy to talk to. Over those twelve miles, she told him a lot. More than she should have, probably, and a lot of it wasn't about Mr. Smith at all. She talked about canine arthritis and what various studies on glucosamine supplements suggested and how she'd picked the spot for Zipper's grave.

He didn't get impatient. He seemed to want to know whatever she wanted to tell him. He didn't get mad when she said, "I don't want to answer," though she had to say it several times because she wasn't sure what it was okay to tell him. She'd have to think about that later.

Most of all, she didn't tell him about Nicky. She protected her friend's secret.

TWENTY-THREE

~~

RULE'S companion hadn't complained once in their four-hour hike, and she'd retained custody of her backpack as if it held her heartbeat. But she was drooping badly by the time they drew near the campsite.

She must have seen the flicker of firelight through the trees. She stopped suddenly and directed an accusing look at him. "You can't have a fire when you're hiding. That's stupid."

"I'm hiding differently. Come on."

The only reason she did, he suspected, was that she was too tired to argue, or to go looking for an unlit hiding spot on her own. He resisted the urge to pick up the pace. The girl with him didn't feel his urgency or his relief. She couldn't see the dark shapes slipping from tree to tree alongside them. She couldn't smell what he did, nor would it have meant to her what it did to him.

Clan. Not Nokolai, but his other clan. Many Leidolf waited for him just ahead. He was surprised at how much the scent welcomed him.

At the edge of the trees she stopped again, staring at the clearing where they'd set up camp. "That," she said in a funny voice, "is not a different kind of hiding. That isn't hiding at all."

The clearing was about a block wide and several blocks long.

Directly ahead, roughly in the center, was the crude stone hearth they'd fashioned for cooking. The tents had been erected on the west end. They didn't have enough of those for everyone—but wolves don't care much for sleeping in tents, and over half those present were on four legs.

What was the best way to hide a wolf? In the middle of other wolves. Humans were not good at identifying one particular wolf unless his coloring was unusual, and Rule's fur was the brindled black-and-silver shared by every other wolf in that clearing. That had been his chief criteria when he'd spoken with Alex that afternoon and asked him to send fifty Leidolf clansmen.

"There must be two dozen of them," she said in a hushed voice.

"Fifty-six now," José said, walking up to meet them. Several of the sleeping wolves had woken at the sound of voices and were looking their way. "Eight more arrived an hour ago."

Rule spoke clearly so everyone would hear. "José, this young lady likes to be called Danny. She is *ospi* and has placed herself under my protection and authority for the next twenty-four hours."

"Twenty hours now," Danny corrected him, "approximately. I didn't look to see exactly what time we made our agreement, but we walked for at least four hours after that."

Rule smiled and went on. "Twenty hours now. She's hiding from the authorities, as I am. Danny, this is José." When she didn't respond, he added gently, "Don't be afraid. They won't . . ." And stopped. The rest of his speech was clearly unnecessary.

Danny was gazing at the piles of wolves with the wide-eyed wonder of a toddler on Christmas morning. She whispered, "Can I meet them? Pet them? I know they aren't dogs, but I . . . it would be so wonderful. Please?"

The girl who didn't much like touching was dying to touch the werewolves. "Mike," he said. "Come here a moment, please."

The wolf he addressed wasn't among those dozing in the camp. He'd been part of the escort Danny hadn't been aware of, and came trotting out of the forest behind them.

Danny spun around. "Oh! Oh, he's beautiful!"

Mike was a handsome wolf, true. He was also unusually

large, even for a lupus, all of whom were bigger than natural
wolves. Rule's nostrils flared as he checked . . . Danny felt no
fear at all, though Mike must have startled her. Good. Nor was
there any trace of desire in her scent, which was a relief. A few
humans took an erotic interest in lupi in wolf-form, and while
he hadn't thought Danny was of that bent, he hadn't been sure.
She'd spoke of fantasizing about him, and she clearly knew
more than most about his people. "Danny, this is Mike. He'll
take you to meet some of the others. They dislike being looked
in the eye. Wait to pet until you're invited. If you aren't sure if
someone is inviting you to pet him, ask."

She nodded seriously.

"Mike, our guest is seventeen. She would like to meet some
of our four-footed clan. I place her in your charge."

Placing her under Mike's protection was probably unnecessary. No lupus would intentionally hurt the girl, protected as
she was by her sex and her age. But a few of those here tonight
lived at Leidolf Clanhome because they lacked the level of control needed to live among humans. Then there was the prevailing attitude in Leidolf about women—the nineteenth century
at its most perverse. Among other things, they considered sixteen the age of consent.

But that was a problem for tomorrow, not tonight. He'd
make his expectations clear when Danny wasn't in earshot. As
she went happily off with Mike, Rule spoke to José. "Have you
had problems with any of them?"

José was the only Nokolai here. Carson remained in town,
keeping track of what the various law enforcement personnel
were up to. In spite of that, Rule was determined to have José
as his second. It was asking a lot of the man, he knew. José was
smart, dominant, and an excellent fighter, but there were a few
here who might think they could beat him—and one who probably could. That one was Mike, but Mike wouldn't challenge
José. Rule had established his wishes on that score quite clearly
last year.

He'd needed to make himself clear to the rest, so before
leaving, he'd spoken to them. He would, he'd said, consider any
resistance to José's authority a formal Challenge to himself—
and if he had to stop looking for his mate in order to kill some
idiot, he would not be happy.

"They're not all smiley faces, but they're behaving."

"That will do for now. None of the patrols have found anything, I take it." José would have told him right away if they had. "And no one with a badge has dropped by for a visit?"

"Not exactly. A helicopter hovered overhead a couple hours ago. State police, by the insignia."

"Hmm. Well, we knew law enforcement would take an interest in us."

Eventually, some type of cops would show up in person. When they did, Rule would be four-footed, and José would explain that they had gathered to look for Lily. Their story had the advantage of being true. Patrols were actively searching for any trace of her or the brownie who'd spoken to her. "Have you heard from Peter?"

"Briefly. They won't let him go beyond the tourist section."

Rule had sent Peter Armstead to the brownie reservation to speak with their elders. He would have preferred to go himself, but he couldn't be two places at once, and confronting HSI's suspect took priority. He'd expected Peter to have trouble pinning the brownies down; he hadn't expected them to refuse to allow Peter into the private area of the reservation. "They accepted Peter as my emissary?"

"Yes. According to him, they were very apologetic, but there's some kind of community ceremony or religious observance going on, and outsiders can't be admitted."

"Hmm." From what he'd seen, brownies were not religious in the human sense. They seemed to be cheerful little pagans, but with a feeling of camaraderie rather than worship. Dirty Harry spoke of the Green Man as if he were an interesting but touchy neighbor—someone he didn't want to offend, but not an object of awe. Still, there was much Rule didn't know about brownies. "Did they answer his questions at all?"

"Oh, they answered—and answered, and answered. Peter said he could hardly get them to stop answering, but he couldn't make sense of anything they said."

That fit what Rule knew about brownies. "Their behavior is suspicious, but not conclusively so. Brownies are slippery little devils, even when they intend to be helpful." And if they didn't intend to be helpful, they could tell you the sky was blue in so many ways that you'd end up believing it was orange. He'd have to deal with them himself. "Peter may as well return."

José sent a quick text, looked up, and smiled. "Your under-age terrorist is having herself a great time."

Danny knelt on the ground, surrounded by wolves. She was scratching Jimmy Bacon behind the ears while Ed Grinowski poked her with his nose, asking for the same treatment. Saul Freeman sat in front of her and presented his paw for a shake, but Claude Bristow, a grim and grizzled veteran, shoved Saul out of the way. He then flopped down in front of her, offering his stomach for a belly rub. She laughed in delight.

"She is, isn't she? The men seem to be enjoying themselves, too."

"We don't often meet out-clan humans who have no fear of us, even in wolf-form."

"Danny's . . . different." In many ways. "Have you heard of Asperger's?"

José's eyebrows lifted. "Autism Lite, isn't it?"

"It's on the autism scale, yes. Some people with Asperger's are extremely successful." Such as Bill Gates, Alfred Hitch-cock, Einstein, Mozart, and Sir Isaac Newton, according to Danny. Rule wasn't sure how accurate her list was, but it was impressive. "Some have more trouble functioning. All have difficulty with facial expressions and social cues. Danny is also an orphan. Her parents weren't married, and her father died before she was born."

"Her mother's dead, too?"

"Four years ago, of breast cancer."

The tumor had been particularly fast-growing, but it should have been caught earlier. Demi had explained at length how it had been missed, what type of cancer it had been, the various treatment options, the type of treatment her mother actually received . . . and why it hadn't worked. She'd spoken clinically, without obvious emotion, and in great detail. It was her way, Rule understood, of reporting on a grief too vast to explain. "She didn't have any family to take her in."

"An older kid with Asperger's, plus she's black—"

"Biracial."

"Either way, I'm betting she wasn't adopted. Foster care?"

"No. Her mother signed over custody to the Bright Haven Refuge for Gifted Young People."

José pursed his lips in a silent whistle. "That's the outfit Ruben is supposed to have secretly funded."

"According to Danny, it's Mr. Smith of the NSA who diverted funds, and until yesterday, she had proof of that. She sent those financial records to the reporter who broke the story. Those records mysteriously changed, and not just the ones the reporter had. Every copy of them, no matter where it was stored, had been altered."

"That's not possible."

"She agrees with you. And yet that's what seems to have happened to point the blame at Ruben." Rule ran a hand over his hair. "I need to talk to Cullen, dammit. I suspect some type of sympathetic magic was used, something similar to what Cullen did to ward our accounts, but I need to talk to him about it." And couldn't. And maybe he'd never speak to his friend again . . . *stop that,* he told himself firmly. Though he did need to give some thought to what kind of enemy could snatch Lily in Ohio and make Cullen vanish in Mexico.

For now . . . "I need to brief you, but I prefer to do so while I brief Theo"—as a Leidolf councillor, Theo had to be included—"and two *nunti.*" *Nunti* meant messengers. The position was mostly obsolete now, but until thirty years ago formal communication between the clans had been handled through these oral messengers. "I think Hal Brownbeck is here?"

"Tall guy, white hair, dark skin?"

"Yes. He used to act as *nuntius* for Leidolf. I'll want him and one other. Present Theo with my compliments and tell him I need him to select someone with an excellent memory to be my second *nuntius.* He'll know who would be best."

"You believe her, then?" José asked.

Rule looked at Danny, who had at last abandoned her backpack so she could romp with half a dozen wolves. They were playing statues—the lupi version, which mixed the human game with tag and hide-and-seek. A couple of two-legged clan stood nearby, grinning. Maybe they'd explained the rules to Danny.

Statues was a favorite game for clan children to play with four-legged adults. The wolves were treating Danny as if she were a lot younger than seventeen. They were right. In some ways, she was very young still. In spite of everything. "She could be wrong about some elements, and she hasn't told me everything," he answered José. "But I believe she's been honest with me. Oh—she's going to need one of the tents and a sleeping bag. After you speak with Theo, you'll have to redo some of the sleeping arrangements." He found a smile. "And while you're hard at work . . . I smell coffee."

"Ed made it. It's strong enough to hop into your cup on its own."

José hadn't exaggerated much. Rule sat near the low fire sipping coffee stout enough to rival the bottom-of-the-pot brew at a cop shop and thought about the girl he was responsible for. For the next twenty hours, that is.

Danny was alone in the world in a way few people are. No family. Her mother's parents had reacted badly when she began dating a black man. They'd cut off relations entirely when they found out they were going to be presented with a biracial grandchild. Danny had never met them and didn't want to. Her father had been a Haitian immigrant, brought to the United States as a child by his grandmother after his parents died, probably killed by Baby Doc. His grandmother had raised him and watched proudly when he graduated from college. A year later, he'd died in a car accident. The old woman had moved in with Danny's mother and helped care for Danny after she was born, but she'd died when Danny was six.

Death on top of death. Danny had been thirteen when she went to the Bright Haven Refuge for Gifted Young People—a large home in the West Virginia countryside where two Gifted children already lived. The place had seemed like a refuge at first. The houseparents had been "nice enough," the rules strict but reasonable, and Mr. Smith hadn't put her to work immediately. He let her get her feet under her at first and see that the other kids weren't being treated as research subjects.

Though that's what they were.

Supposedly the Refuge existed to offer a home to orphaned or abandoned children with Gifts, and to help those children learn how to use their Gifts safely and effectively. To that end, the children were tested and trained—all of them except Danny, whose Gift defied every test they could devise. The essence of touch sensitivity was that it could not be affected by magic, and nonmagical tests were notoriously unreliable in the presence of magic. "But I was very important to the project," she'd told Rule, "because I could find the kids who could be helped. That's what Mr. Smith said anyway, and maybe that part was true even if the rest was lies."

The upshot was that Danny hadn't known much about the tests and training the other kids received. The other kids hadn't filled her in because she hadn't fit in. She never did, she'd told him with a shrug that was supposed to show how little it mattered. When he asked if she'd been bullied, she informed him that the definition of bullying was in flux. According to some standards, the answer was yes. According to others, no. She wouldn't tell him specifically what the other kids had said or done, but it was clear she hadn't been accepted by her peers. That, he suspected, had made the approval of the adults in her life very important.

Adults like Mr. Smith. Especially him, because of his connection to her dead mother. She'd believed everything he told her . . . until a girl named Amanda showed up at the Refuge.

"Stop it!" Danny clapped her hands over her ears, her face scrunching up. "Go away!"

The wolves playing with her froze, looking bewildered. Mike rose to his feet.

Rule did, too, and headed for her quickly. Danny's face relaxed just as he reached her. She dropped her hands. "Oh," she said, looking around at the wolves. "I didn't mean you."

Rule crouched in front of her. "Who did you mean?"

"It's Amanda." She scowled. "That's the second time she's done that, and I don't like it. I don't like it at all."

"Done what?"

"Talked to me in my head."

MANY miles away, Lily muttered and turned over onto her back. Sleep was easing out of her, slow as sieved molasses. As she drifted restlessly into wakefulness, her dream clung.

She'd been looking for Rule, looking everywhere. She wanted to curl up with him again, the way she had . . . sometime. Not very long ago. She'd curled up in his arms recently, but she couldn't find him now.

But she had found someone. Someone she'd found before, whose mind she could speak with.

Her eyes popped open on that thought. She lay still and tried to reach out again. Tried to find that other mind, the one who could hear her. When she failed, her eyes stung with tears. That was frustration, she told herself. Frustration, not fear. She wasn't really crying. She was just frustrated. Bloody damn frustrated. She tried again.

There.

Yes, there was Charles beside her, sound asleep. He'd been allowed to wake sometimes, like her. Wake up so they could pee and eat and drink—and brush her teeth, which she'd done twice now—before being forced into sleep again. Which should not have been possible, because it was clearly magical sleep, but it kept happening. She'd learned that it happened to him, too, when their awake-times overlapped briefly once.

Knowing where Charles was didn't help. He couldn't hear her mindspeech, so what did it matter if . . .

If she knew where his mind was. If she could sense that mental presence as clearly as she saw the uneven rocky ceiling of her cell. No, more clearly, for this sense didn't rely on anything as unstable as the flickers of firelight.

Also: *there, there,* and *there.*

Lily's breath caught in shock. That was . . . those were . . . minds. Other minds, not Charles's. Three of them, roughly level with her and about fifteen feet distant in *that* direction, which put them on the other side of the fire curtain. She had no words to describe this new perception. It was directional like the mate sense, but had elements of vision and touch, too. The minds seemed to glow, yet also felt tangible. Juicy. As if minds were fruit to this new sense—grapes or plums maybe, but not cool like refrigerated fruit. Warm with life. Warm, thin-skinned, glowing fruit that she ought to be able to reach out and touch.

She tried.

Instead of touching, she somehow shifted her perception so that she looked—or reached?—more widely. Another mind.

Not like the others, for if they made her think of fruit, this one made her think of magma: dark-crusted on top, cracked and curdled from the virulent heat burning beneath.

A mind that she suddenly knew was regarding her the same way she regarded it.

This time, she felt it when something flicked the switch that send her plunging down into darkness and sleep. Felt it and screamed, however briefly and silently.

Not in fear. Not in frustration. In rage.

TWENTY-FOUR

~

"ARE you sure it was Amanda?" Rule asked.

He and Danny sat around the fire with José, Mike, and Theo. Danny had her backpack with her, but it rested beside her, not on her. Mike was there because Danny was his responsibility; he'd Changed back to two legs, a process Danny had watched with intense concentration until he finished. Then she'd flushed painfully and looked away until he pulled on a pair of cutoffs. A dozen others, both two-legged and four, would have joined them if Rule hadn't motioned them away. Not that they'd gone very far. His clansmen had taken a shine to Danny. They were also curious.

"Who else could—" She broke off as Claude—who'd also switched back to two legs—approached and handed her a Coke. "Thank you. Um, I'm not sure who you are?"

"Claude," he said in a voice almost as deep as Isen's. On two legs, Claude would make a good television thug, with his heavy brows, burly build, and surly expression. Humans might have guessed his age at fifty or sixty. Rule wasn't sure of his actual age, but he'd fought in the Second World War. So had his oldest son.

"He's the greedy one who wouldn't let anyone else get a belly rub," Mike added.

"Oh, the wolf with the crooked left ear." She nodded firmly. "Claude. I'll remember."

Rule made a gesture that should keep the others from interrupting again. Danny had spoken of Amanda twice now. The first time she'd stopped herself, but it was clear that something about the girl had alerted Danny that things at the Refuge were not as she'd thought. Now . . . "Danny," he said with careful patience, "what exactly did you experience?"

"She tried to talk to me in my head, like I said." Danny was sitting cross-legged. She scowled at one of her feet, apparently unhappy with the way her shoe was tied, because she undid it.

"What did she say?"

"Just questions," she muttered at the shoe she was carefully tying.

"What questions?"

"I don't want to answer that."

"Why do you think it was Amanda who tried to mind-speak you?"

She darted a glance in his general direction. "I don't want to talk about her. Not until I can think things through and decide how much to say."

"It's important." How much to tell her? Most of it, he decided. She had a right to know her own heritage. "Do you know where your Gift comes from?"

"That's a weird question. We don't know why some people are Gifted and others aren't."

"I don't know where other Gifts come from, but I do know where touch sensitivity comes from. Dragons."

Her eyes widened. "That can't be right. I've never met a dragon, and besides, touch sensitives were around when dragons weren't. They've only been back in our realm for a year and a half."

"Apparently it's possible to have both a genetic heritage and a magical one. Magically speaking, touch sensitives have a dragon in their ancestry."

"You can't *know* that!"

"It's what the black dragon told me."

If seeing the wolves had been a marvel, this purely staggered her. Her mouth opened and closed twice without her saying a thing. Finally she managed one word. "How?"

"I don't know what the process is." He doubted that it had been the same for this girl as it had for Lily, whose Gift came from her grandmother. Surely, if dragons often turned humans into dragons, then back into humans, there would be stories or myths about it.

"A dragon," she breathed. "Me. A dragon is . . . my ancestor?"

"Magically, yes. Not genetically, and probably several generations back, since, as you say, the dragons were gone for a long time. Is Amanda a touch sensitive like you?"

She frowned. "Stop asking questions about her."

"I ask because mindspeech is an extremely rare ability. It's not a Gift, but a learned—"

"That's wrong. Telepathy's a Gift."

"Mindspeech isn't telepathy. They're both aspects of mind magic, but they're separate aspects. Telepathy is innate and mindspeech must be taught, just like regular speech. Its use requires training and intention. Telepaths—human telepaths, that is—have no control over their Gifts. They swim in a sea of thoughts, unable to shut them out, until they can't distinguish between their own thoughts and those of others. This drives them insane."

She nodded. "TIFS."

His eyebrows lifted. Very few people had heard of that recently coined acronym, which stood for Telepathically Induced Fragmentation of Self. "That's what the Omega Project calls it, yes."

She blinked. "You know about the Omega Project?"

"They approached Lily a little over a year ago, wanting her to use touch to determine which institutionalized patients suffered from TIFS. She turned them down."

Now her other shoe required attention. Or perhaps it was her sock; she pulled the shoe off. "I wish I had."

"You . . . they asked you to do that?" Rule was appalled. The Omega Project had been formed to investigate the link between telepathy and insanity, with the eventual goal of finding a cure. They'd asked for Lily's help with one specific study. The end result of TIFS was a persistent vegetative state, but the researchers had been interested in what they believed was the penultimate state—catatonia. Catatonia took several forms, all of which would be distressing for a young girl. For anyone, really, but especially someone so young.

"Mr. Smith asked me to work with them. I only did it once. I had a major meltdown." The sock came off. She inspected her foot. "Why did Lily turn them down?"

"Several reasons, but the most important one was the link to the CIA. She . . . do you have a blister?"

She sighed. "Yes. I hate blisters. I'll have to put a bandage on it. Did Lily know about the link to the NSA?"

"No." And neither, he thought, had Ruben—who should have.

"They funneled their contribution through the CIA so it wouldn't show up. Mr. Smith said it would make people uneasy if they thought a domestic intelligence agency was looking for telepaths. Which he was," Danny added. "Stands to reason. If your job is spying, you'd really like to have a telepath on the payroll if you could find one who wasn't crazy."

"But they all are."

She didn't respond. Maybe that was because she was digging though her backpack, looking for a bandage. Or maybe she was digging through her backpack to keep from giving herself away. "Is Amanda a touch sensitive? Or is she a telepath?"

She froze. Then she gave him a dirty look.

"It's important," he repeated softly. "Dragons use mindspeech. The potential for that ability is tied to touch sensitivity, so you could be the only one Lily could . . ." He swallowed. "Danny, the person who tried to mindspeak you might be Lily. That's why I need to know more about Amanda, so I can figure out if it was her, like you think. Or if it was Lily." He wanted it to be Lily, halfway believed that already. Wanted to believe it too much to trust his judgment.

She froze, still hunched over her backpack, but didn't speak.

"Danny, if it was her, that means she probably isn't very far away. It would really help to know that."

"Why did she come here?" the girl whispered. "Was it for me?"

"No, she didn't know about you. She came because . . . well, the reasons are complicated, but they have to do with the murder victim found at that little park."

"Murder victim?"

"Yes, she found the body. A man was killed with magic, though it looked like a sharp blade of some sort—"

She gave a shrill little cry. Her fingers starting playing her invisible instrument. Frantically.

"Would a real flute be better?" he asked. "Would it help you think?"

"I don't have a real flute. It's probably gone forever, like all Mama's things and our photographs and Zipper's leash and *everything*. I don't know what Mr. Smith did with my stuff. He probably threw it all away and I *don't know what to do!*"

Her eyes were wild with grief or panic or some combination. Mike started to reach for her. Rule signaled for him to be still. "Theo," he said, speaking as softly as he would in the presence of a frightened young animal, "doesn't Saul play the flute? Did he bring it with him?"

"I'll see." Theo stood and headed for the group of wolves lingering nearby.

They waited in silence. Danny stared at the ground. Her fingers resumed their motion. Stimming, she'd called it. He needed to find out what that meant. Rule poured the last of the coffee into his cup and sipped at the foul stuff, not looking at her. It was as much privacy as he could offer at the moment. The others imitated him, though Mike kept shooting him hard glances. He wanted to comfort Danny, but Rule's instincts—or maybe his wolf—said that the girl couldn't tolerate touch right now.

Finally Theo returned. Saul—returned to two legs and wearing the usual cutoffs—came with him, carrying a small case. He crouched in front of Danny and held it out.

"It's a Yamaha," she said reverently. "Is it really okay? I can play it?" At his nod, she opened the case and carefully took out the pieces, screwing them together. She held it near her mouth and closed her eyes. Then lowered it. "I haven't played in so long. I won't sound good. Could I . . . is there a way for me to be alone?"

Rule struggled with himself. He wanted answers now. Wanted to know if Lily had somehow reached out and touched this young woman's mind. If she could do it again. If she was all right and could tell them *where she was* . . . he took a deep breath. Danny was tough as nails in some ways, yet fragile in others. If she had truly been a child of his clan, what would he do?

Probably, he thought grimly, he'd continue to browbeat her, as gently as possible. But knowing the attempt at mindspeech had come from Lily wouldn't tell him where she was or what kind of shape she was in. It was of no immediate help . . . except to his raw emotions.

"José found a tent for you," he said at last. "Complete with sleeping bag. It's as much privacy as I can offer. Will that do?"

She nodded eagerly.

"Danny . . . if someone tries to talk in your head again, will you come tell me right away? If it's Lily . . ."

She thought it over first. Then nodded.

Twenty minutes later Danny, her backpack, and Saul's flute were all in the small tent José had cleared out for her. She'd wanted to retreat there immediately, but Rule insisted that her blistered foot be washed, the blister disinfected and bandaged. Then Mike had to show her where the latrine was, since her human nose didn't provide that information, before escorting her to her temporary quarters.

Almost the moment the flap closed, a few uncertain notes floated out. Then, more strongly, a scale, followed by the opening bar to "Greensleeves" . . . high and pure and lovely, with none of the fumbled notes or hesitations Rule had expected. Everyone listened. Most of those on two legs smiled.

Rule did, too. Then he sighed and got down to business. Hal Brownbeck waited about twenty feet away. A much younger man stood with him. "Theo, is the young man with Hal the one you recommended for my other *nuntius*?"

"Richard Swan. He's young and untrained, but his memory's good. I told him to ask Hal for a quick introduction to acting as *nuntius*." The councillor lifted a hand, beckoning. The two men started for them. "A question, Rho, if I may."

Rule nodded.

"What happens to the girl in twenty hours?"

"I will offer to extend my protection."

"Is this wise? She's charming in her vulnerability and lack of fear, but she's also a liability. Hiding her from the authorities may be difficult and exposes us to possible arrest."

Rule smiled. Theo was coming along well. When Rule first became Leidolf Rho, Theo had been exceedingly deferential on the surface and deeply hostile underneath. The hostility was no surprise, under the circumstances. The deference, however, had been excessive. The previous Rho had been a son of a bitch who tolerated no dissent, even from his councillors—whose job was to disagree at times.

Theo was still polite, but a good deal less hostile. He was learning to disagree. Moreover, this was exactly the right sort of question to put when they had an audience. It allowed Rule to reinforce his orders with reason. "Danny is the most important person in this camp right now. There's more to her than the, ah, charming vulnerability you mention. At the age of sixteen, she penetrated the NSA's computers by stealing the log-in information of a high-ranking official there. She used his access to create a ghost persona which gave her ongoing, undetectable access to those computers. She has identified our enemy and may offer the means of bringing him down. I suspect she'll be able to help us hide her. She's been in hiding from the NSA and Homeland Security for nearly a year now, so clearly she knows something about how to do it."

Theo's eyebrows had risen. "I see."

"Any more questions?"

"Not just now."

Rule gave his two *nunti* prepaid Visa cards that shouldn't be on any governmental list and told them how to identify and be identified by their targets. Richard would drive to D.C. to reach Ruben—or Deborah, if Ruben had been arrested. Hal would have to fly to reach Abel in Oregon, but his ID matched his apparent age and he wasn't known to be lupus, so his name shouldn't be flagged.

"I will break my message into three parts," he told them. "Part One. Our principle enemy is Edward Smith, special assistant to the director of the NSA. He is being assisted, knowingly or unknowingly, by a person or persons in Homeland Security. His motives and goals are unclear, as is the extent of his organization, but he does have an organization. The nature and extent of his actions suggest he is smart, patient, and methodical. I believe he is unaware of the existence of the Shadow Unit."

"But—" José started, then clamped his mouth shut and ducked his head low in apology.

Rule continued as if José hadn't spoken. "While he has

targeted both Ruben and myself, in both cases the charges being leveled are fake, based on data tampering. If he knew about our involvement in a clandestine organization but was unable to find proof, he might decide to manufacture evidence—but that evidence would expose or at least suggest the existence of the Shadows. That hasn't happened, which is why I believe he doesn't know about the Shadow Unit.

"It's unclear why he targeted me. His reasons for targeting Ruben are also murky, but obviously include shifting the blame for his own clandestine operation in order to avoid discovery.

"That operation involves using a nonprofit, Bright Haven Refuge for Gifted Young People, to acquire custody of Gifted children and teens who've been orphaned or abandoned. These children and teens are tested and trained and given a drug which enhances their power and control. My source believes that neither Congress nor the administration is aware of what Mr. Smith and his people are up to."

He paused then and had the men repeat what he'd said. Unsurprisingly, Hal did beautifully. Richard needed coaching, but after a few repetitions did fairly well. Rule went on to Part Two—a brief bio of Danny, what she'd done, and how she'd done it, with a description of the records she'd sent to the reporter and how they'd been altered to direct blame at Ruben.

Again he stopped and had them repeat that, then repeat both parts. "Part Three. It seems likely that these records were altered magically. Danny believes it would be impossible to alter records kept in so many places simultaneously and undetectably without the use of magic. This suggests that Smith has at least one extremely competent practitioner at his disposal. Danny doesn't believe Smith himself has the knowledge, experience, or training to do this, nor does she think the children and teens under his control have such training." Rule paused. "Based on comments made by Cullen Seabourne about the nature of the process needed to use magic on computerized records without disrupting the system, I believe Smith's practitioner may be a sorcerer."

AN hour later, the two men had left for their separate destinations. Rule had spoken at greater length with Theo and José, getting their input and speculations. At last he headed for the flimsy sanctuary of his own tent.

Danny was still playing "Greensleeves."

An hour after that, the flute at last fell silent. A soft rain had started, more a heavy mist than drops. Rule stared up at the roof of his tiny shelter, listening to the hushed sound of it on canvas.

For the twenty-one thousand, four hundred and forty nights he had been on this planet, he had mostly slept alone. Roughly ninety percent of the time, according to the calculations he'd performed while trying to bore himself into sleep. You'd think he had the knack of it.

Apparently not. He couldn't sleep alone tonight. No, this morning, for the darkness was softening, stirred by the approach of dawn. He couldn't shut his mind off, couldn't stop from thinking about Lily. Couldn't stop—as his wolf put it—living in a world of terrible maybes. Four-in-the-morning thinking at what must be nearer six than four.

He gave up, stood up, and Changed. A moment later a large black-and-silver wolf trotted out, unbothered by the misty rain. He curled up with a small group of his fellows. They woke; one licked his muzzle briefly.

Warmed by the feel and scent of clan, equipped with a brain less likely to founder on its own imaginings, at last he slept.

TWENTY-FIVE

OUTSIDE, the sun had barely crept above the horizon, but sunlight or the lack of it made no difference in the underground conference room. One of the fluorescent lights hummed loudly.

Edward Smith occupied his usual spot at the head of the table, with the soldierly Greg at his right hand. Sharon sat at his left; the redheaded Chuck was across from her. The man sitting in the chair at the foot of the table was Greg's opposite in every way except gender. Where Greg was tall, upright, and tidy, this man was short, slumped, and rumpled. His pale hair was at least two months overdue for a trim, and his short-sleeved yellow shirt might have been grabbed off a pile of dirty clothes.

At the moment, he was using the tail of that shirt to clean his glasses while he spoke. ". . . twenty-seven heat signatures in the werewolf camp last night, but we . . . um . . ." He put his glasses back on and shuffled his papers. "We have no way of knowing how many . . . um . . . were away from camp. The state has agreed to . . . um . . . additional flyovers, but there are over eleven thousand acres in the . . . um . . . Crown City Wildlife Area. And of course, there are those . . . um . . . homeless men. Can't tell from the air who's homeless and who's . . . um . . . a werewolf."

"Thank you, Barry. You may go."

Barry nodded and did so.

As soon as the door closed, Chuck spoke. "God, but it's painful to listen to him."

"We've got a bigger problem than Barry's speech habits," Sharon snapped. "In case you weren't listening—"

"Painful as the experience was, I heard every word." Chuck sighed. "Times like these I wish I still smoked." He looked at the round little man at the head of the table. "So what are we doing about it?"

"At the moment, planning. Our response will depend—"

The door opened again. "Sorry I'm late," Tom said breezily, not sounding sorry at all. He shut the door behind him. Today the Asian man wore ripped black skinny jeans, a black T-shirt with a smoking skull, and athletic shoes. No socks. His shaggy hair and the shoulders of his tee were damp. "There are too many idiots on the road, slowing down those of us who actually know how to drive in the rain. And this is a pathetically early hour for those of us who don't live in D.C."

Sharon gave him a sour look. "And yet I managed to make it on time."

"That's because you're a better person than me." He smirked at her and sat on Chuck's side of the table, leaving a chair between himself and the other man. "What have I missed?"

Smith answered. "Barry updated us on the number of lupi who've gathered in the wildlife area outside Whistle. Thirty have been confirmed. He declined to estimate how many might be nearby who weren't in camp when the state sent the helicopter."

"Ohio's sharing information freely, then?" Chuck asked. "With us or with Homeland?"

"Homeland, of course. Eric says the state authorities have been most helpful, unlike our brother agency at the federal level. He's annoyed by the Bureau's foot-dragging."

Sharon frowned. "I thought moving Mathison into the head spot at Unit Twelve would take care of interagency problems."

"That was essential, but not sufficient to make the FBI as a whole eager to cooperate with Homeland. You know how arrogant they are. They continue to believe everyone else should cooperate with them. We're getting off-topic, Chuck, how is Prism doing?"

"Buggy as hell," Chuck said promptly, "being still in beta, but I should have some probables within three to four hours. After that, we'll have to pass it to the regular system for full intercept."

Smith nodded. "Sharon, please advise us about Adrian's efforts to find Target Duo among the lupi."

She shook her head. "Still nothing. He can't even get a clear enough image of the werewolf camp for me to confirm Barry's count. We tried increasing the dosage slightly, but he isn't able to penetrate . . . well, he calls it a fog. We don't have an explanation."

Perhaps Smith was the only one who saw the quick flicker of reaction on Tom's face. "Tom? Do you have something to add?"

The Asian man cocked his head as if listening. "Not really, although this convinces me that Turner—"

"No names, Tom."

"—that Target Duo is at the lupi camp."

Sharon's eyes narrowed. "Why?"

"I can't say," he answered sweetly.

"That's not acceptable. If you know something we don't—"

"I know so many things you don't, Sharon. We haven't the time to list them all, much less go into detail."

"And yet," Smith said softly, "this seems especially pertinent."

Tom looked at him. "I can't say. Not won't. This is privileged information under the terms our deal."

Smith's fingers tapped once on the table while he thought that over. Reluctantly he nodded. "Very well. Let's move on."

"Let's do." Tom smiled. "I want to know what you're doing to find Lily Yu."

Smith's eyebrows twitched in an aborted frown. "I believe you were included in the update from Eric which I forwarded last night."

"Yes, and a wonderful example of bureaucratic gobbledegook that was. Translated, it means: 'It's not my fault.'"

"Indeed, it isn't Eric's fault. Special Agent Yu—"

"Vanished." His eyebrows lifted. "That is what happened, isn't it . . . Edward?"

The young man's voice was pleasant. Maybe it was the

deliberate use of Smith's first name which made the question so insolent. The two men's eyes met.

Chuck scowled. Sharon burst out, "The hell with this. If he can't show some respect—"

"No, no." Smith dismissed the protests with a small wave of one hand. His eyes never left Tom's. "Tom is keenly aware that while his interests and ours overlap, they do not coincide. Are you accusing me of something specific, Tom?"

"Specific?" Tom drawled. "No, I merely find myself . . . wondering. How odd it is for Yu to disappear when she did! And you can't seem to find that underage sensitive of yours, can you? She's vanished. Yu's vanished. Now Turner's vanished, too. And so I find myself wondering—am I witnessing an unfortunate level of incompetence? Or might you have arranged one or more of those disappearances and forgotten to mention it to me?"

Surprisingly, Smith chuckled. "Oh, Tom. Yes, certainly I had Target Tres—I really must insist that you use the correct designation—kidnapped. She will make an excellent replacement for Demi. A Unit Twelve agent will be so much more cooperative and easier to manage than a teenager."

After a moment the younger man smiled and flung one hand up in a fencer's acknowledgment of a hit. "Your point. But it is odd that Target Tres disappeared just now."

"Not really. Look at the timing. She disappeared right after Target Duo was arrested. She must have assumed she was a target, too, though she can't have actually known anything. Disappearing is a rather dramatic response to such a vague assumption, but she's a rather dramatic young woman. Not that we can afford to allow either her or Target Duo to remain on the loose—and that, if I may be allowed to drag the conversation back on-topic, is why we're here." He paused for emphasis. "Tom is right about one thing. We have lost track of three people. I am very concerned about Demi connecting with either Target Duo or Target Tres."

"Whoa," Chuck said. "Isn't that a bit of a leap? We've narrowed the area down where Demi might be, sure, based on Tom's triangulation—"

"And a tedious job that was, too," Tom put in.

"—but we're still talking about an area of over a thousand square miles. Unless there's information I'm unaware of—"

"There is." Smith tapped his fingers on the table again, four times in rapid-fire—*tap-tap-tap-tap*. It was an unusual show of agitation. "Two of Eric's people have been making the rounds of establishments in Whistle. A young man who works at a small service station in Whistle bears a strong resemblance to Demi. Two of Eric's people discovered this when they spoke with the young man's employer last night. They then went to have a chat with the young man, who calls himself Danny Stone. He wasn't home. They've since corroborated the resemblance with several other residents of Whistle, including his landlady. The timing of his arrival in Whistle fits with when Demi fled D.C. last year."

Silence. Then, tentatively, Chuck said, "Demi doesn't have any male relatives."

Sharon rolled her eyes. "For God's sake, Chuck! She's been passing as male."

"I know that, dammit. I was eliminating one possibility, not—"

"Then why didn't you say so? If that's her—" Sharon broke off abruptly, her lips clamped tightly.

"She knows too much," Tom said softly. "I've told you that before."

The silence dragged on longer this time. Finally Sharon sighed. "And I've opposed disposing of her. I still think the reasons for keeping her alive are valid. It's not sentiment," she insisted. "We *need* a sensitive."

Smith nodded. "Like you, Sharon, I've opposed eliminating Demi. Unlike you, I will admit that some of my reluctance stems from sentiment. But I have not and will not allow sentiment to interfere with our operation. I have always weighed Demi's potential value against the risk she presents. In the past, her value trumped the risk. Not anymore."

"Are we sure of that?" Chuck looked troubled. "We don't even know definitely that Turner is in the area. The influx of lupi suggests he might be, but I can think of other possible explanations, and he'd be an idiot to go where he told his lawyer he would."

"And even if he is," Sharon put in, "proximity isn't connection. We have nothing to suggest that Demi's with Target Duo—"

Tom snorted. "I had no idea you were such a believer in coincidence. By the time you get confirmation that Turner is in the area—or Yu, if she really is wandering around freely—"

"Quit suggesting that Target Tres is in our hands!" Chuck snapped. "The boss told you—"

"Pax, Chuck. Naturally I accept Edward's assurances. But Target Tres might have gone missing on purpose. I can see her leaving the D.C. area in an effort to assist her husband, just as he broke bail in order to look for her. That would be foolish, but love does scramble people's brains. And yet I don't think we can count on that, can we? Not with so much at stake."

For the next twenty minutes they discussed what was at stake—they agreed about that—and what to do about it. They didn't agree about that. Tom supported Smith's proposal to deploy Cerberus; Chuck vacillated, worried because their stock of Lodan was so low; and Sharon adamantly opposed it.

Finally Smith said, "I have a meeting I cannot postpone. We'll have to end discussion now."

"But if we use Cerberus," Sharon said stubbornly, "the risk of exposure is so much higher than the purely hypothetical risk associated with—"

"Enough." Smith remained pleasant, but his voice was firm. "Despite my preference for consensus, this is not a democracy. Your opinion is noted. However, I judge the risk to be much higher if we do not deploy Cerberus. You will ready them." Smith permitted himself a small, prim smile. "It will soon be clear to local, state, and federal authorities that the werewolves gathered at the wildlife area are extremely dangerous. Therefore, extreme measures to deal with them are both justified and necessary."

TWENTY-SIX

~

MORNINGS and Demi were not friends. That's why she usually skipped them. This one was especially unwelcome for reasons that escaped her sleep-fogged brain. Also weird. Even
before she opened her eyes, nothing was right. Her bed was too
hard. Someone—a man—was talking way too close by, which
made no sense. Mrs. MacGruder didn't allow people to just
wander around on . . .

Her eyes opened. She wasn't in the trailer she rented from
Mrs. MacGruder. She was on the run, hiding out in a tent in a
clearing in the woods. Just outside that tent were Rule Turner
and fifty-six more lupi.

That got her sitting up, but then she didn't know what to do,
with none of her usual morning actions available. There was no
bathroom, no Wi-Fi, no clock. She had to think it through. She
did have clean clothes, but only one set, and since she couldn't
shower, there didn't seem much point in changing anything but
her underwear. But there was a latrine.

She grimaced. A trench, that's all it was, which was why she
didn't much care for camping out. It hadn't been too smelly and
nasty, though. Most of the time, Mike had told her, the lupi
didn't use the latrine, it being simpler to take care of business as
a wolf. At least there was toilet paper.

The tent wasn't tall enough for her to stand up, which made putting on clean tighty-whities awkward, especially since she was sore from last night's hiking. Her thighs, mostly, though her calves were a bit achy, too. She pulled her jeans back on, thought about getting out clean socks, and decided it could wait. Washing stuff wasn't going to be easy here, and she'd put on clean socks last night after bandaging her blister. Then she eyed the coiled elastic bandage she'd set on top of her backpack and shrugged. Didn't seem much point in binding her breasts when everyone knew she was a girl. She didn't have a bra, but the shirt was big and sloppy and her breasts were small, so that shouldn't matter.

She pulled on last night's socks and her shoes, grabbed the roll of TP that Mike had given her last night, and reached for the flute case. She needed to return that.

Her hands were shaky. She looked down at them, surprised. She was scared? She thought hard, trying to identify the fluttery feeling. Happy, scared, uncertain . . . giddy. That was the word.

It turned out her fantasy hadn't been ruined after all. She was practically living it. Fifty-six lupi, half of them in wolf-form, waited on the other side of the canvas flap. She was giddy with lupi.

It was very bright outside. The air smelled like coffee and bacon and spices. There were a couple men near the stone-edged fire, but most of the lupi were at the other end of the clearing—some on two legs, some on four. They were listening to that man who'd talked to Rule Turner when they first arrived last night. She couldn't remember his name, but he seemed to be the only Hispanic person here, so he was easy to recognize. He appeared to be directing them in what looked like a complicated dance. It was fascinating. Wolves and men moved in a complex pattern, weaving—

A cold, wet nose poked her arm. She jumped. "Oh. Good morning," she said politely to the wolf looking at her. She studied him carefully. He was really big, plus his ruff was more black than silver, and there was a roundish spot of paler fur over one shoulder . . . "Mike?"

The wolf wagged his tail once.

"What are they doing down there? Dancing? I—oh. You can't talk right now."

He snorted and looked pointedly at her foot, then at her face.

"I don't understand."

He tapped her heel with his nose, right where the bandage was.

"Oh, my blister? It's okay."

He took a couple steps away, then looked at her.

"You want me to go with you?"

He nodded.

Embarrassed, she lifted the roll of TP without speaking.

He nodded again.

Her fantasy had never involved toilet paper. She sighed.

The latrine was located well inside the trees, so she started walking. She was pretty stiff. Her blister wasn't bothering her, but her thighs were. She liked Mike, but she didn't like him escorting her to the latrine. She knew lupi didn't have human attitudes about bodies. They had no modesty at all that way, but she was human and she did. She told Mike all that. She didn't think he listened because he went with her anyway. After a while, he loped ahead. A few moments later he came back, grinned at her, and sat.

"You're going to wait here?"

He nodded.

"You went ahead to . . ." She thought about it. "See if I'd be alone?"

Another nod.

"Thank you." Maybe he had been listening. "Would you watch this for me?" She set the flute case down beside him.

Once she'd dealt with the difference between fantasy and reality, Demi rejoined Mike and reclaimed the flute and they returned to the clearing. For the first time she noticed the beat-up old pickup parked behind the largest tent. The truck bed held three large coolers. Someone must have driven it bumpety-thumpety across the ground because no roads reached the clearing. It must be hard to feed so many people without electricity or anything. She was thinking about that and about her empty stomach when they reached the campfire.

Two men waited there—an older man with dark skin, white hair, and a smile, and a pale-skinned man with hair that didn't quite manage to be brown or blond, but hit somewhere in between. Both wore cut-off jeans and shoes. Mike gave a little yip. The older man nodded at him, still smiling. Mike trotted off.

She wished he hadn't left. Had she met these men when they were furry, or were they the strangers they seemed to be? They introduced themselves—the smiling older man was Theo and the brown-blond-haired one was John—and told her to sit down and have some coffee. A large coffeepot rested on a stone next to the fire; a huge cast iron pot was suspended over it on a tripod. She peered inside the big pot. Chili, the all-meat kind. Oh, well. They were lupi, after all.

She sat and politely refused the coffee Theo held out. "Water's fine," she told them. "Um . . . I need to return Saul's flute. Do you know where he is?"

"He's four-footed right now," the younger one—John— said. "You want some chili? It's almost ready. Or if you'd like more breakfast-type food, I could fix some bacon and eggs pretty quick."

"Thank you, but I don't eat meat."

No one said anything for a moment. Theo had stopped smiling. He asked, "Are you one of those vegans?"

"No, I'm vegetarian. You're carnivores," she told them, nodding firmly. Nodding was one of those gestures that meant different things, depending on the context. Demi wasn't good at context, but an article she'd read said that people nodded to affirm the other person. This seemed like a good time to add an affirmation. "You're supposed to eat meat. Technically I'm an omnivore, so you'd expect me to eat meat, too, but I like animals too much to eat them. Plus there's substantial evidence that the consumption of meat—some say all animal products, but that's contested—leads to inflammation, which is a cause or contributing factor in all sorts of diseases. I do eat eggs," she added hopefully.

John scrambled her some eggs. Theo emptied the coffee from her mug and filled it with water. While she was eating, Mike rejoined them. He was a man again. She smiled at him so he wouldn't know she was disappointed.

"They're drilling," Mike said, sitting beside her. "It looks like a dance, but it's a drill."

She blinked.

"When I was four-footed, you asked what they were doing at the other end of the field. They're drilling."

Reminded, she looked that way. "Oh! Look at them!" The man-shaped lupi had separated from the wolves and were performing what looked like coordinated acrobatics—leaps and throws and tucks and rolls and things she didn't have a word for.

"The chili smells great," Mike commented.

"It's about ready," John said, adding, "She doesn't eat meat."

Now the wolves joined in, weaving in and out of the moving acrobats . . .

"Danny."

They moved faster and faster, so swift and beautiful she could hardly breathe for the wonder of it.

"Danny!" Mike said loudly.

"What?" She didn't look away from the performance at the other end of the clearing.

"We're not sure what to feed you."

"I eat pretty much everything except meat. Beans, vegetables, eggs, pasta, dairy, all sorts of grains." Nonvegetarians always thought it was hard to cook without meat. She didn't know why. Reluctantly she tore her eyes away from the beautiful wolves. "If you have a smaller pot I could use, I've got a package of dried beans in my pack I could fix. I've never cooked over a campfire, but it can't be too different from cooking on a stove."

"I can cook beans," John said, "but they won't be done for hours."

"I just ate, so I won't be hungry for hours. Where should I wash my plate?" she asked. "I don't see . . . you're leaving again?" she said in dismay to Mike. She didn't know why she felt better when he was nearby, but she did.

"José signaled for me. I'll be back."

John didn't want her to wash her plate right now, but after a bit of discussion, he agreed that she could help with the after-lunch cleanup, so he wanted her to come with him to see where things were kept. Theo assured her he'd watch the flute for her.

The largest tent held supplies, including several five-gallon water bottles. John would clean the pot himself—it was seasoned cast iron, and he was particular about how it was cared

for. For everything else they used four dishpans and six people, set up assembly-line style. It sounded very efficient. She
scraped her plate into the trash sack, then put it in one of the
dishpans along with her fork and mug. John added a splash of
water so everything wouldn't dry on hard.

Last night she'd decided what she should tell Rule Turner
about Amanda. Once she'd been alone and calmed by the
music, it hadn't been that hard to figure out what had to stay
secret because it pointed at Nicky. As they headed back to the
cooking fire, she asked reluctantly, "Where's Mr. Turner? Rule,
I mean." He'd told her to call him that. "I should talk to him."

"Rule's checking something out."

"What?"

"He didn't give me permission to tell you."

She didn't mind putting off her conversation with Mr.
Turner. With Rule, that is. She was kind of dreading it. "Is it
okay if I ask you questions? I have a lot of questions about lupi,
but I can't tell when I'm asking too many or the wrong sort.
You'll have to tell me if I do that."

Theo—they'd reached him by then—smiled. "You may ask
whatever you wish of me, José, or Mike. We won't take offense,
though we may not answer. Don't ask the others. They won't
know what is permitted."

So for a while she wallowed in questions, asking all sorts
of things—stuff she'd wondered about forever and questions
that had just occurred to her. What did the Change feel like?
How many clans were there? Could they truly heal any wound?
How long did they live? (Theo didn't answer that one.) Why
weren't there any female lupi? Did they have jobs? What happened to those jobs when they left to come here? Where were
all their cars?—because obviously, they hadn't walked all the
way here from California, and the only vehicle she'd seen was
that old pickup truck.

That's when she found out that José was the only one from
Nokolai Clan. Everyone else was part of a clan called Leidolf,
which claimed the area around here as its territory. She stared.
"But Rule Turner is Nokolai, and he's your Rho."

"He's Leidolf as well."

"But how did he become your Rho?"

"That's not a question I can answer," Theo said.

"But I—"

"You may ask Rule, if you wish." Something about the way his smile folded into his face made her think of her grandmother. Granmè had died many years ago, but Demi had photos of her . . . at least she used to. She remembered those photos, so she knew Theo didn't really look much like Granmè. Why did he make Demi think of her? "I doubt he'll tell you, but you may ask."

"I need to finish up," John said. "They're about to head back for lunch. Maybe you'd help me carry some bowls, Danny."

She did. She'd read that lupi ate more than humans, and that seemed to be true, judging by the size of the bowls. She made three trips between the supply tent and the cook fire, carrying oversize plastic bowls. John's timing was good. By the time she fetched the last stack of bowls, the men had begun forming a line. One of them brought over one of the big coolers, which she saw was filled with iced soft drinks. John dipped a big ladle into the chili, filled a bowl, and handed it to Theo.

Mike didn't get in line. He came straight to Demi. "I need to talk to you. Come with me while I get some chili," he said. He went straight to the head of the line, ahead of everyone except José, who was filling his bowl.

She put her hands on her hips. "Cutting in line is rude."

"We don't do first-come-first-served." José had finished, so Mike started ladling chili into his. "Since Rule isn't in camp, Theo is served first. You can see that he already started eating— that's so no one has to wait once we get our food. After Theo comes José, then me. Jason would be after me, but he's wolf right now, so . . . never mind the list. Everyone lines up according to his status."

"What's my status?"

"As *ospi*, you may eat whenever you wish."

"Can I get a Coke when I wish? Because now would be good."

"Yes. Get me one, too, please."

She did. Mike selected a spot that looked no different from any other section of ground and sat. She didn't. He looked up. "Sit down, Danny."

"I don't know how close to sit. That's not always easy for

me to figure out with humans, and you aren't human. What's a friendly distance, but not pushy?"

He looked at her in a way that made her uncomfortable, though she wasn't sure why. "Between a foot and two feet, I guess."

She sat one and a half feet from his left elbow. "What about the ones who are wolves? When do they get to eat?"

Mike started eating, but his eyes weren't on his food. He was watching everyone around them as if someone might decide to attack him or steal his food. "About half of them are due to Change soon. They'll eat once they're two-footed. The ones who stay wolf will have some kind of raw meat." He glanced at her. "Does the sight of raw meat bother you?"

"No more than cooked meat does. Why can't the wolves have chili, too?"

He shrugged. "They could, but when we're four-legged, we usually prefer raw meat."

"Is everyone taking turns being wolves?"

"Except for those whose position calls for them to stay two-footed. Take John. As cook, he needs hands and has to be able to tell his helpers what to do. José and the squad leaders have to be able to talk, too. I'm assigned to you, so—"

"Assigned to me?"

"You heard Rule last night. He placed you in my charge."

"I thought that meant introductions."

He gave her another quick glance. This time he smiled. He didn't do that often. Mike had a hard face—not mean, exactly, but hard. She had trouble understanding expressions on normal people beyond knowing if they were smiling or frowning. Mike didn't seem to have expressions. If she'd first met him when he was a man instead of a wolf, she probably would have thought he was scary.

He spooned up the last of his chili. "Introductions are part of it. Danny—"

"What's the rest of it?"

"I take care of you. Keep you safe."

For some reason that made her stomach feel funny. Not an unpleasant sort of funny, but one she couldn't identify.

"In order to keep you safe, I need to talk to you about how

we're going to hide you when the time comes. There was a copter hovering over the camp last night, checking us out. The cops are bound to come in person at some point. Maybe soon."

The not-unpleasant funny feeling vanished, replaced by a familiar tightness she had no trouble identifying. She reminded herself that her fantasy—which had several story lines—had usually included some kind of danger to make things interesting. Real danger wasn't as much fun as the fantasy kind, though. "I'm good at climbing."

TWENTY-SEVEN

~~~

RULE crossed the open meadow at a lope, ignoring the two men who ran with him—Reno on his right and several yards away, Eric thirty feet behind. He was in a foul mood.

Right before she'd been kidnapped, Lily had been planning to speak with the homeless men who lived in the wilderness area. Rule had decided he needed to follow through with that plan. Lily's phone had gone missing when she did, but it had automatically synced with her laptop the night before. The FBI had that laptop, but before giving it to them, José had e-mailed himself the crime scene pictures she'd taken. This morning, Rule had loaded them onto the prepaid phone he was using.

There'd been five men in camp when he arrived; two more had shown up while he was visiting. Their number varied, according to Wheeler, who was their unofficial leader. Four of the seven Rule had met were the camp's founders and had been coming here for years. None of them stayed in camp through the winter; most went to Cincinnati—a fair trek for men with no transportation other than their feet, but they had hope of finding a warm bed in a shelter there. They lived in part by setting traps, Rule knew. His men had spotted a couple of them, and he'd smelled the pelts someone had fleshed and salted. That along with gifts of canned goods from charitable organizations saw them through the warm months. Wheeler made sure they didn't annoy the rangers; they kept the camp clean, packing out their trash.

Not that Wheeler or the others had been eager to chat. They were suspicious and didn't appreciate outsiders intruding into their territory—an attitude he understood—but patience and a few packs of cigarettes had eventually broken the ice.

Six of them had recognized the dead man. The seventh man might have, but he wouldn't talk to Rule. According to HSI, the dead man was named Jason Humboldt, and their agent. According to the homeless men, the dead man's first name was Larry. They were unsure of his last name, but Wheeler thought it had been Hoffman or Stockman. Something ending in "man" anyway.

HSI claimed that their agent had been undercover and on the trail of that dreadful terrorist Rule knew as Danny. They said he'd been in North Carolina until recently and must have followed her here.

The homeless men said Larry had lived with them since April of this year. Before that he'd been in Huntington—"no real shelters, but the Baptists open up their basement when it get cold 'nuff." One of the men had spent last winter in Huntington and had known Larry pretty well. He'd been a good guy, they said—not too bright, but "always ready to help out, you know what I mean?"

They hadn't known about his death. A couple of them were pretty torn up about it.

It was theoretically possible that all of them were lying or mistaken. It was also theoretically possible that Rule would spontaneously combust in the next thirty seconds. He didn't feel he had to take either possibility into account.

The dead man had not been an HSI agent. The two agents who'd spoken to Lily had either been deceived themselves or were part of a more general conspiracy within the organization. Given how helpful Homeland had been to Danny's Mr. Smith, Rule was fairly sure there was at least one highly placed conspirator in the sprawling department, someone able to mobilize HSI in pursuit of fake terrorists.

Rule was badly out of his depth. How could he take on both Homeland Security and the NSA? Even if he hadn't been on

the run, he didn't see what he could do against two governmental behemoths. Ruben might have some chance, with the
resources of the FBI behind him—but Ruben didn't have that
now. He might be facing arrest himself.

Was that why Ruben had been targeted? If so, Rule had
made real progress this morning . . . and it didn't help. It didn't
get him one step closer to finding Lily.

He wanted to hit someone. Several someones. How did he
go about unmasking Smith? How could he learn who in
Homeland Security was working with the bastard? He didn't
know where to begin.

Lily would. Lily was missing.

The hell with unmasking Smith. He wanted to sink his teeth
into the man's neck. And that wouldn't help him find Lily,
either, dammit, much as it might relieve his feelings. *Think,
dammit.* He'd learned something this morning. He didn't see
how it helped him find Lily, but maybe it was why Lily had
been kidnapped—to prevent her from discovering Homeland
Security's duplicity. It would do little good for Rule to
announce their misidentification of the body, but Lily had the
authority to investigate even HSI.

Still, that made little sense. Killing was much easier than
kidnapping, but the one thing Rule knew for certain was that
Lily was alive. Were Smith and Company squeamish about
murder? There was a dead man to say otherwise.

Why was there a dead man? A homeless man who'd been
killed by magical means . . .

Smith had been collecting Gifted children and teens.

Rule considered that for the last mile of his run.

José and the spicy scent of chili greeted him when he reached
the clearing. "All quiet here," José said.

"Good. Any sign of that helicopter?" Rule had glimpsed it
earlier when he was on his way to the homeless men's camp,
but well off to the west.

"It hasn't been back."

"Also good. Reno, bring me a bowl of that chili, please, and
something to drink. Then you and Eric can eat. José, ask Theo
to join me here, please. I'd like to speak with him and you apart
from the others."

He ate standing up, filling in José and Theo between bites.

The briefing didn't take long, but Theo wanted to discuss another subject. Money. They were running low, and John had asked for funds to buy more supplies.

Leidolf was not a wealthy clan. Its finances had been badly mismanaged under the previous Rho, leaving the clan unable to offer its people what Rule considered basic services—college assistance, business loans, jobs in clan-owned companies. Rule had been working to change that, but the rebuilding process left the clan's resources tied up in investments that either lacked liquidity or were difficult for him to access at the moment. He'd been able to tap the emergency fund via Alex, but that was getting dangerously low.

It was frustrating as hell. His own accounts were undoubtedly being watched. It looked like he'd have to liquidate one of Leidolf's investments, even though Leidolf didn't have any it could afford to lose.

Unless he decided he could switch hats.

Rule acted as CFO for both of his clans along with the Shadow Unit—and Nokolai, unlike Leidolf, *was* a wealthy clan. Wearing all three of his hats, Rule controlled assets worth several hundred million dollars. Much of that wasn't liquid, of course, and almost all of it was inaccessible to a man who didn't dare use his ID.

Almost, but not all. Nokolai had three emergency funds. One was held by a bank. One was actual gold, hidden beneath Isen's home. The third was even less conventional and intended for just this sort of situation—a deposit made years ago with a large criminal organization. That account paid no interest and would incur a sizable penalty upon withdrawal, but if he chose, Rule could have nearly three hundred thousand dollars in hand today. Probably within hours.

It was a tricky ethical point. He was entitled to use Nokolai resources to preserve his own freedom and look for his *nadia*, who was both clan and Chosen. But using Nokolai's secret fund to keep from harming Leidolf financially . . . that was skirting close to the edge.

He considered it, frowning, for several moments, then spoke briskly. "We may need funds in the next few days over and above what it costs to feed the men. I'll arrange it." He took out his phone and used one of the few phone numbers he'd memorized. After waiting through three rings he disconnected, then called again. Two rings. Again he disconnected and called back. This time he let it ring until it was answered with a simple "*Bongiorno.*"

He told the man in Italian that he wished to speak to his friend, Charlie. A click, a wait, then a man who asked in American English how he could be of service.

Rule told him.

When he hung up, the other two were watching him—José expectantly, Theo with an expression of gloomy astonishment.

"My Rho," Theo said, ducking his head, "I don't know how you did that—or what exactly you did—but I'm concerned about how Leidolf can repay this debt. Such loans generally come with a very high interest rate."

"There is no loan. There is, however, a debt." Rule drew on the mantles. Both mantles at once. He'd never done that before, and the sensation was distinctly odd. "Theo, José, I call on you to be witnesses for your clans. I speak now as Nokolai Lu Nuncio. Nokolai is contributing that money toward the welfare of its Lu Nuncio and the rescue of the Chosen. I declare that Leidolf incurs no obligation to Nokolai for its use of part or all of these funds. However, I make a claim against Leidolf for the penalty Nokolai pays in order to access the money in this way." He told them how much that penalty was—and switched hats. "I speak now as Rho of Leidolf. I hereby acknowledge the justness of Nokolai's claim and accept the debt on behalf of my clan."

Theo's eyebrows had climbed up his forehead, but there was a small smile on his mouth. "That was a remarkable . . . ah, I so witness."

"I so witness," José repeated.

"Good. The funds will be delivered this afternoon in a mix of cash and debit cards." Time to talk to Danny. "Where . . . ah, there she is. Thank you, Theo, you may go. José, with me." On the way across camp, he briefed José on the man who would deliver the funds so the guards could be alerted to watch for him.

"Got it," José said. "Uh, Rule, do you think Isen will—"

"I think my father has never given me or anyone else cause to doubt that he would honor my word." Isen might not like it. He might dislike it enough to do something Rule would in turn dislike, but he wouldn't dishonor Rule's word.

Danny was on the far side of camp, seated on the grass with Saul beside her, Mike standing behind her, and her open laptop in front of her. Rule paused a couple times on his way to them—once to compliment John on the chili, once to ask after a man's daughter. She was due to give birth to his first grandchild soon. When Rule reached them, Danny's computer was playing a commercial about bathroom tissue. His eyebrows lifted. "You're online?"

Danny looked up. "There you are," she said. It sounded more like an accusation than a greeting. "They wouldn't tell me where you'd gone."

"No, I suppose they wouldn't. How did you get online?"

Saul answered. "Danny's set up a Wi-Fi hotspot with her phone. It's a prepaid, like ours, so they shouldn't be able to track it."

Danny sniffed. "Not like yours. I can't set up a hot spot with that model. Saul bought me a bunch of minutes so we could check the news."

"No word about Ruben," Mike put in, "so I guess he hasn't been arrested."

"That's good to know."

Danny frowned at Rule. "Saul says you don't have a mobile hotspot. Why not?"

"I didn't know such a thing existed. I take it you've had lunch? John's chili is delicious."

"It's meat chili. John fixed me some eggs. They were good."

Mike frowned. "You didn't tell us she's a vegetarian."

Rule had to smile at Mike's consternation. "I didn't know."

"It's not a problem," Danny informed them. "John's going to cook some beans for me for supper. I should go help with the dishes. I got distracted, but I should help now that I've returned Saul's flute. John said I could."

"That can wait a bit. Did you sleep well?"

In the next few minutes Rule learned that she'd slept fine, her blister didn't hurt, and she really ought to go wash dishes. John would be counting on her.

"John can see that you're talking with me. He'll find someone else."

She frowned. "Maybe I don't want him to."

"But I do. I don't suppose anyone has tried to talk to you mentally again?"

She immediately looked at her feet. "No. You really think it was Lily Yu who did that?"

"Who else could it be? Even if there were someone nearby who, without any training, miraculously learned to use mind-speech, your Gift should have shut them out unless their magic is akin to yours. Magic akin to yours means it was another sensitive or a dragon. And it wasn't a dragon."

"How do you know?"

"Did you manage to cut off communication yourself?"

"I yelled at them to stop." She paused, frowning. "It did seem like I made them stop, but I don't know how to tell for sure."

"No one can shut out a dragon."

"I never thought it was a dragon. A telepath with a strong enough Gift—"

"Mindspeech is not telepathy." He'd explained this already, or tried to. "Telepathy is . . . it's all ears, no mouth. Nothing to speak *with*. There's no reason to think a telepath would be any more able to mindspeak you than—well, than I could."

She stared at her feet in silence for a long moment. "I hope you're right about that, because you were right about Amanda. She's a telepath." Another pause, then very softly: "I'm scared of her."

"Do you think she's crazy?"

"She wasn't a year ago. Not with TIFS anyway. I . . ." She stopped. Cleared her throat. "I want to make another deal."

That was not what he'd expected. "What kind of deal?"

"I'll tell you about Amanda and—and about everything else. No more 'I don't want to answer.' But you have to promise . . ." For once, she looked him right in the face. "Have you wondered at all about the kids who were at the Refuge? The house is empty now, according to the news. So where are the kids?"

LILY woke to the feel of something cool and damp poking her cheek. She swatted at it—and her eyes shot open. Charles stood over her, his nose in her face. She opened her mouth. Charles poked that with his nose before she could speak.

He wanted her to be quiet? Lily frowned, nodded, and pushed his head away so she could sit up.

They were both awake at the same time. Had their captor slipped up? Charles's request for silence suggested he thought someone was able to hear them. That might be simple caution, or it might mean he'd smelled or heard someone.

Maybe she could find out. She remembered vividly the way it had felt to touch/see other minds. She didn't remember exactly how she'd done that, but she'd been reaching out, as if she had super-elastic fingers that could . . .

There. That was Charles, his mind glowing like a big, phosphorescent peach. How weird. Fascinated, Lily slid her "fingers" around the glow . . . fuzzy, yes, that's why she kept thinking of a peach. The surface reminded her of peach fuzz. Or fur?

This was very similar to the way it felt to touch magic, yet not exactly the same. There was that glow, and the way she could sense location . . . it was if her mind was mostly processing the new sense from whatever region of the brain handled touch, but some of it got channeled into her visual cortex, and some was handled by whatever it was that let her know where Rule was. Touch, but with a whiff of synesthesia.

The fuzziness was appealing somehow. As if she could pet it and . . . and do something else. Something. She didn't know—

Charles poked her again.

Right. He had no idea why she was just sitting there, staring at him. She patted him to tell him to be patient and tried reaching farther . . . it was easy, as easy as if she'd reached with a real hand. There, on the other side of the wall, was a plum of a mind. The surface of this mind was entirely smooth. Slick, as if it were coated with slippery oil. Her "fingers" couldn't get a grip on it at all. When she tried, her new sense recoiled like a rubber band, snapping back at her.

She was back to using the usual senses—and her head hurt in a familiar way. She rubbed it, frowning. Had that been a hallucination? It had felt so real . . .

Charles lost patience and poked her hard in the shoulder, then took a few steps toward the opening in the wall that led to the outer chamber. He stopped and looked at her.

New sense or hallucination, it was gone now. Only the headache remained. Lily stood. Charles seemed to think there was someone or something they should check out in the outer chamber. Once she was on her feet, he slunk toward the edge of the opening and peered around. He straightened abruptly, ears pricking.

Lily followed quickly—then stopped, staring.

A small, brown-clad person sat on the stony floor near the fire curtain, arms resting on drawn-up knees, face hidden on the arms. Lily couldn't tell if this was the same brownie or another, no more than she could say if it was male or female. The head was bowed, so that all Lily saw was the shiny cap of brown hair.

Slowly he or she looked up, big eyes full of woe. "Oh," the brownie said in a small voice. "Oh, that's not good."

TWENTY-EIGHT

❧

"**Danny,**" Rule said patiently, "I can't promise that."

Her chin was set stubbornly, her posture tense. She'd closed her laptop and was hugging it to her. "You mean you won't."

"I can't promise to find and rescue all the children because it may not be possible."

Her narrow shoulders remained rigid. "You come up with the words, then."

Rule ran a hand through his hair. "I could promise to see that the children are found and helped, if that's possible without undue loss of life."

"It needs to be you. I don't trust other people to save them."

"My priority has to be finding Lily. Once I've done that—"

"But it's probably the same thing," she said eagerly. "Mr. Smith probably took her wherever he's put the children."

"You didn't find records of a second place he's been funding."

"It has to exist. The children are *somewhere*."

That wasn't necessarily true, Rule thought grimly. Bodies were easy to dispose of. Rule knew damn little about Edward Smith, not enough to guess whether he was ruthless enough to kill children. Why had he done what he had? What were his goals, and how much would he sacrifice for them? Danny's account made him sound smart, cold, and manipulative. Was that accurate? Would he remain cool under pressure or react impulsively? Faced with possible exposure, he had smoothly steered the blame to Ruben. But would he think that was enough? He could have decided he had to eliminate all traces of his clandestine project.

Danny was still talking. ". . . not surprising I didn't know about it. I'm not an accountant. I could find the records about the Refuge because I knew where to start—with Bright Haven. Nonprofits have to keep records. They didn't make it easy to trace their supposed donors, but I could work the trail from both ends, since I had access to the NSA's data. But Mr. Smith must not have used Bright Haven to finance this other place. That's why I didn't know about it."

She could be right. If Smith had a hiding place for the children, Lily might be there, too. If not, they still had to be found. Dead or alive, they had to be found. Rule wasn't sure he was the best person to do that, but . . . "If the children are being held in the same place as Lily, I'll try to free them when I free Lily. If they aren't there, I'll use the resources available to me to try to find them."

She frowned suspiciously. "What do you mean by 'resources'?"

"The situation's too fluid for me to be specific. I could be killed. I could be captured and jailed again, which would force me to delegate the search to others. Or I might free Lily and clear Ruben of suspicion without locating the children, in which case we could have the entire FBI looking for them."

She thought that over, then said in a low voice, "Okay, but you have to promise that if you find them, you won't kill them or allow anyone else to kill them."

His eyebrows shot up—then down. "I don't murder children. I don't allow children to be murdered."

"They . . ." She stopped. Swallowed. "Just promise."

He did, finishing, ". . . if I can do so without undue loss of life."

The rigid shoulders slumped in relief. "Okay. Okay, that's good." She freed one hand from its grip on her computer and held it out.

They shook on the deal. That wasn't a lupi custom, but it

seemed to matter to this girl who was uncomfortable with touch. Rule repeated his pledge; Danny promised to level with him about "everything connected to Mr. Smith and the children," then asked if they could talk someplace by themselves.

"We can. May we leave your laptop here and turned on so someone can monitor the news?"

She considered that in frowning silence. He didn't push. Their acquaintance might be short, but it was sufficient for him to know that Danny did not make decisions quickly. Finally she said, "Saul trusted me with his flute. I guess I could trust him with my laptop."

THEY went for a walk. Mike, Reno, and Eric went with them, staying far enough away to give Danny the feeling of privacy, if not the fact of it. For about ten minutes, they walked in silence. The tension had returned to her shoulders.

It was returning to Rule's gut, too. He broke the silence. "Perhaps you could start by telling me why you believe Smith is using mind control."

She shook her head. "The evidence for that is anecdotal, and you'll need a lot of background or you won't understand."

"Hmm. To your knowledge, are any of the people working with Smith nonhuman?"

That startled her. "What?"

"Elves, for example. Or just people whose magic feels different from anything you've ever touched." True mind control was incredibly rare. It seemed impossible that the NSA could have achieved it with a drug.

Her brow wrinkled. "None of them that I've touched have any kind of magic."

"Including Smith?"

"No, he has a small charisma Gift. Pretty minor, but it's there. Could you not ask questions yet? I need to tell this like I planned."

"All right."

She cleared her throat. "I first got suspicious when Amanda showed up at the Refuge because I knew he'd lied to me. Mr. Smith, I mean. Initially, I wasn't going to report any blocked

telepaths I found. I didn't see any reason to. They were lucky
to have a block, and they couldn't do him any good. But Mr.
Smith said he wanted to track them. Blocks can suddenly disappear, or so I was told." She darted him a quick glance. "Is
that true?"

"I don't know."

"I don't, either. Not anymore. But the Omega Project researchers believe that's so. According to Dr. Webb—she's the one who
went with me to St. Elizabeth's—preliminary data suggest that
some, possibly many, telepaths are born with their Gifts blocked,
but puberty disrupts or dispels the blocks. That theory is based on
a statistical analysis of catatonic patients incorporating the age of
onset of symptoms. I didn't know anything about statistics back
then so I couldn't evaluate their methodology, but it seemed
sound. The problem was that their data might be skewed because
they didn't know how accurate their model was for determining
which catatonic patients were telepaths. That's why they need my
help, only I freaked out and couldn't do it."

"And Mr. Smith told you the same thing? That blocked
telepaths might suddenly lose their blocks?"

"Uh-huh. The idea was that maybe, by the time any telepaths I found became unblocked, his people or the Omega
people would have discovered a way to help. It made sense. I
thought it made sense."

"You wanted to help them."

She nodded but didn't speak. When the silence dragged on,
Rule prompted gently. "Then Amanda showed up at the
Refuge."

"She was blocked!" Anger drew Danny up straight and stiff.
"Blocked when I found her, and still blocked when she came to
the Refuge. They thought I wouldn't know. I'd gone off to college by then—"

Rule's eyebrows shot up. "At sixteen?"

"I'm very smart. That's not bragging. It's just a fact, like
having brown eyes or Asperger's is a fact. I wanted to enter
college early so I could get away from the Refuge, so I studied
hard, and once I left, I didn't go back for visits. Except for once.
It was the anniversary of Zipper's death, so I went there to
bring him some flowers. Amanda snuck out. I was at Zipper's

grave, and she snuck out so she could tell me how stupid I was to bring flowers to a dead dog. Amanda," Danny announced like a judge pronouncing sentence, "is a mean little sneak and a braggart."

"It was an unkind thing for her to say."

"She doesn't like me. They had told her to stay away from me—"

"Who?"

"Dan and Sharon, the houseparents. Maybe the others, too. The research people. They thought she'd obey them because she doesn't like me. I'm not guessing about that," she added. "That's what she told me. Anyway, Amanda wanted me to know I wasn't Mr. Smith's pet anymore, that she was more important than me. I said blocked telepaths weren't all that special, and she laughed and said she wouldn't be blocked much longer. She was all puffed up about how important she was, because they were going to unblock her and she was essential to—" She stopped, swallowed, and finished quietly, "To Mr. Smith's plans."

"What plans, Danny?"

She took a deep breath. "The first time I saw a reference to the drug was in a financial report that listed 'LDN1 supplies' but didn't say what LDN1 was. I couldn't find anything more about it until after I ran. Someone slipped up and used its other name in a report—Lodan. A search with that name turned up more reports. No supporting data, but some general reports on a drug they called Lodan. I think they must keep most information about it on computers that are permanently offline. But at least none of those files were changed when the financial stuff was, so I can show them to you. There's one labeled 'Practical Applications of Lodan' and . . . and it's clear they intend to use the kids as weapons. I think . . ." She had to stop and swallow. "I'm pretty sure they used the kids to kill that man. The one whose body Lily found."

Rule spoke in a carefully neutral voice. "Lily said there was magic on the body. That an odd kind of telekinesis had been used to cut the man's throat."

Danny nodded once, the movement jerky. "I need to tell you about Nicky."

* * *

THE woods here had more trees and less brush than the ones Demi had traveled with Rule Turner last night. More trees meant less brush, she supposed, because the heavier canopy cut off too much sunlight for smaller plants to grow well.

The shade felt good. Air-conditioning would have felt even better. She missed air-conditioning.

As they walked, she told him about Nicky. How they'd met, what Nicky was like—an early-admission student like her. An animal lover and vegetarian like her, too, though he took it farther than she had—"He won't own anything made of leather." And his uncle had Asperger's syndrome, so he understood. And he liked her. He was her first real friend since the third grade. He wanted to be a veterinarian, and he got really good grades, and he liked a lot of the nonviolent computer games she did.

Nonviolent because he was a Quaker. It wasn't just that he'd been raised that way, either. He *believed* in Quakerism. She explained about the Society of Friends carefully so Rule would understand.

Nicky was also Gifted.

The words had tumbled out until she got to that part. She liked talking about her friend. She didn't like talking about the rest of it. It felt like betrayal. It *was* betrayal—she was breaking her promise. But he wouldn't want her to keep silent anymore. She had to believe that.

"It felt like a telekinesis Gift?" Rule repeated when she'd stumbled to a halt.

"Almost the same," she corrected. "But it isn't TK. He can't pick things up with it. The only thing he can do is lash out. It's force, he said. Pure force. When he was little, if he got mad, he'd just flail out with it, and sometimes he broke things. Once he hit his mother, and that scared him. As he got older, it got stronger. That scared him, too, because he has a temper. Not so much for himself, but he hates bullying and . . ." She had to stop and swallow. It was Nicky's hatred of bullies that had led Mr. Smith to him.

"But if it's just force," Rule said softly, "not a blade . . ."

"The force could be shaped. Back then, he didn't know

how to do that and he refused to learn. He wanted his Gift to go away."

"He told you that? When?"

"When I first found out about his Gift. I was so startled!" Partly just because he'd touched her. That always startled her. But mostly because she'd never felt magic like his. He'd known something was wrong, and she'd done something she never did. She'd told him about her own Gift. "He made me promise not to tell anyone, so I didn't report him to Mr. Smith."

"Were you supposed to? He wasn't a child, an orphan."

"College students aren't eligible for the Refuge, but Mr. Smith wanted to expand his program by recruiting people who were adult or nearly adult. So after I went to college, I was supposed to report any Gifted students I found, but there were only a couple. I couldn't go around grabbing people, could I? Mostly I didn't touch the other students, so I only found two who were Gifted. And then Amanda showed up at the Refuge."

"And you stopped trusting Smith."

Her forehead wrinkled in a confusing wash of feelings. One of those emotions she could identify, though. "I was so angry! I said I'd quit if he didn't come talk to me. And he did, too. He came to see me at the dorm. He claimed his people had figured out how to help telepaths, but only if they could be treated while they were still blocked. I said that Amanda told me they were going to unblock her, and he said that was the only safe way to do it. Tests showed Amanda would be one of the unlucky ones who came unblocked at puberty, so they had to remove her block themselves to do it safely." She sighed. "He made it sound reasonable. He even said I could take a sabbatical and see if Amanda did okay before I looked for any more Gifted kids for him. But he couldn't explain away one thing."

"Why not?"

"Isn't it obvious? If everything was like he said, why hadn't he told me earlier?"

"About Amanda?"

"He should have come to me and said, 'Danny, I have good news. We can help any blocked telepaths you find, but we have to bring them to the Refuge right away.' But he didn't do that. He waited until I was gone to bring her there, and when I showed up, they told Amanda to stay away from me. They didn't want me to know about her. So I didn't believe him, but I didn't have actual evidence that he'd lied. I needed facts."

"So you hacked into the NSA computers."

"No, I talked to Nicky. Then I hacked into the NSA. It was Nicky's idea."

Rule seemed surprised about that. She explained why she'd decided she could tell Nicky about Mr. Smith. It went against the agreement she'd signed, but when Mr. Smith broke his word by bringing Amanda to the Refuge, she wasn't bound by hers anymore, either. Not that the courts would see it that way, but she did.

"The elves would agree with you."

She thought about that for several moments. "That makes me extremely curious, but this probably isn't the time to ask about elves."

"Probably not."

"Getting full access took a long time. I got into the NSA computers within a week of getting Mr. Smith's log-in, but I had to find the place where he'd hidden all the Bright Haven data. That was slow. And I didn't know about the drug yet, not until after Nicky went missing."

He needed her to explain that, so she told him how Nicky was suddenly not at college and his parents didn't know where he was, and how she thought of Mr. Smith right away. "I don't know why exactly. Lots of things might have happened to Nicky that didn't involve Mr. Smith. But I knew he'd have loved to get hold of someone with Nicky's Gift, and I couldn't stop thinking about that, so I went to the Refuge to find out if he was there."

She told him what had happened at the Refuge—the uniformed guards, how Mr. Smith had found her, and what he'd said. She described seeing Nicky and how odd he'd acted, and how confused she'd been until he pretended they'd been boyfriend and girlfriend. That had been so absurd she'd realized he was lying—and if he was, it was because of Mr. Smith. Then he told her to run.

"And you did. Just like that?"

"Yes, but that's not the important thing. You can see that Nicky did several things he would never have done if Mr. Smith weren't controlling him somehow."

"Is that why you think Smith has developed mind control? Because your friend did things that were out of character?"

"That's part of it."

"What's the rest?"

"I can't tell if you believe me about Nicky."

"I can't helping thinking that if your friend was under Smith's mental control, he wouldn't have told you to run."

"He only managed that one word, and he couldn't even say it out loud."

Rule nodded. She still couldn't tell if he believed her, and was about to ask again when he said, "I'm impressed with the way you reacted. Not many people would have the courage to take off like that, without money, without anything."

"Oh, that's because of my strategy. When you have an enemy who's much more powerful than you are, you have to take him by surprise. What's the one thing no one ever expects?"

"Aliens?"

She stopped and frowned at him.

"I never expect aliens. Demons, perhaps, but not . . . it was supposed to be a joke, Danny."

"I don't always get jokes. I have a sense of humor, but jokes often depend on context, and I often miss the context."

"I see. So what is the one thing no one expects?"

"For you to use the maximum force to achieve a goal instead of the minimum."

"That . . ." he started, then fell silent. When he went on, it was in a different kind of voice. ". . . is rather brilliant, actually."

She smiled, pleased.

"Though there are exceptions. Suicide bombers spring to mind."

"No, because they think they're doing the minimum necessary to achieve their goal of martyrdom. You have to put their actions in context, which is hard for me, but I think that's why I figured out that everyone always uses minimum force, because I've thought about context a lot."

"Are you talking about social context or worldview?"

"Both, because for neuro-norms, social context is a huge part of their worldview. I didn't understand that for a long time. It's like the way a blind person lacks the context that sighted people take for granted. Blind people can do a lot of the same things sighted people do, but they have to use a different approach, and some things that are obvious to sighted people aren't part of a blind person's world at all. I'm socially impaired. I get surprised all the time by people saying and doing irrational things. Take gay marriage. Why would some people get so upset that people they didn't even know wanted to get married?"

"For the same reason men denied women the vote for so long. It threatens their status and their understanding of the world."

She beamed, delighted that he saw it, too. "That's right! I had to think and think to figure that out. Though I still don't see why they're so scared of changing their minds."

"Because the world is a dangerous place. If it doesn't work the way we believe it does, the danger becomes unmanageable."

The *ping!* of sudden understanding gripped Demi, holding her motionless. That fit. That fit so very well. "That's why I was so shaken up about Amanda," she breathed. "It wasn't as if I'd ever liked Mr. Smith all that much, but when I found out he lied, the world didn't make sense anymore. Then when I saw the guards at the Refuge . . . and when I saw Nicky there and knew the lies were even bigger and more terrible than I'd guessed—" She stopped and swallowed. It didn't help. So many feelings clumped up in her throat that she couldn't squeeze a single word past them.

She'd tried so hard! But she hadn't made anything better. Instead, things were falling apart. She'd messed up. Nicky and the kids were still in Mr. Smith's hands. Rule was an escaped prisoner. Lily Yu had been captured. And Mr. Smith had made Nicky kill someone. A homeless man.

How would he ever get over that?

"Danny?" Rule said in that soft voice he used sometimes.

She swallowed again and managed to answer. "What?"

"Are you okay?"

"Of course. I haven't been hurt. Were you thinking of my blister? It hasn't bothered me much today. The bandage protects it."

"I meant emotionally okay."

"Oh. I don't know how to answer that."

"I'm going to hug you for a minute so we can see if that helps. If it doesn't, tell me and I'll stop."

Because he'd warned her, she had time to close her eyes. Sometimes that helped keep her from overloading. He put his arms around her the way he had last night. She ducked her head, eyes tightly closed, and was hit with so many sensations—the pressure from his arms, arms she didn't control that were connected to a body so solid . . . he was taller than her, and stronger. Separate from her. His T-shirt was soft against her face. She could smell him, and the scent made her feel . . . she couldn't find the word at first, then it came to her. Safe. She felt safe.

Maybe this was how a father's arms felt. She'd always wondered.

His phone vibrated. It was in his pocket and set on silent, but she heard the faint hum from it vibrating. "Should you—"

"It can wait."

But she felt tense again. She had to make sure he understood about Nicky, then tell him about the drug. "You can let go now."

He did.

She automatically stepped back. Should she tell him his hug helped? He'd said to tell him if it didn't, not if it did. Maybe she should say thank you. While she tried to figure that out, he took out his phone.

It had been a text, not a call, she saw when he opened the message window. And maybe it had mattered, because he frowned when he read it. "I have to call José."

While he did that, she tried to line up clearly in her mind what she should tell him about the drug and how to say it so he'd understand her conclusions. She'd planned that out that last night, but she wasn't sure she'd convinced him about Nicky, so she needed to—

"Shit!"

That interrupted her thinking.

"When?" he asked, and, "That was the exact wording?" And then he didn't say anything for a while. He wasn't frowning, but he'd cursed, so he must be upset. "How are people reacting?" A pause. "Not surprising, but not good. Not good at all. Carson should have called about this. He didn't, so . . . yes.

Try to reach him. I'll call back in minute." He disconnected
and raised his voice slightly. "Come in close."

"What's happened? Who should come in?" Her stomach
was jittering around like crazy.

"Mike, Reno, and Eric. Danny, you know how you needed
time to think last night? I need that now."

She nodded. She knew how that was, how you couldn't
stand to have people talking at you when you were trying to
think through something complicated. But it was hard to stay
silent when she *needed* to know what was going on.

One second she and Rule were alone. The next, Mike was
there, startling her so much she jumped. He nodded at her. A
moment later, two more people joined them—Reno and Eric.
At least, she assumed the chunky one was Eric. She knew the
other one was Reno, having met him last night. She remembered because she liked his name and he looked kind of like
her—skinny, with skin the color of caramel candy.

Rule didn't seem to notice. He was still thinking.

Finally he nodded, but not really at them. At whatever he'd
decided, probably. "I just heard from José. The national news is
reporting that three people have been killed near Whistle. Eric
Ellison from Homeland Security just held a press conference.
He claims they've confirmed that the victims were savaged by
a large predator or predators. Asked if he meant wolves, he said
that was unconfirmed, but according to José, he made 'unconfirmed' sound like 'hell, yes.'"

Killed. Demi's brain froze, wrapped around that word. Two
other phrases battered at her: *three people* and *a large predator or predators.*

By the time her brain thawed, Rule was back on the phone,
giving instructions to someone. Probably José. He spoke
crisply about evacuating the camp, paused, then said *shit* again.
"Bring him along. All due courtesy, but bring him." He gave
instructions about what to bring, where to meet—Fallback
Two? Where was that?—and about the sentries and search
squads. He told José to keep an eye out for "that damn helicopter," then asked about Carson, paused, and said, "They must
have either picked him up or killed him."

Killed him?

"No," Rule said forcefully. "It wouldn't help. Those people were killed to give our enemies reason to come after . . ." A short pause. "Yes. From what Danny's been telling me, Smith's got a Gifted youngster who could do it. Questions? All right. Don't forget Danny's backpack." He disconnected.

"You heard?" he asked.

"No!" Danny said. "Who was killed? I know people in Whistle. I've got a friend there."

"I don't know. The names haven't been released to the press. Danny, we'll be running all or most of the way to the rendezvous. You wouldn't be able to keep up, so Mike's going to carry you. Piggyback, if you prefer, but you must be carried."

Everything was happening too fast. She couldn't think what to do. When Mike squatted and told her to get on, she just stared. Not refusing. Just unable to act.

"You're still under my care," Rule told her. "This is the best I can do to protect you."

She must have believed him, because she did climb on Mike's back. She felt awkward and shaky and unlike herself. She didn't like any of this, not at all. Mike hooked his arms under her knees. His arms were thicker than Rule's and very strong. "Hold on," he told her. "Try not to choke me."

Mike took off.

It wasn't dark this time, so she could see how fast they were going—at least she could for the first couple minutes. After that she closed her eyes. As she was carried through the woods at a run for the second time in less than twenty-four hours, one thing was clear: piggyback was better than over the shoulder, but it was still scary.

TWENTY-NINE

~⁓~

RULE set an easy pace, about that of a human marathoner. Fall-back Two was less than ten miles away, but some of those were rough, uphill miles, and Mike was carrying over a hundred extra pounds on his back. Rule didn't want to exhaust him getting there. They probably wouldn't stay long.

He was buying time. Time to think. The authorities knew where they'd been camped, so they had to clear out. That much was obvious. What he should do beyond the obvious . . . Rule hoped like hell he'd have figured that out by the time he reached the rendezvous.

Fortunately, there was time for an orderly evacuation. José was sending watchers to keep an eye on all the roads. They should have warning well before the cops could reach them. Plus they'd have money. His first reaction when José told him the courier with the money had just arrived was that the timing sucked, but that was wrong. An hour ago might have been optimum, but now was better than not at all. Since the courier couldn't give the money to anyone but Rule, he'd be brought to Fallback Two. They had to make sure nothing happened to the man. Rule didn't want to damage his relationship with that organization.

One of the first things Rule had done when he joined his

men at the camp yesterday was to establish three fallback points—two within the wildlife area and one in the federal forest that abutted it. Fallback One would have been quicker for Rule—it was north of camp, and so was he. But Claude hadn't marked that route yet.

Most lupi were good at navigating, even in unknown territory. Lily claimed that Rule was like a migrating bird—equipped with a mysterious sense that wouldn't let him get lost. That was an exaggeration, but he always knew where the moon was, and in a way he couldn't put into words, that kept him oriented. But while most lupi shared his sense of direction, not all were good at reading a map. He'd wanted a rendezvous point even the map-impaired could find when they were two-footed—because he'd ordered that everyone go as men, not wolves.

Law enforcement outfits of all stripes had strict guidelines about when lethal force was allowed. Those guidelines weren't always followed, especially with his people—court rulings were a muddle of inconsistency about what measures were reasonable with a lupus suspect—but they did create some reluctance to shoot first, ask questions later.

It was entirely legal to shoot wolves. No explanations needed.

Rule and the others had been running for about ten minutes when the land turned choppy. Fallback Two lay in rocky foothills, outriders to the Appalachian range. He had ten or fifteen more minutes before he reached the rendezvous. He wouldn't be the first to arrive—those at camp were closer, and José would have sent some ahead quickly to secure the area. The rest would pack and bring a few basic supplies, so would take a bit longer.

He still didn't know what orders to give when he got there.

Homeland Security seemed to be running this investigation, too—or at least HSI was heavily involved. Eric Ellison, the new head of HSI, had already held a press conference about the murders. Rule had run into Ellison once at a Washington party. An ambitious man, and one who liked cameras.

Was Ellison Smith's partner or his stooge? Because Smith was behind the killings. There was no doubt in Rule's mind about that, given the method and the careful way they'd made sure everyone blamed wolves for the deaths. It certainly hadn't been any of Rule's people. He hadn't told Danny this, but two of the victims were women. He might not be sure how much control some of his Leidolf had, but none of them were insane. Only genuine madness could bring a lupus to kill a woman.

Rule leaped over a fallen tree and thought about those victims. Smith had ordered three innocents killed. He was coming after Rule in a remarkably ruthless way, and using the biggest guns he had to do it. At least Rule hoped like hell these were his biggest guns. Why?

Smith must consider him a threat, however little he felt like one right now. In spite of all he'd learned from Danny, he still didn't know what Smith wanted. What did he expect to do with the Lodan drug that was worth risking so much? Did he covet fame and glory? What was his ultimate goal, and how did Rule stand in his way?

He swerved around a brushy thicket, slowing as he saw the tiny creek ahead. He thought this was the spot . . . yes, the scent was unmistakably lupus. In this form he couldn't identify it as Claude's urine, but he didn't need to. He turned and followed the little creek up the hill.

Maybe Smith wasn't desperately trying to kill *him*. Maybe his real target was the girl riding on Mike's back.

That thought clicked into place like a puzzle piece finding the spot it had been made for. It raised other questions, however. How could Smith know Danny was with Rule? And why was he suddenly desperate to get rid of her? She'd been hiding from him for nearly a year. Was this the first chance he'd had to eliminate her, or had something changed?

He couldn't answer the last question, but clearly Smith had known Danny was in the area. The HSI agents had said so when they showed Lily Danny's photograph. If Smith knew about Danny's romantic fascination with Rule . . . and he might. Danny lacked the filters most people possessed, so she might have talked to Smith about Rule back when she still trusted him. It wasn't a huge leap for the man to suspect that Danny might try to find Rule when news reports suggested he was in the area.

But Smith had killed three innocent people and might be planning to kill a great many more—assuming Smith considered lupi to be people. Some didn't. Doing that based on mere suspicion *was* a leap. Rule filed that theory under "possible" and turned to the next question: why now?

Smith had kept his operation deeply hidden for years. Now he was moving almost openly. Kidnapping an FBI agent. Framing the head of Unit 12. Framing Rule. Killing innocents. And now, all but declaring war on Rule and his people— possibly in order to kill Danny. He could see only one reason for the change.

Whatever Smith's goal might be, it came with an expiration date. And that date was soon. Probably very soon.

By the time Rule drew near enough to the rendezvous to smell clan nearby, he'd gotten his wish. He knew what he needed to do next. He slowed, then stopped, looking for the sentry. There, in the elm. The man gave a low whistle, notifying the others.

Reno and Eric stopped alongside him. Mike was slightly behind. "You doing okay, Danny?" he called.

"Are we there? I hope we're there."

"We are." Close enough anyway. Just ahead, the path bent around a rocky outcropping. Two men came around that out-crop. One was normal-sized. The other was not.

"Rule!" Little John called out cheerfully. "'Bout time you showed up!"

Rule was surprised to see Little John, who'd been given his nickname for obvious reasons: he looked like Robin Hood's oversize sidekick. Unlike some big men, he could move fast when he wanted to, but he very seldom wanted to. Not to put too fine a point on it, Little John was lazy.

The man with him was Jason, who was next in rank after José and Mike. Jason looked like a model for a U.S. Army ad. He slapped Little John on the side of the head. "I report to the Rho first—*then* you can run your mouth." He gave Rule a quick wink. "José bet him he couldn't deliver your guest here before you arrived."

That was one way to get Little John to move quickly. The man might be lazy, but he hated to lose a bet. Rule grinned. "Congratulations, Little John. Jason, how many are here, and where is my guest?"

"Six, and he is—"

"Here," said another voice, and a third man came around the rocky outcropping.

He was slim, blond, and dapper in pressed khakis and a green polo shirt. He held a bulging Priority Mailer in one hand. His loafers looked comfortable, but they weren't a great choice for running through the woods. Good thing he hadn't had to run, then. Rule was sorry he'd missed seeing Little John carrying him.

Danny slid off Mike's back. "Thank you," she told him politely. "I hope I never have to do that again."

The blond man chuckled. "It looks like you had as interesting a trip as I did."

"As a favor to me," Rule said, "please don't remember the young woman you just spoke to."

"What young woman?" was the bland return.

Rule nodded his thanks. "There's a strong south wind today."

"South winds favor haste."

"So do I. I'm Rule Turner."

"Yes, you are. Call me Bert." The man smiled. "Are you ready to take delivery?"

"I am." As Bert came forward, more of Rule's men moved around the rock. The official meeting point might be slightly farther on, but lupi would naturally gather where their Rho stood.

Up close, Bert smelled faintly of gun oil. Rule wondered where the weapon was. An ankle holster perhaps. There was just a whiff of fear, but overall he was very calm for a man surrounded by lupi. He held out the mailer. "The cash."

Rule accepted it.

He then offered Rule a wallet. "Cards. You'll want to count the cash, of course. To check the amounts on the cards we'll have to—"

"We'll skip that this time," Rule said dryly. "Bert, are you familiar with this area and able to escape through the woods without being spotted?"

"Not at all. Especially since I have no idea where I am now. I take it there's a problem."

"One that will probably involve large numbers of law enforcement officers. With your permission, I'll get you away from here as quickly as possible."

"I accept your offer."

"Excellent. I regret that I can't offer any refreshment, unless you're fond of jerky—" Rule stopped when John cleared his throat. "Yes?"

"I've got a little alcohol stove. I could make coffee, if you like. I have to do it one cup at a time, but I've got what I need for that."

"Ah." Alcohol burned clean—no smoke to give them away. He turned to his guest. "You'll have a ways to go, whether you walk or ride the way you did to get here. Would you like a cup of coffee before you leave?"

Bert's sigh was heartfelt. "I surely would."

There was also a bottle of water for Danny, who was reunited with her computer. The rest of them could refresh themselves with water from the creek—not sanitary for humans, but fine for them—and jerky. By the time Rule had drunk his fill, five more clan had joined them, bearing backpacks with clothes and a couple sleeping bags. The others wouldn't be here for another ten minutes or more. They were carrying more supplies.

Rule led everyone on around the rocky outcropping. A small clearing there gave them more room. John set up his tiny alcohol stove and started making coffee. Bert stood near him, chatting easily. Rule had a quick word with Jason and gave him a large part of the cash in the Priority Mailer. The rest went in the wallet Bert had thoughtfully provided. Then it was time to talk with Danny again.

She sat on a fallen log. Mike sat cross-legged in front of her. He was explaining the way the sentries had been placed. She seemed to be listening, though it was hard to be sure when she directed her intent gaze at the ground, not him.

"How are you holding up?" Rule asked, joining her on the log.

"I'm not hungry or sleepy. I don't hurt anywhere. I'm not panicked or having a meltdown. So I guess I'm holding up okay, but I'm not—I don't—" She stopped, drooping. "I don't know what I am."

"I thought it would help to know what's going on."

She perked up a bit. "It would. I can see why you abandoned the camp, but why did we come here? Why didn't we just keep going? Not that I want to keep going, but why aren't we? I asked Mike," she added, "but he just said, 'If the Rho says go there, we go there.'" She frowned in disapproval. "He doesn't have much curiosity, does he? Though he seems smart enough otherwise."

Rule smothered a laugh and avoided looking at Mike. "He didn't want to speculate out loud on my reasons, though I imagine some of them were obvious to him. We came here because we needed to go someplace we could reach quickly. Other spots would have worked, but this one had a marked route. We're waiting now for the rest to join us—except for those keeping watch, that is."

"Who's keeping watch where? You told José something about that, but I wasn't paying attention."

"I'd been keeping two squads out at all times, searching for any trace of Lily or the brownie—"

"What brownie?"

Had he not mentioned that to her? "I'll explain later. The men from those squads, along with the camp's sentries, have been redeployed to watch the roads into the wilderness area. We should have word when the authorities send in their posse."

"They can't watch the entire perimeter."

"They don't have to. A couple of men could easily slip in, but the authorities aren't going to send a couple of men after us. They'll assemble a large group of heavily armed officers—no less than forty, I'd think, and possibly more. Unless they decide to wait long enough to bring in the National Guard." It had been many years since the authorities had gone hunting his people en masse, but he knew the stories. He knew what kind of tactics the government had used—everything from state troopers to the massive deployment of the National Guard that had resulted in the infamous Bridgetown massacre.

He wished he knew what was being said in the media and online. José had said that people "were pretty worked up" about the killings. How much of a frenzy had Smith been able to whip up?

Danny's eyes were wide. "The National Guard?"

"That's unlikely to happen right away. Our enemy has great leverage at the federal level, but he'll need the governor on board to call out the Guard."

"My friend Jamie says the governor is an idiot, so he might go along with that. And Mr. Smith had soldiers at the Refuge. If he gets the U.S. Army to come after us—"

"I suspect they only looked like Army, Danny. Even if Smith does have a general in his pocket, deploying soldiers to guard the Refuge would leave one hell of a trail. They were probably mercenaries of some sort. My first concern now is that we not linger. If our enemies are smart, they'll encircle us. We need to be gone before they can."

"You're going to disperse us?" Mike said.

No point in waiting to announce it, he decided. "The non-fighters will be heading back to Clanhome."

Danny's forehead wrinkled. "Don't all lupi fight?"

A couple of them chuckled. "Certainly," Rule said. "Especially if no dominant is around to knock some sense into them. But not all are trained. I'll keep the trained fighters with me, or nearby. But not here. I've got one major resource our enemy lacks and she's wasted out here, where she doesn't have quick and easy access to the Internet."

"Me." Danny sounded pleased.

"You," he agreed. "And for the rest of us . . . it's time I stopped playing by human rules."

"What does that mean?"

"It means that I know who my enemy is. It's time I—" He broke off to listen.

A whistle sounded from the elm that held a sentry—two short notes, followed by a rising crescendo. Two notes meant clan approaching. The crescendo warned of possible danger. Rule jogged back around the rocky outcrop; Jason shadowed him. He stopped beneath the elm and spoke softly. "Who?"

"José and the rest. I don't see any pursuit, but they're running flat out and I don't see packs on their backs."

Something was wrong. Rule spoke crisply. "Jason, start distributing the money. Be quick. John, put out your fire. Everyone else except the sentries, to me. We'll wait for José and the rest, but be prepared to scatter. Danny, I'd like another twenty-four hours."

She'd rounded the outcrop with the others, but stopped dead at that. "What? What do you mean?"

"I'd like to extend our agreement about your protection for another twenty-four hours."

She was pale. Frightened, but not—as she put it—having a

meltdown. "I—I—okay." She came forward and held out her hand.

Solemnly he shook it. "We'll take care of you, Danny."

"What's wrong?"

"I don't know yet." He would soon. He could hear José and the rest now. They weren't trying to run silently. "Mike, Danny remains in your charge. Bert, I'm sorry there won't be time for coffee. We need to get you away." Claude would be best for that. He knew the area, knew how to fight—and just as important, when not to fight—and was damn good at traveling unseen. Rule knew that because the man had once led a Leidolf squad onto Nokolai Clanhome land and lived to tell of it.

José came pounding up the trail toward Rule, a long tail of winded men behind him. All of them were shiny with sweat. José started talking before he stopped running. "Got a call on the way here. Checked with . . . others. Summarizing. They've spotted . . . our watchers."

"All of them?" Rule asked sharply.

"I think so. Two"—he stopped in front of Rule—"may have been picked up. Or shot. Mark heard shots fired to the south of him, and that's one of the pairs not answering their phones. Another pair had state cops show up while I was talking to them—half a dozen, armed with rifles. I told them to pull back. I dumped the supplies and got here stat. Figured we could go back for them if needed."

"You did right." Rule scowled, thinking. Someone among his enemies was too smart for comfort. He must have guessed that Rule would send people to watch the roads. Dammit to hell. "Text the other watchers. Everyone is to leave their posts and join us here. Jason's distributing cash—a thousand each. We'll be splitting up. Mike, Danny, José, and Jason will stay with me. Nonfighters are to return to Clanhome. Jason—" Danny had reached him and was tugging on Rule's arm. "A moment, Danny. Jason, when you've finished passing out the money, you're in charge of getting Theo back safely to Clanhome. I want Claude—"

"Rule!" Danny said urgently.

"Not now. I want Claude with Bert." He searched the throng behind José until he spotted the older man. "Claude, your job is to get Bert to as safe a spot as you can find. A city or small town. You'll get extra funds. Fighters are to scatter like everyone else, but will rendezvous later. You'll be instructed about where on your phone. If you—"

"Ruletheymaybelisteningtoyourphones!"

Danny delivered the words in a single, rapid-fire burst that took him a second to untangle. "We're using prepaids purchased under names the government doesn't know. They can't have our phone numbers, so they can't listen in."

"They can! It's the NSA, Rule! Collecting, storing, and sorting massive amounts of data is what they *do*. I wish I'd thought of it sooner, but I didn't. I'm sorry. I'm really sorry. It's so obvious!"

"What's obvious?" he asked with strained patience.

"They know you're here, so they know what cell towers are handling your phone traffic. They'd have to query all the cell towers in a twenty-mile radius because calls aren't always routed to the nearest one. You'd think that included everyone who places a cell call in an area of about three hundred square miles, but in practice that's reduced to about a hundred square miles because of the directional antennae. That's still a lot of cell numbers, but they can either find out from the phone companies involved which numbers are newly activated, or they might do a sort to eliminate calls placed from numbers that have made calls in this area before you got here. That would be trickier than it sounds, but—"

"Speed it up," he said. "Please."

The strain of not explaining made her pant, but she managed. "It's possible for them to find your phone numbers. I don't know how long it would take, but if it's possible, they've already done it or are in the process of doing it. Once they have the numbers—"

"They can listen in real time." And had, it sounded like. Quickly he sorted through what he'd said over the phone—and what he hadn't. They knew Danny was with him. He'd mentioned that. They knew about the watchers and evacuating the camp, but he hadn't specified where Fallback Two was, so . . . shit. The squads José broke up to create the watchers wouldn't have known where Fallback Two was. He must have told them.

"José. How did you describe the location of Fallback Two when you contacted the search squads?"

"Too well," José said grimly.

"Dammit. New plan. Everyone—"

A single short, rising whistle from the sentry. Incoming—and hostile. "Who?" Rule snapped.

"Helicopter. It's headed straight for—oh, hell! That's not DPS. It's some kind of military copter."

"You're sure?"

"Yes! It's five or six minutes out!"

This time, Rule shouted. "Sentries, abandon posts. Everyone, don't use your phones. Nonfighters, scatter now! Go!" Men started to peel off. "Fighters—"

"Rule!" José broke in, fast and urgent. "Mother bird!"

"No, dammit, I'm not going to—"

"You damn sure are! You're their damn Rho, and that copter probably has machine guns! Let me do my job!"

"Bloody hell." Rule wasn't the only one at risk. There was Danny, whom he was sworn to protect. And everyone else. "Yes. A squad, no more. Don't get yourself killed."

José didn't answer. He was too busy calling out names.

"Mother bird" was one of the basic tactics known to everyone who trained under Benedict. José would lead his squad away from Rule—and make sure they were seen. Just like a mother bird pretending to be wounded to draw the danger away from her chicks.

Rule called out names, too, even as he revised his plans. "Little John, get Bert on your back. Danny, get on Mike's back. You're with me. Claude, you're point for my party. Take us roughly south, with overhead cover as much as possible. Move!"

José and the men he'd chosen were already running back down the trail. The rest scattered every which way. The second Mike and Little John had their charges securely aboard, Rule gave Claude the signal. He took off. Rule raced after him, trailed by the encumbered Mike and Little John.

Five minutes later, machine gun fire shattered the quiet of the woods into bloody shards.

THIRTY

~~

THE brownie's name was Shisti. Her call-name anyway.

"Fathers choose the first call-name," she told Lily and Charles, looking down at her busy hands weaving five thin strips of leather into a complex braid. The strips were anchored by loops hooked around her toes. "That's what the child will be called until zhe's nine. Most of us change our call-name several times before we reach adulthood. Not so often after that."

"The father gets to pick the baby's call-name? Seems wrong to leave out the mother."

Shisti's round green eyes grew even rounder in astonishment. "But she chooses the birth name!"

"Is a birth-name like a true name?"

"No. Yes." One of Shisti's little hands abandoned its task to flutter in the air, then scoop it as if cupping water. "It holds together like a true name, but it is not one."

"But it's kept secret like a true name?"

"Of course. Only mothers know the birth name. They whisper it into the baby's ear when zhe has three days, and when zhe has three moons, and when zhe has three years, and every three years after that until zhe's an adult. Also if zhe gets sick," she added. "Not little-sick, but bad-sick, but that doesn't happen much. We don't get sick all the time like you humans." She gave Lily a pitying look.

"Zhe? Is that from your language?"

"No, it's English. You haven't heard it yet?"

"No."

"You will." She resumed her weaving.

Shisti was not the brownie Lily had followed into the woods, though her hair was the same ash brown color. She wore a single mother-braid, not three, and lacked the fine lines around her eyes Lily had seen on the other brownie. Shisti's eyes were also a bit more widely set, her chin more pointed.

The three of them sat in what Lily thought of as the foyer near the fire curtain. Shisti had pulled off her shoes so she could anchor five thin strips of leather with her toes—she'd pulled them from a pouch at her waist—and was braiding them in a complicated pattern. Charles lay beside Lily, looking sleepy. He'd eaten. They'd both emptied their bladders, Charles by directing the stream into the fire-curtain, where it hissed into oblivion. Quite a tidy solution really, considering how difficult it would be for him to use the camping toilet. Lily was munching on the trail mix Shisti had brought. She was bloody damn sick of trail mix.

Putting together a few things the brownie had said with a great many she hadn't, Lily was pretty sure Shisti had been serving as their waitress, delivering food and water, and chambermaid—emptying the bag in the camping toilet. She hadn't expected them to wake up, or to be trapped here herself. Both things upset her. She refused to tell them why, or how they'd repeatedly been put to sleep, or why they'd been captured, or anything else related to their imprisonment. She'd happily answered other questions, though, once Lily abandoned the forbidden topics.

So Lily had kept her talking. Suspects and witnesses often reveal a good deal through indirect questioning. She now knew that brownies counted age based on the year they became adult rather than their birth year. By this reckoning, Shisti was twelve. She had a young son called Aire who loved to climb; she was a *dada*, whatever that meant (when Lily asked, she'd said, "I *geesh* the *prelli*. I also nag. I am very good with *prelli* and getting better at nagging"); her favorite food was chocolate, but worms were nice for snacking; and "shisti" referred to her ability to move soundlessly, a skill the little brownie was very proud of. "I have the softest feet in Home," she'd announced. "The bear can't hear me. The cat can't hear me. Certainly none of you Big People can hear me."

Lily's headache was almost gone. She decided to try . . . but the moment she *reached* with that other sense, a sharp stab of pain made her wince and rub her head. Which was suddenly pounding again. "I don't suppose you have some ibuprofen in your pouch."

"I-bu-what?"

"It's a painkiller."

"What hurts?" The little brownie looked alarmed. "Is it your head? Did you hit it? Are your brains scrambled? Are you knocked silly? Will you—"

"No, none of that. I have a headache."

Shisti clucked in sympathy. "I've never had a headache. I know humans get them. Why is that? They sound unpleasant."

"Brownies don't get headaches?"

"Not unless we hit our heads. I was knocked silly once. It hurt a lot and my words stayed tangled for hours."

Lily ate another handful of stupid damn trail mix. "That word you used. 'Zhe.' What does it mean?"

"*Yayo.* None of your languages have a word for *yayo.* Isn't that ridiculous? Elves do. Gnomes do. We do. But you don't, so we decided to give English a word for *yayo.*" She paused expectantly.

"Um—thank you?"

Shisti beamed at her. "You're welcome. Some thought it should be she-he, but all your other pronouns are only one syllable, so that would be hard to insert. Besides, she-he sounds like tickling giggles, doesn't it? And 'zhe' could work for other languages, and we might want to give it to one of them, too, later on."

"That's planning ahead." Conversation with brownies was always interesting. Not necessarily informative, but interesting. "So 'zhe' means 'he or she'?"

"Or 'his or hers.'" Shisti had finished her braid. Carefully she removed it from her toes and tied off that end. She held it up, admiring it—and promptly untied it and took the strands apart.

"Why did you do that? It looked pretty."

"I need something to do, of course." Her busy fingers were looping the strands around her toes again.

"You think you'll be here with us for much longer?"

"I don't know." She paused in her task, her forehead wrinkling. "She's not listening anymore."

Lily resisted the urge to ask who Shisti meant. "That makes you sad."

Brimming green eyes met hers. "We've tried so hard! We're doing everything the *ithnali* says, but we aren't enough. Even the great-mothers can't get through to her now, or I wouldn't be on this side of the fire."

"Great-mothers?"

"Grandmothers? Or great-grandmothers. Or great-great-grandmothers. Or great-great-great-grandmothers, but we don't have any four-greats now except for Old Talla. She can't come because she's busy dying."

"I'm sorry to hear that."

"No, no. She's doing splendidly." Shisti smiled with fond appreciation. "We all knew she would."

"Oh, ah . . . good. So this—what's going on—it's for mothers only?"

"Well, of course! Except for you, but you're different because . . . uh-oh. I think I wasn't supposed to say that."

"Charles isn't a mother, either," Lily pointed out.

Shisti gave the sleepy wolf a dubious glance. "I don't know why he can be here. No one told me, but I'm just a one-mother. I think it's because he's dying—"

"Wait a minute. How do you know that?"

Shisti's big eyes rounded in astonishment. "It is obvious."

"Can you go into more detail about why it's obvious?"

Her face screwed up in concentration, then she shook her head. "I don't think so."

"But that's why Charles can be here, even though he isn't a mother. Because he's dying."

She shrugged as if she'd lost interest in the subject and looked away, her cute little face tight with worry.

Worry and adorable just didn't look right together. Lily

reminded herself that harmless little Shisti, mother of one, had helped keep her and Charles prisoners. "Cheer up. I'm sure the, uh, the great-mothers will fix things. Have some trail mix."

"That's for you."

"It looks like you'll be here awhile, and you have to eat."

Shisti drooped all over. Her knees came up and she pillowed her head on them in the dejected posture she'd been in when Lily first saw her.

Charles stood, went to the little woman, poked her with his nose, and lay on his stomach beside her. She looked smaller than ever next to the big wolf. Shisti lifted her head. "I don't speak wolf. What does he want?"

"I think he's trying to comfort you. Humans often find it comforting to stroke furry animals." ·

"Oh. We do, too." She stretched out a tentative hand. "Is it all right if I pet you?"

He nodded and laid his head on his front paws.

Shisti stroked carefully. "Oh, that is nice."

A stream of unintelligible speech in a high, piping voice erupted on the other side of the fire curtain.

Shisti called out, "No, no! They're not—"

The fire disappeared.

"—asleep," Shisti finished.

Lily was already on her feet. She darted forward, ducking to get through the low opening without "knocking herself silly." Her head hurt enough as it was.

There were mage lights and brownies on the other side. Four brownies, she thought, though she didn't pause to count. A couple of them shrieked in surprise and one didn't get out of the way fast enough. Lily knocked her down. There was only one direction to take so she took it, racing off down a curiously rounded tunnel with Charles right behind. Her head pounded with every footfall.

"Come back!"

"Nidilistrionamason—"

"Not him! Not him! Stop him!"

The last must have meant Charles, who pushed past her to take the lead. She let him. The tunnel was dim to her eyes, and what light there was lay behind her so that she ran always into her own shadow. No one shot at them—always a good thing.

Brownies kept calling for them to come back. After about fifty feet the tunnel curved, plunging Lily into deeper murk as the rocky wall cut off the brownies' mage lights. She stumbled, nearly falling, and had to slow so she could trail one hand along the rough wall.

It wasn't completely dark, though. There was a glow ahead. Behind them the piping voices of the brownies drew closer. Lily trotted quickly after Charles, who'd gotten well ahead of her. Was it getting hotter in here?

Charles froze, a low growl erupting from his chest.

Oh, good, an enemy who was not a brownie. Charles didn't growl at brownies, even when they kidnapped him. Lily wouldn't have to worry about hurting this enemy's feelings. If only she had some other way of hurting him—a gun, a knife, a club. Especially a gun. Her Glock. She really wanted her Glock. She kept going.

It was definitely hotter. That wasn't her imagination. She stepped out of the tunnel a couple feet behind Charles—and stopped dead, staring.

She always had that reaction to dragons.

This rocky chamber was much larger than the one where she'd been held prisoner, with a ceiling so high she couldn't see it. There was light, though, streaming in through an opening high in one rock wall. Sunlight, which she hadn't seen since she was brought here. Vaguely she noted a ledge running around three sides of the chamber. Vaguely, because most of her attention was caught by the way sunlight struck fire from scales that varied from glistening ruby to garnet, its slant draping shadows around the huge body looped in lazy coils on the sandy floor of the chamber some fifteen feet below.

She took special note of the large triangular head lifted high above her own.

His eyes were yellow and looking straight at her. "Mika?" It was him, surely. None of the other dragons were that bright, gaudy red. Only he looked bigger than she remembered. It was hard to tell with his body looped around itself like that, but . . .

"She stopped!"

"I can see that, idiot, get out of—"

"You must come back with us!" A small hand tugged at Lily's shirt. "She isn't—"

"Maybe she can talk to her." This voice was just as high-pitched as the others, yet it carried the feel of age. "Lilyu, can you speak to her?"

"Of course!" piped one of the others. "That's why she's—"

"No, that's not why she's here, dummy! If she—"

"Quiet," the older voice snapped. "Lilyu?"

"She?" Breaking the spell of the dragon's eyes, Lily turned to face the brownies. Five of them clustered around her and Charles, who stood a few feet inside the chamber, stiff-legged, still growling. "What do you mean, she? Isn't that Mika?"

"Oh, yes." The speaker nodded firmly, sending her braids dancing—a couple dozen braids, snowy white. Lily had never seen an old brownie, but she was looking at one now. Even her wrinkles were adorable. "Mika was he. Now she's she, and not in her right mind, which is natural and normal at this stage, but something of a problem. That's why we hope you can speak to her, though not too long, which might hurt you, and it would be good if you persuaded the wolf to go away. She might be in a mind that doesn't know she allowed you to bring him."

"I didn't bring—"

"Of course you did. Or was that the Lady?" The brownie tapped one finger on her round cheek. "Maybe so, but either way, you—"

"Mika." She faced the dragon again. "What in the world is going on? Why am I here? What—"

The huge, red-scaled head shot forward, jaws gaping. Brownies scattered. Lily jumped back—but Mika wasn't aiming for her.

Charles might be old. He might be dying. But he was still fast. Before those jaws could close on him, he was elsewhere—leaping several yards into the chamber to land heavily near one rock wall. The dragon reared back and screeched, an ear-splitting cry of rage.

"Mika!" Lily cried sharply. "Stop that! He's with me!"

Lily Yu?

The mental voice was familiar, but not because it was Mika's voice. It wasn't like any dragon's mind-voice she'd ever experienced. This voice was hot, not cold, seething with passion and power. Hot and glowing, like magma. A volcano mind—which, she suddenly realized, she was touching with her other sense.

As she'd touched it before. This mind had sent her into sleep.

"Damn you!" she cried, her head pounding viciously. "Don't you dare put me to sleep again!"

This mind lacks the precision for such work. The male must . . . the words were interrupted by a sort of tactile hiss that scraped along her other sense like a rasp. It hurt. *Go away, Lily Yu. Speak with the ones you call brownies. They will speak truly. Do not attempt to leave. Do not mindspeak me again while I am* . . . Another burst of that staticky, rasping sensation, then, clearly: . . . *strong risk of insanity.*

THIRTY-ONE

∽

"Is Mika the one at risk of insanity, or is that me?" Lily demanded.

She sat in a different rocky chamber on a cushion that looked a lot like a dog bed. It may have been a brownie bed; they'd dragged it in from another room. A dozen brownies sat in a circle with her on much smaller cushions. It was a fairly large room, some sort of public or shared space, with a ceiling high enough for Lily to stand without fear of bashing her head.

Not so the tunnel that led here.

Lily had agreed to go with the brownies because (a) they'd promised to tell her what was going on; (b) Mika would probably eat Charles if she didn't get him away; and (c) she couldn't get out past eleventy-dozen feet of dragon anyway. The brownies had wanted Charles to return to the chamber where they'd been held captive. He refused to leave her side. After a quick discussion in their own language, they'd given a collective shrug and decided not to worry about it. He lay behind Lily now, dozing.

They'd traveled back along the tunnel she and Charles had run down. This time, with light, Lily had seen several openings. Turned out there was a regular warren of tunnels here—wherever "here" was—tunnels slanting up or down, tunnels opening off other tunnels. Mostly they were sized for brownies. Lily was glad she wasn't claustrophobic. Rule would have been really uncomfortable here, she'd thought as she followed the white-braided brownie down one low tunnel, bent over uncomfortably to keep from braining herself on the rock overhead. That had brought a flood of other thoughts—useless thoughts, sad thoughts, worried thoughts. Especially the worried ones.

The four brownies who'd gotten rid of the fire curtain were among those seated with Lily now. So was Shisti. She was the only one with a single braid, though Lily had seen other single-braid brownies on the way here. The others in the circle had multiple braids in hair that varied from mostly brown to pure white, and most had wrinkles in their cute little faces.

None had as many braids or wrinkles as the little white-haired woman, who seemed to be in charge. She'd asked what refreshments Lily would like. Lily had devastated them by requesting coffee. They didn't have any. It took a while to persuade them that something else would do—"as long as it isn't trail mix. Or worms," she'd added, thinking of Shisti's preferred snack. A couple of single-braid brownies had scampered off to fetch what Lily was assured would be a real treat.

The smallest brownie—seven braids, white-streaked hair—answered Lily's question. "You. Mika's not crazy, she's just—"

"—not in her right mind, which is a human term for crazy—"

"But she isn't. Don't confuse our guest, Shisti," the one with the most braids said. She looked at Lily with huge eyes as brilliant a green as those of the youngest of them. "Mika is in a primitive mind just now. She's dangerous, not crazy."

"Is that supposed to make sense? Because it doesn't." Lily dragged a hand through her hair and longed, briefly but intensely, for shampoo. And a shower. And deodorant.

"You ought to understand," another one piped up. "Humans are many-minded, too."

"Unlike us," put in the brownie who Lily had followed into the woods. "Brownies are single-minded all the time."

"Like cats."

"Not dragons, though. They're many-minded, but they know how to use their minds constructively, unlike you Big People—"

"—who are confused all the time."

That sent them all off into giggles.

The matriarch sobered first. "Mika is pretty single-minded right now. She'll stay that way until after the *nithelien*."

They all looked grave and nodded at each other.

"What," Lily asked with all the patience she could muster, "is *nithelien?*"

Everyone chattered at once, only not in English. A couple of them burst into song. In the midst of the clamor, the pair who'd left came running up to Lily. One presented her with an apple. The other beamed and held out a can of Coke.

"Thank you," Lily said. It was warm, not cold. Everyone watched her eagerly. None of them had any drinks, she noticed. "Um—are we sharing this?"

Several of them assured her that they hated the nasty stuff, but they knew humans loved it, and to please go ahead and enjoy herself. She popped the top. Warm or not, it was almost as good as coffee, sliding down her throat in an acid-and-sugar rush. After a few swallows she made herself stop.

Another contingent of brownies arrived, this group bearing trays with small cups and bowls, which were passed out quickly. The cups held a liquid the color and consistency of motor oil. One glance at the bowls made Lily glad she'd already vetoed worms.

The white-haired matriarch sipped her motor oil. "Ahh. It was a good batch this year. Your Coke is good?"

"Wonderful." Maybe the caffeine in it would help her head. The pain had subsided from the initial ice-pick stage, but a dull throbbing lingered. "What am I to call you?"

The wrinkled face creased in a smile. "Gandalf."

"Um . . . I thought that was a man's name."

"It is a wizard's name. I," she said complacently, "am a wizard."

Lily knew what a sorcerer was. "Mage" and "adept" were familiar terms, too. But wizard? As far as she knew, that designation didn't exist outside of Tolkien. She wanted badly to ask what the little woman meant, but caught herself. If she followed every conversational oddity the brownies threw out, she'd spend the rest of the day down the rabbit hole. "Gandalf," she said firmly, "I was kidnapped."

The woman nodded and selected a worm.

"You've held me captive—"

Her eyes rounded in distress. "Not us! We have taken care of you. The wolf, too. Mika kidnapped you. Mika holds you here. We bring you food and water and make you as comfortable as we can."

"But you're helping him—"

"Her."

"Whatever. You're accomplices. I don't want to stay here, and you're helping keep me here. Even if it weren't for the little problem of potential insanity—"

"But that's why you were in a place with lots of earth between you and Mika," Shisti explained, leaning forward. "Contact with her mind hurts your brain. She explained that earlier, before she got stuck in her primitive mind. You must be kept away from her until you figure out something."

"What?"

The brownie shrugged. "Don't know. That's none of our business. But you must be kept separated—"

"—with plenty of rock and earth between you," another one finished, nodding wisely. Her eyes were a darker green than the others and nestled in fine wrinkles.

"Except that you went running to her!"

"Yes," said the one on Lily's right, "and *you* said she should talk to Mika. That was stupid. She isn't supposed to do that!"

"But she'll have to sometime, so maybe then was the right—"

A snort. "Your mother must have dropped you on—"

"Enough," Lily said loudly, and went on in the brief, startled quiet, "Even if there wasn't a problem with me maybe going crazy, I can't stay here. I have duties, and Rule must be frantic."

The one on Lily's left patted her knee. "But that's why Dirty Harry left. To tell your mate that you're fine."

"Harry might have trouble doing that if Rule's still in jail."

"Jail?" Gandalf turned to the others. "What is jail?"

One answered in a quick burst of that other language.

"Ah. A strange custom, this jail. But so many of you grow big without growing up. I guess you must do something with youngsters who behave badly. But why would Rule be there? He's an adult."

Lily tried to explain. She didn't think she succeeded. She wondered if she should warn them. They seemed to think that Harry could pop up, tell Rule she was fine, refuse to tell him where she was or anything else, and Rule would be okay with that. They were seriously wrong, but was it her job to correct them?

She decided it was not.

The matriarch patted her arm. "Don't worry. Harry can get into your jail if he needs to."

"He's very strong in dul-dul," said the one with dark green eyes. "And so good at the game!"

"We all like Dirty Harry," Shisti added. "He is dependable, even if he is slow to grow up."

"He has a good laugh," said the littlest one.

Shisti nodded. "And a very fine penis."

Lily choked. "That's what us Big People call too much information."

That made them all laugh. They agreed with each other that Big People were very funny about sex. Shisti leaned forward to say that she knew about Harry's penis from before she grew up, of course. The others chimed in with additional explanations.

"You are confused because you Big People don't know what 'marriage' means."

A snort from Lily's left. "They know. They don't do."

Giggles. "They do this one, and that one, and the next one—"

"—only youngsters go around doing sex with everyone. Rule is an adult. Even Big People must notice that, so they'll let him leave this jail of yours."

Lily gave up explaining about law and jails. "I need explanations. Gandalf. You're in charge here?"

"No, of course not. I'm the boss."

Cheerful grins all around. "She is very bossy," one agreed.

"But you can answer my questions."

"Ah," she said, nodding. "Yes. You are an *efondi*."

Eleven heads bobbed along with her. One them hummed a snatch of melody; two of them repeated, "*Efondi*."

"You are permitted to know," Gandalf went on. "Mika told us to tell you. But first, you must pinkie-swear to never, ever reveal what I am about to say."

"No."

Brownie babble erupted. Three of them sprang to their feet. Some forgot to use English. Shisti burst into tears. The gist seemed to be that Lily absolutely, positively had to pinkie-swear.

Lily raised her voice over the babble. "Mika told you to tell me. Don't you have to do what he says?"

"What she says, silly!"

"Yes, but she doesn't—"

"No one can know!"

"She has to—"

Lily raised her voice more. "Mika told you to tell me. She did not say I had to pinkie-swear." Lily was gambling now. Dragons could mindspeak one person or many; Lily hadn't been privy to whatever Mika said to the brownies. Shoot, she didn't even know what all Mika had said to her. The painful static had drowned out parts.

Dead silence. It was wonderful. It didn't last. Gandalf said slowly, "Mika didn't say you *didn't* have to swear silence."

"No, she didn't. But dragons are very precise in their speech. If Mika had wanted me to pinkie-swear, wouldn't she have said so?"

Gandalf's cute little wrinkled face screwed up in thought. She said something in her language. Some of the others responded in the same tongue—a lilting sort of speech, suited to their high-pitched voices.

That went on for a while. Lily drank more Coke. It wasn't getting rid of her headache, but it tasted good. She took a bite of the apple. It was delicious, sweet and tart in just the right way.

She'd almost finished both apple and Coke when Gandalf spoke in English again. "We cannot decide what Mika intended. We can't ask her. We used much power making her listen long enough to let down the fire, and now . . ." She sighed. "This isn't in the *ithnali*, and it has been long and long since we served. We have no guide other than the *ithnali*. Mika did not say you had to pinkie-swear, but she does not think so clearly in her current mind. Maybe she assumed . . . still, she did not say, so we are not wrong to tell you without the swearing, and she said to tell you. But if you tell someone else, very likely Mika or another dragon will kill zhe."

"Or tamper with zhe's mind," another one added seriously. "The black dragon could do that without destroying the mind. I think. Maybe."

"But probably just kill," Gandalf said.

A dozen adorable heads bobbed in agreement.

"And the dragons will find out, if you tell. They watch for such knowledge. So I think you shouldn't tell anyone who you want to live."

"Ah." Lily's mouth felt dry. She finished her Coke. "This is a big-deal secret to the dragons."

Everyone nodded again, including Gandalf, who leaned forward. "Listen and heed," she said in a singsong. "In the way-back time, when brownies first came to be, we were friends with squirrels and birds, as now. Then as now, we laughed with the trees, played with raccoons, and teased the badger. But we were few and then fewer, for we were small, and we had no dul-dul."

A chorus of hisses, sighs, and head shakes greeted that announcement.

"The dragons came to us and offered to make a great change, to give us the dul-dul. In return, we would serve them at their *tinaitha*. They needed us. We needed them. This was *af'-Yaldo*—The Big Deal. No one knows of *af'Yaldo*, save only brownies and dragons."

"And *efondi*," put in the littlest one.

"And *efondi*," Gandalf agreed, "But *efondi* are either dragons or dragon-descended. And possibly the Queens . . . we are not sure about the Queens. They may know. They have lived a long, long time. But otherwise, only brownies and dragons—"

"And the Queen's Hound," piped up the smallest brownie. "He knows."

This was one interruption too many. Gandalf snapped, "We do not know if he knows."

"The dragons don't like him."

Gandalf sniffed. "He lives, doesn't he?"

An argument sprang up, not always in English. Most seemed to think that the Hound's continued existence proved that he didn't know about The Big Deal, though a couple of them disagreed for reasons unclear to Lily, as they were expressed in terms of brownie logic. In other words, they made no sense at all. The discussion might have gone on indefinitely, but Gandalf cleared her throat loudly and the others subsided. She folded her hands in her lap and finished. "And so it has been, down through the ages."

"So it was and is," the others chorused.

Shisti turned to grin at Lily. "Isn't that cool?"

That started them off again. This time they argued about the word "cool." It was a subject they felt passionate about, with half of them disdaining the word—which, one of them said, didn't deserve any encouragement—and the other half vociferous advocates. Gandalf tried clearing her throat again, to no effect. So she bopped the two sitting next to her on their heads.

"Ow!"

"Why did you do that?"

"Did we come here to talk about cool? I think not." Gandalf straightened to her most dignified. Brownies were not all that good at dignified. "Do you understand, Lilyu?" The way she said it made one name out of two.

"No. I understand that dul-dul came from the dragons and that you serve dragons at, ah, *tinaitha*. I don't see what that has to do with me—with why I was kidnapped and am being held captive. And what," she added with rising annoyance, "is *tinaitha?*"

"Ah!" Green eyes twinkled. "Adult dragons are the most rational, the most controlled, of sentient beings—except during *tinaitha*, when they are driven by instinct so strong even they cannot master it. Brownies are the only ones who can be with a mother dragon without triggering her need to kill."

"A . . . mother dragon." For some reason the two words didn't seem to go together. "A mother dragon?"

"Yes." Mischief glinted in those bright eyes. "Lilyu, had you ever noticed that all the dragons were male?"

Her mouth opened. Nothing came out. All the dragons who'd come back with her from Dis were male. She knew that, but . . . surely at least one of them was . . . no. Not one, and she'd known that without exactly noticing it, but that made no—

The brownies burst into peals of laughter. They laughed for some time, eventually winding down into giggles and grins.

"You looked so funny!" Gandalf wiped tears of mirth from her eyes.

Lily scowled. "They're all male. All of them. And I never thought about it, what that meant. How could I not have noticed?"

"Because the dragons didn't want you to. Everyone knows the dragons are male. No one thinks about it. Except us, of course."

No one? All over the world? Dragons had mind magic out
the wazoo, but that was flat-out unbelievable. "They couldn't
do that. Not to everyone. The world's too big."

"You are sure?" Gandalf's eyebrows lifted in lofty surprise.
"Then find someone, somewhere, who has noticed that the
dragons are all male. A U.S. scientist who worries about their
species going extinct, maybe. A child in Argentina. An old Rus-
sian man. Maybe an aborigine in Australia. They know that all
the dragons are male. They do not think about it. At all."

That level of mental tampering . . . an entire world? "That
can't be possible."

"Oh, possible, impossible . . ." The old brownie shrugged.
"Never mind if it is possible. It is so. Dragons are born male.
They remain male until they decide to be female. It is a difficult
transformation, requiring a great deal of gold—"

"Gold?"

Gandalf giggled. "Did you think they liked it because it's
shiny? I won't speak of their process. It's very secret, and also
I don't know anything about it."

"Except that gold is required."

She nodded. "They eat it. So Mika—you know she is the
youngest? When she was male, he longed for the third birth
very much—"

"Third birth," Lily repeated.

"Oh, yes," piped up another one. "Dragons have three births."

"One when the eggs are laid—"

"Two when the eggs hatch—"

"Three when they transform to female," Gandalf finished
firmly. "Which they may do only once or several times, but
only the first time is their third birth—which, as I said, Mika
longed for, but it wasn't allowed. Or do I mean enabled?" She
tapped her chin. "Yes, I do. He was born in Dis, you see. Dis is
not a good place to raise children. Even dragon children."

It wouldn't be. All those demons . . . "A dragon can't, uh,
transform without the help of other dragons?"

Gandalf's eyebrows shot up. "I didn't say that. Did I say
that?" She looked around at the others. They assured her that
no, she hadn't. "Not quite," Shisti added cautiously. Gandalf
frowned hard at Shisti. That round, wrinkled face couldn't

look fierce, but she tried. Shisti wilted. "Where was I? Oh, yes. So Mika transformed and mated with the others."

"Mika's a girl," Lily said, dazed. "And she mated. With all of them?"

"Oh, yes, that is very important. Unless one or more of them are her parents, of course. Dragons do not mate with their offspring, but parentage is a private matter for them. I don't know if any of these dragons begat or birthed Mika. Other than parents, they must all mate with her, or the others will kill them. Not right away, but later, after the fledging, which doesn't take place until quite some time after the eggs hatch—"

"Eggs." Lily couldn't seem to stop repeating things the brownie said. "Dragon eggs. I didn't see any eggs."

Gandalf looked shocked. "You wouldn't. Mika may be in a primitive mind, but not that primitive! But you'll see the wee little dragons when they hatch." She nodded encouragingly. "You're the *efondi*."

"You used that word before. What is an *efondi?*"

Gandalf cocked her head. "Midwife? Godmother? No . . . you don't have a word for it. The *efondi* should be a dragon, of course. A female dragon. If a male dragon entered Mika's territory, she'd kill him. If she couldn't kill him, the others would. Dragon instincts are *very strong* about such things. But . . ." She sighed. "There are no other female dragons at this time, and Mika didn't want to wait and let one of the others transform first. It was her turn."

"But if he—she—can't transform without help from the others—"

Gandalf did her best to look fierce again. "I did not say that."

"But . . ." Lily sighed and gave up. "Never mind. What does an *efondi* do?"

"I don't know." The old brownie smiled sunnily. "That's not in the *ithnali.*"

"None of our business," piped up another one.

"But I'm sure you'll do it well," Shisti said, "whatever it is. If you don't go crazy."

"But what am I supposed to—you can't just tell me—oh, hell!" Lily pushed to her feet. "I'm leaving."

Gandalf rolled her eyes. "Oh, *that* will work."

It didn't. Fire sprang up in front of Lily as soon as she left the chamber. "Shit."

"We told you and told you," Shisti said. "We don't hold you here. Mika does."

"She may be in a primitive mind," another one added, "but she knows fire in all her minds."

"Look." Lily turned back to face the brownies crowded up in the doorway looking at her with expressions ranging from disapproval to sympathy. "This is no good. You have to give me some idea what I'm supposed to do to help Mika."

They insisted that they couldn't, since they didn't know. But it was a great honor, being asked to be *efondi*.

"No one asked! I was *kidnapped*. Kidnapped is not asked!" Lily ran a hand through her hair—her dirty, unbrushed hair—and growled. It wasn't much of a growl compared to Rule's, but it was probably better than throwing things at their cute little distressed faces. One of them—the littlest one, whom she absolutely *could not* hit—started patting her on the leg, up-tilted face filled with concern, saying, "There, there. There, there."

Couldn't hit them. Couldn't even shove the one patting her away. Lily gritted her teeth and went on in a tightly controlled voice, "And why wasn't I asked? What reason could there be to force me here instead of asking?"

Something about the patterns, they thought, though they didn't understand about patterns. That was a dragon thing, and maybe she'd feel better if she had something to do? They all had suggestions. After breathing in and out for a few moments, getting her temper under control, Lily had a suggestion, too. A bath.

They loved the idea. They got so excited that it worried Lily—with reason, as it turned out. But how could she have known that brownies considered a bath a major social occasion? Washing-up was a personal chore, but baths were big, splash-happy parties. Plus they considered her "invitation" to bathe a sure sign that she wasn't mad anymore about the whole kidnapped-and-held-captive thing.

They bathed Japanese-style, though without the decorum of a Japanese sentō. Everyone was supposed to wash and rinse before getting in the rocky pool fed by a hot spring that Mika had somehow created or otherwise arranged for them.

Lily could handle the naked part. She didn't have many hangups about nudity, probably because she had sisters. Stripping with a bunch of tiny, giggling strangers wasn't exactly comfortable, but she had reasons to go along . . . right up until she found out that bathers did not wash themselves. They washed each other—and expected Lily to take her turn lathering and being lathered—and they had no concept of hands-off zones. Lily had to tell them that humans simply did not touch each other in some places unless they planned to have sex.

That led to a lot of giggling and a fascinating discussion about brownie sexuality. TMI in some ways, but fascinating. Then they all got in the pool and tried to drown one another.

Back in her prison chamber—without the fire curtain this time—Lily tried to untangle her hair with a teeny little comb the brownies had provided. They'd left her a mage light, too, which was good. It would have been way too dark in here otherwise.

Her hair was clean. That comforted more than maybe it ought to. And somewhere along the line her headache had gone away, which really helped when she had so much to think over. She'd learned a lot. Most of it was stuff the brownies intended to tell her. During the bath she'd asked what brownies did to serve a mother dragon during *tinaitha*. Many things, they assured her, but their main purpose was to sing to her. They sang songs from the *ithnali* in the true tongue, which was what they called their own language. They sang to remind her of who she was. Without the singing she would forget too much for too long.

Lily had also learned a couple things that they hadn't intended for her to know—like where they were. She was pretty sure she'd figured that out. She scratched behind Charles's ear and leaned down, speaking softly. "So were you able to sniff out which tunnel leads outside?"

He nodded once, looking about as smug as a wolf can.

"Good. Excellent." She had a plan. It was shaky, maybe foolhardy, depending as it did on one small guess, one big guess, and her new ability.

Which meant she'd better practice. Better get started. She didn't know how much time she'd have. She stretched out next to Charles, but instead of practicing, she thought about her shaky plan. She hadn't exactly lied to the brownies, but she had deceived them. She was pretty sure Rule wasn't in jail. Nokolai could afford good lawyers. He'd be out on bail by now, and she knew what he'd done the moment he was free.

How long would it take him to find her? Or to find her general location anyway. Not long, she thought. Not once Harry caught up with him, which was why she needed to practice now, dammit. But one other question kept rearing up, distracting her.

What, exactly, was she going to do when he did?

THIRTY-TWO

~

THE sun was headed offstage, but it took a damnably long curtain call this time of year. Golden light slanted across the front of the concavity where they'd collapsed; at its rear all was shadowed. Rule slid his phone back in his pocket and leaned against the rocky rear of the hollow, his chest heaving. The muscles in his thighs, back, and shoulders burned and twitched. He'd carried Danny the last nine or ten miles, after a bullet tore up Mike's thigh.

Danny, whom Rule had just set down, pulled off her backpack and crawled over to sit next to Mike, looking worried. He was panting, too, his head on his forepaws. Wolves can run on three legs pretty well, so when Mike was hit, Rule had told him to Change.

They'd stopped because they had to, but at least they were out of the wildlife area now. Out of Ohio entirely, if Rule's reckoning was correct. And they'd been lucky—the hollow he'd spotted in the side of a rocky hill wasn't quite a cave, but it was deep enough to keep their heat signatures from showing if that gods-cursed helicopter should pass overhead.

Little John was the last of them to enter. The moment he did, he dumped Bert. The human man staggered, but didn't fall. Little John did, collapsing as if he'd been clubbed.

"Hey!" Bert said, dropping down beside the man who'd carried him so long. "Is he—"

"He'll be . . . all right . . . in a bit." Little John had run roughly twenty miles, often at damn near top speed, while carrying a hundred and sixty pounds on his back. He'd done that after racing to Fallback Two carrying Bert. Even his strength had limits. He wouldn't be getting up right away.

All of Rule's small party was here now. Claude wouldn't be joining them.

Rule gave himself another moment to get his breath under control, then moved closer to Mike. He sank to his knees. The bullet had torn out a chunk of meat on what had been Mike's left thigh and was currently his left haunch. Now that Rule got a good look at the wound, he was pretty sure it had hit the bone. Not good.

That bullet had come from a rifle, not a machine gun, the result of pure bad luck. Claude had been about fifty yards ahead of the rest of them, acting as point. He'd practically run into a large armed group—maybe a dozen people, some in sheriff's department uniforms, some not. Not his fault. The group had been downwind and in a shallow ravine, so he hadn't seen or smelled them until he was almost on top of them. He'd turned and run.

The instant Rule had seen Claude flip direction and start racing back, he'd done the same. They'd run away as rifles fired. Bullets pursued them, but they'd been farther from the shooters than Claude, with lots of trees in the way. Pure bad luck that Mike had been hit.

Claude's luck had been worse.

Rule's hands fisted. *Not now*, he told himself. *Not yet. Think about that later.*

The helicopter had never come near them. José had seen to that. José and six others. They'd done what they set out to do. The moment Rule had stopped and let Danny slide down off his back, he'd sent José a text. Just one word: Reply.

He hadn't heard back.

Rule stuffed the anger down, where it wouldn't be heard or smelled, before he spoke to Mike. "Aren't you a bloody mess. At least it's an in-and-out, not lodged. The bone is probably broken. I need to examine it to be sure."

Mike grunted.

"Hold still." Mike's control was excellent. Rule reinforced it anyway, pulling on the mantle slightly as he gave the order. That would make it easier on Mike. He ran his fingers over the wound, lightly at first, then more firmly. Mike whined, then yelped. He didn't move.

Rule sat back on his heels. "There's good news and bad news. The bad news is that your femur is broken a few inches above the patella. The ends are badly out of alignment, and—as I'm sure you noticed—there are bone fragments. The good news is that there's no way I can set a femur properly, so I won't maul you around trying."

He got another grunt in reply.

Danny's face screwed up. "If you can't set it—"

"It will still heal, and the bone fragments will work their way out. Bones that are this badly aligned, however, tend to heal crooked." Given how bad the break was, probably very crooked. "Our healing is more concerned with getting the bone knit than with its straightness. Eventually the leg would straighten, but that might take months. For some reason our healing doesn't prioritize that. Mike may want to have it straightened surgically." Rule dropped a hand to the ruff at Mike's neck and gave him a rub. "For now . . . he's hurting, but he'll be okay."

Unlike some. Carefully Rule shut that thought away for later.

What did his small band need next? Food and water. They were all dehydrated. That wouldn't be hard to mend; he'd smelled water as he approached the hollow. Food would take longer, but they all needed fuel, especially Mike. The Change burned calories. Healing a broken bone burned through them like a wildfire in dry brush. "Bert, I need you to step outside so you can watch the sky. Keep a lookout. Little John will join you when he can."

The man rose without a word and moved to just outside the hollow.

Rule had stuck two pieces of jerky in his pocket at Fallback Two, not thinking he'd need them, but from habit. He pulled them out, bit into one, and fed the other to Mike. Keeping one for himself might be selfish, but was good sense. He'd be doing the hunting, so—

"Rule?" Danny's voice shook. "Is Claude dead?"

He stiffened. She needed to be comforted. He could hear it in her voice. In that moment, he hated her need. He was so angry . . . "I don't know. Do you have food in your backpack?"

"Yes. I can share—"

"Share with Bert, if you have enough. The rest of us will have rabbits soon." He stood.

"If you don't know if Claude's dead or not, how could you leave him?"

He didn't answer. Couldn't. Anger filled him, ready to spill out—

Surprisingly, Bert answered for him. "He had to. Sure, he probably could've gone back for Claude if he dumped you and me. He would've had to kill every one of them, though."

He'd wanted to. Still wanted to. Wanted to go back and rip open the throats of those who'd shot Claude, shot Mike, who could easily have killed the girl who'd just asked that damnable question. Then go on and find the ones who'd fired on José and the others.

"I don't know if they could have done that," Bert was saying. "Even for lupi, that's a tall order, killing a dozen armed people. But say he pulled it off. Then what? He's guilty of killing law officers. It doesn't matter that they fired first and without provocation. His enemies get what they want—proof that he's too dangerous to be allowed to live. He and everyone with him are as good as dead."

"I'm going to hunt," Rule said abruptly. He'd kill something, anyway. Hopefully several somethings. "Once Little John is able to keep watch, you can go in pairs to the creek to drink." Without bothering to pull off his clothes, he Changed.

FIVE rabbits and a raccoon later, he was back on two legs, scowling at his phone.

Hunting had been easy. It was a wildlife area, after all, in the middle of summer. He'd eaten the first two rabbits before he started bringing his kills back, and the food had restored much of his control. His anger wasn't gone, but it was a cold fury now. He could use it instead of being used by it.

José still hadn't replied to his text.

He jammed his phone back in his pocket, cursing himself for telling everyone not to use their phones. He'd been making decisions in one hell of a hurry, but a blanket ban was foolish and unnecessary. Their phones lacked GPS, so they couldn't be tracked that way. They just had to be careful what they said. It would tell the NSA very little if his men were to text him to let him know they'd made it, that they were alive.

If they were alive, that is.

"Time for an after-dinner drink," he told his small party, "before it's fully dark."

They followed him, talking a little among themselves. Everyone felt better after the rest and food. Not that they were truly full. Summer rabbits were plumper than winter ones, but Rule could have eaten all five himself without feeling stuffed. Danny had shared her protein bars with Bert—who might have preferred rabbit, but not raw. Mike and Little John had dined as wolves, that being easier and more appealing, given the nature of their food. They'd taken their meals slightly away from the hollow to avoid distressing Danny. She might not be bothered by watching others eat tidily packaged meat purchased from a grocery store, but Rule had a feeling watching them chow down on cute little bunnies would have been more reality than she needed to deal with after a day like this one.

Rule kept an eye on Mike without being obvious about it. He was in pain, of course, but he was moving well. Rule had made sure he got three of the rabbits. At the creek Rule stood aside, keeping watch while the others drank. He'd drunk his fill while still four-legged. He worried about the humans drinking untreated water, but they didn't have many options. Danny had many useful things in her backpack, but not bottled water. At least this was moving water, not stagnant.

No sign of the helicopter or other threats, though in the failing light his range of vision was limited.

Damn that copter. And damn Edward Smith. How had he gotten the Guard to use shoot-on-sight when they had to know they were firing on men, not wolves? They hadn't issued even a token warning, hadn't asked for surrender. They'd just opened fire with their bloody be-damned machine gun. Rule had expected an attack, but one cloaked in the trappings of legality. How could Smith hope to cover up what he'd caused to happen?

Maybe he wouldn't bother. Maybe whoever had issued that order was himself disposable.

The sun was fully down now. Dusk wrapped the world in tired gray. Gray to Rule, at least—probably the humans couldn't see much at all. "When you're finished drinking, I'll fill you in on our next steps," he told them.

They must have been finished, for they gathered around him—Little John and Mike lying down to seem less threatening, Danny sitting next to Mike, Bert with a few wary feet between him and the two big wolves. Rule stayed on his feet. Four pairs of eyes—worried, tired, trusting, or simply waiting—met his.

All of them dropped their gazes immediately, even Bert. Perhaps Rule didn't have his anger hidden as well as he'd thought. "We'll sleep in the hollow tonight. It should be warm enough that humans won't be uncomfortable sleeping out-of-doors, and the skies are clear. Little John and I will split the watch. In the morning . . . if I've led us right, we're between five and ten miles from the brownie reservation."

Bert looked disappointed. "From the private section of the reservation maybe, but that's no help. They only let visitors into the public section, and that's on the east side, and we aren't. I may not know where we are, but I've taken one of their tours, and I know what that section looks like. There's a small lake and—"

"We're northwest of the reservation."

"Whatever. They don't let anyone into that part."

"No, they don't. Not even law enforcement. It's in their charter."

Bert snorted. "Which might be useful, except that we can't get in, either. They've got those magical whatsits—wards—to make sure no one wanders onto their land."

"I can get in."

Bert still looked skeptical. "You think they'll invite you?"

"It doesn't matter. I can get us in."

"That's a bad idea," piped up another voice.

He sat on a small rock on the other side of the narrow creek, a cocoa-colored little man dressed in brown. His eyes were large and green. When he smiled, dimples popped up in his round cheeks.

He wasn't smiling now. "A bad, terrible, awful idea," he went on. "If you—eeps!"

Brownies are fast. Rule was faster. He sailed across the ten feet separating them, arriving just as the little brown man vanished. Rule's right hand closed around one small leg as he hit the dirt and rolled, ending up on his feet with an armful of squirming, invisible brownie.

Dul-dul doesn't work on touch.

"Dirty Harry," Rule said, showing his teeth in what might be called a smile, "how good to see you again, however briefly."

"Harry!" Danny sounded amazed. "That's Dirty Harry, Rule! He's my friend. You can let him go."

"I don't think so. You might as well let me see, Harry. I'm not turning loose of you."

Dirty Harry popped into visibility. His round face, only inches from Rule's, was screwed up in indignation. "What kind of way is that for friends to say hello? I came here to help you!"

"All right. Help me. Where's Lily?"

"I can't tell you that, but—eep!" he said again as Rule squeezed. "Don't do that! And don't show your teeth at me that way! I came here to tell you that she's okay. Well, first I went to the government city, but you weren't there. Trust you not to be where you're supposed to be! You'd been told, but did you listen? No, and I had to hunt and hunt—"

"Harry." Rule squeezed again—not hard, but enough to make his point. "I'm a little on edge. I've had a bad day. My men have been fired on. Some are probably dead. And my mate is missing. Kidnapped. But you know that, don't you? And you know where she is."

"I—I kinda sorta do. Not exactly, but—Rule, I *can't* tell! It's like a pinkie-swear, only more so!"

Rule's voice lowered to a growl. "You made a pinkie-swear deal with my enemies?"

"But it's not your enemies who have her! I can't tell you who does, but I swear that it's not your enemies." He paused. "Uh—just who are your enemies this time?"

"The NSA. Homeland Security."

"Those are government people."

"Yes."

"That's not good. They probably have a lot of guns. A lot of people to shoot them, too. But they don't have Lily. I'll pinkie-swear about that." He tried to tug one imprisoned arm free, with a predictable lack of success. "At least I would if you'd let me."

Rule didn't loosen his hold. Brownies might be small and seem helpless, but they were incredible escape artists. He didn't need a pinkie-swear anyway. He believed Harry. It made no sense. Who else might have grabbed Lily? And yet he believed Harry. "Everyone," he said, turning to face them. "I apologize for the change in plans, but we're going to have to go on to the reservation tonight, if you're up to walking. No rides available this time, I'm afraid. If you're not up to the hike—"

Bert pushed to his feet. "I couldn't miss seeing how this ends up."

Danny scowled and stood. "You shouldn't be treating Harry this way, Rule."

Little John and Mike simply rose to their feet. Three feet, in Mike's case.

Harry sighed as deeply as his constricted position allowed. "This is such a bad idea."

THIRTY-THREE

~~

LILY woke suddenly. She hadn't been asleep long—just long enough to slide into a dream she wanted back. A dream that left her body warm and aroused and tingling in places that made her think of . . .

Rule. She sat up, wide awake now.

There. He was *there*, a point as clear in her mind as if she'd been able to see it. And he was less than three miles away. That was close, achingly close, but well beyond the limit they'd been living with during her "period of adjustment." Less than three miles and headed her way—not straight at her, but in her general direction. He was moving slowly. Walking, she guessed, and she waited, every muscle tense, for her sense of him to jump, splinter, go wacky again.

It didn't. Her mate sense was working properly. Which wasn't as huge a surprise as it might have been.

She could mindspeak now.

Not well, not easily, and at this point it went only one way—she could speak but couldn't listen. Surely that meant her brain had finished adapting.

"Charles," she said in a voice that sounded much calmer than she felt. "It's time."

The old wolf awoke. He stood and shook briskly, as if shaking off sleep.

She leaned close and spoke so softly she barely heard herself. "He's three miles away. Let's go." She rose and laid a hand on his back, turning her attention to her new sense.

She'd practiced for a long time before going to sleep. Hard to say how long, without a watch or clock, but it had left her exhausted. No headache, though. That was encouraging. And no hallucinations. She hadn't had one since she woke up here the first time. She must have finished adapting.

Practicing had taught her a lot. First, she could only clearly sense minds that were very close. With effort she'd sensed some that were more distant, but it was like groping through sand while wearing thick gloves, hunting for tiny pebbles. Muffled and frustrating, in other words. That made sense, considering how much rock and earth were around her.

There was one exception. It did not make sense. In spite of all the rock between them, Mika's mind was so tactilely vivid that it took real effort to focus on anything else. It was like looking away from a forest fire, or trying to ignore the mountain lion crouched overhead. Possible, but not easy.

The rest of what she'd learned . . . or thought she'd learned, because she was guessing about some of it. But the mindspeech part was definite. She'd had a hunch her new sense was good for more than seeing/touching other minds. She'd been right, though she'd stumbled across the trick more by chance than design. But the important part couldn't be tested, so she was relying on a smidgeon of experience and a big guess.

She'd find out soon if she was right, wouldn't she?

Practice had also taught her how to use her new sense more gently, not so much reaching with it as allowing it to unfold. Using it now felt as if something had been curled up snugly inside her, and she had only to give it a nudge for it to uncoil, stretch . . . and *there* and *there* were the bright little plums that were brownie minds, slick-skinned fruit she could sense but not affect. They were in the tunnel outside her chamber, about ten feet away.

When she and Charles left that chamber, two brownies turned startled faces toward them. "Do you need something, Lilyu?"

That was Hergrith, the one who'd led her through the woods

to a clearing where Mika could zap her into sleep, then snatch her. Lily had learned her name when they teamed up against a trio of brownie matriarchs in a knock-down, drag-out water fight during their joint bath. "I need to leave," she told them.

"Silly. You can't leave," said the brownie with Hergrith, a one-braid Lily hadn't met.

She used one of Rule's favorite responses. "Mmm." And kept walking.

"You're acting funny," Hergrith said, more puzzled than suspicious.

"It's not you who's keeping me prisoner, though, is it? So you won't try to stop me."

"Mika will," the one-braid said.

Hergrith nodded. "And she's very good with fire, no matter what mind she's in."

"I remember." They'd reached a juncture with one of the other tunnels—a narrow, twisty worm of a tunnel. Charles paused, sniffed, and turned into it. Lily ducked down to follow him. Wouldn't you know? This was the lowest one yet.

Both brownies shrieked—first just noise, then words as they pattered after Lily.

"No, don't!"

"You'll get burned!"

"Come back!" That was accompanied by a tug on Lily's shirt.

Lily ignored them. Their presence was helpful, though. They'd brought their mage lights with them. "Charles," she said firmly, "stop and let me get in front."

The wolf did stop, but he was still blocking her. He gave her a stern look over his shoulder.

"You know why." Mindspeech was still too difficult and inconsistent—not to mention one-sided—for her to use it often, so before they went to sleep, she'd used her softest voice to explain her plan to Charles. Talking softly shouldn't make a difference when there was a dragon around; it was hard to keep secrets from a telepath. But Mika wasn't in her right mind, was she? "Scoot over."

Reluctantly, he did. And thank goodness for that. Ten more steps and a sheet of fire sprang up, close enough for her to feel the heat.

Her mouth went dry. She was suddenly sure she was insane

to do this. And yet she let her sense uncoil a little farther, until it brushed against the bright, burning fascination that was Mika's mind. "You need me." She said that out loud, but at the same time she felt her new sense ripple with the words, ripples that washed over that other mind . . . "I'm going to walk forward. If you want me to live, you'll remove the fire."

She took a step forward, hunched over so she wouldn't hit her head. The fire still burned.

What if she was wrong?

The logic seemed inescapable. Mika needed her alive for some mysterious purpose; therefore, Mika would not burn her. The fire was a bluff. She'd thought out every angle she could, and had come up with one possible flaw in her simple plan. Dragons could and did set up automatic defenses. If the fire was on autopilot, something Lily's presence triggered, she could get crisped whether Mika intended that or not.

So she had to make sure Mika was paying attention. That's why she'd practiced and practiced . . .

Lily took another step. She was feeling sunburned.

The only one she'd been able to practice on was Charles—whose mind was nothing like a dragon's. Not to her mindsense anyway. But that was all to the good. All that texture she perceived in Mika's mind—that was what *took in* what she sent. She felt intuitively sure of that.

In other words, she was guessing. But her guess was based on some experience. She couldn't mindspeak a brownie. She'd tried. Their mental frequency, to use what Sam had always considered a poor metaphor—she could see why now—made their minds completely slick to her. But Charles's mind was fuzzy. Practicing with him had seemed to confirm her theory; the fuzziness meant it was possible for him to receive what she sent with those ripples. Not easy, but possible.

Learning to send those ripples had been surprisingly easy. Doing it consistently was hard. She had to pay close attention to two things at the same time—her mindsense and the words she wanted to send. It helped to speak those words aloud. She'd done it by accident the first time when she started cursing in frustration and felt the way her sense rippled, then the way those ripples found purchase in the textured surface of Charles's mind.

Charles had felt it, too. He'd jolted and given her such a look.

Just now, it had felt as if her ripples had reached Mika, as if they'd sunk easily into the rich texture of his mind. Her mind. Whatever. But what if the dragon was so far into her primitive mind she couldn't think rationally anymore?

Another step.

The fire vanished—and a word exploded in Lily's mind. Not a normal word, not an intellectual abstraction meant to convey a concept. This word was the direct and immediate carrier of meaning—a howling, primitive vastness of meaning— *NEED!!!*

Lily found herself on her knees. "Yes," she whispered, then remembered to send that word out in a ripple . . . "Yes, I understand." She stood, shaky. Now her head did hurt, pounding like it was trying to detach itself. "I have to go." *Rule. Rule is so close . . .* "But I'll come back."

THERE were many kinds of wards. Rule had listened to Cullen discuss the subject enough, often in great detail, to claim some familiarity with the various types. The ward around the brownies' private zone was a simple keepaway—simple, but powerful. Most people wouldn't be able to come within ten feet of it. A man with great determination might get closer, but a point would come when he could not take another step.

It was a good thing Rule didn't need to rely on determination. He set Mike down carefully. "Your turn, Little John," he told the man—for Little John was on two legs again, having Changed so he could keep hold of the prisoner.

Danny, Mike, and Bert were on the other side of the ward. Rule was glad to see that Bert was beginning to stir. He'd had to knock the man out to get him across. Danny, of course, hadn't had any trouble. Sensitives couldn't be turned away by wards. Nor could those with really strong shields—not this type of ward anyway. Keepaways used a type of mind magic.

Rule didn't have shields, but he didn't need them. The brownies had altered their ward to admit him when they became allies of the Shadow Unit, united against the Great Bitch. He had sworn not to use the privilege except in an emergency. No doubt the brownies had meant an emergency caused by *her*—but they hadn't included that in the vow, and he wasn't bound by their intentions. Only by his words, and this was certainly an emergency.

Rule had heard the helicopter twice on the way here. It hadn't come dangerously close, but clearly the authorities had expanded their search. "Keep a tight grip on Harry," Rule reminded Little John, and heaved the big man up in a modified fireman's carry.

They'd used Bert's belt to fasten Harry's arms firmly to his sides, so Little John needed only one arm to keep the brownie pinned. The brownie and the oversize man made an untidy bundle, but Rule didn't have to go far. He started forward. "Don't struggle," he ordered the moment he felt Little John twitch, reinforcing the order with a pull on the mantle. "Be still and keep hold of Harry."

He'd learned, in carrying Mike across, just how strong this ward was. He took two steps, three—and the pull on the mantle rose as power was sucked out to enforce his order. Then he was across. He took another few steps and lowered Little John. "You all right?"

The big man was pale and clammy, but he had both arms around Harry, who was looking pretty woebegone. "Yeah, but I hope I never have to do that again. That felt like . . . I don't know what. I couldn't move, but I had to. I couldn't stay still, but I had to."

Mike came closer and poked his fellow clansman with his nose, then snorted—meaning something along the lines of, "You're here, so get over it." Mike wasn't known for coddling those under him. He'd half kill himself rescuing any one of them, but once they were safe, he'd explain in clear terms just how stupid they'd been to get in that fix. He had a knack for finding nice, simple words for such explanations. Four-letter words mostly.

Bert sat up and scowled at Rule. "What the hell! You hit me!"

"I apologize for that," Rule said. "You were struggling so much I was afraid of injuring you."

"Getting belted on the jaw is a whole lot like being injured."

"More seriously injured. I suppose I could have put you down and let you—" He broke off, his eyes widening. And turned toward the east.

Lily. Lily was *there*. Not splintered, fragmented, all-over-the-place in a hideous distortion. Right *there*.

"Rule?" Danny's voice was high and worried. "What is it?"

His breath whooshed out as a burden he'd carried way too long evaporated, leaving him giddy. The mate sense was working. He could feel her. As surely as he felt the ground beneath his feet, he felt Lily. And she was close. He couldn't tell precisely how close. She'd always been better at that, but within an easy run—no, not easy, not in these rocky hills. But she was *close*. "Lily." His voice was hoarse. "She's not far. I have to . . ."

Go to her. But he also had to take care of his small company. Mike was injured, Danny didn't know what to do, nor did Bert. Little John might be unhurt, but he was hungry and exhausted and not a leader. But—

Mike poked Rule with his nose this time. Hard. And snorted.

"Better go, then," Little John said. "That's what we're here for, right? Rescuing Lily. Do I go with you?"

He had no idea if the mate sense would stay functional. It might fritz out again. "Yes. I mean no, you stay with the others, Little John. Mike's in charge. Follow me, but with caution. I don't expect any problems, but I don't know what's going on. I—"

Mike poked him again.

"Yes," Rule agreed. And took off.

LILY stepped out into open air. And night. And brownies.

A couple dozen of them, at a guess. All female. And all talking in their high, piping voices. "My head hurts. Shut up."

They didn't. They desperately wanted her to go back, and they all told her so, and told her, and told her. "Charles. Cut me a path through them."

The wolf moved in front, and that helped, but it didn't get rid of them. Charles didn't want to hurt the brownies. Lily didn't, either—not really, though her temper was peaking along with her headache. That *word* Mika had sent had made her mind-sense recoil. It lay curled up inside her now. She wasn't tempted to nudge it. Not until her headache died down.

It had seemed to take forever to reach the outside. That

twisty wormhole of a tunnel had devolved into a long stretch she'd had to travel on hands and knees, with Charles following in a crouch. But the fire curtain hadn't come back. She'd made it, and the air smelled sweet and the stars were putting on a dazzling show overhead and Rule was *so close!* But all those desperate, damnably cute little brownies would not get out of her way.

She gave up and stopped. Waiting.

He came racing over the crest of the hill in front of her, leaping from rock to rock to land on a twisty path. Which he ignored, bounding down like a two-legged mountain goat. The fire of his nearness burned through everything else as he landed on the relatively level ground at the base of the hill a dozen yards away.

He'd been going fast. Now he speeded up. Brownies scattered.

And at last, at last, they came together—his arms around her, her arms around him. No words, no caresses, nothing but the sweet ease of his breath stirring her hair, his heart beating so close she could feel it, his arms whole and strong, her arms tight, tight around him . . . for a long moment they stood motionless beneath the night sky and held each other. Just that. And everything that had been wrong in the world gradually righted itself.

Without her thinking about it, something uncoiled inside her. And spread out a bit . . . oh! Oh, of course his mind felt like that, so dear and familiar even though she'd never sensed it like this before . . .

Guess what I can do? she said—then, out loud: "Ow."

"What the—that was—are you okay?"

"My head hurts, that's all, and I gave myself an owie just now—but I can do it! I can mindspeak. That's why the—ah, that's why you could find me." Couldn't speak of the mate bond in front of all those pint-size witnesses. "I'm not good at it, not yet, but I know the basic trick. But mindspeaking Mika left me with such a headache . . . shit." She shouldn't have mentioned the dragon. But surely they—the dragons—didn't expect Mika's changed condition to be a secret forever?

"Mika?" He straightened enough to frown down into her face. "What do you mean?"

"Long story, and I can't . . . but you're okay? You got out on bail?"

"Not exactly. That also is a long story. Come on. We need to get out of here. Whoever snatched you—"

"Isn't really an enemy."

"You must define enemy differently than I do."

"It's complicated." The scattered brownies had begun to clump up again a few feet away—all of them chattering madly, of course. She raised her voice to be heard over them. "The brownies aren't enemies, either, though I'm not too happy with them. They did aid and abet the one who snatched me."

His eyebrows drew down. "And held you prisoner."

"And held me prisoner, at first by keeping me asleep all the time."

"You were drugged?"

"No drugs. After a while it wasn't possible to keep putting me to sleep and I figured out that the fire was a bluff, so Charles led me out and we escaped. We just walked out, really, though I did have to crawl part of the way."

For once, Rule was flunking poker face. Confusion flickered in his eyes. Urgency or anger tightened his mouth. When a couple of the brownies darted forward and tugged on Lily, he bared his teeth at them.

They squeaked and jumped back. Another brownie stepped forward.

"Rule Turner," Gandalf said sternly, frowning with all the severity her round, wrinkled face could muster. "Behave yourself."

"Address your corrections to your own people, *t'laptha*."

"But you are here with my people, on our land." Gandalf shook her head. "This was a bad idea, wolf. A very bad idea."

For some reason that made Rule burst out laughing.

THIRTY-FOUR

≈

"**A** terrible idea. I told him!" Dirty Harry told the other brownies. "But how do you make a stupid, stubborn werewolf listen? I sure couldn't!"

There were a lot of others for him to address. Everyone had gathered in the village green—that's what they called it, though it was mossy and tree-shaded rather than open and grassy. A vast mob of brownies nodded, exclaimed, and called out questions or suggestions on how to get a werewolf's attention.

Lily paid little attention to them. She had a hamburger. A big, juicy hamburger with lots of pickles.

At Gandalf's strenuous urging ("We have to get that stubborn wolf away from you-know-who! *He's* not dying! You know he can't be here, Lilyu!"), they'd walked to the brownie village. One of the villages anyway. There were at least two—one in the tourist section, where Big People could snap pictures of the adorable little people churning butter or whatever. And one where the brownies actually lived.

Most of the brownie great-mothers had stayed at the tunnels, but Gandalf, Shisti, and three other brownies had accompanied them. Lily had agreed to go on one condition: they had to bring her things to her. Purse, weapon, everything. They agreed, but at first Rule didn't. He wanted to wait for the rest of his party, which consisted of a wolf, a teenage girl, and two men, one of them human, the other one lupus and carrying Dirty Harry. The wolf was wounded. They would all be tired and hungry, Rule had added. Especially the wolf.

That had elicited worried glances and Gandalf's quick assurance that the men, the wolf, and the girl would be brought to the village, too. They'd call the horses and everyone who wanted to could ride, though someone might have to help the injured wolf—no, no, don't worry, Happy Feet would carry a wolf if they asked him to, he was not at all excitable, and of course there would be food, but brownies didn't eat animals so they couldn't offer—

"My people do eat animals," Rule had said, "and it's easier for us to be calm and rational when we eat meat instead of thinking about how much we want to eat meat."

More worried glances.

"You have meat. You sell hamburgers and hot dogs to tourists in the public area. Four or five hamburgers apiece would be about right. My people are very hungry right now."

"You mean I could have had a hamburger?" Lily had said indignantly. "All this time I've been eating trail mix, and Charles has had to get by on jerky—"

That had brought on a burst of brownie chatter, the gist of which was that brownie mothers could not touch meat, that was in the *ithnali*, not for the whole time they were serving. But the males could—it wasn't forbidden in the *ithnali*—so maybe it would be all right for male brownies to bring hamburgers to the village. "But not *here*," Gandalf said urgently. "We need to go to the village. We need to go now."

"They're right about that," Lily told Rule. "At least I think they are. Explanations later, okay?"

So they had walked to the village, talking on the way. Mostly it had been Rule who talked, at Lily's request. She couldn't tell him who had kidnapped her—not without thinking it through, at least, and maybe not at all. He didn't like that, but he seemed to accept her assurance that they weren't in danger.

He'd been right. His story was long. Also complicated, scary, and in spots it hit pretty high on the shocked disbelief scale. She tried not to interrupt, but he kept tripping her "Oh, shit!" switch. Especially when he told her about breaking his house arrest.

She'd stopped and stared, stricken. "That's not going to go away. Even if—when—we prove you were framed—"

"Later," he told her. "That isn't our priority. We'll deal with it later."

Twice as they walked, she felt something brush against her mind. Felt it with her new sense, and knew who and what it was. Mika was keeping track of her. By the time they reached the village, Rule had finished briefing her. He'd done a good job of summarizing, but it was still a summary, and she had a gazillion questions. She didn't get to ask them. That's when the others in his party joined them—riding enormous horses. She hadn't known horses came that big.

The village was—surprise!—adorable. Rather than using a clearing, the brownies had built their little houses in and around tall pines, oaks, and cedar—with "around" meaning that some of them were literally built around the trunks of trees. Mage lights glimmered and danced among the trees. No electric lights; brownies were selective about where they used electricity. Mostly they didn't. Aside from the tourist area, only a few public buildings were wired.

They didn't much care for right angles. The little adobe houses seemed to have sprouted from the earth like oversize mushrooms, their walls festooned with vines or pebble mosaics, their roofs like moss-covered caps—some coming to jaunty peaks and others more like berets. Most of those houses must be empty, she thought as she finished her hamburger, judging by the number of brownies gathered on the green. For the first time she saw brownie children. She couldn't tell which were boys, which girls. It didn't matter. Even the ear-splitting pitch of their voices didn't matter—at least, not much. Brownie kids took cute to a whole new level.

They'd even carried someone out on a litter which they set down carefully near Gandalf. The litter's occupant was tiny, shrunken, muffled in covers, and looked comatose. Actually she looked dead, but Lily didn't think even brownies would bring a corpse to the party.

Still . . . brownies. To be sure, she oh-so-gently nudged her mindsense in that direction. A couple of ibuprofen from her recovered purse had her headache on its way out, but it wasn't gone. Sure enough, there was a shiny brownie-mind associated with that unmoving body. Lily let her sense coil back up inside her. "Is that the oldest great-mother?" What was the name . . . "Old Talla?"

"Oh, yes," Shisti said. She'd managed to wedge herself in on Lily's left side despite considerable competition. "She wouldn't want to miss this."

Charles and Rule had already finished their hamburgers. Charles lay behind Lily, dozing again. Rule sat on Lily's right, talking with the alleged terrorist, who'd chosen trail mix over meat. At the moment the terrorist was exhausted, possibly traumatized, and enraptured by brownies. Rapture, with Danny, took the form of lots and lots of questions. Lily could relate, though she hoped she wasn't quite that much of a pest herself. Danny went in pursuit of brownie facts with the single-minded excitement of a puppy chasing its tail.

She was also apparently capable of nearly defeating the NSA single-handed. Nearly hadn't been enough, but Lily badly wanted to talk to that young woman.

". . . and their horses!" Danny's hands flew out, narrowly missing Rule's nose. "Aren't they the most beautiful things you ever saw? I'd read someplace that brownies kept horses, but I thought that meant little ponies. You know, brownie-size. But they're Clydesdales!"

The three nearest brownies all started explaining at once that their horses were not Clydesdales, but a breed called Shires, which were superior to other horses in every way. They set out to explain each and every one of those ways.

Lily leaned against Rule, mostly because she could. He put his arm around her, probably for the same reason. "You haven't told me a bloody thing," he murmured.

"I know." She was almost as unhappy about that as he was, and he was pretty damn unhappy. Again that shivery, barely there touch brushed her mind. She didn't have to uncoil her own sense to feel it. She wanted so much to tell Rule about it. "I have to figure out—"

"Rule Turner." That was Gandalf, rising to address him. "We have fed you. Are you calm?"

"Moderately."

"Then explain to us why you violated your sworn—eep!"

Rule had moved suddenly, rising to his feet. "Be careful. Be very careful what you say."

Gandalf tilted her head back to glare up at him. "You were not to use the privilege of entry save when it was utterly necessary in the war against our common enemy."

"I swore not to use it save in an emergency. Is there something about being chased by a helicopter spraying machine gun fire which doesn't strike you as an emergency?"

"You know what was intended—"

"I know what I swore. If you intended something else, why did you not put that intention in words?"

The brownie babble that arose was summed up pretty well by Harry's comment: "Got you there, Gandalf."

Gandalf did her best impression of a fierce scowl. She looked so damn cute, trying to scowl. "You shouldn't be here. You weren't supposed to come here. You were supposed to stay in the government city."

Rule's voice was low and every bit as fierce as Gandalf's wasn't. "My mate was taken. Did you think I wouldn't come looking for her? No," he said more loudly when a couple dozen of them protested that they hadn't snatched Lily. "Don't tell me you didn't actually kidnap her. You were part of it." His voice kept gaining volume. "All of you conspired with someone else—someone whom no one will name—to kidnap and hold my mate against her will. My people have gone to war for such an act!"

The last sentence rolled out like thunder. No one spoke. Or moved.

Rule let the silence drag out before breaking it. "We have been allies. Because of that, I give you a chance to explain. Were you forced to cooperate? Did you act against your will?"

The brownies responded like a class of unruly, overeager philosophy students prompted by their teacher. They burst into discussion. What was the real meaning of force? Could fulfilling a racial duty be considered acting against your will? What did "act" mean in this usage? What about "will"? It wasn't the same as intent, but did it encompass intent, or was it the other way around? Before long, they were locked in multiple debates about the meanings of various words.

"You invited them to talk," Lily told Rule. "You actually asked them to talk."

Gandalf, still standing nearby, sniffed. "Because he wants something. The wolf doesn't plan to make war on us."

Deliberately, Rule sat again. "Why is it, *t'laptha*, that you keep referring to me as wolf? You know that is only part of my nature, and what my wolf wants right now wouldn't please you. You might do better to address the man."

A grin popped out. She quickly wiped it off her face, but the twinkle in her eyes said it hadn't gone far. "All right, man. What do you want?"

"Sanctuary here for all those of my people who need it, for as long as they need it."

Gandalf's eyes widened to excessive roundness. "You don't ask much, do you?"

"A great offense requires great reparations."

"The government Big People would come. They can make trouble for us."

"They won't even find you unless you allow it."

This time it was Lily's eyes that widened. Did Rule mean that dul-dul could be extended over the entire reservation?

Gandalf shook her head dolefully. "Such a thing would take much power. It would also interfere with the tourists. Tourists bring money, and feeding your people would be expensive."

"It may be possible to reimburse some portion of your expenses."

Negotiations were clearly open. This might take a while. Lily leaned close to whisper, "I'm going to see if Danny will have a chat with me."

He turned to look at her, his face very close. "All right, but we need to talk."

"But not now, I think. Or with so many people around."

THIRTY-FIVE

~

IT wasn't that simple, of course. First Lily had to find out where the brownies were putting them for the night. The public area had a couple human-size buildings for the tourists, but it was some distance away—and not part of the thou-shalt-not-enter zone. Everything in or near the village was way too small for humans . . . with one exception.

They'd be spending the night with the horses in their big stone barn.

It wasn't easy getting away without a couple dozen brownies eager to help them make their beds from the available supplies—straw and horse blankets they could lay in empty stalls—but Lily insisted that she needed something to do. That resonated. She'd thought it might.

Getting Danny to come along was easy. She slipped her backpack on, ready to go see the horses the moment Lily suggested it. But first Rule had to place Danny officially in Lily's charge so Mike didn't hobble along with them. Then Lily had to turn down the mob guy's offer to help. Little John didn't offer; maybe Rule had given him a cue, or maybe he didn't want to move. He'd done a lot of moving today.

She and Danny had company anyway—pint-size company in the person of Dirty Harry to guide them, plus four-legged company. Lily had thought Charles was sound asleep. If so, he sure woke up fast when she started to walk away. Invisible company, too. Mika kept checking on her, making sure she didn't go far. She was glad the dragon didn't try to mindspeak her. Her headache had finally gone away.

The barn wasn't far, she was told—just outside the village on the edge of a meadow. Brownies might prefer trees to a clearing for their own homes, but they knew horses needed space.

Not surprisingly, Danny wanted to talk about horses. Dirty Harry obliged, which was just as well since Lily had nothing to contribute on the subject. Harry's chatter did make an interesting addition to her growing collection of weird-things-brownies-say-and-do. They did not imprison their horses—"imprison" was Harry's word—so neither the barn nor the stalls had doors. Nor were there any corrals. Sometimes the horses performed weighty tasks like moving boulders, but mostly they acted as brownie buses. Currying the horses was a coveted job. Lily couldn't figure out how the task was assigned—Harry's explanation employed a lot of brownie logic—but some kind of point system seemed to be involved.

Danny was disappointed when they arrived. Of the two dozen stalls, only four were occupied. Most of the herd slept elsewhere when the weather was good, Harry explained, though they'd show up in the morning for breakfast and grooming. They loved to be groomed almost as much as the brownies loved to groom them.

Harry introduced them—including Charles—to the four horses, who were amazingly calm about meeting a wolf. He told them to take their pick of the empty stalls, which looked surprisingly clean, Lily noted with relief. She'd had some qualms. Superior as these horses might be, she doubted they were housebroken. Charles lay down to finish his nap, and Harry showed them where the blankets were kept and demonstrated the pump where they could get water for drinking or washing. Someone had already tossed down a pile of straw bales that were about half the size Lily vaguely imagined normal bales would be.

"Use as much of it as you need," Harry said. "Oh—I forgot to find out what the password is this week. I'll have to find out and tell you later. I've been gone, and we change it every week."

Danny's eyes glowed. "You mean for Wi-Fi? You've got Wi-Fi?"

Harry snorted. "You've heard of brownie cams?"

Everyone knew about the brownie cams. Brownies.com was one of the most popular sites on the Internet. "Those are in the public area," Lily said. "We didn't know you had it here, too."

"We've got Wi-Fi everywhere. This *is* the twenty-first century, you know."

They had Wi-Fi everywhere but not electricity, and they pumped their water by hand. Brownie logic strikes again. Lily thanked Harry and sent him away. Firmly. You had to be firm with brownies.

When she turned back to her witness, Danny was petting the nose of one of the big Shire horses. The horse was a lot taller than Danny. It had a coat the color of a stormy sky and long bangs. Danny's back was half turned to Lily and her shoulders were slightly hunched. Tense.

"You seem to be good with horses," Lily said. "Have you been around them much?"

Danny shook her head. "We didn't have horses at the Refuge. I didn't know I liked them until now, but I do. A lot." She sighed. "If it weren't for all the terrible things that keep happening, this would be a wonderful adventure."

"Adventures tend to be messy that way." Lily headed for the pile of straw bales. "Lots of discomfort, moments of amazement, and the occasional stretch of sheer terror. Would you like to give me a hand with this?"

"No, thank you," Danny said politely, then, "Oh. Was that a real question or a request for assistance?"

"I'd like some help."

"Okay." Danny joined her. "How do we undo them? Those knots look pretty tight."

"I've got a pocket knife." She had all her stuff again, which was a great relief. She couldn't use her phone, but at least she had it. "We should probably put them where they're going first so we can use the twine to carry them." She picked up two of the bales, one in each hand. Maybe twenty pounds apiece, she thought. That was a heavy load for a brownie.

"That makes sense." Danny followed suit with another two

bales. "Why did you say that about adventures? The terror part, I mean. You don't get terrified."

Lily snorted. "Human being here. I'm real familiar with terror." She dumped her bales in one of the empty stalls.

"But you don't panic or freak out or freeze up. You're a hero. If you do feel terror"—she sounded skeptical on that point—"you must be really good at mastering it."

"The thing about terror is that it's physical. Regular fear is only partly physical, but real terror is an instinctive brain-body response." Two more bales. The twine cut into her fingers. "You can't master it, no more than you can master the flu. Fortunately, it doesn't last near as long as flu does, so you just keep doing what you need to do. After a while it subsides and you're left with regular fear."

Danny had stopped moving. She frowned down at the straw bales. "Where does panic fit? Is it like terror or like regular fear?"

"Hmm." Something in the girl's expression made Lily think this was important to her. "I think panic is what happens when terror hits and you don't have any training to fall back on. Without training, it's easy to panic when you're terrified."

Danny gave a satisfied nod and picked up two more bales. "My lists. I use my lists when I'm panicking. I can't think straight then, so they let me know what I need to do. They're like my training."

"I like lists. They organize my thoughts and keep me on track."

"I know! I don't understand why everyone doesn't make lists, but lots of people don't. Not even grocery lists." She shook her head, marveling at this odd behavior, and dropped her bales in the next stall. "How many do you think we need?"

"I'm not sure. I'm going to start cutting the twine and spreading out the straw so we can see how much it takes to make a bed. Would you bring some of those horse blankets?"

"Sure."

Lily watched as Danny walked to the back of the barn, where the tack was kept. The girl's shoulders were looser. Good.

Rule said Danny had Asperger's syndrome. Lily knew a little about that. A key witness in a homicide she'd investigated a few years ago had been an Aspie, though with more severe symptoms than Danny seemed to have. That's why she'd set things up so she and Danny could work at a task together—to help the girl relax, feel more at ease. It seemed to be working.

She was spreading straw when Danny returned carrying a pile of horse blankets. "You talked in my mind, didn't you? I thought it was someone else, but Rule was sure it was you."

"That was me, yes." Lily reached up for the horse blanket Danny handed her. "I didn't do it on purpose. I hadn't figured out how to mindspeak consistently when I did that."

"Can you do it consistently now?"

"With some people, not everyone." Which reminded her . . . Lily sent a tendril out to sample Danny's mind.

"With me?"

"You'd be easy." An orange, Lily decided. That's what Danny's mind reminded her of—a glowing orange with an invitingly nubby surface. Easy to sink a ripple into that.

"I'd really rather you didn't." Her words were polite. Her face was alarmed.

"I won't, then, unless it's really important." Lily smoothed a second blanket over the straw. Blankets for Shire horses were big, but it took two of them to make a human-size bed. "Two bales per bed seems about right. Do you mind if I ask you some questions?"

"I think I've already told Rule everything."

"And he passed on the basics, but we didn't have time for him to go into detail, so I may cover some of the same ground you've already covered with him. I need to know more about the drug Smith's people are using on the kids. Rule said you'd started telling him about it, but you were interrupted. Did they ever try it on you?"

"I didn't even know it existed until after I ran away."

"Rule said you're certain the drug has mind control properties."

She frowned. "Did he tell you about Nicky?"

"Briefly. Danny, mind control can only be achieved through spirit or through magic. Nothing you've said suggests Smith has a god pulling spiritual strings for him, so if you're right about the mind control, magic must be involved. The drug's other properties indicate that, too. Which means we can't call it a drug. If magic's involved, Lodan must be a potion."

"Does that make a difference?"

"Yes. Among other things, it makes this my case. Using unauthorized magic on minors is highly illegal and very much Unit Twelve business. About this Lodan potion—it's supposed to give a magical boost to a Gift?"

"Yes, though the increase isn't consistent. It ranges from thirty percent to four hundred percent."

"That's a lot of variance."

"Due to their small sample size, they can't be sure, but they think the difference is due to the type of Gift involved." She hesitated. "The four hundred percent increase was Amanda."

"The telepath." Lily nodded thoughtfully. "I see. Is this increase permanent?"

"Oh, no. It decreases with time. Looked at proportionately, the decrease is consistent regardless of the Gift involved. Two months after the drug—or potion? I guess it is a potion—has been administered, its effectiveness has decreased by fifty percent. In another month, any lingering effect is too slight to be measured. I need to tell you about Cerberus. I didn't have a chance to tell Rule. One of the reports outlined what dosage was necessary to achieve Cerberus, but didn't say what that meant."

"Cerberus—that's from Greek mythology, isn't it?"

"He's the three-headed dog with a serpent's tail, a lion's claws, and a mane made of snakes. Sometimes he's shown with just one head, and once in a while with lots of heads, but mostly it's three. He guards the gates of hell."

Cheerful. "Was Cerberus mentioned anywhere else?"

"In the report on practical applications, but it just listed Cerberus as one of the applications with a note to 'See R.R. 1180; Harris, B.J.' The purported author, B. J. Harris, is one of Mr. Smith's researchers, and the numbered reports seem to be the ones that aren't on the NSA's system."

"Hmm. What Gifts are represented in the kids?"

They finished making everyone's beds well before Lily ran out of questions. Danny claimed one of the stalls for herself by moving her backpack there. Lily sat next to her, still asking and listening. Danny was a good witness. She sidetracked easily, but didn't mind when Lily prompted her back to the original question. And she had a phenomenal memory.

At last Lily fell silent, turning over what she'd learned. Danny sighed. "I wish Harry would come back and tell me that password."

"Brownies have a different sense of time than we do." Rule's sense of time was fairly human, though. She'd expected him to show up by now. Was he still negotiating? "I'd like to hear more about Edward Smith. We don't know what his goal is. What's your impression of the man?"

Danny grimaced. "I'm not good at people. I can't read expressions and body language and sometimes my theory of mind hiccups. About all I can say for sure is that he's a liar."

"That's an important datum, but don't undervalue yourself. Rule said that Smith has a minor charisma Gift. It's possible he's test-driven that potion himself, which would mean his Gift isn't minor anymore, but—"

Danny's eyes were big. "I never thought of that!"

"It's something to keep in mind. But he must be accustomed to relying on his Gift to make people like him and trust him. His Gift never worked on you, though."

"No, he managed to fool me without any magic."

"When you were thirteen, yes. It's not that hard to fool a thirteen-year-old. But did you ever like him?"

Danny frowned, thinking it over. "No. I didn't dislike him, but I didn't . . . he was just this adult who was not a friend, not family, but important."

"That's factually accurate, isn't it? He was extremely important in your life. And that's the other thing you've got going for you. Because you don't have much instinctive understanding of people, you're used to trying to understand them logically. There's nothing wrong with relying on instinct. It's a powerful tool, but so is logic."

Danny brightened. She liked that.

"Let's talk about what can logically be deduced about Edward Smith based on what you know of him. I'm going to stipulate that he isn't insane, not in the irrational sense. If he were truly irrational, someone at the NSA would have noticed."

"So we assume his actions make sense. That there's logic behind them."

"Exactly. Let's start with your mother. She worked for him a long time. She must have talked about him sometimes."

"Well . . . she trusted him, but that was because of his Gift, I expect. And, um, let me think." She did just that, remaining silent so long Lily had a hard time not prompting her. Finally she gave a nod. "She thought he was really patriotic. That nothing mattered to him as much as protecting the country."

"Did you observe anything to support or contradict that?"

They talked for a while about things Danny remembered about the man she always referred to as Mr. Smith. "He wants to be in charge," she finished, sounding surprised, as if she hadn't known that until she said it. "That's my observation, based on—oh, lots of things, but my mom said something like that once. He wants to run things. He thinks he can run things better than anyone else."

A small brown head peeked around the opening to the stall. "It's 'firefly.'"

Lily blinked at Dirty Harry. "What is?"

"The password. 'Firefly.'"

Danny had her laptop open and was typing madly. "Firefly. And the network is Browniehome, so—yes! I'm on!"

So much for questioning her witness. Lily had a feeling it would take dynamite to get Danny's attention away from her computer. Still, she'd covered the ground she most wanted to. "Can you check the news? See what they're saying about the murders. And about calling in the National Guard."

"Sure." Danny happily typed "national guard Ohio" into the search box. Apparently it didn't matter greatly what she did online, as long as she get could online.

Lily's satisfaction evaporated quickly. "Gaddo bullets? There's no such thing. And that supposed expert who advised the Homeland Security guy—he was discredited years ago. Disgruntled former MCD agent," she added. "He wanted lupi put down with extreme prejudice, not just rounded up and branded, back before the Supreme Court made the whole registration thing illegal. And that's Franklin Foster," she said when they checked another headline. "Good God. How can anyone take him seriously? He doesn't know enough about lupi to . . ." Her voice faded as she read quickly. "Shit. Harry. Go get Rule. Tell him it's important."

"Wow," Danny said, scanning the article, too. "What they said about Ruben Brooks—is that true?"

"Danny. Can you make a secure phone call with your computer?"

"Sure, but about Mr. Brooks. Is he—"

"It's really important that the NSI doesn't hear what I say on this call."

Danny's lip curled in scorn. Her fingers danced over the keyboard. "They haven't caught me yet. You may see some delay because of the way I'm routing this, but it won't trip any of their flags. Unless they've already flagged the number you call, that is. Who do you want to call?"

Lily had her phone out, scrolling through her contacts. "Dr. Xavier Fagin." Fagin was the world's foremost expert on magical history. He was also a friend, a fellow touch sensitive . . . and a member of the Shadow Unit.

THIRTY-SIX

⤳

CHARLES sat beside Rule. Together they watched the video clip playing on Danny's computer. Forty seconds into it, Charles growled. Rule didn't, but he was every bit as angry. "That son of a bitch."

To most people, that was a garden-variety curse. Not among lupi. If one lupus called another a son of a bitch, Lily knew, he'd be challenged—if his opponent didn't just go for his throat. Lupi meant the phrase literally. Call someone a son of a bitch and you accused him of being the product of bestiality. To be specific—and lupi considered it a very specific insult—you claimed that the man's father had impregnated a female dog while he was in wolf-form.

"I'm guessing you mean Smith," she said, "not Eric Ellison."

"He's a son of a bitch, too." Rule scowled at the computer as it played the rest of the news clip. He was shirtless. He and Gandalf had reached an agreement which included having the brownies seek out his men and bring them here. His shirt had been ripped to shreds to give to the searchers, along with the name of Alex's adopted daughter. His scent on the shirt scraps plus a name only those in Leidolf Clan would know should reassure his men that the summons came from him.

He finished watching the son of a bitch give his press

conference, then clicked to end the video. The moment he did, Danny spoke. "So did Mr. Smith make this up, like he did all the other stuff, and Ruben Brooks isn't really a lupus? I asked Lily," she added, aggrieved, "but she wouldn't answer."

Rule glanced at Lily. She shrugged. It seemed that the truth was out, but it wasn't up to her to confirm or deny. At least the bastards didn't seem to be aware that Ruben was Rho of Wythe. The public didn't know that clan existed, and Ruben wanted to keep it that way for now.

"He is lupus," Rule said in a dead-level voice.

Bert gave a low whistle. He and Little John had accompanied Rule, as had an undetermined number of brownies. Amazingly quiet brownies. Lily was pretty sure they thought they were hidden. They hadn't come into the barn, and Lily had only caught a couple glimpses of small, brown heads peeping around the door. Mike hadn't come with them. Rule said one of the brownies was a healer who was supposed to be good with broken bones.

"If it's true," Danny persisted, "why are you so mad? You are mad, aren't you? Your face doesn't look mad, but you cursed. You didn't curse when people were shooting at us."

Rule's mouth twitched in what was probably unwilling amusement. "I was too busy to curse then. But this is why people shot at us. Why some of my men may be dead and two women are dead. Smith is guilty of murder and attempted murder and inciting the country to genocide—"

"Genocide?" Bert said. "That's extreme."

"You heard a sampling of what's being said," Rule replied. "Smith's tools are fanning the flames with every stupid, hate-mongering lie ever leveled against my people. He's out to get all of us."

"Maybe," Lily said.

Rule's head swung. "Maybe?" He made the word sound like it, too, was a curse.

"I'd bet that he fears and despises lupi, but I don't think destroying you is his main goal. He wants lupi discredited, but mostly he wants Ruben discredited. That's essential to his real goal."

Rule's eyebrows lifted. "You know his goal?"

"I think this all started as an extreme form of interagency

rivalry. No, listen," she said when he started to speak. "Edward Smith considers himself a patriot. A true patriot, a man who puts the welfare of the country ahead of everything else. But he's also a narcissist. Maybe not clinically, but he's like Victor Frey." She named the previous Leidolf Rho, who hadn't seen any distinction between what was best for him and what was best for his clan. "He *knows* that he has to be in charge. Behind the scenes maybe—I suspect he prefers that—but he has to be the one pulling the strings. He's the only one with the intelligence and integrity to do what's necessary to protect the country. Everyone else in positions of power is venal, weak, incompetent, or stupid."

"That's him!" Danny exclaimed. "That sounds just like Mr. Smith. I never put it all together like that, but that's how he thinks. It's like you know him. Did you really get all that from what I said?"

"A lot of it." Reminded that there were a lot of ears present, she said, "I'm sorry, Danny, but I need everyone except Rule to leave for a bit. Out of hearing range."

Danny stiffened. "I don't want to."

Rule spoke. "Perhaps you could go see how Mike is doing."

Lily didn't think the girl was going to agree, but after a moment she bent and picked up her laptop, hugging it to her. "I don't like being sent away, but I do want to see if that healer helped Mike."

"Little John, I put Danny in your charge for now. Bert, if you wouldn't mind . . ."

"Not at all," the mob guy said politely.

"Charles—"

"He knows," Lily said.

Rule's eyebrows lifted. "Does he now." And then he waited for the others to leave. "Where were we? Ah, yes. You were claiming that this whole business has been a power play designed to promote the NSA."

"No, I'm saying that's how it started. Unit Twelve used to be a small, relatively unimportant branch of the FBI's Magical Crimes Division. Most people didn't know it existed. That's how Ruben wanted it because of the prejudice against using the Gifted in law enforcement. Smith wouldn't have seen the Unit as a rival back then, but he probably kept an eye on it. Maybe it even inspired the Refuge by opening his mind to possibilities.

He was going to have Gifted agents, too, only his would be better than Ruben's. They'd be used by the important agencies—his own, the CIA, Homeland Security—not that piddling little Unit Twelve. His influence would grow, which would help him protect the country. But he didn't want to recruit adults. Gifted adults had too much power. They couldn't be trusted. He wanted youngsters who could be indoctrinated. He wanted—still wants—control. So he got his Refuge up and running—and then the Turning hit."

Rule's eyes lit with understanding. "And Congress gave Unit Twelve unprecedented power."

She nodded.

"That's why you believe his goal is to discredit Ruben and dismantle Unit Twelve. The Unit is the one segment of government with both the integrity and the authority to threaten him. I'll bet he tried to get to Ruben somehow, to influence him or put one of his people in the Unit. And failed. If a Unit agent learned about the children he's been experimenting on—"

"Exactly." She was grimly pleased he'd caught on. "And it was after the Turning that Smith and Company escalated their criminality. The first report on the Cerberus potion was dated five months post-Turning."

Rule's eyebrows lifted. "I didn't realize that. I didn't make the connection." His lips tilted wryly. "I've needed you for more than personal reasons. In a couple hours, you've figured out some of the key pieces that baffled me."

"Which I could do because you'd pieced together the rest of it. And because . . . well, the next part builds on something you don't know. You said it would take a sorcerer to change the financial records the way Smith and Company have done."

"So I suspect. Using magic on electronic records requires such delicate work, according to Cullen, that only someone with the Sight—" He broke off, his eyes narrowing. "Cullen. He disappeared, like you. There aren't any brownies in Mexico, or anywhere on the West Coast, but—"

"I'm pretty sure he was snatched by, ah, someone connected with the one who snatched me. He should be fine," she added quickly. "Mad as hell, but fine. The point is—"

"The point is that you haven't told me who kidnapped you."

Rule had spoken quietly, not using his Rho voice, nor with

the icy control that meant he was seriously pissed. But there was no mistaking the intensity behind those words. She sighed. "Yes, and I think I have to."

An explosion of brownies burst upon them. A couple dozen of them anyway, racing in the open doorways at both ends of the barn, every one shrieking that she mustn't, not on any account, *don't tell him, oh no oh no, you promised, no she didn't stupid, please don't, oh no oh no, burn him to a crisp!*—and those were just the ones who shrieked in English.

"*Silence!*" Rule roared.

Every one of them stopped—some so suddenly that a couple collisions took place. In the sudden hush Lily heard only one voice—Dirty Harry saying sadly, "But I like Rule Turner, even if he did tie me up. I don't want him to die."

"I'm going to try to see to it that he doesn't," Lily said. "Rule—"

The next roar didn't come from Rule. It came from overhead—and it was much louder.

This time the brownies' screeches weren't directed at Lily. Their heads were all tilted up.

"Not the barn!"

"The horses—please don't—"

"Not here! Don't burn him here!"

Mixed with brownie cries were the screams of a couple of the horses, who knew a threat when they heard one. So did Lily. She grabbed Rule and pressed herself close so Mika couldn't burn him without getting her, too. Then she unfurled the power inside her and gingerly touched the lava-mind circling overhead, sending a ripple as she spoke aloud. "Way to go on keeping a secret, Mika. Show up and roar."

As if she'd been making a suggestion, another roar shuddered through the air. As it did, the ripple traveled back to her, only stronger. Much stronger. *DO NOT TELL.*

Ow. She winced. Headache again.

"It was Mika, then," Rule said very low, almost a growl. "I thought so, when you said . . . Mika kidnapped you."

"Um. Yes, but that isn't the part—"

A small hand tugged on her pant leg. "Lilyu, would you please take him outside so zhe doesn't burn the horses by accident?"

Lily scowled down at Gandalf. "I thought she wasn't listening anymore!"

"She?" Rule said.

"Zhe can still listen," Gandalf assured Lily. "It's hard, but zhe can, but it's nearly *regarre*, so zhe just hears you now, but not all the time, only sometimes. We don't understand that part, but it's in the *ithnali*. This close to *regarre*, zhe can only talk and listen to an *efondi*."

Lily frowned, trying to untangle that. "You mean that sh—"

"Zhe!"

"—that *zhe* doesn't have telepathy now? Only mindspeech, and only with me?"

Gandalf shrugged. "I know what's in the *ithnali*. Zhe can only listen and speak to an *efondi* now."

"Who is 'she'?" Rule demanded again.

"Rule." Lily turned so she was looking up at him. This was not going to be easy. She wanted Mika to "hear" what she said and what Rule said. She didn't know if she could do that, but she needed to try. "You know that old joke, 'I'd tell you, but then I'd have to kill you'? It isn't a joke to everyone."

"I got that impression, yes."

"You often distinguish between your roles—Lu Nuncio and Rho. As Nokolai Lu Nuncio, you can't promise to keep a secret no matter what because if your Rho needed to know about it, you'd have to be free to tell him. As Rho of Leidolf you could make such a vow, only what the Leidolf Rho hears, the Nokolai Lu Nuncio will hear, too. So there ought to be a way for you to promise to keep something secret, but I don't quite see how. How can we do that?"

Rule frowned. "It's a matter of duty. Conflicting duties, in this case, but the duty of a Rho to his clan supersedes all others. I would need to promise first that I would hear you only in my role as Rho—then, speaking in that role, promise never to reveal what you tell me."

Relief made her knees soft. "Good. Then—"

"I didn't say I'd do that. I said that's how we could do it, if I agreed."

"This is kind of life and death."

"Give me a moment. I have to be sure."

Did you hear? she sent. *He knows his life is at stake, but he won't promise unless he knows he can keep it.*

. . . *MUDDY*, came the answering ripple. For the first time, the mindspeech sounded like the Mika she knew. Still hot instead of cold and way too loud, but that was a familiar complaint. *YOU'RE . . . [rasping static] VERY MUDDY.*

"Yeah, well," she muttered, "you aren't so clear yourself right now. Plenty loud, not so clear."

"What?"

"Sorry. It's really hard to mindspeak without vocalizing."

"You're talking to Mika."

"I'm trying to talk to both of you. It isn't easy."

Rule looked at her a long moment. "You want me to give this promise."

"Yes. I don't think there's any conflict with your duty to either clan. I can't say there will never, ever be such a conflict, but I can't see it happening. And your duty to Leidolf"—in spite of her efforts, her voice rose—"will be a whole lot easier to fulfill *if you're not dead.*"

That amused him, which made her want to hit him. "Very well. I promise to hear what you say next only as Leidolf Rho. You have my word as Rho that I will not reveal it."

THIRTY-SEVEN

~~

FIFTEEN minutes later, Charles was napping again and the brownies were gone. Rule had strongly requested their departure when they interrupted Lily's account one time too many. Now he sat in stunned silence.

Dragons were few. He'd always known that, without giving thought to what it meant—no more than he'd given thought to the screamingly obvious fact that every dragon he knew about was male. Such remarkable incuriosity . . .

"Rule?" she said. "You're really quiet."

"I'm absorbing." He'd thought Lily was exaggerating the danger when she insisted on his vow of silence. If anything, she'd underplayed it. He wondered if she realized how deadly her knowledge was. It was, he thought, the most confoundedly complicated system of reproduction he'd ever heard of. It was the dragons' one big weakness. They'd dulled the minds of an entire world on the subject because they could not afford for their weakness to be known.

That is not the only reason.

The mental voice was as cold and precise as an ice crystal. It was also about that size—a tiny voice he wouldn't have noticed if not for its impossible precision. "Sam," he whispered.

"Yes!" Lily leaned forward. They sat facing each other on their makeshift bed in one of the stalls. "You see it, too?"

Do not tell her I speak to you. Mika might pluck that knowledge from her mind. The outcome would be widespread disaster, death, and destruction.

Rule took only a second to decide to follow the black dragon's suggestion. If Sam spoke that definitely of widespread death and disaster, there would be widespread death and disaster. "Sam sent you here for this. To be an, ah, *efondi* to Mika. Whatever that is."

"That's just it. He didn't send me here. He sent me to Whistle, Ohio, where I found that body—and we still don't know why he was killed, do we? But Sam could have sent me to the brownie reservation, making it easy for Mika to grab me. He didn't. He had a reason for that, something beyond whatever stupid-ass reason Mika had for abducting me instead of just asking for help—which probably has to do with dragons being the epitome of arrogance, unable to humble themselves enough to—"

"No, that isn't it," Rule said absently. Half of him was listening for more from Sam, who was perversely silent. The black dragon shouldn't have been able to mindspeak him at all from the other side of the continent. Aside from the sheer distance involved, the curve of the earth ought to put too much earth and rock between them.

Perhaps he hadn't. Perhaps he was close by.

No.

"If that isn't it," Lily said, exasperated, "maybe you'd like to tell me what is."

"Ah. Yes. Mika couldn't ask because in order to do so, he—she—would have had to tell you the secret of dragon reproduction. The taboo against speaking about it must be extraordinarily strong, especially since she'd have to broach the subject when you weren't an *efondi*. What if you didn't agree? Then you'd never be *efondi*, so you'd have to either be killed or have your memory altered. And I gather Mika's not up to altering memories now."

"So Mika abducted me because he—she—had my best interests in mind."

The sarcasm in her voice made him want to smile. He

restrained the impulse. "Yes, from the dragons' point of view—which isn't ours, but that is how they'd see it."

She tilted her head. "You sympathize with her. With them."

"Mmm. I suppose I do. That doesn't mean I'm not angry about what they've done, but . . . Lily, you—or humans, rather, as a species—have always had the luxury of certainty about your race's survival. Some individuals might be unable to have children, but the race as a whole reproduces like crazy. You know humanity will continue. You know this in such a fundamental way that it's hard for you to imagine what it's like to lack that certainty. Humans are *fertile*. Amazingly so, from the perspective of those of the Blood. None of the innately magical races can take fertility for granted the way humans do." He paused. "In general, as innate levels of magic rise, fertility decreases."

Rule didn't add the obvious—that dragons were among the most magically powerful beings in existence. He didn't have to. She was clearly adding it herself, frowning over what he'd said. Finally she sighed. "In other words, I shouldn't hold my breath waiting for Mika's apology."

"That would probably be wise." Should he point out the difference between apology and debt? A true apology required both regret and amends. Debt was amends without regret, the acknowledgment of inequity or imbalance. Mika would feel no regret for having appropriated Lily, not if Lily was vital to her offspring in some way. She would feel a debt. Perhaps all the dragons would, which was why Lily was safe from them despite her dangerous knowledge.

Rule, not so much. "I am very glad you convinced me to promise silence. There's no way I would endanger either of my clans, or anyone else, by passing on such knowledge, but obtaining my vow makes that impossible. I hope the dragons find that reassuring." He hoped Sam was still listening and could testify to the bone-deep honesty of that statement.

"Yes, but I can't help wondering how they expect to keep their secret. People are going to notice if baby dragons start dive-bombing them."

Amusement ghosted through Rule's mind, so faint he couldn't be sure he hadn't imagined it. "We'll leave that problem for the dragons to deal with. We have enough on our plates."

"True. Getting back to that, what I was building towards before we got sidetracked is that Sam intended for us to tie these things together—Mika having babies and Smith's plan to take down Unit Twelve."

Rule's eyebrows drew down. "I don't see how."

"I don't, either, but there's a link. There has to be. Sam wouldn't have sent me to discover that body if—"

"I'm not arguing. I just don't see the connection. Unless . . ." He frowned. "Is Mika threatened somehow? Or the secret of their reproduction? She's temporarily impaired, you said."

"She's got no telepathy and very limited mindspeech, so she probably can't use other forms of mind magic, either."

"But if there was a serious threat, either to Mika or to their secret, surely Sam would deal with it. I know you said he can't come in her territory now without repercussions, but if—"

Would you rape your son to save the lives of strangers?

Lily frowned. "You've got the weirdest expression on your face."

"I suddenly thought of something Sam said to me once." As in, Sam had only said it once.

"What?"

"I'm pretty sure I'm not supposed to repeat it." Absolutely certain. "But it makes me think that, to Sam, entering Mika's territory now would be a violation so extreme it's unthinkable."

"Huh. Well, Gandalf said that dragon instincts overwhelm their rationality on this subject, proving they've got more in common with humans than they'd like to think. Sex muddles things for all of us."

"I don't know about that. Often it clears my head wonderfully." He wouldn't mind clearing his head right now.

Her mouth twitched. "You're going to have to clear it on your own tonight. Too much company."

"Not at the moment. *Carpe momento.*"

"First, Charles is still here. Asleep, but here. Second—do you really think the brownies left just because you told them to?"

He looked around quickly. "Are they—"

"Not in the barn, and I admit I've only seen one of them peeking through the doorway, but I'll bet there's more."

When the attack comes, Lily must lead your side.

What? What did that mean?

She is Unit Twelve. The government must . . . The small, precise voice faded out, then returned. *Too far. Cannot . . .*

That was it. All Sam could say. The last part meant that Sam couldn't maintain the connection any longer, but the rest of it . . . Rule shook his head, trying to think.

Lily shrugged. "I'm not going to argue about it. Listen, about the potion—Danny calls it a drug, but I'm sure it's a potion. That's obviously key to whatever Smith has in mind. I don't know enough about potions myself, so I called Fagin to—"

"You used your bloody phone? Hell, we might as well send Smith a text, telling him where—"

"Chill! For God's sake, how stupid do you think I am? Not with my phone."

"Sorry." His heart was pounding. Too much alarm and emotion today. Beneath the sudden infusion of fight-or-flight hormones, he suspected, lay exhaustion. "I'm twitchy on the subject."

"Plus you're muddled because you were just thinking about sex."

He didn't argue. He—or a portion of his body—was still thinking about sex, undeterred by either physical or mental eavesdroppers.

"I asked Danny if she could use her computer to place a call the NSA couldn't track. She said she could. She's an A-list hacker, right? One who's managed to elude the NSA for nearly a year. She ought to know."

"She's probably a damn genius, but it still makes me nervous."

"I also asked Fagin to use one of those crystal thingies Cullen developed that disrupt any listening devices."

"Sheer paranoia on my part." Probably. He waved that away. "What did Fagin say?"

"He's going to look for historical accounts of potions that supposedly give Gifted people more power, more control, or both. It may take a while. He says that rumors of potions and other ways of getting a magical power boost have abounded for centuries. Most of them are bunk, but there isn't exactly a database of credible accounts. I'll call him back tomorrow to see what he's learned."

"He's not looking for a mind control potion?"

Lily grimaced. "I did mention that, without going into detail, but . . . Rule, it seems so unlikely."

It did. He hated to think of how it would affect Danny to learn that her friend had been a willing killer, but mind control was so very unlikely.

"But I did ask Fagin to keep an eye out for any mention of a potion credited with helping telepaths control their Gifts. He's skeptical about finding anything. Very little is known about telepathy, except that nothing seems to help."

"You've covered all the bases. I can't think of anything to add." His head felt too thick for thinking, period. He'd been right. The adrenaline rush was fading, and he was tired. Really tired. He rubbed his face. "If you were wanting to brainstorm together, I'm no help."

She rubbed his arm. "Tomorrow will do."

It would have to. "I should have thought about using Danny's computer to call Alex. He can tell me who's reported in." He forced himself to stand. It was harder than it should have been. "I'll do that now."

Lily rose with him. "You look ready to fall over."

"It's been a long day." A long few days . . . how many? When had he learned about Lily's capture? He added it up and was amazed. "Three days. It's slightly over three days since you were taken. It seems so much longer."

"Three days I spent sleeping while you were doing everything but sleep, I bet." She reached for his hand. "You know, José might have just lost his phone. He might even have thrown it away because he couldn't use it."

"Perhaps." If José had turned suddenly as stupid as his Rho, unable to think beyond the immediate crisis . . .

"Shut up."

His eyebrows lifted. "I beg your pardon."

"Whatever you were thinking, you need to shut up about it. Not to me. To yourself."

"Ah." It was good advice. He wasn't sure he could take it, but it was good advice.

The moment they started to move, Charles joined them. The old wolf had been so quiet Rule had forgotten about him. "You can go back to sleep, Charles. I'll watch out for Lily."

Charles looked from Rule to Lily . . . and shook his head.

Impertinent pup! Rule bared his teeth. "I said—"

"Rule." Lily squeezed his hand. "He's not yours."

No. No, Charles was Wythe, and Ruben's to command. He closed his eyes and took a slow breath. "I'm having some trouble with my temper."

"I hadn't noticed," she said dryly.

He'd been angry for days, banking that anger, waiting for the chance to use it to destroy the enemy who'd snatched his mate. Suddenly that enemy . . . wasn't. He couldn't rampage among the brownies, who'd been fulfilling a racial duty. Nor could he attack Mika, who'd been fulfilling a different sort of racial imperative. For one thing, the latter would be suicide. But it would also be wrong.

"Charles," he said, opening his eyes to see that the wolf was hunkered down submissively, "are you under the impression that the Lady put Lily in your charge?"

Charles nodded.

Rule sighed. "Come along, then."

Lily had been right. There were lots of brownies lurking near the barn. Rule saw about a dozen, but there might have been dozens more using dul-dul so he couldn't see them. At his request, a couple of them ran off happily to tell Little John and Bert they could return to the barn. Some of the others went with him and Lily to find Danny.

She and Mike were together, and sound asleep. Danny lay on her side, curled up protectively around her laptop. Mike lay on his side, too. And Danny's out-flung hand rested on Mike's furry back.

Mike was wounded. He should not have been able to sleep with Danny touching him. Even if the healer had put him in sleep—a healing trance of a deeper state than normal sleep, but not unconsciousness—he should have roused at the touch of anyone not clan. Any touch at all, really. Mike had been schooled in distrust by an expert.

The little brownie sitting nearby was braiding several strips of leather, using her feet as well as her hands. Rule recognized her, though they hadn't been introduced. She was the healer who'd offered to help Mike. She looked up as they approached, smiled in a motherly way, and whispered, "They look so sweet when they're asleep, don't they?"

LILY lay on her side with her back to Rule's front, his arm draped over her, listening to his soft, even breath. It was rare for him to fall asleep ahead of her, proof of just how exhausted he'd been.

The barn was dark, but not wholly silent. Now and then one of the horses moved or an owl hooted outside. She shifted slightly. Straw didn't make a very comfortable bed, but that wasn't why she was still awake.

The world hadn't really come right again, however much it had felt that way the moment Rule's arms closed around her. There was one whole hell of a lot seriously wrong, and her mind couldn't stop turning over the facts, looking for what linked them. She couldn't stop thinking about dragons and a mysterious potion and a man who considered himself a true patriot.

A few stalls down, someone shifted on his straw bed, making it rustle. Bert, she thought, from the location. Charles was in the stall on her left, Little John on the right, with Bert one stall beyond Little John. Mike and Danny weren't here. Mike needed to remain in sleep to speed his healing, and Rule hadn't been willing to wake the girl. He could wait until morning, he'd said, to call Alex.

Danny mattered to him. Mattered enough for him to wait another night to find out how many of his men lived. Let it be all, Lily thought at the darkness around her. Please let it be all of them. However unlikely that seemed, it was possible, so until she knew otherwise, she would think of them all as alive.

Especially José. They all mattered, but losing José would hurt—hurt her and wound Rule, leave him limping worse than Mike. Some breaks couldn't be mended by a healer. So for now, she'd believe José was all right, just as she'd told herself it didn't matter that she and Rule couldn't make love tonight. They'd have other nights. Mornings and afternoons, too. She intended to go right on thinking that though she knew no one was guaranteed another breath, much less another day.

But what did it help to think about that? Pain wasn't paint.

She couldn't thin it out by starting on it early, as if there were a fixed amount she could spread around so no one spot got too much. Starting on the hurt before she lost someone just meant she'd hurt longer. She knew that; she'd tried it, and it had crippled her, and how was that useful? So she'd go on thinking that José was alive and that she and Rule would have another day. And then another. To hell with the odds. He was here now, and . . .

Something brushed across her mindsense, making her shiver. Mika, checking. Making sure she was still around.

What did the dragon need from her? What did Mika's changed state and the eggs Lily hadn't been able to see have to do with Edward Smith? Where were the Gifted children Smith had perverted to his ends?

No, being with Rule again hadn't made everything right. So much was wrong and scary and bad. But the world made sense again. Not the figured-things-out kind of sense, but a deep-down sort which made the figuring-out seem possible.

That was good. There was a lot to figure out.

THIRTY-EIGHT

⟨flourish⟩

LILY had fallen asleep still trying to figure out how the potion, the dragon, and the patriot connected. She woke up knowing.

"Son of a bitch," she said, sitting up. "It fits. It damn sure fits." She paused. "I think it fits."

Rule wasn't there. Her mate sense told her he was in the village. When she stood, she could see that no one else was in the barn, either, except for Charles. Even the horses were gone— but maybe not far. She heard brownies giggling nearby, and comments that suggested they were doing grooming things with one or more horses. The light streaming in from the open doorways was bright and strong.

How late had she slept? Didn't matter, she supposed. She spared one wistful thought for the coffee she didn't have and stuck her feet in her shoes, then grabbed the little plastic glass, toothbrush, and toothpaste the brownies had provided when she was a prisoner instead of a guest.

Charles awoke, stood, and stretched. She took a moment to scratch behind his ears, which he seemed to appreciate. Then she headed out to the pump.

Four brownies were brushing one of the horses. Two of them sat on his back, one working on his mane, the other on his hips. One of the others was doing something with his hoof;

the last one was combing out his tail. They greeted her without pausing in their work and asked if she was hungry.

"Getting that way."

"Hot dogs at the green!" one of them piped up. "For you and the wolf. You just tell someone. They'll get you hot dogs."

Hot dogs were an unconventional breakfast, but at least they weren't trail mix. She pumped water, brushed her teeth, and drank a glass of water. The whole time she was turning her theory over in her mind, looking for holes. She found one. A big one, too. And yet the rest of it fit so well . . . she didn't have enough data, but she knew one place to get more.

Teeth brushed, she went back in and got her comb and an elastic from her purse. In a few moments she was as present-able as she was going to get. She donned her shoulder holster, but left her jacket draped over the side of the stall. It was going to be hot today. She set off for the village with Charles.

There was something odd about the path she followed. She hadn't noticed last night, but this morning the difference between it and the land around it was obvious. It was harder than it should be, and lighter in color. She bent and tapped it. It was hard, almost like adobe. Brownie magic did feel a lot like Earth magic. Not identical, but as if that was its basis. Had they spelled their path to resist water?

Shortly before she reached the village green, she ran into Mike. He was standing on all four legs—much to Shisti's dis-pleasure. "You are not to be walking on it!" She shook a finger in his face. She had to reach up to do that. The little brownie could have walked under the wolf's stomach without ducking her head.

Mike looked confused and took a step back.

"Use three legs! You—oh, hi, Lilyu!" The little brownie beamed at her. "I'm practicing my nagging."

"That was pretty good," Lily said. "But if you want a lupus to mind, you need a Rho to back you up."

"A *dada* has to be able to nag her patients herself," Shisti said seriously, and turned to frown up at Mike. "Your healing is good. My *geeshai* is very good. But that bone isn't hard yet. Use three legs!"

Lily kept going. There weren't many brownies around, and the few she saw seemed to be in a hurry to get someplace else.

They all greeted her; one of them called out that breakfast would arrive soon. A few minutes later, she saw Rule, Danny, and Little John just inside the mossy village green. Also four more men. After a second she recognized one of them. Jason was a high-ranking Leidolf guard. Another man looked familiar, though she couldn't think of his name.

Looked like the brownies had already found a handful of Rule's men. She hoped they'd find more. Find everyone.

They were all staring intently at the laptop screen. As she got closer, she heard a voice coming from the speaker. She couldn't hear clearly—the speaker was aimed away from her—but she recognized Alex's voice and caught some of what he said. Her heart twisted.

"Not Saul!" Danny cried suddenly.

"I'm sorry," Rule said. "But James confirmed it."

"No!" She shook her head. "He was nice! He let me borrow his flute. He—" Her face crumpled.

Rule tried to put an arm around her. She pushed it away, turned, and ran.

A huge, dark wolf raced past Lily, running after the girl— on three legs.

Rule watched them for only a moment before looking back at the laptop. "Thank you, Alex. You won't be able to reach me, so I'll call again later."

The men parted to let Lily come close. They looked grim. Her mouth was dry when she asked, "How many?"

Rule had his face in lockdown. No emotion in his voice, either. "Thirty have reported to Alex. Ten of them were injured. Three have been confirmed dead." His gaze flicked briefly in the direction Danny had vanished. "Including Saul. As you see, four have reported here. That leaves eleven unaccounted for, counting Carson. We're fairly sure at least two of them were arrested."

She asked the hard question first. "Who's dead?"

"Saul Cotton. Dave Wells. Roger McConnell. They were all on the squad José led to draw the helicopter away. James is the only one from the squad who has called Alex. He reported the three deaths. Of the remaining squad members, he thought one was dead but wasn't sure, as he was hit at the same time and was briefly unconscious. When he came to, José ordered him to leave."

"José was alive yesterday, then."

"Alive then, yes. He'd lost a great deal of blood, mostly because of his leg, which James thought must have taken multiple rounds."

"No word about Claude?"

He shook his head.

She absorbed that in silence for a moment. "If one of you doesn't die right away, there's a good chance his healing will keep him alive."

"Unless an enemy comes across him and finishes the job."

"The Guard troops thought they were shooting gaddo bullets, not regular ammo." Gaddo was the drug used to keep lupi from Changing. It had others effects, too, all of them unpleasant. "You and I know that's ridiculous. There's no such thing. But the men in that copter thought they were preventing their targets from turning wolf, not committing murder. It's a big step up from that to deliberately killing wounded prisoners."

"It depends, doesn't it? On whether the person who found José saw a man or a monster."

Lily didn't argue. He was partly right. Edward Smith was doing his damnedest to make people see monsters, but Lily couldn't accept that everyone would tip so far, so fast into fear-driven violence. Some would, but not everyone. But she hadn't experienced the years of suppression and bigotry that Rule had. It would be easy for him to think that humans would kill his people out of hand. It had happened.

She glanced at the silent men around her. The other lupi found it easy to believe, too. They weren't as good as Rule at keeping what they felt from showing. They were angry. Deeply angry.

She couldn't argue with that, either. So was she. "I need to call Fagin. I think I know what Smith's after."

His gaze sharpened. "It's connected to the potion?"

"The potion and what it takes to make it. I'd like to talk to Fagin before I tell you what I'm thinking. It, ah, it sounds kind of crazy."

"I'd like to know what you're thinking, crazy or not."

"I can't talk about it in front of everyone."

His gaze flicked over the men around them. "Little John, Danny knows you. Please go after her and see if she's up to placing another call for us. The rest of you find something to do out of hearing range. Completely out of hearing range, unless I shout. If you hear too much, your life is likely forfeit."

RULE watched his men scatter, with Little John taking off in the direction Danny and Mike had run. He looked back at Lily, and some of the grief he felt lightened. She was here, he was with her, and world was not wholly dark. One of her cheeks was smudged with dirt. Her clothes were in much worse shape.

"Where's Bert?" his smudged, dirty, beautiful Lily said.

"He offered to help fetch hot dogs. I won't risk having my men go into the public area. The authorities seem unaware of our presence here, but we can't count on that. Bert assures me his record his spotless. Even if cops are there, they'll have no reason to bother him."

"That's just wrong. Your people have to hide, but the mob guy—"

"We don't refer to him that way."

"You don't, maybe."

"We don't have much time before Little John returns, hopefully with Danny."

"Right." She took a deep breath. "I dreamed about Grandmother last night."

He raised one eyebrow. "Much as I respect Madame Yu's abilities, I doubt she was offering advice in your dream."

"No, she kept nagging me to speak Chinese. It wasn't a mindspeaking, Rule, just my subconscious yelling at me about something. Danny called the potion Lodan."

"She did. And—"

"She hasn't heard anyone say the name, though, has she? I've been pronouncing it the way she did—accent on the long *o*. That's why I didn't realize it until I dreamed about Grandmother. Put the accent on the second syllable."

He tried that. "Lodán?"

"Close, but . . . you know how English speakers don't hear Chinese correctly? First because it's a tonal language, and second because some of the sounds just aren't Western. Well, Danny never heard anyone say the name of the potion. She's just seen it written, and it was almost certainly written by an

English speaker who doesn't know that *g* is unvoiced in Chinese. Someone who might hear *lóng dàn* and write Lodan."

The way Lily said the first version was much more musical than the second, but . . . "They do sound similar to my English-speaking ears. Not identical, but close. What does *lóng dàn* mean?"

"Dragon egg."

Rule didn't stagger physically, but he felt like she'd knocked his legs out from under him. "You can't mean—that's—how could he even know about Mika?"

"That's the big hole in my theory," she admitted. "I can't come up with any way he could know, but Mika's not at her best. No telepathy, so she can't check to see if anyone's thinking thoughts they shouldn't. Maybe that means she can't blank everyone's minds on the subject, either."

"But the potion was created long before Mika's, ah, transformation. If—" He broke off, looking to his left. Little John, Mike, and Danny were coming. They weren't close enough for Danny to overhear, but the lupi would.

Lily followed his glance, then lowered her voice to a whisper. "The sorcerer. The one you think has to be working for Smith. If he's Chinese . . . there was no Purge in China, Rule. A lot of chaos during the Revolution, and before that—"

"You think he could be an adept?"

"Shit, I hadn't thought of that." She scowled, thinking. "I guess that's possible. Let's hope to hell not. I mean that some of the knowledge that was lost in Western countries during the Purge wasn't lost in China. A lot of it, yeah—as the level of magic decreased, the communities who'd preserved that sort of knowledge dwindled and mostly died off. And more was lost during the Revolution, but it's possible that some family or group retained and passed down a lot more spellcraft than people in the West did. Maybe they passed down something tangible, too—like fragments of dragon eggs. And China is where Sam and the others used to live. They were there for centuries. If anyone knows how to—"

"Lilyu! Rule Turner! Lilyu! Rule Turner! Come! Come with us!" A swarm of agitated brownies raced toward them, shouting. Brownies ran amazingly fast for anything with only two legs, much less beings so small.

Harry was in the lead. He skidded to a stop. "You've got to come right now!"

"—right now!"

"They're lying about her!"

A chorus of agreement that someone was lying.

"We're coming," Rule said. "Where?"

"The *wewishal*," one said.

"That's like a gathering hall," said another.

"It's the TV place," Harry said, tugging on Rule's jeans. "Come on!"

The TV place was the largest building in the village—huge by brownie standards, but still too small for any of the Big People to enter. Rule lay flat on his stomach so he could look through a window. Lily did the same at the open door. A flatscreen TV held pride of place at one end of the long, rectangular room—not one of the enormous flatscreens, but it was still taller than the brownies gathered to watch it. Around three dozen stared at it intently. None of them spoke, and the ones who'd come for Lily and Rule fell silent, too.

". . . go to Angie Sommers with our affiliate in Charlottesville now," said a familiar newscaster. "Angie, what have you learned?"

"I'm speaking to Greg Price, who works in the gardens at Monticello. He'd just arrived at the gates this morning when the fire started. Greg, tell us what you saw."

"They just burst into flame! Everything was normal, then all of a sudden, the trees were on fire!"

"Did the flames seem to come from somewhere, Greg?"

"No, ma'am. I've never seen anything like it. I braked—didn't think about it, see, that was automatic, and then I just stared because it didn't make any sense. Then I got my phone and called it in and they told me to move my car so the fire trucks could get in. They didn't want me to go any closer to see if anyone needed help getting out of the house—there was some folks coming out by then, see. Running out the front door. I did like they said and got my car out of the way." He shook his head. "That fire was sure hot. It ate up those trees like they were dry kindling."

Angie came back with a question about whether the fire spread to the house, but when Greg started to answer, they were interrupted by the newscaster, who had more breaking news. Another mysterious fire had occurred, this one in forested land just outside Lewisburg, West Virginia. Firefighters were on the scene and the cause was unknown, but . . . "We've received confirmation that radar picked up a bogey over Lewisburg similar to that reported at Monticello just prior to the fire's occurrence. That's three fires started in the space of three hours, all of them tied to a mysterious bogey visible on radar but not reported by anyone on the ground—a bogey that Eric Ellison of Homeland Security has said is almost certainly the missing Washington, D.C., dragon. Tom, what have—"

All around him, brownies burst into angry cries—"They lied!" "They're lying about her!" "Why do they lie?"

"Quiet," Rule said sharply. "Quiet. I need to hear."

This being an all-news channel, they repeated everything they'd just said, using different words and adding a lot of speculation and a few more details. The first fire had occurred in the early morning at a small manufacturing plant in eastern Virginia; a security guard had been the only person on the site of the blaze, and he'd been killed. Casualties at the last two fires were still unknown.

Rule listened a little longer before sitting up. He met Lily's eyes.

"One of the Gifted kids Danny told me about has a Fire Gift," she said. "A strong one. They're doing it to Mika now. What they did to you to, Ruben, to Danny. They're framing Mika."

"Yes. You were right." Rule's voice sounded hollow in his own ears. He understood now why Sam had said what he had about Lily and the Unit. "Smith intends to break the Dragon Accords."

THIRTY-NINE

~~

DEMI didn't hear the whole newscast, having arrived a little behind Rule and Lily, but she heard enough to be shocked. At first no one would answer her questions, but after a bit of confusion Rule got the brownies and everyone else to adjourn to the middle of the green, where they could talk. Just as they settled there, Bert arrived, carrying several paper bags. Demi smelled hot dogs.

That distracted her. Hot dogs were one of the few meat products she missed sometimes, maybe because they didn't seem like they'd ever been part of an animal. Lily—she'd told Demi to call her that—hadn't had any breakfast, so she took a couple of hot dogs. The lupi wanted some, too. Lupi always seemed to be ready to eat.

Fortunately Demi wasn't all that hungry, having had some trail mix when she woke up, so she could ignore the way the hot dogs smelled. Mostly. Then Bert passed around Cokes. She took one of them, and it tasted great. She didn't usually have Coke in the morning, but that rule wasn't as important as the "no meat" rule, and she didn't want to wear out her prefrontal cortex. She needed it working right now. The sugar in the Coke would help with that. Then one of the brownies—his call-name was Mallum, he said, which meant "young oak"—gave her an apple. That helped, too. It was a good apple.

While Lily Yu ate, Rule Turner explained what was wrong. Demi tried to listen, but most of it she already knew. She kept thinking about Saul. She didn't know why she'd run off when she heard he was dead. How did that help? It was a strange reaction, but she felt strange. Like someone had hit her in the stomach and she couldn't get her breath, only of course she was breathing just fine, but she didn't want Saul to be dead. She'd only talked to him twice. She didn't know why it hurt so much.

Mr. Hawkins was dead, too. He wouldn't go to the Tip-Top ever again so he could eat and be with people without talking much. So were two people from Whistle she didn't know, or at least she hadn't recognized their names. The article she'd found last night that gave the names of the victims of the "large predator" hadn't had photos, just names. She'd been so relieved that Jamie's name wasn't on that list, but she knew Mr. Hawkins. He wasn't exactly a friend, but she knew him.

No, she *had* known him. He was dead now. Demi had understood how real death was ever since her mother died. She hadn't understood how often it happened. Oh, in her head she'd known. She's seen statistics. Now her whole body knew.

Was it Nicky who'd killed them? Had her friend cut up Mr. Hawkins with his Gift until he died?

Bert's exclamation got her attention. "He's trying to frame a dragon? How can he think he can get away with that?"

"Because he keeps getting away with it," Demi said. She hadn't seen the dragon last night—which she deeply regretted—but she'd heard her. "He's good at it. He can plant pretty much anything in a system that relies on electronic data. That's how he was able to create those radar bogeys. His weakness is that he thinks that's what it takes to win—that if the data is on his side, the people involved don't much matter." She stopped, frowning. "Why are all of you staring at me?"

"I guess we were surprised," Lily said. "You're a computer geek yourself, and geeks often think the data is the important part."

"It is important," Demi agreed. "But the difference between him and me is that he thinks he's good at people. I know I'm not. I get people wrong all the time, so I know from experience that getting the data right isn't enough."

"True," Rule said, "but for the moment he's ahead on the people front, too. He's using the media to get his message of fear out."

She frowned at him. "Even I know you can get people to do bad things if you can scare them enough. That's easy. It doesn't make Mr. Smith good at people. He thinks he is because his Gift has always helped him get what he wants. But his Gift won't work on millions of people watching the news the way it does on whoever is right there with him. You're the one who knows how to do that. You're good with people one-on-one or in bunches or over the television. I bet that's why he wanted you out of the way—so you couldn't go on television and calm everyone down when he wanted them to be scared."

Rule had a funny look on his face. He glanced at Lily, who raised her eyebrows at him. "You may be right," he said. Demi wasn't sure if he meant her or Lily. "But if so, he got what he wanted. I can't go on TV and calm people down right now."

She thought that over. While she was thinking, the others were talking and talking. At one point they got loud as if they were arguing, but she didn't let that distract her. She had an idea. She thought about it for quite a while before she got it lined up right, then she spoke. Loudly, because someone else was talking and this was important. "You don't need TV."

Everyone stared at her again. "What?" Rule said.

"The brownie webcam gets millions of hits a day. The brownies should bring it to this part of the reservation, where police can't come and arrest you again. Then you go on the webcam and explain to people what's really going on and why they don't need to be afraid of lupi. You should have brownies with you, and they should talk, too. Everyone loves brownies. People will trust them."

"That . . ." Rule did the look-at-Lily thing again. "That's a very good idea. It would give away my location and probably Danny's, too, but the potential gain is substantial."

"What about me?" Lily said. "I can't exactly arrest Smith over the Internet, but if I—"

"The only reason you're still on active duty is that you're missing in action. We need to keep it that way."

Even Demi could see that Lily didn't like that, but after a moment she nodded. Then she looked at Demi. "I suspect you didn't hear what we were discussing just now."

"No, I was thinking."

"What you suggest is important and might help. But our first priority has to be stopping Smith. I, ah—I recently learned that the president had the Pentagon work up contingency plans in case there was ever a need to take out one of the dragons. Those plans call for using the military. I don't know what the other dragons would do if that happened, but it would be bad. Dragons aren't just big, smart animals who dislike visitors and soak up magic. They're powerful. More powerful than I think most people realize, including Smith. Do you know where they lived before they returned to Earth?"

"Sure. In hell."

"Yes, otherwise known as Dis, the demon realm. When the dragons first arrived in Dis, they killed a demon lord and took over his territory. You wouldn't know how powerful a demon lord is when he's on his territory, but I don't think any of our tech could accomplish that. I think that if we dropped an atomic bomb on a demon lord when he was in his own territory, he'd laugh and eat the fallout."

That made Demi feel cold. Shivery cold. "A fission bomb or hydrogen? Because a fission bomb delivers the equivalent of twenty thousand tons of TNT, while a modern thermonuclear weapon, which is often called a hydrogen bomb, releases a blast equal to one-point-two tons of—"

"Let's just leave it that demon lords are incredibly hard to kill on their territory, and incredibly bad things would happen if our government violated the Dragon Accords."

Demi nodded, still feeling cold. "Dragmageddon."

"Uh—what?"

"Dragon plus Armageddon. Dragmageddon."

"That's pretty much right."

Rule said, "We know who is behind this. Edward Smith. Others are part of it, but if we stop Smith, we throw his people into chaos. A man as bent on control as Smith is would have total control of his organization; without him, the rest will flounder. I see only three ways to stop him: we kill him, we kidnap him, or we arrest him. Setting personal preferences aside, killing him would have severe consequences for my people because it plays into the narrative he's established. Smith's people wouldn't need to know who killed him to blame it on lupi. Kidnapping him carries the same risk. Arresting him is the only thing that might work. That's what we were discussing."

"You mean Lily?" Demi asked. "She could arrest him?"

"Maybe," Lily said. "It's complicated. The Fourth Amendment means that I almost always need a warrant to make an arrest, but getting one is likely to tip off Smith—if I even could, based on hard evidence. That's pretty skimpy at the moment. Felony arrests without a warrant are permissible in a public place based on probable cause, or if the law officer is in hot pursuit, or if there are "exigent circumstances"—which usually means an immediate emergency, like shots being fired. This is certainly an emergency, so a case could be made that it's a lawful arrest, especially given the gravity of the charges. But—"

Rule broke in. "It is, as Lily said, complicated. It's also moot, because Lily says she can't leave the reservation."

"Mika needs me here," Lily said. "I promised I'd stay."

"Why does she need you here?"

For some reason that startled Lily. "She?"

"Mika," Demi said impatiently.

"Ah . . . I can't go into that. It's part of my promise. But among the powers granted the Unit by Congress is one most people aren't aware of. I can temporarily skip the paperwork and bring someone into the Unit immediately on my own authority. They'd have to be approved later, but until they were recalled for that procedure, they could act with full authority."

"Lily wants to induct me," Rule said. "I think that's a bad idea."

Demi nodded. "You'd just get arrested yourself, wouldn't you? Probably before you ever got to Mr. Smith. Your face is pretty well-known."

"No, he wouldn't," piped up Dirty Harry. "That's where we can help. We can spread dul-dul around a little bit. Not for very long, but if he can do most of the sneaking himself, a couple of us could go along and hide him when he needed hiding."

Rule shook his head. "As I was about to say when Danny told us about her idea, arresting Smith isn't enough. He has to stay arrested. No law enforcement officer or agency in D.C. is going to believe me when I claim to be a Unit agent—particularly," he said with a quick glance at Lily, "since I won't have a warrant. They'll let him go and keep me."

"Who, then?" Lily demanded hotly. "Who could I tap? The same problem arises no matter who it is. If I inducted Jason into the Unit, they'd probably arrest him for impersonating a Unit agent. They'd have to drop the charges later, but they'd take Smith's word over his. Smith would still go free."

Everyone was very quiet for a moment. Lily spoke first. "We'll just have to get in touch with another Unit agent."

"Who?" Rule asked. "Abel and Martin are among the ones who've been relieved of duty pending the results of the investigation. Doesn't that mean they currently lack the authority to make an arrest?"

"I didn't know that." Lily sounded discouraged or mad or something. She was frowning, but frowns didn't always mean anger. "Did you tell me they'd been relieved of duty? I don't remember it."

Rule ran a hand through his hair. "Perhaps I forgot. I can't think of anyone else who'd listen to us."

Lily shook her head and didn't say anything.

Demi did. "Mr. Brooks would, I bet. Has he been relieved of duty, too? Or put under arrest? Or was he just removed as head of the Unit?"

"I don't know," Rule said slowly. "The press didn't use that term—'relieved of duty.' Officially he's still under investigation, but he hasn't been arrested. Being lupus isn't technically a violation of the law. Some of the television pundits claim that he can't be employed by the FBI at all due to his status as a lupus, but that would have to be litigated. Lily?"

She was still frowning. "There are procedures that have to be followed. It's possible that Ruben was removed as head of the Unit without actually being relieved of duty. It depends on . . ." Her voice drifted off. "Ida! Did Ida stay on as secretary to the head of Unit Twelve?"

"I have no idea," Rule said. "How would that help? Are you thinking of making her a Unit agent?"

"No, I'd have to go there to do that—can't do it over the phone. I'll bet she's still the top guy's secretary. Smith wouldn't think she was a threat. People don't think of secretaries as having power, but even this idiot they brought in to run the Unit must know he has to keep the monster fed. The bureaucracy, I mean. Bureaucracies can't function without paperwork, which means secretaries and clerks who know how to feed the monster the proper forms." She grinned. "Or not. If anyone knows how to delay or bollix up the paperwork, it's Ida."

"You think she did?" Rule asked.

Lily's fingers were tapping her thigh. "She may not have needed to. The way the Unit is set up is so different from the rest of the Bureau. On an organizational chart, Unit Twelve looks like part of MCD, but if you read the fine print, the head of MCD has no authority over us. The director of the FBI does, but it's largely limited to appointing or removing the person who runs the Unit. He can tell that person to remove agents from duty, but he can't do it himself because the paperwork has to originate with office of the head of Unit Twelve."

"Ruben didn't remove himself from duty."

"No, and this guy who's taking his place is regular FBI. There's a good chance he wouldn't realize that when Ruben was removed from command, he wasn't automatically removed from duty, too. He might not know that was up to him to do. And Ida wouldn't point it out."

Rule seemed excited about that possibility. So did Lily. They wanted to call Ida, but weren't sure how to do it without the NSA listening in. Ida would be at work and that number was bound to be spied on, and maybe her personal phone was, too.

Normally Demi would have spoken up because that was her kind of problem. She didn't. She was thinking again.

This problem was a lot harder. She didn't like the answer she kept coming up with, but no matter how she looked at the data, she got the same thing. So she started listening again, hoping that someone would say something that changed the data. They didn't. They'd decided there was no safe way to talk to Ida over the phone, so someone would have to go there in person to find out if Mr. Brooks had been relieved of duty or not. The question was who to send.

Demi sighed. No way around it. "Me. You need to send me. First, I'm the only one of us who knows Mr. Smith on sight. Second, it's possible he's used some of the Lodan potion himself, increasing the strength of his charisma Gift, which might be a problem for someone else—but his Gift doesn't affect me. Third . . ." She sighed again. She did not like this part. "It might be important to stay in touch, and Lily can do that mindspeech thing with me even when there's a lot of miles between us. We know that because she did it. Twice. She talked to me in my head and she heard me, too. We don't know if she can do that with anyone else when they're far away, and we don't have time to find out."

TWO hours later, Demi was an agent of Unit 12 heading for Washington, D.C., in an old Buick. She'd had to tell Lily the name she'd been born with: Demi Alicia McAllister. She'd told everyone they could still call her Danny if they wanted to. She liked being Danny.

Mike had Changed back to being a man so he could drive and, when they got there, so he could explain to Ruben Brooks who she was and why Mr. Brooks should listen to her. Four brownies went with them—Dirty Harry, Mallum, and a pair of twins called Twix and Hershey. They'd named themselves after their favorite candies.

Rule had argued about sending her. That made her feel good. He made it clear he didn't want to risk her, and he couldn't protect her personally if she was in D.C. But he couldn't come up with data that changed her reasoning, though he had made one good point. The brownie reservation was almost twice as far from Washington, D.C., as it was from where Demi had been when Lily mindspoke her before. They didn't know if Lily would be able to reach her in D.C.

Still, Lily had a better chance of reaching Demi than anyone else. Like it or not, Demi had won the argument.

"You sure this gas gauge works?" Mike asked.

"I don't know," Dirty Harry said. "Do you know about gas gauges, Twix?"

Twix didn't. Neither did Mallum or Hershey.

The car belonged to the brownies. Sort of. Who'd have thought brownies would have a car? They were too small to drive. A tourist had abandoned it in their parking lot a few months ago and they'd claimed it. Demi didn't think they'd actually taken care of the paperwork to put it in their names, but it hadn't been reported stolen. She'd checked. So it should be okay for them to take it to D.C.

They knew the car worked because, while they didn't drive the car on roads, they did drive it, going around in circles in the parking area after the reservation was closed to tourists. Doing that involved two of them steering, two manning the brake and gas pedals, someone whose job was to shift gears, and someone else perched on the hood, calling out directions. Dirty Harry claimed that no one had been seriously hurt playing with their car. Sometimes Dirty Harry didn't have a lot of sense.

Lily had practiced mindspeaking with her before they left. Several times. That was to get Lily used to finding her mind, and so Demi could get better at talking back to her. It seemed to work best if she spoke her response out loud and paid close attention to what she was saying. She still didn't like the way mindspeech felt, but it wasn't as creepy now that she knew it wasn't Amanda talking in her mind. That was good. She was going to be experiencing it a lot because Lily would check with her pretty often.

Making Demi a Unit 12 agent was a fallback thing. Lily said the appointment wouldn't stand up because she was underage. But for now, she was a law enforcement officer, an agent of the FBI, sworn to uphold the constitution of the United States. It thrilled her. If for some reason they weren't able to connect with Ruben Brooks, she would try to arrest Mr. Smith herself.

She was hoping hard that they found Mr. Brooks.

"You're sure quiet," Mike said.

"There's a lot to think about. I don't understand why Lily didn't make you a Unit Twelve agent, too."

"Conflict of interest."

"That's what Rule said, but I don't understand it."

He gave her a small smile. "You'll honor your duty. You may be a very new, very temporary agent, but you take it seriously, don't you?"

"Of course."

"I can't make the promise you did. I'm not going to follow anyone's orders but my Rho's, and my job is keeping you alive. If I have to violate the constitution to do that, I will."

That made her stomach feel really weird. Not bad exactly, but weird. "I'm breathing, but I don't feel like I'm doing it right. Do you think I'm having a new kind of panic attack?"

"Don't."

She put her hand on her stomach and paid attention to her breathing for a few moments. This wasn't panic, she decided. It was what Lily called ordinary fear, only it was a really big big ball of ordinary fear because she was scared for so many people. For herself, sure. She didn't want to die. But for Mike, too. In trying to keep her alive, he might get killed himself the way Saul had. Plus she was scared for Rule and Lily, who were facing some kind of attack from Mr. Smith back at the reservation. And the brownies. She was scared for them, too.

She had lots of friends now. She hadn't realized that having lots of friends meant a much bigger ball of fear in her gut.

"I brought cards!" Dirty Harry called from the backseat. "We should play gin rummy. Not you, Mike, because you're driving. Do you know how to play gin rummy, Danny?"

Demi swallowed. "Sure."

"Better watch out," Mike said. "Brownies cheat."

"It isn't cheating," Dirty Harry said, "unless you get caught."

FORTY

~

THE conference room held five people when Edward Smith walked in with Greg—Sharon, Chuck, and Barry, plus a gray-haired woman and a young man with hair the color and texture of straw. Tom Weng wasn't there. Most of them were talking. Voices ranged from anxious to angry to excited.

Smith's lips were tight as he went to the head of the table. Barry pulled out the chair on his right and sat. Smith remained standing. One by one, the others fell silent. He let that silence drag out for a moment before saying, "Operation Retrieval is about to commence." Before they could respond, he added, "That is not, however, why I asked you to come here."

That startled everyone.

"You all know your tasks in Operation Retrieval. You don't need me to tell you again what's at stake or what part you play. Unfortunately, you do need another sort of reminder. We have accomplished some of our most important goals. Target Prime has been revealed for the inhuman monster that he is. Public opinion is shifting toward a more sensible attitude about were-wolves, and Unit Twelve is virtually paralyzed. It will continue to degrade once we have time to turn our attention to other Unit Twelve agents. However, some matters have not proceeded as we intended."

Smith shook his head, a schoolmaster unhappy with his students' performance on a test. "Many of you seem to regard this
as a crisis. Indeed, a few seem to be only a breath away from
panic. Did you believe everything would unfold precisely
according to plan? In what world does that ever happen?"

"This is more than a minor hitch," the gray-haired woman
said. Her voice was deep enough to pass for a man's. "Target
Duo has Demi. The two of them have escaped and we can't
find them. Target Tres is still missing, and we have to suspect
she might be with Duo. And we are now out of time to look for
them."

"Target Duo is not superhuman," Smith said dryly. "He's not
any sort of human. True, he's likely to complicate matters. If I
didn't believe that, I wouldn't have authorized the use of Cerberus. But realistically, what can he do? He has two useful skills
and one significant resource. He can fight. He can summon
other werewolves to fight with him. And he performs well on
television." A small smile. "He won't be going on the *Tonight
Show* anytime soon, though, will he?"

Some of the tension in the room eased. Barry actually
chuckled. "Like to see him try."

"Exactly. Let us look at the worst-case scenario. Assume
that somehow Target Duo has managed to locate the dragon,
which I think we all agree could only happen with help from
the brownies. It's unlikely that a bloody-minded werewolf and
a timid, defenseless people like brownies would be friends, but
for the purpose of our assumption, we will say that this is so.
Perhaps Target Duo once rescued the brownie chief's son from
certain death and earned his everlasting gratitude."

More chuckles greeted that sally.

"In this scenario, the brownies helped Target Duo escape
the National Guard and—for some unguessable reason—
made him aware of their other guest. I'm afraid I can't come
up with a story to explain how Duo then became aware of our
plans. My imagination isn't sufficient for that task." His voice
was very dry now. "Have any of you a better imagination?"

"Demi," Chuck offered. "Something she told him made him
suspect it."

"What?" Smith asked pointedly. "I believe you were present at other meetings when we discussed what Demi knew or

might guess. We concluded that there is simply no way she's aware of Cerberus. She might have heard of the Lodan potion. It's unlikely, given her ostracization from the children, but possible. Amanda might have said something to taunt—no, Sharon, don't object. Amanda insists that she didn't, but we all know the child is difficult to control. But it is quite a leap from hearing vaguely of Lodan's existence to guessing at what we undertake in Operation Retrieval."

The others gave Chuck slightly hostile looks. "Hey, I just wanted to cover all the possibilities," he protested.

"That is one of the things we value you for," Smith assured him. "Now, back to our scenario. I can't explain why Duo might decide to risk his life, and perhaps those of his men, in defense of the dragon's clutch. Unless one of you would like to suggest that the dragon is herself aware of us and our plans, and passed that on to Duo?"

Sheepish looks now.

"Good. Because my imagination truly falters at the prospect of explaining why, knowing about our intentions, she has done nothing." Another look around the table. No one spoke.

He nodded. "We can conclude that Tom's information about her was accurate. Still, in order to construct our worst-case scenario, we will factor even that into our assumptions—that Duo means to stop Operation Retrieval and gathers some of his men to oppose us. What happens then? Some of the troops we send will die." He looked grave. "That would grieve us all. But even in this, the worst-case scenario, we will still accomplish our goal. He and whatever men he might call upon cannot, with tooth and claw, stop troops armed with M16s, grenades, and missile launchers."

Tentatively, Barry spoke. "And Duo will be in real trouble then, won't he? He'll have killed U.S. soldiers."

"Very true. Though we hope to avoid that outcome, if it should happen it only strengthens our position." Smith smiled faintly. "Tom is, I suspect, the reason for some of your unease. He's not one of us, however useful he has been. He's contrary, arrogant, and he enjoys baiting people. That makes it difficult to have confidence in him, but I keep a close eye on Tom. Do any of you lack confidence in me?"

"Of course not!"

"—complete confidence—"

"Never!"

"—ridiculous. Of course we trust you."

"We'll follow you to the end, Edward. You know that." That came from the gray-haired woman with the deep voice. "One thing does worry me, though. Your safety. Duo's a born killer. We know that, even if the general public needed to be forcibly reminded of the fact. Because of Demi, he knows who you are. What's to stop him from coming after you?"

This smile was fuller now. "Thank you for expressing that concern. I am only one man, however, and hardly the most vital. I—" He had to stop while they all assured him that he was indeed the most vital and his safety meant everything to them. "Thank you," he said again. "Your words touch me, even if I can't agree. If it eases your mind, Sharon, I've implemented additional security at home."

When he looked around the room, meeting each pair of eyes briefly, he was a proud papa surveying his brood. "We all know what our jobs are in Operation Retrieval. Most of you can go on to your regular jobs for now. Sharon, Chuck, Greg— please remain. I have some additional instructions for you."

Dragons Break Their Silence, Speak as One

Governors of fourteen U.S. states, as well as the leaders of China, France, and Italy, report being mentally contacted by the dragons in their regions. The contacts appear to have taken place either simultaneously or within a very short time span. All of the dragons made the same announcement. They denied that Mika, the missing Washington, D.C., dragon, bears any responsibility for the mysterious fires in Virginia and West Virginia.

The dragons warned against any attempt to seize or harm the red dragon or otherwise violate her current lair, stating that this would be an "irredeemable breach" of the Dragon Accords which would nullify the Accords in their entirety.

While the content of the announcement appears to have been consistent with each recipient, some leaders reported additional statements from their dragons. The Chinese president, Chen Wei, stated that the dragons are extremely angry with the United States. French Prime Minister Nicolas Bellamy said that *Le Érudit*, as the Paris dragon is known in his country, is very reluctant to leave France, but he would have no choice if the Accords were breached. Prime Minister Bellamy urged the U.S. to act with extreme caution and restraint.

The fires the dragons referred to took place in Virginia and West Virginia earlier today. All three fires are now out. One person died in the fire at the Roanoke, Virginia, plant; two were injured at the Monticello blaze, one of whom remains in critical condition. No injuries took place at the fire near Lewisburg, West Virginia.

While no witnesses have reported seeing who or what caused the fires, the FAA has confirmed that radar sightings of bogeys took place at all three fires at or near the moment of combustion. The bogeys were too large to be drones and flew too low for most conventional aircraft; experts say that their manner of flight was inconsistent with any known type of aircraft. Prior to the dragons' announcement, many officials had been attributing the attacks to the missing Washington, D.C., dragon, because of the size of the bogeys and their motion, which suggests winged flight. Eric Ellison of Homeland Security has reiterated that claim, pointing out that the inability of witnesses to see anything supports that conclusion. Dragons are known to be able to go unseen.

Officials speaking off the record indicate that the president is meeting with officials from multiple departments, and that she does not intend to act precipitously.

———————

FORTY-ONE

~~~

AFTER the brief ceremony, Rule lounged on the mossy ground of the village green, propped up on one elbow. He loved the smell of moss. The entire reservation smelled good, but the scents were especially welcoming here. He drew in a deep breath, savoring the moment as any warrior must in the pause before battle.

He drew in his mate's scent along with the moss. Lily sat next to him, writing in her spiral notebook. Making a record of what had just taken place.

Along with those scents were many more . . . brownies, of course. Not a lot of them, since many of them were busy. They might have started out frantically trying keep him from learning about the eggs, but now that those eggs were threatened, they were his enthusiastic supporters. He was coordinating their defense with an old brownie called Codger. "You see," he'd told Rule when they met, "when Gandalf changed her name, I decided I would, too. Keeps things even between us."

"You're Gandalf's husband?"

Green eyes nested in fine wrinkles had opened wide in astonishment. "Well, of course!"

"And you're in charge of the reservation's defense?"

"No, I just tell them what to do. I'm not as bossy as Gandalf," he said with pride, "but I do okay."

Rule also smelled lupi. His lupi. Leidolf. Ten more of his men—all fighters—had found their way to the reservation, giving him a force of fifteen. They sat or stood nearby, chatting with each other or simply waiting. Lupi knew how to wait—unlike brownies, who were no good at it at all. If a brownie wasn't sleeping, he was doing—working, walking, talking, playing. Most of the ones nearby were playing tag.

Amid their shrieks and laughter he could hear the television in what Harry called the TV place. Rule had asked them to turn up the sound so he could keep track of the news. He kept half an ear on that while they waited for Gandalf. All the newspeople now referred to Mika as "she," just as Danny had done earlier. No one noticed that this was not the pronoun they'd used for the red dragon in the past.

Rule had decided to think about what that meant later. He had enough to juggle mentally right now.

They'd called Fagin before Danny left. What the old scholar told them confirmed what they both suspected. Dragon scales were mentioned in numerous references to potions and spells—including the more credible accounts of potions that purported to increase a spellcaster's power. Due to the dragons' long absence from Earth, their eggs were more a matter of myth than historical record, but Fagin was confident that they would be even more potent than the scales.

All the great-mothers and many of the mothers were now at the tunnels with Mika—singing to her, Lily said. Gandalf had promised to come listen to Rule's proposals soon, but it was hard to know what a brownie considered "soon." Many of the brownies weren't in the reservation at all. They were acting as scouts. If some kind of military or police buildup occurred nearby, Rule would learn about it quickly. They were keeping watch even though most of them thought there was little danger. The bad government people didn't know where Mika was. Even if they did somehow learn that, now that the dragons had made their joint announcement, the Big People wouldn't dare act. And if they acted anyway, the wards would stop them.

The brownies were wrong. Rule was convinced of that. The fires had taken place in what was nearly a straight line leading to the reservation, with the last one less than an hour's drive away. Rule didn't know how Smith had learned where Mika was. According to Lily, one of the Gifted children was a Finder; maybe, in Mika's current condition, she'd been unable to prevent the child from Finding her. Or maybe the sorcerer had some secret knowledge about how to find dragons. Whatever the means, Smith knew where Mika was, and he knew about the wards because everyone did. Which meant he had a way to get past them.

And the dragons' announcement? It had bought them time, that was all. The government wouldn't be eager to send troops to deal with a supposed rogue dragon when they risked having all the other dragons quit their jobs as magic sponges. No one wanted tech to start crashing regularly the way it had after the Turning, and without the dragons soaking up excess magic, it would.

They risked a lot more than that, though Rule doubted they were aware of it.

But Edward Smith was a fanatic. He'd do whatever it took to turn the tide in his direction. Rule was very much afraid they'd hear about an atrocity soon. A daycare burned, or a school, or a major shopping center. Something that forced the government to act. When they did, they'd use massive strength. No bombs, because Smith wanted the eggs. Ground troops of some sort.

And Rule had fifteen men.

Still, if fifteen men weren't enough, fourteen would have been little worse. He should have sent Little John with Mike and Danny. Demi. Dammit, he was sticking with Danny for now. If she . . .

A finger poked him in the ribs. "Hey. You're doing it again."

He looked up at Lily. "Doing what?"

"Worrying."

Lily shouldn't have been able to tell. It didn't show on his face or in his body. He knew how to make sure of that. "I don't like sending a child to do an adult's job."

She nodded. "I can't promise that she'll be okay, but she's better off away from here. If Smith uses Nicky . . ."

He sighed and sat up. "I know."

Lily had made that point earlier, when they were arguing

about whether to send Danny to D.C. Lily had drawn Rule aside and pointed out quietly that Danny's friend Nicky might be part of the attack they expected. How better to kill a dragon than from a distance? Danny didn't need to see her friend kill. She didn't need to see what might happen to Nicky, either. Rule had promised to help the children, but he'd left himself a back door, hadn't he? He'd vowed to help them if he could do so without "undue loss of life."

If Nicky killed Mika, the number of lives lost would be undue as hell. Rule didn't know what form the other dragons' anger would take, but Sam had spoken of widespread disaster, death, and destruction. That was probably as good a description as any. He understood the last part of Sam's message very well now.

When the attack comes, Lily must lead your side, Sam had said. And: *She is Unit Twelve. The government must . . .*

The rest had been lost to distance, but Rule had figured out what Sam meant. To keep the Accords from being broken, those with official authority who acted against Mika had to be stopped by someone with greater official authority. In effect, the government must stop itself, or even the attempt to violate Mika's lair would break the Accords.

Unit 12 agents were way up on the official authority ladder. They could, in an emergency, issue orders to the military. And as Sam had pointed out, Lily was Unit 12.

So, too, were Rule and his men now. She'd just sworn them in.

Not that anyone would take his word for it. That wasn't the point. Legally, they now had the necessary authority, so whatever actions they took to halt an attack on Mika would be done in the name of the government.

Rule was hoping—they were all hoping—those actions would be limited to getting Lily to whatever officer was in charge of the force sent to kill or capture Mika. That officer shouldn't doubt Lily's authority—her face had been all over the news—and would have to comply with her orders.

Danny's friend Nicky was another story. He might not be with the troops or under the command of whoever led those troops. How do you stop someone who kills from a distance?

First you had to find them. They had no idea how close Nicky needed to be to his target, and that was only one of—

"Lilyu!" one of the brownies called, running toward them with a mobile phone in his hands. It was the smallest phone on the market, but still looked huge in the brownie's hands. "Felix Thompson wants to talk to you."

With Danny gone, they'd lacked a way to make secure phone calls. That, it turned out, was easy to solve once the brownies realized what they wanted. Brownies loved cell phones almost as much as they loved chocolate—and dul-dul, he'd been informed, worked on phones.

"Ah . . . how?" Rule had asked one of the brownies who'd told him. "I thought dul-dul didn't work on sound."

Dilly had giggled. "There's still sound, silly. You have to be able to hear each other, or why call? Dul-dul's for hiding, so it hides the call. No one can listen in because they can't find the call."

Rule had tried to translate that explanation into what he knew about electronic eavesdropping. He'd come up dry, but the brownies were certain of their ability to hide calls. He and Lily had decided to take them at their word.

The little brownie with the phone climbed into Lily's lap and held it to her face. He had to keep the phone in his hands to make the dul-dul work. "Mr. Thompson?" Lily said. "This is Special Agent Lily Yu. Thank you for calling me back."

"Curiosity is my downfall sometimes. When my voice mail included a message from someone claiming to be the missing FBI agent, I had to call."

"Did you honor my request not to tell anyone?"

"I did, but before we continue, I need some kind of proof that you are who you say you are."

Lily's eyebrows lifted. "That's reasonable, but I'm not sure how . . . ah, hold on a moment." She covered the tiny phone with one hand. "Can you hide text messages, too?" she asked the brownie.

He could. Lily dug out her ID and held it up to her face. The brownie took her picture and sent it to Felix Thompson—the expert Ruben had recommended days ago when she wanted information about telekinesis. A moment later, he called again.

The brownie answered, then held up the phone for Lily to talk. "Your secretary has a very high-pitched voice," he said when Lily greeted him again.

She grinned. "I suppose so. I need to ask you some questions about TK."

"Shoot."

"You know that I'm a touch sensitive?"

"Yes, of course."

"I've encountered magic recently which feels very similar to TK, but not identical. I'm told this magic came from someone with a Gift that allows him to use pure force—and that force can be shaped into a weapon. He can't pick up a spoon with it, but he can batter someone or shape the force into a blade that cuts."

"Oh, sure. I've run into a couple people like that. It's still TK, but the person got only part of the skill set that usually comes with the Gift. See, all TK is force. That's how we move objects around, by applying force to them. Most TK'ers experience our Gift kinetically, as if this force were a physical part of us that can reach out and pick things up. Like it's a hand, usually, though I've met one guy who said it felt like a tentacle. Creepy, if you ask me. The people who get the half-assed version—it's like they have an arm without a hand. They can use it to whack away, but they can't grip things. The funny thing is that they're a lot stronger than most TK'ers. The two I've met were anyway. I don't know why that would be so, but those guys had a lot of power. Not much control, but lots of power."

"And they could shape this force into a blade?"

"I don't think the guys I met could, but that doesn't mean it's impossible. It probably wouldn't be easy. That form of the Gift is hard to control. But with practice, sure, someone might learn to do that. Shoot, I could probably learn how myself, if I wanted to spend the time and effort. A hand's a lot more useful, though."

"That's a big help." Lily was jotting notes madly. "Another question. I've been told that a TK-Gifted has to see an object to use TK on it. Is that so?"

"Absolutely. The Gift is triggered by vision. If I close my eyes, I can't use my Gift. Same if I'm in a really dark room. I can't use TK on an object unless I can see it. I can't use it at all if it's too dark to see. Funny, isn't it, that I experience TK kinetically, but it's triggered visually? But that's how it is. And it's not just me. Every TK'er I've ever met is the same way."

Lily exchanged a quick glance with Rule. "Including the ones who only got half the skill set?"

"Sure."

Lily asked a few more questions, narrowing down how well he had to be able to see to use his Gift. Finally she thanked him for his time, disconnected, and thanked the little brownie for the use of his phone. He giggled and jumped out of her lap, phone in both hands.

She looked at Rule. "That was interesting."

"It means we probably don't have to worry about Smith sending Nicky against Mika at night." But there were hours of daylight left, so that wasn't entirely reassuring.

"Probably." Her fingers tapped on her thigh. "I keep wondering how Nicky could have seen the homeless man clearly enough to kill him. Or the victims in Whistle, for that matter, though I don't have much information on those murders. Maybe he stood right in front of them, but he didn't stand in front of the first victim."

"Was he the first?"

"Shit. I hadn't thought of that." She was quiet for several moments. "There's no motive for killing the homeless guy, is there? Unless he was practice."

"An ugly possibility, but logical. You don't go into battle using a weapon you've never tested."

"So maybe there were other victims involved in getting that weapon tested and ready. Seems like I read about a body or bodies . . . I can't recall the details, dammit. But on the way to Whistle I read up on recent events in the area, and I know there was something about another unexplained death."

Rule nodded, frowning. "Have you ever touched someone with two Gifts?"

"Other than Cullen, you mean?"

"Other than him, yes. I'm wondering if it's possible Nicky has a minor secondary Gift. A farseer could peer around the corner in order to target someone with TK."

"Danny would've told us."

"Maybe she didn't notice. We don't know how strong her Gift is."

"It's hard for me to imagine missing something like that. Farseeing feels nothing like TK. I suppose, if she didn't know how TK is supposed to feel, she might not realize she was feeling two Gifts instead of one, but . . ." She shook her head, then glanced at her watch. "It seems unlikely, but it's nearly time for me to check in with her anyway. I'll ask."

Rule watched as Lily's eyes lost focus and drifted closed. It fascinated him, this new ability of hers. And frustrated him. He had no way of sharing it with her, no way to really understand what she experienced. Did she feel that way about his ability to Change?

Dumb question. Of course she did.

She still hadn't reached Danny. At least he didn't think so; her lips hadn't moved. She'd gone from needing to vocalize to needing only to physically shape the words she sent, leaving them unvoiced. He frowned. It seemed to be taking a—

Lily swayed and started to topple over.

Rule caught her. "Lily!"

Her eyes popped open. "Whoa." She blinked several times. "Are you okay?"

"Yeah. Dizzy, though. Give me a minute." She closed her eyes. After a moment her posture firmed up and her eyes opened again.

He kept his arm around her, just in case. "What happened?"

She rubbed her temple with one hand. "I learned what happens when I stretch too far."

"Headache?"

She shook her head. "That only seems to happen with Mika. I'm tired, that's all. Though it's a funny kind of tired." She frowned. "Maybe this is how it feels to be drained. Magically, I mean. Kind of like I stayed up all night writing reports."

She wouldn't have experienced that before, given the way her Gift operated—constantly soaking up magic without allowing her the use of it. Until now. "That seems reasonable. Your mindsense uses magic, so . . ." Rule's voice drifted off. "I hope that's Gandalf."

The hoofbeats he'd heard slowed as the horse reached the trees, but the big Shire horse was still moving at an easy lope when he came into view—and what a sight that was, over a ton of horse loping up to the green with thirty pounds of brownie on his back. No tack, no saddle, but the little brownie seemed to have no trouble staying on.

The horse slowed and stopped just outside the green. Gandalf slid off, landing with her knees flexed, unfazed by dropping three times her height. Rule had known that brownies were incredible athletes. He hadn't realized that old brownies were nearly as athletic as the gymnasts so often featured on their webcam.

"What's all this about the webcam?" she said.

Immediately she was swarmed by the other brownies, all explaining at once. And arguing. This was why Rule hadn't made his webcam appearance yet. Brownie governance was a slippery beast, but it was essentially a matriarchy. When it came to decisions affecting the whole community, everyone got to express an opinion. If most of them agreed, they went with that. When there was substantial disagreement, the great-mothers had the last word. The brownies had not been able to agree about putting Rule on the webcam, so they'd appealed to the great-mothers—who were all busy singing to Mika. Gandalf had agreed to come make the decision. She was the eldest, and besides, as one had explained, "She's the bossiest anyway."

Rule was still waiting for her to reach him so he could explain why he wanted to appear on the webcam when Gandalf waved a hand. "Enough. Bring the webcam. Let the wolf talk to the Big People. Maybe they'll stop being stupid."

One of the brownies was stubborn enough to say, "The government Big People will make trouble when they know he's here."

"The government Big People already intend to make trouble." She stopped in front of Rule, scowling as much as she was capable of. "What is this they tell me about you wanting to bring guns into the reservation?"

That was the other thing he needed her permission for. He'd given Bert back a large chunk of the money Bert had brought him. The man was on his way back to the reservation now with three AK-47s and an Uzi. Even the mob couldn't lay hands on more than that this fast. "The soldiers who come after Mika will have guns. We need guns to stop them. We won't use them unless we have no choice, but—"

"No. No guns. We made an exception for Lilyu's gun because

Mika kidnapped her, gun and all, but no more guns. The young-sters would start playing the Game with them, and the next thing you know—"

"We would not let your youngsters get hold of them."

She rolled her eyes. "Debitty, give the wolf back his phone."

A very small brownie giggled and handed Rule the phone he didn't know he was missing. He checked to make sure it hadn't been turned on and put it back in his pocket.

"You see?" she said. "No guns."

"These guns are much larger than a phone." He indicated the size with his hands. "Your youngsters are very good at the Game, but they won't be able to sneak AK-47s away from us."

"Why take the chance? You won't need them."

"Soldiers will come, Gandalf. I know you find that hard to believe, but—"

"The government Big People can't be that stupid! The drag-ons told them Mika didn't make those fires, and dragons don't lie, so they won't—"

"Rule," one of them called. "You have a phone call. It's Hamp."

Hamp was in charge of one of the brownie troops who were acting as scouts. "Excuse me a moment, Gandalf." Rule crouched so the brownie with the phone could hold it up to his face. "This is Rule." He listened to the excited voice on the other end, then said, "I think you'd better tell Gandalf, too."

The brownie passed his phone to Gandalf. Rule stood and met Lily's eyes. "Army troops have started arriving in Sum-mersville."

Summersville was less than ten miles from the reservation.

A few moments later, Rule had permission to bring in guns.

FORTY-TWO

~

WHEN Ruben Brooks opened the door of his big house and saw Demi, he blinked once. "Ah. That's what I've been waiting for." He didn't explain what he meant, just told them to come in.

As they did, Mike told him who she was. Demi started to tell him why she was there, but he wanted them to come sit down first.

Demi was very curious about Ruben Brooks. He looked about forty-five, but she wasn't good at figuring out ages so that might be wrong. His glasses were black except for one temple, which was brown. His hair was messy and he was skinny like her. He had smart eyes, she thought as they entered the kitchen at the back of the house.

His wife was there. Mrs. Brooks was very pretty, with thick, dark hair and pale skin. She told Demi to call her Deborah, then got drinks and snacks for everyone. Then she asked if this was a private conversation.

"Yes," Demi said, "but I don't know if that means private from you or not." She looked at Mike.

He thought a moment. "I think it's okay for her to know, since Rule didn't say otherwise. But it's dangerous knowledge."

Deborah looked at her husband, who looked back. Neither of them said a word, but she sat down at the breakfast nook just as if they'd discussed it and decided she should stay.

"Mr. Brooks," Demi began, "I have a lot to tell you, but first I need to know if you've been relieved of duty. Lily thought maybe you hadn't been."

His eyebrows went up. "Lily told you that?"

She nodded. "She made me a Unit Twelve agent and sent me here."

"I think," he said slowly, "you had better call me Ruben."

BACK at the village green, Rule was making his webcam appearance with four of the brownies while several others were busily engaged in custom leatherwork, making harnesses for some of them to use. Brownies didn't eat meat, but they had no problem working with the hides of dead animals. Brownie logic strikes again.

Lily had a different task.

Turned out there was one way to make sure brownies didn't play the Game with something: make it the property of an *efondi*. *Efondi* were almost always dragons, and dragons did not like it if you messed with their stuff. Brownies didn't have much use for rules, but even the most scatterbrained brownie would not play the Game with an *efondi*'s possessions.

Lily now owned three contraband AK-47s and an extremely illegal Uzi. "Rule says you three are the least likely to shoot each other instead of the enemy," she told the lupi in front of her. She gave them a slow and skeptical appraisal. "We'll see. I don't know you. You don't know me. Let's get acquainted. Jason, how many kills do you have?"

The man acting as Rule's second spoke coolly. "Five."

"Luke?"

He cleared his throat. "None. I've fought, but—"

"Never mind that for now. Manny?"

"Two."

She nodded. "I've got two kills as well, if we just count humans. If we add in demons—"

"You've killed demons?" Manny exclaimed.

"In Dis, yes. I'm not sure how many of the demons I shot

died, but some did. Jason, Manny—how many of your kills were with a gun?"

"Well . . . none," Manny said.

Jason simply shook his head.

"All but one of my kills were made with a weapon." She let that sink in. Lupi didn't much like guns. There was a reason for that. Mostly they fought each other—in personal challenges or the type of surreptitious, undeclared war that had existed between Nokolai and Leidolf clans for so long. Guns couldn't be used in a challenge, and using them anywhere near humans tended to draw unwanted attention. "I'm told all of you can use a rifle. Luke, here, won the clan's sharpshooter competition." A brand-new competition, begun by Rule three months ago. "So you know some of the basics. I'm going to teach you how to handle an AK-47 and an Uzi. Two of you will get one of the AK-47s; one will get the Uzi. Who gets what will be my decision."

"Who gets the third AK-47?" Jason asked. "Rule?"

"No. I do. Your Rho shouldn't be out front, firing and drawing return fire. Also, I'm better with it than he is. He can use one, don't get me wrong, but I've stayed in practice. He hasn't. Before we start, I want to make one thing clear. These weapons will be our last resort. If we get to the point where we have to kill U.S. troops, we're pretty well screwed. Rule will do his damnedest to keep from using you three. Got that?"

Manny and Luke nodded. Jason didn't.

"Jason? Got something to say?"

"No."

The terse answer managed to combine obedience with a clear lack of respect. Jason had been told to obey Lily. He would, but he didn't like it. Women weren't supposed to give orders to men—especially not when it came to combat.

Lily had run into his type often enough, both among humans and with lupi, but the attitude was especially virulent in Leidolf. It was an attitude neither of them could afford. People had died when another Leidolf lupus decided his opinion counted for more than hers in the midst of battle. Lily couldn't adjust his attitude the way Rule would have. She wasn't bad at hand-to-hand, but that was against humans. Against lupi, she had no chance.

So she stared at him. Stared right into his eyes. Six seconds passed. Eight. Ten . . . and his gaze dropped.

He immediately looked up again, but now his eyes were slightly wide. Startled. He hadn't intended to look away, but he had. He knew it. So did the other two.

Lily went on as if she hadn't just challenged and won. "The good news is that these weapons are made for dummies. Almost anyone can use one. The bad news is that every one of those soldiers is going to be twice as good with his weapon as you will be with yours." She paused. "Manny? Got a comment?"

"Well—yeah. They're humans. They don't have our reaction time."

"They don't need it. Ever heard of muscle memory? They'll be carrying M16A4s. AK-47s are good weapons, don't get me wrong. But M16s are better. And these guys know their weapons like you know your arm. Each one of them can field strip his rifle in three minutes or less. Right now, none of you know how to load your weapon, much less strip it. Which is why we'll start by learning how to load the magazines."

DEMI talked for a long time. Ruben asked a few questions, but not many, and Mike broke in once to add something, but mostly it was up to Demi to explain why she was now a Unit 12 agent. She would rather it was Ruben who arrested Mr. Smith, she told him as she finished, but she would follow orders if he told her to do it.

He tilted his head and said, "It's funny. When I first brought Lily into the Unit, my only real concern about her was that she'd be too by-the-book."

"It sounds like you can stop worrying about that, doesn't it?" Deborah said.

He smiled, but not for long. "I can't give you orders, Demi. I lack that authority now. Lily was right, however. I haven't been relieved of duty. I suppose I should have made Mathison aware of that omission, but I had a feeling it was best he didn't know."

"You get hunches, right?"

He nodded. "Unfortunately, I'm not getting one about this."

Demi's forehead knit in sudden anxiety. "You don't believe us?"

"I think you've spoken both truly and accurately. That's both gut feeling and logic. What you've told me fits with conclusions I'd already drawn. It was obvious that another arm of government was involved in the frames on Rule and on me. Given the nature of those frames, my suspicion had begun to turn towards the NSA. The fake radar sightings today confirmed that for me."

Demi blinked, surprised. "How did you know they were fake?"

"If Mika had truly gone mad—gone rogue, as many in the media are putting it—the other dragons would know and would already have dealt with her. That's in the Accords, which each dragon swore to uphold. It is barely possible that one dragon might violate his sworn word. It's inconceivable that all of them would." He drummed his fingers on the table. "I wish I knew what Smith wanted with Mika."

That was one of the questions he'd interrupted Demi to ask. She'd had to tell him she didn't know, but Lily and Rule did, only they couldn't tell anyone because of a promise. Tentatively she offered, "I think it has something to do with the Lodan potion."

He flicked her a glance. "Hmm. I have some questions about that, but they'll wait." He didn't say anything more. He went on saying nothing for quite a while. Demi figured he was thinking, so she kept silent, too. She hated it when people yammered at her when she needed to think.

Finally he reached out and took Deborah's hand. "I have to do this."

"Of course you do. Those people can't be allowed to get away with this." She smiled when she said that, but it looked like she was holding Ruben's hand really tightly.

"There's no going back, no matter what happens. I'm known to be lupus now. I won't serve as head of Unit Twelve again."

"I'll settle for you coming back alive."

Ruben smiled. "I'll do my best. Now—Danny, Mike." He let go of his wife's hand and gave them each a nod. "I do still have the authority to arrest Smith. Keeping it a legal arrest will be tricky because I can't go to a judge for a warrant. We lack the time and the evidence."

"Lily explained the exceptions that permit a warrantless arrest."

"Did she? I believe we'll have to rely on the courts to agree that this is a pressing emergency, and that I didn't have time to get a warrant. And who knows? Smith may simplify matters by attempting to commit a felony, such as assaulting an officer, while I'm arresting him."

"That doesn't sound simpler," Demi said. "That sounds dangerous."

"This is going to be dangerous. You need to understand that, because I'm about to make a request. Edward Smith has been trying to catch you for nearly a year, Demi, for very good reasons. He might not come to the door to speak with me. He'll do so if you're with me. He'll have to, given what you know. Are you willing to come with me when I make the arrest?"

"Of course," she said, though the thought made her stomach jittery. "You should probably know that sometimes I panic, and when I do, I can't think straight. I do better if I have a list, but we don't know enough about what might happen for me to make a list. So I'll try to not panic, but it's possible I will."

Mike snorted. "You didn't panic when a machine-gun-equipped helicopter chased us. You didn't panic when a dragon flew over our heads, roaring. I'd say you don't panic easily."

She thought that over. "I think you're right," she said, pleased. "I'm getting better. But Mr. Smith knows me pretty well. If anyone can make me panic, he can."

"If you start to panic, let me know," Mike said. "I'll tell you what to do so it won't matter if you're thinking straight or not."

"I can delegate the thinking?" She considered that and nodded. "That makes sense."

Ruben cleared his throat. "The question we must consider next is whether to make the arrest as soon as possible—which would mean going to NSA Headquarters—or waiting until Smith is at home. Here, I'm afraid, we'll have to rely on logic, not hunches. There is one important point in favor of arresting him there and two against it. The point in favor is that it's legally a public place, making an arrest without a warrant simpler. However, that's his territory. Security staff there are likely to obey him, and he almost certainly has co-conspirators there. Also, I don't think I'd be able to get you two into the headquarters. It's probable that I'd have to go in alone."

"That doesn't sound smart."

He gave her a quick smile. "I suspect you're right. However, we don't know when Smith will go home. We can't even be sure that he will. We don't know enough about how his conspiracy is organized to guess what place he considers his command post—home or NSA—but with matters reaching a crux, he'll wish to be where he can coordinate his people. That might mean remaining at NSA Headquarters."

"Seems pretty clear," Mike said. "You need another Unit agent. One of you can go to the NSA and the other to Smith's home."

"I'm a Unit agent." Demi felt she had to point that out.

"Yes, but I believe it would be difficult for you to convince others of that. However, we're in luck. Another Unit Twelve agent is due to return to Washington later today. I have no authority to send him anywhere, but I believe he'll attempt to make the arrest if I ask it of him."

"How long will it take for him to get here?" Demi asked anxiously. "NSA is an hour's drive from here. So is Mr. Smith's house."

"His plane should arrive at four thirty-two, so we need to leave soon to pick him up."

"Who is it?" Mike asked. "Anyone I know?"

"Abel Karonski."

Danny frowned. Lily and Rule had used that name earlier. "I thought he got relieved of duty."

Ruben smiled. "He was supposed to be. I'm told that something went wrong with the paperwork."

COPS do a lot of waiting. Lily should have been used to it, but this wait was rubbing her nerves raw. Maybe because the stakes were so high. Maybe because she had nothing to do—nothing that mattered anyway. Though that was pretty much the definition of waiting.

". . . most in the government know nothing about," Rule's voice was saying on the iPad mini on Lily's left—the proud possession of a brownie who went by Guido. "But a few do. And those few will stop at nothing—even murder."

He was followed by a brownie's high, piping voice. "There are soldiers coming! Soldiers with guns and tanks!"

"They're not tanks, stupid."

"They've got big guns on top and—"

"They're IFVs, not tanks."

"IFVs, tanks, whatever—they've got *big* guns on top," the second brownie said. A third one chipped in: "The government Big People promised this wouldn't ever happen. They said this was *our* land. Our home." And a fourth: "They wrote it all down that way in laws, but it's happening anyway!" All four brownies: "Please help us!"

The show she was listening to was *Town Hall Live*, the biggest pundit talk-fest at this time of day. The last bit, followed by the brownies' plea, was the part of Rule's webcast the news channels kept playing. Lily had heard it over and over. Brownies, she reflected, did pathos really well.

Rule had relied on emotion more than fact in his webcam performance. Lily had objected to that. "I don't need to prove my case in court," he'd told her. "I need to change the conversation, make people start asking why all of this is happening. If I simply tell people what's going on, the story becomes two-sided: my version versus the official one. Everyone would then pick a side and stop listening. People don't ask questions when they've decided they already have the answers."

He'd been right, of course.

Lily frowned at her cards—little bitty cards, less than half the size of normal playing cards. The face cards featured adorable brownies. They were a hot item, she was told, in the reservation's gift shop.

"Are you going to play or not?" Shisti demanded.

"Sure," Lily said, and laid her hand down. "Gin."

Shisti squeaked in dismay.

About twenty yards away, Jason and Luke were practicing

stripping their AK-47s. Manny had been given the Uzi. He was showing it to two of the other lupi.

Rule wasn't with them. Codger wanted him to see a defensive installation on the east side of the reservation—something about a "potential pit," whatever that meant.

She'd mindspoken Mika when soldiers started arriving in Summersville, explaining what was happening, trying to get the dragon to understand the need for her to go to Summersville and order the Army to stay away from the reservation. The only thing that had gotten Mika's attention was the part about her leaving the reservation. If Lily tried, Mika would bring her back. The dragon had made that emphatically clear.

Lily didn't want to take any more rides clutched in a dragon's talons. She'd wait for the CO to come to her, all the while hoping he didn't. Of course, there was no guarantee he'd listen to her when she did reach him. But it was their best hope.

She glanced at her watch: 5:35. Sundown today would be at 8:25, with civil twilight lasting until 8:55. If Smith and Company intended to use Nicky to attack Mika, they'd move before it got dark. She looked at the rifle at her side. If the Army did manage to cross the wards, they had to be stopped. She accepted that, but the idea of firing on men and women who were serving their country made her ill.

"Lilyu," Shisti said in a sad little voice.

"What?"

Shisti looked up at Lily beseechingly from big, green eyes shiny with unshed tears. "Could we play this hand again?"

Lily snorted. "Forget it."

Shisti huffed. "You don't react the way Big People are supposed to."

"Nope. I'm a cop." And that was part of her problem with using one of those weapons. Soldiers were trained to kill and to fight strategically—to take a hill or defend one. She had been trained to apprehend criminals, not to kill them. Deadly force was only for situations when the bad guy was going to harm you or others. If necessary, she could fire on someone who was trying to kill Mika. But to shoot at people who simply crossed a boundary they shouldn't have crossed . . .

"My deal," Shisti said brightly, gathering up the cards.

"Wait a minute. You didn't lay your hand down."

"I had two unmatched cards, but I laid them off on your run."

"You can't lay off on a gin."

"Sure I can. I'm not supposed to, but you weren't looking."

"You really like cheating, don't you?" She didn't think they'd played a single hand in which the little brownie hadn't tried to pull something. Still, if it cheered her up . . . Shisti had been devastated when Gandalf told her not to come to the creche for the singing. "If the stupid Big People come," Gandalf had said, "you'll be needed out here."

She was right. If the soldiers came, the brownies might well need their healer.

Lily glanced to her right. Rule was loping toward her with his communications officer riding his back like a jockey, courtesy of the leather harness Rule now wore. Dilly was one of the smallest brownies, but he was no youngster. He had crow's-feet, a wife, a husband, and two children with a third on the way.

Lily stood. "We'll finish our game later."

"I win," Shisti said happily.

"The game isn't over yet."

Rule stopped in front of Lily. Dilly pulled his feet out of the loops that served him as stirrups and somersaulted to the ground in one of those casual displays of gymnastic skill brownies excelled at. "Be right back!" he called cheerfully and ran off.

"Important business?" Lily said, eyebrows lifted as she watched the little brownie scamper off.

"He wanted to say good-bye to his husband and children." Rule lowered himself to sit beside her. "Just in case. His wife's with Mika, so he can't see her now."

Lily took a slow breath and refused to picture what a round from an M16 would do to a little brownie body. Easy to forget how much the brownies were risking on behalf of Mika and The Big Deal—they were so damn cheerful. "Is the 'potential pit' going to be useful?"

A quick grin. "Definitely. There are three of them, it turns out. The ground over each is stable now, but if the brownies pull the trigger—I gather Earth magic is involved—they'll collapse. On another front, I heard from one of the scouts a few minutes ago. Two of them got into the mobile command unit. The tech is new to them, but they'll do their best to bollix things up. Oh, and we now know the name of the officer in charge. Captain A. A. Martin."

"That's who I'll need to talk to, then."

He nodded and took her hand, glancing at the iPad, which was still displaying *Town Hall Live*. "Anything significant on the news?"

"The short version is that you got what you wanted. The talking heads are asking all sorts of questions—some of them pretty stupid, but not all. They play the bit with the brownies a lot. Smith may have to back down. People really like brownies. The idea of sending the military against them is raising a lot of hackles. And that," she added, looking at his frown, "isn't making you happy at all."

"Public opinion is turning in our favor, and our enemies haven't done anything to change that."

"I'm okay with that."

"Hmm. How's your head?"

"Thank God for ibuprofen." Every time she mindspoke Mika, the headache started up again.

For a few minutes they just sat there, neither speaking. Holding hands. Eventually Rule stirred. "I wish I knew what was going on with Danny. And with Ruben."

Lily had stopped trying to reach the girl. The last attempt had left her so tired she gave up. The drained feeling had passed, fortunately. "I don't know how much it will help if Ruben does manage to arrest Smith, not with the Army already at our door. They'll follow through with their orders. If we could have done it sooner . . ."

"I know." He squeezed her hand. "Pity Smith didn't hold off a little longer."

Off in the distance, thunder rolled—and a dozen brownies cried out.

"What?" Lily looked over at Shisti. "You're scared of thunder?"

"That's not thunder!" Shisti's eyes were wide with distress. "The earth jumped!"

Lily had been in earthquakes. She knew what they felt like. "I didn't feel anything."

Shisti rolled her eyes. "You're a Big Person."

Maybe brownies could sense movement in the earth that Lily couldn't. "Can you tell what happened?"

"Yes. The earth jumped."

"Hellfire," Rule said suddenly and grabbed the iPad off the ground. He fumbled with the volume control. A moment later Lily heard what Rule had.

"—repeat, this just in. A major explosion has occurred just outside Summersville, West Virginia."

FORTY-THREE

~

THE passenger pickup area was crowded. Mike had managed to edge out another car, though, and pull up to the curb. Ruben Brooks and Dirty Harry were up front with him; Demi sat in back with Twix, Hershey, and Mallum. Ruben had sent one of his men into the airport to look for Abel Karonski, who didn't know Ruben intended to pick him up.

It turned out that Ruben Brooks wasn't just a lupus. He was a Rho, like Rule. That was super secret, and Demi had promised not to speak of it to anyone unless she was sure they already knew. His clan was called Wythe, and the man he'd sent to find Mr. Karonski was a Wythe lupus.

The radio was on, tuned to an NPR station. No one spoke.

". . . train with multiple tankers carrying the highly flammable Bakken crude exploded today just outside Summersville, West Virginia. Troops have been massing in the small town for what is rumored to be an assault on the missing Washington, D.C., dragon, although there has been no official confirmation. The dragon is reputed to now be laired on the brownie reservation, making such an assault highly controversial because the brownies oppose it.

"While it is not yet known what caused the initial blaze which ignited the tankers, the FAA reports a low-flying bogey similar to those seen at three other fires today was spotted near the site of the explosion. Homeland Security has identified that bogey as the missing dragon, an allegation that is strongly denied by the other dragons.

"Firefighters cannot yet approach the blaze and casualties are unknown. The Army has closed access to the entire town, citing safety reasons, and is not responding to questions from reporters. However, reports from both townspeople and on-site reporters indicate that some portion of the assembled troops were within the blast area at the time of the explosion. No Administration officials have yet issued a statement, but Eric Ellison of Homeland Security is expected to speak with the press soon.

"The unique legal position of the brownies and their three U.S. reservations has raised questions about what conditions might permit federal intrusion onto the West Virginia reservation. Joining us now is Jim Debussy, Professor of—"

Ruben stabbed the button that turned the radio off.

Demi broke the sudden silence. "Ruben? What does that mean? Did Mr. Smith kill some more people? Soldiers?"

"Some people consider soldiers infinitely expendable." He reached for the phone he'd brought. Not his usual phone, but one he'd assured her couldn't be traced to him. "And that means that I'm going to have to break a few rules myself."

FORTY-FOUR

～

"**GOOD** work," Rule told the brownie who'd called, then added to Dilly, "You can hang up now."

The brownie reservation in West Virginia covered over twenty thousand acres of the roughest, least usable land the government had been able to find. Brownies managed to grow hay for their horses, as well as apple, pear, and peach trees in spite of the thin, rocky soil, but even their earth-based magic couldn't make it support most crops. The Appalachians had never been good farming country.

That rough terrain was their first line of defense. There had been two possible entry points for vehicles. Now, Lily thought, there was only one. "The bridge is down?"

"Yes. They'll have to either come in where we want or abandon their vehicles."

Rule had recalled almost all the scouts. He and Codger had other jobs for them, such as taking down that bridge. The brownies still hoped their wards would stop the soldiers, but they were taking preparations for an armed invasion seriously.

Lily had contacted Mika when they first heard about the fire. The dragon had told her to quit worrying about a few soldiers, and no, she hadn't started that blaze.

Lily believed her. Even if Mika could send fire to a location that far—and she might be able to; Lily had no idea what the limits were on dragons' use of fire—the radar bogey was obviously a fabrication. Also, it was probably impossible to use mindspeech to lie. Sam had said it was, and Lily had checked by having Rule and Jason lie to her while she mindspoke them. The ripples returned gibberish.

Dilly, perched on Rule's back once more, had just slid his phone into his backpack when it chirped again. "Yes? Okay!" He held it to Rule's ear. "For you."

"This is Rule." He listened briefly. "All right. You know what to do." A pause. "That's right. Hamp's troop is to report to Codger at the gate. Pass the word. Dilly, hang up now."

"Showtime?" Lily said. Her voice was steady, which surprised her. They were about to go to war with the United States Army.

"The first of the IFVs just turned onto SR 670." Rule looked to one side. "Jason!"

The young man acting as Rule's second broke off his conversation with two of the brownies and loped toward them.

Lily reached for the AK-47 she was loath to use, slipped the strap on her shoulder—and winced.

"What's wrong?"

"Mika." The dragon wasn't just brushing against Lily's mind this time. She was jabbing. Hard. Lily rubbed her temple and let her mindsense unfurl, reaching for that compelling mind . . . "What do you want?"

The answering ripple was clear and simple: *Come now.*

"The soldiers are coming now. Even if they don't worry you, the Gifted guy I told you about should. He may be with them—the one with a form of TK that lets him kill at a distance. I need to order the commanding officer to—"

Brownies fool soldiers, Rule Turner kills soldiers. You come.

"There are a lot of soldiers. Nearly a full company. That's too many to—"

COME!

"But if—"

Something wrenched at Lily's mind, or was it Mika's mind? She couldn't tell, but *something* was wrenched open and emotion flooded in. Need—overwhelming, imperative. Demand—wordless, insistent. And almost lost in the torrent of feeling, Mika's voice, not clear at all, but small and raw. *My babies. Efondi, my babies need you.*

A dozen brownie shrieks split the air, followed by a dozen brownie voices crying out the same thing: "The wards! The wards are gone!"

Lily stared at Rule. Her hearted pounded. "I have to go to Mika. I have to go now."

His eyes were dark with the same conflict she felt. "Go. But"—a smile flickered at the corners of his mouth—"stay in touch."

She started to slip the rifle off her shoulder.

"No. Keep it. If they get as far as Mika's lair—"

"If they do, we're screwed anyway." But she kept the rifle, hesitated one more second—then grabbed him and kissed him once. Quickly, but like she meant it. "Don't die." And she took off at a run.

Charles took off with her. She told him to stay behind, that Mika wouldn't tolerate him in her creche and he couldn't come with her.

Charles didn't listen worth a damn.

She headed for the entrance to the creche, not the tunnel they'd used to escape. Gandalf had told her how to get there. That entrance was at ground level from the outside, but it would open onto a sheer twenty-five-foot drop to the floor of the creche. There was a rope ladder for Lily to use, but wolves can't use rope ladders. She explained that to Charles in panting breaths as they ran.

Of course, wolves could jump twenty-five feet, but surely Charles wouldn't be that crazy.

She hated leaving Rule to deal with the soldiers Mika had so cavalierly dismissed. Sure, let the brownies trick them, then Rule could kill some. Never mind how many lupi might be killed in the process, or what the consequences would be. Mika could massacre the rest when she got around to it.

And it would be a massacre. Two hundred soldiers armed with assault rifles were serious overkill when pitted against eleven lupi—and that left out the IFVs with their machine guns and cannon. Rule believed the brownies could seriously slow them down, even stop some of their vehicles altogether, but eventually a lot of soldiers would reach the creche.

Where they'd face a dragon. And die.

Unless Mika died before they arrived.

The red dragon was impaired, unable to use telepathy, ensorcellment, or any other form of mind magic, including mindspeech. It was Lily's mindsense that allowed them to communicate, not Mika's. The one thing Mika could still do, it seemed, was find Lily's mind and poke at it until Lily opened communication between them. But the dragon didn't need mindspeech to kill a couple hundred people. Fire would do just fine.

Did Smith know that? Was Nicky nearby, prepared to start slicing and dicing a mother dragon so Smith's troops could claim the eggs?

The wards were down. Soldiers could enter the reservation. Nicky might already have done so.

Why wouldn't Mika listen to Lily? Was she incapable of reason now, or did she have some defense against TK she hadn't bothered to mention? Lily was afraid it was the former. Primitive mind, the brownies called it, but to Lily's mindsense, Mika's mind was magma—molten, churning, burning.

It was hard to reason with a volcano.

And why did Mika need Lily? What could Lily do for her babies? If the dragon just needed someone with hands to do what she could not, there were dozens of brownies with her already.

The opening yawned ahead, a gaping, shadowed hole in one rocky hill. As they drew near, Lily heard music. She slowed, struggling to catch her breath. Listening.

The brownie mothers and great-mothers were singing to the dragon. Impossibly pure and high, their voices floated out from the cave. They sang in their own language, not English. Gandalf had spoken of songs from the *ithnali,* songs that had been passed down, generation to generation, for God knew how long. Millennia? How many—two, three, four thousand years? The harmonies were intricate, inhuman, and haunting. They reminded her of dragonsong.

Lily crouched near the entrance and spoke to Charles. "Listen. Listen to me. Whatever the Lady wants of you, it can't include getting eaten by a pissed-off mother dragon. How would that help? Mika will not tolerate you entering her creche. You know that. Stay up here, okay?"

He thought it over. Finally he nodded.

One thing had gone right, at least. Impulsively Lily hugged him, then gave him a quick rub behind his ears. Then she walked up to the gaping entrance, which wasn't truly dark. Shadowed, yes, compared to the sun's light, which was still bright at this hour, though it arrived at a slant now. But there was a dim radiance belowground. Mage lights, she guessed. They provided enough light for her to spot the rope ladder she'd been promised, fastened on this end to iron spikes set securely in stone.

It was a brownie-size rope ladder.

She stared at it in consternation. She could maybe get one foot in at a time . . . kneeling, she pulled it partway up and tried that. Good thing she had narrow feet. She tested its strength as best she could, leaving her foot jammed in between the rungs and pulling with both hands. It seemed sturdy enough to hold her weight, but there was only one way to find out for sure. She shoved it back over the edge, lay on her belly, and lowered herself over the edge.

The singing never faltered as she descended. The worst part was finding an opening to thrust her foot into; her weight pulled the thing down in a way that made the two sides draw together. Several muscle-straining minutes later, she let herself drop the last few feet to land in soft sand.

Five feet away was a red coil of dragon. Mika's tail, to be precise. On the ledge way above her, brownies stood, singing. Above them rose Mika's head. The glow from hovering mage lights struck crimson sparks from her scales. Yellow eyes glowed with their own light.

Lily's mindsense quivered, wanting to reach out. It took only her permission for it to uncoil and touch the mind behind those glowing eyes. "Now what? What am I supposed to do?"

Come close.

That great body shifted slowly, coils sliding, one of them lifting to make an opening. One Lily could slip through if she ducked. Her heart pounded as she approached. The dragon's body radiated heat like a sidewalk that's baked in the sun all day.

Sam's body wasn't this hot. She'd been close to him often enough to know. She ducked down and squeezed herself through that small opening.

It was like stepping into a sauna. There was sand beneath her feet, soft and hot. Mika's coiled body radiated and trapped heat on this section of sand . . . where five eggs rested.

They were the biggest eggs she'd ever seen. They were beautiful. And pink. The eggs were the softest of pinks, the color of the sky's first blush at dawn, and each one was beautifully marbled with another color. Blue marbling in that one. Copper and yellow swirls in the one beside it. In another, turquoise; in the fourth, a bright green much like brownie eyes. And in the fifth . . . that one was marbled with crimson, like Mika's scales. And cracked. As Lily stared, the egg rocked slightly. "Mika?" she whispered.

Touch me.

"I am."

Touch with flesh and mind.

Lily backed up a couple feet. She slipped the AK-47 off her shoulder and laid it down carefully, then laid her palm on hot, slick scales. Her palm heated from more than physical warmth as she touched dragon magic—heat and chaos, order and power all mingled in an indescribable tactile sensation. And her mind-sense sank deeper into Mika's mind.

Efondi. Mika's voice was different. Not clearer, exactly. More intimate. The ripples carrying the dragon's words resonated deep inside Lily. *I will explain your duties now. You know I cannot mindspeak at this time.*

"Yes. Mika, I—I don't sense the babies' minds."

Their shells protect their minds now. As each one emerges from his shell, he loses that protection. You must touch his mind with yours while linked with me this way.

"I don't know how to touch two minds at once. Not fully enough to mindspeak them. I don't think—"

Do not think. Do. Touching with flesh and mind together makes a link. You must touch my babies while you and I are linked and mindspeak each one. Dragon babies must be touched and spoken to this way in the first moments outside the shell, while their minds are fully open. If this does not happen, they will never speak. Never touch another mind. Never develop

*telepathy or other forms of what you call mind magic. Their
minds will be locked in forever.*

Lily wanted to be somewhere else. Almost anywhere else.
Fighting a demon, maybe. Surely that would be easier than being
responsible for keeping baby dragons from growing up trapped
in their own minds, unable to communicate. "Forever?"

*Yes. You understand I will kill you if you reveal this to
anyone except your mate.*

"Goes without saying." And Lily wished she hadn't said it,
though she was surprised Mika had made an exception for
Rule.

A second crack appeared on the dawn-and-crimson egg.
Panic made her voice almost as high as a brownie's. "What do
I say?"

You name them.

NSA Headquarters was a huge, dead black building in Maryland next to Fort Meade. Demi had been there twice, but she
didn't go there today. Abel Karonski would go there because
it was a public place. Demi wasn't sure why that meant Mr.
Karonski should go there instead of them, but it had something to do with his career not being over the way Ruben's was.

She had never been to Mr. Smith's home. She knew it was
in Laurel, Maryland, about eleven minutes away from the NSA
Headquarters if Mr. Smith took the Baltimore-Washington
Parkway. She knew what his house looked like, having looked
it up using Street View once. He and his wife lived in a two-
story Federal-style home with white siding. It felt beyond weird
to drive past that big white house with its flat front and sym-
metrical windows.

There were a lot of cars parked near Mr. Smith's house—
cars in the driveway and parked along the street, as if Mr.
Smith was having a party. Surely he wouldn't do that when so
much was happening, but why so many cars?

Maybe it was his wife's party and he wasn't home. Demi
had never met Mrs. Smith, but she knew that her first name was
Annabelle, that she had very conservative political views, liked
cats, and enjoyed cooking. Mrs. Smith was on Facebook.

Another car followed theirs, but that was okay. It held four

Wythe lupi and two brownies. Ruben didn't think Mr. Smith was going to just stand there and let himself be arrested. If he was even there, that is. With or without a bunch of guests. They'd find out soon.

They turned a corner and drove halfway down the block, then Mike pulled over. The car behind them did, too. Ruben, who was in the front seat, turned around to speak to two of the backseat passengers. "You know what to do?"

Twix and Hershey nodded. "Go see who's there," Twix said.

"Especially see if the round man's there," Hershey added. "Count up how many people and see if they have guns, if we can."

"And don't let ourselves be seen," they chorused, as if they'd practiced it.

"That's right," Ruben said. "Don't be brave. Be careful. Demi, you can let them out now."

She opened the door and the two brownies climbed over her to get out. Twix and Hershey were confident they could get in Mr. Smith's house and get out again without being seen. She hoped they were right.

"How are you holding up, Demi?" Ruben asked.

She realized she'd been rubbing her stomach, which felt very uncertain. "It's just ordinary fear," she assured him.

RULE crouched low in the shrubby undergrowth, watching as three IFVs advanced on the tree line at the boundary of the reservation's public sector. The rest of the company straggled out behind—a pair of armored personnel carriers and several squads of foot soldiers. Those soldiers had started out in APCs and IFVs which had suffered mysterious calamities on the way here. Brownies were appallingly good at breaking things.

Two of the soldiers in the nearest squad suddenly stumbled for no apparent reason. Another fell flat on his face. Rule didn't doubt that others, farther back, were also tripping over small invisible obstacles. Some of them would suddenly be missing some item of their gear. Their squad radios, he hoped. That's what he'd suggested.

People had largely forgotten why the government created the brownie reservations in the first place. Brownies loved to pla tricks on Big People—especially Big People who'd harmed or offended them. With the advent of the Industrial Revolution, some of their tricks had become costly. Mills, factories, or foundries had been shut down when their equipment suffered strange mishaps. A few had wanted to get rid of "those little troublemakers" altogether—but most people, then and now, loved brownies. Public outrage had made pariahs of those few who'd advocated for a final solution. They'd been pariahs with both power and money, however. Hence the reservations.

Three dozen brownies came skipping out of the woods, singing at the top of their lungs, some holding hands, some holding flowers. The IFVs—which did look rather like tanks, with their treads and turrets—slowed. And were quickly swarmed by brownies, who climbed up on the vehicles, tossing flowers around like manic flower girls at the world's oddest wedding. A few brownies hung back, pointedly aiming their phones at the scene. The Internet community would be very interested in those videos.

The brownies were singing "It's a Small World"—one of the most insidious earworms ever invented.

Rule smiled. On his back, Dilly convulsed in silent laughter.

"We got this," Codger whispered from beside Rule. "Go."

Rule nodded and slipped away. The brownies would continue to slow the troops as much as possible. He and his men had another focus: finding Nicky.

FORTY-FIVE

~~

BABY dragons don't have wings.

That was one of several surprises Lily had experienced as she sat on the hot sand, her hair limp from sweat, mentally midwifing Mika's babies as they hatched—which, she'd been happy to learn, they did one at a time.

A shiny blue length of dragon stretched out limply across her lap like two feet of reptilian ribbon. He was drowsy, tired from the exertion of breaking through the shell. The warmth of her body probably felt good; he wouldn't be able to regulate his temperature without help until he was older, according to Mika. A few feet away his older brother tried to run, wobbled, and fell into a crimson heap. He opened his mouth and meeped in surprise.

She smiled. Big dragons roared. Babies, not so much.

Overhead, seventeen brownie mothers and great-mothers sang. They took it in shifts, she'd learned, so that no voices grew overly tired and as many as possible could participate. But the number of singers remained constant at seventeen.

A coil of Mika rested beside Lily so she could keep one hand touching the dragon.

Keeping her mindsense anchored in Mika's mind was effortless while her hand was pressed against the dragon's bulk. Touching another mind at the same time was harder, but not as difficult as she'd expected. Mostly it was a matter of attention—rather as if she had to force herself to notice she was already touching that mind.

Directly in front of her was an egg. A small blue-green snout thrust through the crack, bit down on the ragged edge of the shell, and snapped off a large piece. With that, the rest of the shell cracked, came apart. A tumble of turquoise spilled out— along with a burst of strange magic.

The magic prickled over Lily's skin, wilder or more primitive than Mika's. She closed her eyes and thought of her mind-sense as if it were a diffuse fog already present in the rocky creche, already touching every mind here . . .

"Ohhh." The new baby's mind was without texture, pure and clear as water, though there were textures beneath the surface. She couldn't touch those textures, couldn't go that deeply, but she sensed them, shiny white patterns sliding around in a crystalline bubble.

Those textures influenced her choice in a way she couldn't describe. With her mind both linked to Mika's and touching that water-crystal mind, she spoke: "*Bái.*" White, she named him. White for those shiny patterns. As she did, Mika sent a pulse of shaped power along Lily's mindsense—a peculiar sensation.

The naming sank gently into the baby's mind.

Mika had terrified Lily by telling her that the names she gave the babies would shape them, eventually becoming the first syllable of their true names. For now, the names would be Mika's entry into their minds, allowing her to speak to her babies, to teach them how to speak back—and when necessary, to control them. But until a baby grew beyond his birth name, it could, potentially, be used by someone other than his mother. Mika assured her that was unlikely. Simply pronouncing a name correctly was not the same as using it, and very few in this world knew how to use a name. But why take a chance? By giving them Chinese names, Lily greatly reduced the number of people who could say them properly. On this side of the world, anyway.

Plus she'd just thought Chinese appropriate. These babies were American dragons. They'd probably have English call-names, but their parents were immigrants. Their roots stretched back to China. And probably to someplace even more remote as well, but none of the dragons had seen fit to confirm or deny that idea when Lily asked. The babies would have to settle for names that reflected their earthly roots.

Bái wobbled up onto his feet for the first time. Lily beamed at him. *Good*, she told him. *Good for you.* She even got a reply, though not in words—a sort of delighted hum. Carefully she withdrew her mindsense from him. *I'm going to check on Rule*, she told Mika. *And on the invaders you're ignoring. I'll have to break the link.*

No response. Mika was lost in the bright fascination of her babies.

Lily sighed. Single-minded, the brownies had called the dragon. She had to agree. She took her hand away from the dragon's hot body—and swayed as her mindsense snapped back into her and pain stabbed through her head.

She'd expected that. While she was linked with Mika, her head didn't hurt. The moment she broke the link, it did. But the worst pain would subside if she waited a bit.

She sat without moving. It seemed to take longer this time and hurt worse. Finally, though, the pain ebbed to a dull throbbing.

Carefully she moved the blue baby off her lap—*Fēng*, she'd named him, Wind—then stood and stretched. The hot sand was littered with brightly colored shell fragments, glossy shards of pale pink streaked with fiery red, deep blue, and now turquoise.

Lily checked on the last two intact eggs. Neither were cracked, but when she crouched to get close, she could hear tapping from the one marbled in copper and yellow.

She settled beside it and closed her eyes. That seemed to help when she wanted to mindspeak someone who wasn't close by.

Rule was easy to find. Oh, it took effort to push her mindsense out far enough to touch his mind, especially when she was already tired. Even before she nearly fainted after overextending herself, Lily hadn't liked the way it felt to extend her mindsense very far. It was disorienting, for one thing. It made her feel stretched and precarious and, if she pushed too far,

downright tenuous. But with Rule she didn't have to go looking. The mate sense guided her right to him.

She touched his mind very lightly, not wanted to distract
him, and sent the softest "voice" she could. Her lips shaped the
words as she sent them. *I'm here, if you can talk.*

. . . hold . . . a minute.

Funny how his mental voice sounded exactly like the one
she was used to hearing. Did her brain just interpret it that way,
or was it an innate property of mindspeech—something his
mind did, not hers? She'd have to check that out with people
whose voices she didn't know . . .

Sorry. Had to get some distance from . . . following me.

I missed some of that. Who's following you? Giving really
was better than receiving when it came to mindspeech. For her
anyway. She could send quite clearly, according to those she'd
practiced with, but she often missed part of the response.

*A couple squads. Keeping them . . . while the others look
for Nicky. No luck. Brownies . . . half a dozen soldiers in one
pit and IFV in another.*

His amusement came through clearly, making her grin. *Go,
brownies. Is it going well, then?*

A few problems. No major injuries, but when . . . A frus-
tratingly long break then, followed by, *You're okay?*

Sure. There are now three baby dragons. Two more to go.

Baby dragons. It's hard to picture. Are they cute?

*They're dragons, just very little ones, so mostly they're stun-
ningly beautiful, but there are moments of cute. They meep.*

They what?

*Big dragons roar. Baby dragons meep. It's adorable. I missed
what you said earlier about—shit! What was that? What just
happened?* It had felt as if his mind had been jostled or jolted.

Got to go.

She stayed in touch with his mind, but didn't try to speak to
him. That abrupt departure could only mean something was
happening that needed his attention. A fight. Bullets. It might
be some more benign event, but the ones that seemed most
likely all involved threat, danger, possible injury.

But not death. He hadn't been killed. At least she knew that
much. She drew a shaky breath and, at last, let her mindsense
coil back up inside her. Things were not going well, though she

wasn't sure how bad their position was. Rule had been careful not to tell her. A few problems, he'd said. No major injuries. Whatever she'd missed would likely have been more of the same, a way to tell her as little as possible because he didn't want her to worry.

She snorted. As if that would work.

Mika's tail shifted across the sand, coming to rest beside her. She shook her head, trying to dispel the anxiety that chilled her in spite of the overheated air of the creche.

The egg in front of her had developed a long crack. It rocked slightly as its occupant attacked it from within.

Lily's hands were resting in her lap . . . in fists. Slowly she straightened her fingers and shook them out. Time to get back to her midwifery. She stretched out a hand and her mind and touched the dragon.

FORTY-SIX

As they approached Mr. Smith's house, Demi grew sick with nerves. It was just her, Ruben, and Mike—Ruben in the lead, her and Mike behind him. The door was recessed with a semi-circular fanlight above it. The porch was tiny, too small for Demi and Mike to step up onto it with Ruben when he rang the doorbell. They waited, listening to the voices coming from the backyard.

Mr. Smith really was having a party.

They'd discussed how to do this—at least Ruben and Mike discussed it. Demi didn't have an opinion. Mike had wanted to go straight to the backyard, where the brownies reported that seventeen people were gathered, including Mr. Smith. More room to maneuver, he said. There were people in the house, also—two in the kitchen who were probably a caterer and a waitress. Plus one man had come in to use the bathroom, and four more men wandered throughout the house. Those four were armed, the brownies said. So were at least two of the people in the backyard. Ruben and Mike both thought the armed men were mercenaries.

Almost all the guests were male. The brownies had seen only three women.

Ruben wanted to go up to the front door, and he was in

charge, so that's what they did. There were legal reasons for that, but mostly he wanted it because of the two people standing on the edge of Mr. Smith's small front yard—a skinny man and a chubby woman. The woman held a camera with the WGVT logo on its side.

A desperate man might behave rashly, Ruben had said, but having a television camera aimed at him would strongly discourage a violent reaction.

Someone was sure taking his time answering the door. Ruben rang the bell again. Demi rubbed her stomach.

Mike leaned close and whispered, "I won't let anything happen to you."

"I don't want anything to happen to you, either."

"It won't. Nothing I can't heal anyway."

"Your bone isn't finished healing. If you—"

The door opened.

It was not Mr. Smith. This man had a hard face, skin much darker than Demi's, and he wore a black jacket over his black shirt, even though it was July and hot. He didn't say anything.

"We need to speak with Edward Smith," Ruben said.

"You aren't on the guest list."

"Tell your employer that Ruben Brooks and Demi McAllister are here to speak with him. I believe he'll overlook our lack of an invitation."

The hard-faced man did something with his chin and talked at the air. He had a radio, she realized, like the police sometimes used, with the mic on a thingee around his neck and an earbud in one ear. Then he stood there, staring at them, not saying anything.

"He gives me the creeps," Demi whispered to Mike.

Mike didn't whisper. "He's trying for intimidating. He's not there yet, but I'll bet he takes comfort in knowing he can creep out a seventeen-year-old girl."

The man did not like that. He scowled at Mike. That made Mike smile, but it didn't seem to be a friendly smile somehow. Then his radio talked to him. She couldn't hear it very well, but the lupi with her probably could. "You can come in," he said, stepping back and opening the door wider.

"Thank you, but no," Ruben said politely. "Mr. Smith needs to come to us."

More talking to the radio. More waiting. Demi's stomach didn't like waiting. She started stimming, moving the fingers of one hand down at her side where it wouldn't show too much. "Greensleeves" was such a soothing song.

Suddenly Ruben turned around and gestured at the two people waiting on the sidewalk. They jogged forward just as Mr. Smith came to the door.

He looked so much the same. That was the only thought in her mind as she stared at him. He was still a round little man with a shiny forehead. He didn't look scary at all.

"Ruben Brooks?" Mr. Smith said. "I certainly hadn't expected you to turn up on my doorstep. And Demi." His voice got all sad. "I'm glad you're all right, but—" He broke off, staring behind Demi. "Who are you?"

"Morrie Peterson, WGVT News," said the skinny man. "Are you Edward Smith of the NSA?"

"I don't give interviews. If you—"

"Edward Smith," Ruben said firmly, "you are under arrest on charges of conspiracy to commit murder, conspiracy to commit arson, and multiple counts of the unlawful use of magic. There will be further charges," he added, "once we've recovered the children you've abused, but those will do for now."

Mr. Smith looked at Demi with eyes meaner than Mrs. MacGruder's had ever been. The hate was so clear that Demi took a step back—then it vanished beneath his usual expression. "You've been listening to this poor girl. She's not stable, you know."

"She's been very helpful, but we're hardly going to rely solely on the testimony of a minor." Ruben cocked his head. "It wasn't really a very good conspiracy, you know. As long as no one suspected, as long as we weren't looking, you went undetected. Once we knew where to look, however—"

"Get off my porch. Off my property."

"No, sir. You are under arrest. Please step out onto the porch."

"This is absurd! You can't arrest me. You've been removed from your position."

"I am still a legally empowered agent of Unit Twelve, however."

"I don't believe you." Mr. Smith's pink tongue darted out

and licked his upper lip. He half turned and said something Demi couldn't hear to the hard-faced man, then he demanded, "Where's your warrant? I insist on seeing a warrant."

"Did you think Jim Mathison was wholly your creature? Or that ambition would prevent him from listening to me?" Ruben shook his head. He sounded as if he felt sorry for Mr. Smith, which made no sense to Demi. He also made it sound like he'd spoken with the current head of Unit 12, and he hadn't. It must be some kind of trick. "Your Gift allows you to manipulate others when you're with them, but the effect isn't permanent, and you don't really understand the people you use. Take Eric Ellison, for example. When he—"

Mr. Smith moved to one side. "Nick. Get them out of here."

And Nicky stepped forward—only he didn't look like Nicky anymore. He looked like a drug addict or an AIDS patient or a Holocaust victim—haggard and rail-thin, with long, dirty hair. His arms hung down by his sides as if they were too heavy to lift. And his eyes weren't right. They weren't right at all.

Ruben and Mike flew backward.

Mike collided with the camera-carrying woman. And someone seized Demi's wrist and yanked her. She tried to resist, but it was the hard-faced man who'd grabbed her, and she couldn't even slow him down. He dragged her into the house as easily as if she were three years old. Someone slammed the door shut.

"Nicky!" she cried. Mr. Smith was talking—yelling—but she didn't listen. "Nicky, you have to stop doing what he says!" Nicky was looking at her with those terrible eyes. She wasn't sure he knew who she was. She wasn't sure he knew who he was anymore. "He's a bad person, Nicky, a really bad—"

Mr. Smith slapped her. Hard. "Shut up. Just shut your stupid mouth, you stupid little slut. You won't be testifying for—"

"Don't," Nicky said. His voice sounded flat. Like a synthesized voice. Like no one was really speaking at all.

Mr. Smith seemed to try to gather himself together. He was breathing hard. "Nick, she's hysterical. I had to slap her to—"

"That's Demi," Nicky said in that no-one's-home voice.

Someone screamed out back.

The front door boomed. Wood cracked and splintered and the front door fell all cattywampus, two of the hinges having pulled loose along with the lock, but not the third, so that it dangled from that one anchoring point. Mike came barreling in and a gun went off once, twice—and just as Demi realized no one was holding her anymore, Mr. Smith grabbed her.

He was almost her height and nowhere near as strong as the other man. She fought him. She might have gotten loose, but something hit her hard on the side of her head.

The bright, ringing pain stunned her. Not for long, but long enough. By the time she could pay attention again, Mr. Smith had one arm around her waist, holding her tightly against him. His other hand held a gun to her head. The muzzle pressed right where he'd hit her. It hurt. "Stay back!" he screamed.

He had to scream because of all the noise out back—people screaming and guns firing. The hard-faced man lay on the floor. He wasn't moving. Mike and Ruben were both inside now. Mike was sort of crouched, as if he was about to spring. Ruben was on the other side of the door, and he looked ready to attack someone, too. But neither he nor Mike moved.

Demi bit her lip. The noise out back told her that Ruben had signaled for the other part of his plan to begin—the part they'd hoped not to use. Two of the Wythe clansmen were now wolves, racing around stirring everyone up. That was to create a distraction. The other two would have stayed men and they'd come help as soon as they could.

But the other mercenaries inside the house got there first— two men who came racing down the stairs and a third man— Demi didn't see where he came from—who stopped beside Mr. Smith. They all had their guns out and looked angry and ready to shoot.

"I need to be extracted," Mr. Smith told them. "You two— Brooks and whoever you are. Get on the floor. Flat on the floor. Now," he cried when they didn't move. "Do as I say, dammit, or I'll shoot her. I swear I—"

Nicky interrupted. "But that's Demi." A thread of emotion had crept into his dead voice. He sounded . . . puzzled.

"Nick." Mr. Smith still sounded angry. He took a deep breath, and when he spoke again, his voice was persuasive, almost caressing. "You trust me, don't you?"

"I trust you." The words were rote, mechanical.

"You need to go with one of these men. Our nation's enemies

have caught up with us, and we have to retreat. But he'll take care of you, and I'll join you shortly."

"Nicky," Demi pleaded. "He's lying to you. He's a liar."

Nicky's face didn't change. His arms still hung limp at his sides. But he turned to face Mr. Smith. "You hit Demi. You hurt her. You promised you wouldn't hurt her."

"I didn't have a choice, Nick. You can see that."

"You lied to me."

"No, of course not. She's misguided, Nick, confused. You can't—"

He stopped talking and screamed. Something warm and wet splashed on her shoulder and her head. The arm around her waist went loose and the gun barrel was suddenly gone and she dropped to the floor and rolled, getting away. Shots rang out and they were loud, so loud she couldn't stand it, and she huddled in on herself, her head down, her hands over her ears, and she was screaming, too, like the people out back, but she couldn't get away from the deafening sound.

All of a sudden it stopped. All of it. The shots and the screams—even hers, because her voice shut itself off as if surprised by the silence.

Someone came up to her. Her eyes were squeezed shut, her head buried in her arms, so she didn't see him. But she knew who it was.

He rested a hand on her back. "You're okay," he informed her.

"Mike." That's all she could say. "Mike."

"I'm going to do your thinking for you now. You said I could. Keep your eyes shut." He didn't wait for an answer, lifting her easily to her feet and holding her the way Rule had done a couple times. He pressed her head to his chest with one big hand. "You don't want to look yet."

"He's still alive," Ruben said.

"Mr. Smith?" she asked in a wavery voice.

"No," Mike said. "Your friend. Your friend killed Smith and Smith's men shot him. They're dead now. Ruben and I didn't have time to stop them without killing them."

"I need to see him. Mike, I need to see Nicky."

After a moment he nodded and took her to see her friend. She tried not to look at anything—anyone—else, but couldn't quite manage it. There were a lot of bodies.

Ruben knelt beside Nicky. He stood when Mike and Demi got there and gave a nod of his head, then started telling people what to do. His men were there, she realized. The ones who hadn't turned into wolves.

She paid no attention. Her legs kind of gave out and she sat suddenly. "Nicky."

So much blood. His whole front was bloody. Blood dribbled from the corner of his mouth when he looked up at her. He was very badly injured. Maybe he was dying. But his eyes . . . they were blurry, unfocused, yet his eyes looked like him again. "Nicky," she said again. "It's Demi. I tried to rescue you. I tried really hard. I'm sorry I couldn't do it."

Slowly his eyes came into focus. "You're okay?"

She nodded, then realized he might not be seeing very well. "Yes. You're not."

His mouth twitched as if he wanted to smile. "Are you crying?"

"Of course I am."

His eyes closed. "I tried not to believe him. At first I didn't, but after a while . . ."

"That's his Gift. His charisma Gift. You couldn't help it."

She wasn't sure he heard her. "Amanda. Don't let her near you."

"She's scary."

"Evil. She's evil. Cerberus . . . takes over. And the drug. The drug made me bad. I did terrible things. I thought . . . he said they were enemies . . ."

"The drug is really a potion. It's magic, too. It wasn't your fault, Nicky. None of it was your fault."

His eyes opened again. This time he did smile. His lips moved just a little as if he was trying to say something, but no words came out. He lay there smiling up at her until his body jerked and his breathing stopped. A little more blood came out of his mouth. And his eyes died.

FORTY-SEVEN

～

RULE ran. Every footfall sent a bolt of pain through his head. He ignored that. The small body in his arms was so limp. Limp and bloody.

He'd been running from one squad when he ran into another one. They'd been doing that awhile, he and the others with weapons—spraying a few bullets to get the soldiers' attention, then running away. Luring them away from the lair. It wouldn't have worked if the brownies hadn't stolen a lot of their personal radios—and twice disabled the CO's comm unit.

They hadn't yet resorted to shooting at the soldiers, but it was only a matter of time. They'd failed entirely to find Nicky.

At last he reached the village green. There—there she was, the little brownie healer. Shisti. She was bent over another patient.

"It was shrapnel, I think," he gasped as he reached her and dropped to his knees, laying his small burden in front of her. "Not a bullet. It hit him in the back." And Rule hadn't realized it. He'd been creased by a bullet himself. He'd gotten away, dizzy but knowing he'd been lucky. He'd run, unaware of the small life bleeding on his back until he stopped.

"Ah," she said sadly, and stroked Dilly's ashy cheek. "Bend down more. I have to touch your head to help it."

"I'm fine. Help Dilly."

Big green eyes blinked once. "Rule, I can't. He's dead."

Dead? No. He couldn't be dead. Rule had run so fast, tried so hard—and Dilly had died in his arms, his passing unnoticed. Dimly he was aware of having closed his eyes. Some stupid, instinctive effort to hide the way they'd filled with tears.

"Rule!" someone called.

Jason. That was Jason. He forced the tears back, swallowed the grief, and became Rho once more. "Here." He stood.

Jason was hurrying to him, talking on a phone. He sounded excited. "No, I found him. Here. You tell him." He held the phone out to Rule. "It's Ruben Brooks. He called on the only number he could find for the brownies—the reservation hotline."

"Ruben? This is Rule."

"Good. I request strongly that you cease all attacks and harassment immediately. The Army should begin retreating at any moment."

Rule almost dropped the phone. "What? How did you—"

"Smith is dead, killed when I went to arrest him. Several of his people were at his house at the time. One of them fell apart quite nicely and confessed. With that on record, I was able to get through to the president. She's still angry with me for having become lupus without her permission," he said dryly, "but at least she was willing to listen. She's ordered the troops withdrawn."

"It's over." He spoke with more disbelief than relief.

"Your end is. Things will be messy at this end for some time yet."

"And Danny—Demi—is she okay? Mike?"

"Mike's fine. Demi got knocked around a bit, but nothing serious. She's grieving, though. Her friend was killed."

"Nicky?" Rule's voice was sharp. "Why would he be there instead of here?"

"Apparently he was supposed to provide emergency security. That didn't work out the way Smith intended. When Smith threatened Demi, it shattered the man's hold on Nicky. He killed Smith, but Smith's men shot him." Ruben sighed. "He was in rough shape. Very rough. Whatever they'd been doing to him . . . and we still don't know where the other children are.

The man who confessed—Charles Bradley, goes by Chuck—didn't know much about that end of things, and the others have lawyered up. Oh, you should know that two of the conspirators are unaccounted for—a woman named Sharon Plummer, who acted as houseparent and headed up the research staff. Also a man named Tom Weng whom Chuck says supplied the potion."

Weng? Rule thought of Lily's theory. "Is he a sorcerer?"

"We'll ask, but Chuck may not be aware of distinctions of that sort. For people who've invested heavily in magic, they don't seem to know much about it. I . . ." His voice moved away from the phone as he told someone he'd be right there. "I have to go. Lots of mess to deal with still."

Ruben disconnected before Rule could ask more questions, and he had several. He needed to know what had happened with some of his men. With José. But maybe Ruben didn't know, either. Not yet.

They'd find out soon. Rule looked at Jason. The younger man was grinning. Slowly Rule nodded. It wasn't in him to smile. Dilly was still dead. Barring extreme ill luck or outrageous stupidity, though, he'd be the last to die. It was over—except for the messy parts, such as whether he'd be arrested for today's actions or jailed for having escaped his earlier arrest. But no Dragmageddon.

"We need to get the word out," he said. "Jason, call Luke and Manny. I'll borrow a phone and call Codger and see that he—" He cut himself off, listening.

Hellfire. Another bloody helicopter—not directly overhead. Not yet anyway. "Someone get up a tree and find out where that damn copter's going!"

"Xīn," Lily said. New. Which was true of all babies, but struck her as particularly apt for this fresh, shiny mind. The now-familiar pulse of magic traveled from Mika to the baby along her mindsense, and the baby's mind absorbed his new name. A moment later, he thrust up on wobbly legs and took his first step.

Little Xīn had taken his time about hatching. Lily had wanted to help him, but Mika had been adamant that the babies must break through the shells by themselves. Lily didn't know whether custom or reason lay behind that dictate. Maybe the act of breaking through the shell triggered important physiological changes in the hatchling. Maybe it triggered something magically that was equally important to a being built as much from magic as from flesh.

Or maybe dragons had simply always done it that way, she thought, and stretched without removing her hand from Mika's tail.

She didn't think she'd be too drained. It had dawned on her after the fourth hatchling emerged that when she touched Mika, the dragon's magic buoyed her, soaking in through her skin much faster than she could absorb magic normally. So although she'd given her mindsense a workout, she shouldn't be totally depleted. But she was not ready for the headache that would hit the moment the link was broken. Those had gotten worse each time, so this one was apt to be a doozy. She wished Mika weren't quite so distracted by motherhood. She'd asked the dragon twice why—

The volcano her mind was linked with went suddenly calm. Still.

The change jolted her. Her hand fell away from Mika's tail and she moaned as she doubled up, hit by the headache to end all headaches.

It felt like getting shot. Not that she'd ever been shot in the head, but she'd taken a bullet elsewhere, and this white-hot pain was way too much like that. Finally agony began fading into mere pain—still mind-dulling, but not strong enough to wipe out everything else.

The brownies were upset. She blinked and tried to pull her thoughts together. They weren't singing anymore. She heard her name amid the high-pitched clamor, made a huge effort, and lifted her head. "What?"

Most of them feel silent. "She fell asleep!" Gandalf cried. "Mika fell asleep and won't wake up!"

"Maybe she's tired." God knew Lily was.

"No, it's wrong. She isn't supposed to sleep now, and dragons don't sleep like this, so soundly they won't wake."

Lily looked around. Mika's head no longer hovered up above the rest of her body. With a groan, she got to her feet. Briefly she was dizzy, but that passed.

All she saw was coils of dragon, sand, shattered eggshells . . . and the babies, of course. Three of them were awake and practicing walking, lurching now and then into unsuccessful attempts to run. As she watched, the red one snapped at his brother's tail. Two had curled up next to their mother's heat, sleeping. "The babies seem fine."

"Mika is not fine. Wake her up, Lilyu! She must wake up."

How do you wake a sleeping dragon? She tried poking Mika with her hand. Nothing. Could she wake someone with her mindsense? She had no idea. Time to find out. She urged the magic coiled inside her to uncurl. It responded sluggishly, either because she was depleted or because her head hurt. But it did respond.

Lily hadn't noticed any difference between a sleeping mind and a waking one, yet she'd known it the instant Mika fell asleep. So on some level, she was aware of a difference. She wanted to bring that awareness up to the conscious level, so she resisted the pull of Mika's mind and studied the babies first.

Their minds weren't clear bubbles anymore. They shone with shifting dawn colors now, and the surfaces she touched were beginning to acquire texture. The change was most noticeable in the ones who'd been hatched longest, but even the brandnew baby's mind had begun taking on color.

At first that was the only difference she noted. Gradually, though, she realized that the patterns she dimly sensed beneath the surface were different in the sleeping babies' minds. Farther from the surface, maybe.

She let her attention be drawn to Mika's mind. And frowned. What had always felt like seething lava was now quiet. Motionless, as far as she could sense. It seemed an unnatural stillness, but she didn't know if that was because—

A brownie screamed shrilly.

Lily spun around.

"Freeze!"

She did. A man stood in the mouth of the tunnel she'd used the first time she came to the creche. Five-ten, Asian, slim, maybe thirty-five, part of her mind noted. But most of her mind was fixed on the gun he pressed to Gandalf's head. He stood there smiling down at Lily with the little brownie securely pinned against his chest and a 9mm held to her head. "Lily Yu!

What a surprise. And to think I accused Smith of having secreted you away somewhere. Hold your hands in the air, please. Very good. Now, all you little brownies hop down there with her."

"He can see us!" one of the brownies exclaimed.

"Yes, I can, so don't try your cute little brownie tricks."

"It's a fifteen-foot drop," Lily said.

"They're excellent little acrobats. And I'm impatient. Jump!" Abruptly he twisted Gandalf's arm.

"Ow!" she cried. "Ow, ow, ow!"

Some of the younger brownies did jump. Two landed in sand. Two landed on Mika. The older ones began to slip off the ledge to climb down.

The AK-47 lay buried beneath a coil of Mika, but Lily had her Glock. She nudged her mindsense open. The first time someone "heard" mindspeech was startling. If she could distract him even for a moment—

The sharp crack of his gun was shockingly loud in the enclosed space. Sand shot up near Lily's feet. The babies all meeped loudly. Those who'd been playing hurried in their unstable way to the shelter of their mother's body.

"No magic." He wasn't smiling now.

Her heart pounded in time with her head. He wasn't there. He was, but he wasn't. "I'm a sensitive. I can't do magic."

"And I'm a sorcerer, so I know you were trying something— some type of mind magic. That won't work on me, but the ban stands. No magic."

No, she thought, mind magic probably didn't work on him. To her mindsense, Gandalf was alone on the ledge. This sorcerer's mind was as invisible to her new sense as the baby dragons had been before they hatched. Completely shielded.

"Now, what to do with you." The gun stayed aimed steadily at her head.

"Are you taking suggestions?"

His smile flashed white in the dim light. "I think not. You're quite the unexpected complication. Or do I mean bonus?" He sighed. "Decisions, decisions. Have you been here all along? No, that's the wrong question. Why are you here?"

"To help Mika."

The brownies sent up a chorus of protests. Most of them were perched on various parts of the sleeping dragon. A few were on the sand near Lily.

The intruder ignored them. His eyebrows lifted. "Tell me more."

"She needed my hands. Often the hatchlings can't emerge without help."

"And yet brownies seem to have hands."

"They aren't immune to magic. I am. The hatching sets loose a lot of odd magic that can have dangerous effects." She lifted her eyebrows. "If you're a sorcerer, as you claim, you must be able to see the remnants of it."

He studied her a moment. "Part truth, part lie. Perhaps we'll have time later to sort out which is which. For now, it's time to get busy." Abruptly he tossed Gandalf away from him. The old brownie landed on Mika with a cry of pain. Several of the brownies hurried to her.

Lily didn't move because his gun hadn't. It remained aimed at her head. "Is she all right?"

Several brownies answered at once. She picked out enough from the torrent of words to be somewhat reassured. Gandalf was alive, but her arm was probably broken.

"Time to get to work. Brownies, this is for you." His free hand tossed out something—a sack or tote made of camo fabric. "Lily, I need you to unbuckle your shoulder harness slowly and carefully. I'm feeling nervous. Do try not to alarm me."

She did as he'd bade. Slowly. As her hands went through the routine task, she became aware of something that had been in the background, unnoticed.

Rule was coming closer.

"When you get it off, throw it behind you. Throw it nice and hard so it lands on the other side of the dragon. Don't worry about waking her. You won't."

"And why is that?" She slipped off the shoulder harness, letting it dangle from one hand. And tried not to notice Rule.

"Little Amanda put the dragon nighty-night."

The sorcerer had seen it when she used her mindsense. He might be able to see the mate sense, too, if she were actively using it. The mate bond itself was part magic, part spirit, but was that true of the sense that told her where Rule was?

Closer, yes. He was coming this way.

"Do get rid of that shoulder harness like I told you, Lily. This place is chock-full of hostages to your good behavior. I could kill two or three and not miss them at all."

Seventeen brownies and five baby dragons made for a lot of hostages. She turned and threw her shoulder holster, weapon and all. It didn't land on the other side of Mika's coils, but fell in between them, which was just as damn unreachable. "Amanda's a telepath," she said, turning back to face him.

"So she is. Nasty child. Lily, sit down right where you are. Very good. Brownies, start gathering up every tiny fragment of the shells. Put them in that tote for me. I'm not at all squeamish, but neither am I bloodthirsty. Do as you're told and no one needs to die today. Not even Lily."

The brownies didn't hurry, but they did obey, starting to pick up bits of eggshells.

"Very good." He lowered himself to sit on the edge of the ledge, his legs hanging off it. "Now, Lily, I'm quite curious about you. Let's get acquainted."

"Excellent idea." She sat in the hot sand with her head tipped back, watching him. "What's your name?"

He smiled. "Tom."

"Was it you who took down the wards, Tom?"

"Why, yes, it was. Though I'll admit I had help. Very strong wards, they were. What type of magic were you trying to do earlier?"

"I hoped to turn you into a toad. You want the eggshells for the lóng dàn potion. Not the whole eggs. Just the shells."

"Heard about that, did you?"

He was enjoying himself, she thought. Now that she'd gotten rid of her weapon and the brownies were obeying him, he could relax and enjoy his own cleverness. He probably hadn't had much opportunity to brag. "You fooled Smith for a long time."

He chuckled. "That idiot! It wasn't hard. Smith thinks it's the potion that makes Amanda so strong. Oh, it's necessary for some things, but really! He's such a joke. Do you know, he thought he could kill the mama dragon, steal the eggs, and raise his own dragons to be good little secret agents?"

She stared, horrified. "That . . . hadn't occurred to me."

"Dragons are telepathic, you know." His voice mocked the absent Smith.

Not without an *efondi* to name them when they hatch, but neither Tom nor Smith could know that. "Did he think the babies would grow up to obey him?"

"Remarkable, isn't it? He desperately wants more telepaths, you see. When I suggested he raise his own, he loved the idea. Stupid man, but his particular combination of ignorance and monomania let me get where I am now, so I suppose I shouldn't complain." He glanced at his watch. "Speed it up, little brownies. Or I might put a bullet in one of you for motivation."

The ever-chattery brownies didn't say a word. They just began working faster.

So he had a schedule to keep, did he? No doubt Mika couldn't be kept asleep indefinitely. "Why did you say Amanda put Mika to sleep? Telepaths can't do that even with humans, much less with a dragon. It isn't part of the Gift."

"Ah, but Amanda has help, too."

"I assume Amanda had to get close to Mika to put her to sleep, but she isn't with the soldiers."

"Modern technology is a marvel. A helicopter brought us."

"Us? How many is that?"

"Did you not find out about Cerberus?" He shook his head. "I do hate it that Smith was right about something. He was sure you didn't have a clue, but I thought you might stumble to it. You're fairly bright, and that little sensitive of Smith's is brilliant with computers. Limited in other ways, but within her limits she's quite a marvel."

"Danny found a mention of Cerberus, but no description."

"Ah. Well, you do know that Cerberus was the three-headed dog of myth? Smith's Cerberus is three-headed, also. But Amanda's head is always the one in charge. At the moment she's linked with a farseer and a Finder."

"Linked," she repeated slowly. He was telling her too much. He intended to kill her when he'd finished crowing . . . and he was glancing at his watch again. She didn't have much time. "Is that how they were able to murder people? This link must have let Nicky see what the farseer saw so he could use his form of TK on them."

"More or less," he said agreeably.

"And the fires—that was Cerberus, too." There was a Fire Gifted among the children. Amanda must have linked the farseer with the fire-starter. "Your potion makes it possible for Amanda to link telepathically to two other children?"

"It's necessary, but not sufficient. Come, now, Lily, I've dropped a couple hints. Do you not have even an inkling? No? Shall I tell you?" He smiled sweetly. "Why, yes, I think I will. Amanda and I have been receiving help from someone you know. Someone who knows you, too. Someone who finds it very useful to have a telepath in this realm bound to *her* service."

The blood drained from her head.

He laughed. "Oh, the look on your face! Yes, *that* someone. Did you not guess? It takes a great deal of power to incapacitate a dragon, even one who's temporarily limited by motherhood."

Amanda was in telepathic contact with *her*. With the Great Bitch, the Great Enemy . . . and Tom was in *her* service, too. Sam had been wrong. The Great Bitch was very much involved. Lily's mouth was so dry she had to lick her lips before she could speak. "Tell me—is she currently wanting me dead or kidnapped? She keeps changing her mind about that."

"Oh, she doesn't object to your death. Not at all. But she'd just love to get her hands on you alive." He stood. "Time's about up, little brownies. If you don't have the last pieces in the bag by the count of five, I start shooting. One . . . two . . . three . . . there!" he exclaimed as they dropped the last handfuls of tiny fragments into the tote. "I knew you could do it. Now take the bag to Lily."

The tote was almost as big as one of the brownies. Two of them carried it to her together, their faces tight with worry. And silent. It was eerie, all that silence from brownies. She took it from them.

"Zip it up, Lily, and sling it on your shoulder. Now go over to that wee little rope ladder." He started walking along the ledge, keeping his gun trained on her, stopping where the ledge did about fifteen feet below and five feet short of the opening to the creche. "Very good," he said when she reached the bottom of the rope ladder. "Climb it."

Was he finally making a mistake? He couldn't reach the rope ladder from where he stood, but maybe he was good at rock climbing and intended to cross the distance between him and the ladder Spider-Man-style. But he couldn't keep his gun trained on her while he went up that rope ladder. It wasn't possible.

Lily grabbed a rung and started up as quickly as she could. She kept expecting to feel the ladder tugged down by his weight, coming up it behind her. It didn't happen.

When she was halfway up, she heard a mechanical roar somewhere overhead. A helicopter. She glanced quickly at him. He still stood on the ledge, gun aimed her way. "Keep going." He made a small motion with his gun to encourage her.

When she'd nearly reached the top, sudden knowledge froze her for a moment. She stole another glance at him. He smiled, leaned forward—leaned right out into the empty air. And started rising.

Son of a bitch. Son of a bitch. He could teleport? That was impossible.

He kept smiling. Kept rising. And made that little gesture with the gun again.

Her fingers numb and clumsy with shock, she managed to pull herself up the last bit, rose to her knees—and saw him land several feet away. Too far, dammit. Too far for her to tackle him when she wasn't on her feet yet.

A helicopter slid into view, coming over the top of the rocky hill, then dropping lower.

Tom the sorcerer smiled with his mouth, but some mask had dropped away. His eyes were cold now. Viciously cold. He raised his voice to be heard over the chopper's noise. "Quite the showstopper, that little trick, isn't it? Cousin."

Cousin? What did—

He said something, but the chopper was so loud now that she couldn't hear his words. It hovered some twenty feet up and maybe forty feet away. As she watched, someone dumped out a rope ladder. It unrolled to almost reach the ground.

Two black-and-silver wolves leaped down, down from overhead—one from the right, one from the left. Leaping straight for the man who'd called her cousin.

Lily dropped, the gun cracked—and the sorcerer burst into flame. One wolf fell short of his goal. The other completed his leap to crash into the burning man—knocking him down, only to be seized by arms that seemed made of flame. Burning man, burning wolf, rolled together on the ground for deadly seconds—rolled close to Lily, who pushed to her feet and stumbled back.

And immediately dropped to the ground again as machine-gun fire spattered the ground and rocks nearby. The helicopter. They were firing from the helicopter. She lay flat but turned her head, desperate to see the other wolf, the one who'd been shot—

Tom the sorcerer, no longer burning but covered in ash and blood and scraps of burned cloth, kicked her in the head.

He was barefoot, his shoes having burned off, so the blow wasn't as bad as it might have been. She didn't black out. But she lost a few seconds to a pain-wracked daze, and when her eyes would focus again, she was alone. Tom must not have been hurt badly, in spite of the blood. He'd reached the chopper's dangling rope ladder—and he had the tote.

A few feet away, the corpse of one of the wolves smoldered. And it was a corpse. No breath stirred ribs with fur and flesh burned away. Charles. Charles, who she'd forgotten was up here, waiting patiently and loyally while she named baby dragons—waiting and no doubt listening, maybe pacing, when the sorcerer arrived, watching for his chance to act.

Then Rule had arrived while she was on the brownies' rope ladder. She'd tried not to notice, tried hard not to use the mate sense, but he couldn't be so close without her knowing. He and Charles had attacked together. Fate or luck let only one of them connect with his target—and die for it.

Lily pushed to her feet, shaking. And saw the other wolf pushing to his feet, his side bloody. Reality took a quick dive into impossibility, a sudden Möbius-strip twist impossible to follow with eyes alone, and Rule stood on two legs, one hand holding his side, where blood dripped.

Lily staggered toward him, dizzy but determined. And the chopper rose with Tom partway up the rope ladder. Rose up and away.

She stopped. "Goddammit!" They were getting away, and she had nothing, no way to stop them.

Rule managed a few wavering steps and she hurried to him, tucking her shoulder under one arm to prop him up. "How bad—"

The earth shook with the dragon's roar.

Mika. Mika had woken, either because the chopper and its occupants were too far away or because Amanda just couldn't keep her asleep any longer. Fuzzily Lily tried to open her mindsense so she could tell Mika to stop them, that the bad guys were getting away—

Before she could, the red dragon shot out of the opening to the creche in a huge leap, narrowly missing knocking them both down—a leap that exploded into flight. She roared again.

And the helicopter burst into flame.

FORTY-EIGHT

~⟋

As Rule had expected, there were a lot of messy bits. Those bits kept them in Washington for days, though they stayed in Nokolai's Georgetown house instead of with Ruben and Deborah. Rule was satisfied that he and Ruben had established that they could share a house. Staying in another Rho's territory when he was wounded and vulnerable was not necessary. Not very smart, either.

He'd be less than fully mobile for a while. The bullet had missed his heart, but it hadn't done his stomach much good. The rib it broke was healing nicely, but gut wounds healed slower than most. Fortunately, Nettie had been able to fly out to put him in sleep for the surgery. Unfortunately, she'd put him on a liquid diet for the first two days, followed by disgustingly bland food "until I tell you otherwise."

He was propped up on the couch trying to work—trying not to think about steak—when Lily returned. He heard her on the porch. "No, I've got it," she told the guard who'd gone with her. "Just get the door. Thanks."

His heart lifted in anticipation. He closed the laptop and swung his legs off the couch as Lily came in . . . pushing José in a wheelchair.

"Don't you dare get up," she told him, parking the chair near the couch. "You'll set a bad example."

He ignored her, of course, standing so he could hug his friend and get his back pounded in return. He'd known that José had survived since waking from his surgery. It was the first thing Lily had told him. But he hadn't been able to go to him, hadn't seen him until now.

José had nearly bled out before being found and taken prisoner. The military doctors had given him blood, which was good, but they'd also decided they had to take off his leg at the hip. They'd been quite surprised when their unconscious, anesthetized patient woke up when they started to make the incision. Bloody fools. They'd known he was lupus. They should consider themselves lucky he'd been too weak from blood loss to do more than knock out the surgeon.

They'd been half right, though. Even lupi healing could only do so much. José did lose his leg below the knee, but Nettie had been present to put him in sleep for that surgery yesterday.

Once they'd greeted each other, Rule told José to sit down before he fell over, then he did the same. They talked awhile, mostly meaningless things. Rule said that regrowing a limb was a bitch, especially when José couldn't use crutches until the hole in his shoulder finished healing. José said yeah, but at least he could eat real food while he healed. Rule called him a couple of rude names. Then José asked about the firnam—when and where it would be held.

Not for another two weeks, Rule told him, and at Leidolf Clanhome. They should both be well enough for it by then.

Silence fell.

Rule had lost friends, people he valued. Five of the dead had been his men—Andy, killed by a scared cop; Saul, Dave, and Roger gunned down by the National Guard; and Claude, shot by a gods-cursed vigilante. The people in uniform Rule had seen had been deputies who were trying to get the damn vigilantes to go home. Five wasn't a lot maybe, considering their enemies had included the national government. But they'd been good men. Men who shouldn't have died fighting their own countrymen. The firnam would honor them and others who'd died in battle, but firnams were also for the living, meant to help those who'd survived. Rule hoped it would help José. He hoped it would help him, too.

He'd lost men before. It didn't get easier with repetition.

"Will you hold the *gens amplexi* then?" Lily asked.

He flashed her a smile, appreciating her effort to turn the conversation to a happier subject. "I don't know yet if there will be a *gens amplexi,* but Demi will be here soon, so I expect I'll find out. And you," he told José, "had better get up to bed. You look like hell."

José didn't protest much, proving that it was, indeed, time to get him horizontal. One of the guards came in to carry him upstairs. The house was not convenient for a one-legged man.

Lily came and snuggled next to him. "Did you make up with your lawyer?"

His mouth twisted wryly. He'd been having that conversation when Lily left to pick up José. "She's mostly forgiven me. Largely, I think, because she's relishing the suit for false arrest I plan to bring."

Lily snorted.

No one was in jail. No one was going to jail. That was an unexpectedly good outcome, and one he'd had nothing whatsoever to do with. He'd been only half a day out of surgery when he picked up his phone and the person on the other end asked him to hold, please, for the president.

Rule didn't know what the black dragon had said to the president, but he'd clearly been persuasive—rather, he thought, in the way that nuclear bombs can be called persuasive. She'd sounded shaken when she promised Rule that there would be no arrests, no fines, and that all expenses incurred on behalf of the dragons would be reimbursed by the government. She'd added that Sam had asked her to let Rule know that he would be in touch when Rule and Lily returned to his territory.

Later that day, she'd given a press conference in which she said publicly the same things she'd told him privately, praising Rule and his people for their actions, and going on to praise the brownies lavishly.

As she damn well should have. Sixteen brownies had been injured, to varying degrees.

Dilly was the only one who'd died.

Guilt rose, a smothering miasma. His thoughts ran through the usual cycle of if-only's . . . if only he'd turned faster, dodged better, run straight for the healer instead of just trying to get away . . . if only he'd not taken the little brownie on his back in the first place. The thoughts were as inevitable as they were useless, his brain trying to rewrite reality.

Lily stirred. "I heard the news on the way here. That damn fool in charge of the Ohio National Guard finally stepped down. The one who told his troops they were firing gaddo bullets. I hope they hang him."

So did he. "Add him to the three at NSA who've resigned, the five who are under arrest, Eric Ellison and the other two who've resigned from Homeland Security and will probably end up indicted—"

"Don't forget the slimy bastard," she said, using her pet name for Jim Mathison, who'd taken over the Unit for such a short time.

"—and the slimy bastard, and I think we can say that the nation's security apparatus is undergoing a major upheaval."

"Yeah." She sighed. "Ruben says he's satisfied. I don't believe him."

Technically, Ruben Brooks was still on the FBI payroll, an agent of Unit Twelve. But he wasn't on active duty. He wasn't running Unit Twelve. "Ever since he became one of us, he's said that eventually he'd have to step down. His secret couldn't be kept forever."

"I like Croft. I'm trying to be glad that he got the job. I haven't managed it yet, but I'm trying."

He gave her a gentle squeeze. "He's a good man."

"He is still looking for Tom Weng," she said as if that proved it.

"Or for any sign that the man ever existed?"

"That, too."

Weng's body hadn't been found. He'd been on the rope ladder when the helicopter exploded, which Lily was convinced meant he'd managed to teleport away. The first time she brought that up, he'd pointed out that being able to rise fifteen feet did not mean the man was Mary Poppins. He'd been a couple hundred feet up, not fifteen. Maybe he had teleported a short distance—enough to make his body hard to find. The helicopter had gone down in a particularly rough section of the Appalachians.

What about the way no one could find any record of him? That, she claimed, suggested he was alive. He knew how to use magic to change computer records, after all. Rule had retorted that Weng's partners in crime at the NSA knew how to do it without magic. Obviously they had, for some reason, removed all traces of Tom Weng. For God's sake, they'd both seen the helicopter explode. Weng was dead.

She'd given him a look and said she'd be glad when he could eat meat again.

Beside him, Lily stirred. "You need to get your feet up."

"I'm five days out of surgery, not one. I don't need to spend the day in bed."

"I didn't say go to bed. I said put your feet up. You're hurting." She stood, crouched, and lifted his feet for him.

He allowed that, even helped swing his legs around. She was right. His stomach hurt like blazes when he sat up for long. He was tired of it. He and Lily had managed to make love last night, but he disliked the care they had to take because of his bloody wounded stomach. He told himself to be patient. He scowled at his own advice.

The doorbell rang, followed by brusque words from the porch. "It's me."

Rule perked up at the sound of Mike's voice. He'd sent Mike to pick up Demi. When he and Lily returned to D.C., they'd offered Demi a bedroom for as long as she wished, but she'd turned them down. She'd wanted to go to Whistle and see some of the people she'd gotten to know there. She needed to explain why she'd deceived them, she said.

He hoped that had gone well. He doubted it had, but perhaps his view of people was jaundiced.

Sean unlocked the front door. A moment later, Demi entered the living room. She wore old khaki shorts and a faded T-shirt with a hideous zombie shambling across it moaning, GR-R-RAINS!

"I see your things caught up with you," Lily said, pleased.

One of the many things Lily had done while Rule was lying around, in bed or on the couch, was to track down Demi's possessions, abandoned when she fled Edward Smith. She'd thought there was a good chance they hadn't been disposed of "Smith thought he was a super-spy," she'd explained, "but he was really just a geek bureaucrat. Bureacracies may lose things, but they never throw anything away."

"Yeah." Demi smiled, looking down at herself. "Thanks for that. It feels weird to have stuff again."

"Good weird or bad weird?"

"Good weird. Especially because of my mom's stuff, the photos and all. There's this necklace she used to wear all the time. I'd forgotten about it until I opened the box it was in, and then . . ." She stopped, clearly unsure how to put words to that moment. "It's good to have it again."

"I'm glad," Lily said. "Can we offer you anything? A Coke maybe?"

"A Coke would be great."

Lily left. Demi stood there looking awkward. "I'm not good at chitchat."

Rule smiled. "That's all right. I am. Have a seat." As she did, he added, "You're looking good."

"Better than you do, I imagine. Do you hurt a lot?"

"Sometimes more than others. I'm healing. Demi—"

"Where's Mike?" she said suddenly, looking around as if she'd just noticed he hadn't come in with her.

"He tactfully absented himself so I could talk to you about something important."

Wariness slid over her face. "What?"

"I'm speaking now as Rho of Leidolf. My clan owes you great debt."

"No, you don't."

"It's not necessary for you to agree for us to feel the weight of that debt. Without your actions, I'd be in prison or dead. is . . ." He hesitated over how to phrase this. "It is very bad for the clan when a Rho dies. Many other terrible things would have happened as well without your determination and courage, but I'm speaking now of what Leidolf owes you. In recompense for that debt, we are willing, eager, to pay for your college—room, board, tuition, books. However, we would rather handle it another way."

"What do you mean?"

"I would like to make you clan, Demi."

Her jaw dropped. Her eyes opened wide. She didn't say a thing.

"I can't make you lupus," he added, making sure she understood. "But I can make you Leidolf, if you wish. It's rare for a clan to adopt a human this way." Aside from Lily, who was Chosen, he couldn't think of any modern examples at all, though there were a few historical ones. "But I've spoken with Theo and a few others. They—we—want to claim you, if you agree."

She was still staring at him in silence.

"There are female clan, you know. You wouldn't be the only non-lupi in Leidolf."

She nodded mechanically. "Your daughters. Not yours personally, I mean, but any daughters born to lupi. They're considered clan."

He smiled. She'd been a member of his fan club, hadn't she? And obviously had read the information he provided. "Exactly. You don't need to give me an answer right away. It's a big decision. But you're alone in the world, and that's difficult. If you did agree, there would be no debt between us, but you'd be entitled to have your education paid for. You'd have a home at Clanhome if you wanted it. In addition to the rights and protections the clan offers, however, you'd assume some responsibility to the clan. Female clan don't have to give their Rho the unconditional obedience expected of male clan, but you would owe me . . . ah, let's say you should grant my authority respectful attention rather than blind obedience. If you—"

"Do you mean it?" she demanded, leaning forward. "I could be clan?"

"That's what I'm saying, yes."

"I can't—it's just so—it's so perfect!" Abruptly she jumped to her feet. "I thought you'd ruined my fantasy, but then I started liking you in spite of the way you grabbed me that night. Then I met all those wolves, and Theo, and Mike, and Saul, and everyone else, and it was even better than I'd thought it would be, and—and you said they want me, too?" She stopped, swallowed. "It's my fantasy coming true," she whispered, her eyes shining with unshed tears. "Only better."

"Ah . . . your fantasy?" he repeated.

"Yes, you—" She broke off, eyeing him. "You have a funny look on your face. I can't tell what it means."

He might as well confess. "I thought you had a different sort of fantasy in mind."

"You mean like a sex fantasy? Oh, no." She gave him a perfunctory smile. "I don't think about you that way. You're kind of old. And I don't see why people make up fantasies about sex anyway. It's not hard to find sex. Even I can, if I want to. But a family . . ." She blinked misty eyes. "That's worth making up stories to dream on, isn't it?"

FROM *NEW YORK TIMES* BESTSELLING AUTHOR

Eileen Wilks

UNBINDING

A Novel of the Lupi

After questing through the sidhe realms with her ex-hellhound lover, Nathan, Kai Tallman Michalski has finally returned home. But she knows Nathan will eventually be called back to serve his queen—and Kai will have to decide whether to enter Her Majesty's service as well. Sure, the job comes with great bennies, but there's one big downside: she would have to swear absolute fealty to the Queen of Winter.

For now, though, Kai is glad to be home, and glad that Nathan completed his mission with surprising ease. But what seemed to be a quick conclusion turns out to be anything but...

PRAISE FOR EILEEN WILKS

"Eileen Wilks writes what I like to read."
—Linda Howard, *New York Times* bestselling author

eileenwilks.com
facebook.com/eileenwilks
facebook.com/Project ParanormalBooks
penguin.com

M1706T0715

EILEEN WILKS

RITUAL MAGIC

A NOVEL OF THE LUPI

When Lily's mother suddenly loses all her memories after age twelve, Lily knows that she is under the influence of something even stronger than magic. And when she learns that others have fallen victim to the same fate, she must discover what dark force connects them…

eileenwilks.com
facebook.com/eileenwilks
facebook.com/ProjectParanormalBooks
penguin.com

BERKLEY
SENSATION

Penguin
Random
House

M1460T0715